**Gerald stared at the lion and the
lion stared back.**

On the nightstand on the right-hand side of the
bed, a tower of ancient texts. The stench of unwholesome incantations was so oppressive he could
practically taste the dark magics contained within
their covers. The ether shivered with them, a subliminal note of evil on the very edge of sensation.
He could feel his *potentia* shrivel like a garden slug
sprinkled with salt.

*And here's me, come to take that evil into myself. Come to
let it devour me alive . . .*

Praise for the Rogue Agent series:

"Mills' whimsical prose keeps the plot jumping and
the reader laughing." — *Publishers Weekly*

"A world that's magical, yet believable, and great fun
to read." — *Romantic Times*

"A fun mix of steampunkish fantasy, spy adventure,
and screwball comedy." — *Locus*

Books by Karen Miller

Kingmaker, Kingbreaker

The Innocent Mage
The Awakened Mage

The Godspeaker Trilogy

Empress
The Riven Kingdom
Hammer of God

Fisherman's Children

The Prodigal Mage
The Reluctant Mage

Writing as K.E. Mills

The Rogue Agent series

The Accidental Sorcerer
Witches Incorporated
Wizard Squared

wizard
squared

✥ rogue agent book three ✥

K.E. MILLS

www.orbitbooks.net

This book is a work of fiction. Names, characters, places, and incidents are the product of the author's imagination or are used fictitiously. Any resemblance to actual events, locales, or persons, living or dead, is coincidental.

Copyright © 2010 by Karen Miller
Excerpt from *The Prodigal Mage* copyright © 2009 by Karen Miller
All rights reserved. Except as permitted under the U.S. Copyright Act of 1976, no part of this publication may be reproduced, distributed, or transmitted in any form or by any means, or stored in a database or retrieval system, without the prior written permission of the publisher.

Originally published in paperback by HarperCollins*Publishers* Australia Pty Limited.

Orbit
Hachette Book Group
237 Park Avenue
New York, NY 10017
Visit our website at www.orbitbooks.net

Orbit is an imprint of Hachette Book Group. The Orbit name and logo are trademarks of Little, Brown Book Group Limited.

Printed in the United States of America

First edition: July 2010

10 9 8 7 6 5 4 3 2 1

*To the two fabulous young ladies I met at
the Adelaide Nation 2009.
Thank you for reading, bright sparks of the future.*

Parallel worlds, Gerald. Alternate realities. They've got to exist, right? I mean, they've got to be within the bounds of thaumaturgical possibility. Haven't they? At the end of the day, aren't they just one more metaphysical dimension? I'll bet they are, you know. And I'll bet it would be brilliant to actually go visit one. Don't you think?

Professor Monk Markham,
Member of the Masterful Company of Wizards.

wizard squared

CHAPTER ONE

*A different New Ottosland, eighteen days after the
Stuttley's staff factory debacle . . .*

Love at first sight.

Monk Markham, sprawled on a not-terribly-
impressive carpet in a totally awkward and
compromising position, looked up into a face that
until now he'd only seen through the ambivalent lens
of two different crystal balls.

The face belonged to Her Royal Highness Princess Melissande of New Ottosland.

"What the hell?" Her Highness demanded. "*You're*
not Gerald!"

Just like that, no warning, no reprieve . . . the world
was abruptly divided in two: the time Before this
moment, and the time After it. And without anyone
bothering to ask his permission, he suddenly wasn't
the same man and never would be again.

Princess Melissande's face wasn't beautiful, like

his sister Bibbie's. It was plain and round and pinkly embarrassed, with severe green eyes and a scattering of freckles and a framework of springy rust-reddish hair and a pair of prim spectacles sliding down its blunt nose. It was a face full of character—and determination—and courage.

The first time he'd seen it he hadn't actually *seen* it, because it was hidden behind a voluminous veil. As for the second time, not only was it distorted by Dunwoody's truly cheap and nasty crystal ball, it had been mostly crowded out by Dunwoody.

Gerald and a princess, sitting in a tree . . .

Except it wasn't a tree, it was a fountain. And though it had been a bit tricky to tell, he was almost sure Her Highness had been what polite society called *squiffed.*

Mind you, given what Gerald's been getting up to while my back's turned, I'm in the mood to get bloody squiffed myself.

Never in a million years would he have said that kind and gentle and above all else *ordinary* Gerald Dunwoody could ever land himself in this kind of trouble.

But then I never would've said he could turn a cat into a lion, either. Third Grade wizards who used to be probationary government compliance officers—until they accidentally blew up a staff factory—can't do Level Twelve transmogs. Everybody knows that.

Well. Everybody except Gerald, apparently.

And now some mad king's trying to kill him or worse, he's about to incite an international incident and I've got a used-to-be-human talking bird telling me what to do.

Having wearily flapped herself onto the nearby royal bed, she was telling him now.

"—lying about like a ratty old rug and find our boy Gerald before something *else* terrible happens to him!"

Ignoring Reg, he managed to smile at startled royalty. Waggled his fingers at her and hoped she couldn't tell she'd tipped him ass over teakettle.

This is ridiculous. I don't believe in love at first sight. It's a side effect from the portal. Some kind of chemical imbalance in the brain. It'll wear off. It has to. I'm far too busy to be in love.

It took him two tries before he could unstick his tongue from the roof of his mouth.

"Hi there, Your Highness. Monk Markham. Remember me?"

Please. Please. Say you remember.

"Vaguely," Her Highness snapped, haughtily repressive, and shuffled herself backwards. "How did you get here?"

He sat up. "Long story. Where's Gerald? Because he's not in his apartment."

"I neither know nor care," said the princess, frosty as mid-winter. "I consider myself gravely deceived in Gerald Dunwoody."

"*Deceived?*" Catapulted headlong into battle, her weariness forgotten, Reg chattered her beak. "You watch what you're saying about that boy, madam, there's not an ounce of deception in him! And not for want of my trying, either. A good wizard needs a dash of the devious but will he listen? No, he won't."

"Is that so?" The princess glared at Reg. "Then why did he hex my doors so I can't get out of my apartment after he swore blind he'd help me?"

"How should I know?" said Reg. "I haven't been

here. But I'll bet you a new hairdo it wasn't Gerald. Or if it was he had a very good reason. Probably something to do with saving you from yourself. The ether knows you could do with it. Those *trousers*, girl! With that shirt? With *any* shirt?"

Monk looked at her. *Really, Reg? Really? You think this is the time for a fashion critique?* "Um—look—maybe we should be concentrating on—"

The women ignored him. "Of course it was Gerald. Who else could it be?" Her Highness retorted. "And what do you mean you haven't been here? Where have you been? And what are you doing in my *bedroom*? With *Markham*? Answer me!"

So Reg answered, at length, all her acerbity given free rein. To pass the time as she pontificated he clambered to his feet and gave his portable portal a quick once-over, just to make sure it was still in working order. When Reg was finally done explaining, the princess rounded on him. Behind the prim spectacles her green eyes blazed with temper.

As if this is my fault. Well, it's not. I'm just along for the ride.

Except maybe, sort of, it was his fault. Or partly his fault.

Because if I hadn't shown Gerald that stupid Positions Vacant advertisement . . .

"Well, Mr. Markham?" the unexpected love of his life demanded, and used a handy chair to haul herself upright. "Don't stare at me like an idiot. If Gerald is missing, then *why* is he missing? What the *hell* is going on around here?"

It took quite a long time to tell her, because Reg insisted on interrupting and making trenchant personal observations about the princess and one-upping her about how *she* was the former Queen of Lalapinda and so forth, which inevitably led to more acerbic exchanges and a certain amount of meta-phorical hair-and-feather pulling. If he'd not been so worried about Gerald and exactly *why* there'd been such an enormous spike on the Department of Thaumaturgy's etheretic monitors he would have found it rather amusing. Like vaudeville.

At least, it was like vaudeville until he got to the part about how King Lional was suspected of some very nasty goings-on and likely had something truly horrible planned for Gerald. It broke his heart to tell the princess that. Seeing her pain, feeling her shock, his pleasure at impressing her with how he'd casually invented the portable portal evaporated.

"Come on, ducky," Reg said gruffly, breaking Her Highness's stunned silence. "You don't honestly expect us to believe you never *once* looked at Lional sideways, do you?"

Arms folded, head turned towards the window, the princess—*Melissande*—shrugged.

Monk flicked Reg a reproving glance—which naturally the bloody bird ignored—then took a hesitant step towards the woman who'd turned his life inside out just by existing. "Don't mind her, Melissande. I'm sure—"

"No," said the princess. "Actually, the bird's right. I just—I didn't—I *couldn't*—I mean, I never thought he'd actually *hurt* anyone . . . but—" Her voice caught. "It's true I've always known he could be unkind. And I don't recall inviting you to call me *Melissande*, Mr. Markham."

The last bit was said snappishly. That was all right. He could live with snappish. He could live with anything but seeing that blinding misery in her eyes. "Sorry."

She turned. "So. We're in a pickle. Don't suppose you've got any bright ideas about how we're going to get out of it, do you?"

"Maybe," he said. "But first things first. We can't do anything while we're stuck behind locked doors."

"Then what are you waiting for?" said Reg. "Get out to the foyer and unlock them, Mr. Markham!"

But that was a whole lot easier said than done.

One touch to the apartment doors' binding incant and he broke into a cold and sickly sweat. Snatching his hand back from the polished timber, he shook his head.

Oh, bloody hell. Just when I thought things couldn't get any worse.

"You're right. They're hexed. But Gerald didn't do it."

Standing off to one side, the princess glared. "Don't be silly, Mr. Markham. Of course he did."

No. No. I've got a first name. You can use it. "Call me Monk," he said, then pressed his palm flat to the doors a second time. For her, not for him. He already had his answer. The same sickly surge of thaumic energy roiled through him, tangled and twisted and hideous. Bile rose in his throat, burning.

"Well?" Reg demanded, perched on the back of a book-laden chair. There were books on the floor, too. There were books *everywhere*. Her Royal Highness Princess Melissande was as big a book fiend as he was.

Bloody hell. She's perfect.

Distracted, he looked at Reg. "Well what?"

"Well can you get us out of here or can't you?"

With an effort he focused on the job at hand. "I don't know. Maybe. It's the most powerful barrier hex I've ever come across."

"Then it *has* to be Gerald's," Melissande insisted. "Because there isn't anybody else in New Ottosland who could've put it there."

"Mel—Your Highness—I wish that were true," he said. "It'd make my life a whole lot easier if it was."

Melissande started tapping her toes. "Fine. Then who was it if it wasn't Gerald? And *don't* say Lional, because he's not a wizard."

Bloody hell. I don't want to tell her. Except he had to. Not only was she ranking royalty and had the right to know . . . he had no right to protect her. And if he tried she'd probably smack him.

"Look. Your Highness. I know this is going to sound crazy, but—"

"Then it must be true," said Reg, snippy. "*Everything* in this cockeyed kingdom is crazy."

"Thank you," Melissande said coldly. "Mr. Markham?"

"The doors were hexed by a single wizard," he said quietly. "But there are five First Grade thaumic signatures in the hex."

"So?" said Melissande, her arms folded tight and her chin lifted, as though she could hold the terrible truth at bay.

"So we have five missing First Grade wizards, all of whom reported to your brother the king—and who all disappeared before Gerald got here."

She didn't want to believe him, couldn't bear the

thought of her brother murdering five innocent men and stealing their *potentias*. So he made her prove it to herself using a thaumically-charged gift the missing wizard Bondaningo Greenfeather had given her.

It was the cruelest thing he'd ever done.

I'm sorry. I'm sorry. I didn't have a choice.

Giving her a moment to compose herself, he turned to Reg. "A non-wizard stealing *potentias*? I've never come across anything like it."

"You wouldn't have," the bird said darkly. "Seeing as you're a nice young man who doesn't read that kind of grimoire. But I've known men who do, Monk. Crazy or not, you've hit the nail on the head. It's true that mad bugger Lional's not a wizard, but all it takes is one tiny thaumaturgical spark to start the fire. Now get us out of here so we can rescue Gerald before he becomes victim number six."

Breaking the mad king's filthy hex nearly finished him. Sick and shaking he forced himself inside its intricate workings. Tried not to hear the faint, terrible screams of those five dying wizards as he unraveled the incant strand by dirty, stinking strand.

The power of its final unbinding blew him clear across the foyer.

Melissande rushed to his side. "Monk—*Monk*! Are you all right?"

And suddenly the blinding headache and nausea were worth it.

He groaned. "I think I'm going to be sick."

"Not in my foyer you're not, Mr. Markham! Just you pull yourself together!"

She put her arm around his shoulders and helped him sit up. The urge to collapse into her practical embrace was almost overwhelming. But Gerald needed him, so . . .

"I will," he mumbled. "I promise." Blearily he blinked around him. "Reg?"

Lalapinda's former queen was hovering between the splintered remains of the foyer doors, wings flapping up a hurricane. "Yes, that's me! Now get off your skinny ass and let's *go*, Mr. Markham!"

Melissande's fingertips brushed against his cheek. "Are you really all right? Are you sure you can do this? Find Gerald, stop Lional? Save my kingdom?"

Mesmerized by her stern and steady gaze, Monk nodded. Cleared his throat. "Yes. I think so."

"Good," she said, with the swiftest, sweetest smile. "I think so too. Now you heard the bird, Mr. Markham. Get up off your skinny ass. You and I have work to do."

The warm glow of her touch, and her smile, carried him through the fear that he'd not be able to locate Gerald—fed into the ebullient joy when his best locating incant did find him—and lasted right up to the moment they saw the dragon.

On the other side of a palace skylight's sparkling glass, lazily floating on an updraft like an enormous crimson and emerald striped seagull—with teeth and talons—the fantastic creature opened its massive jaws and belched a fearsome plume of fire.

Staring astonished at the impossible beast, Monk felt a fresh wave of sickness crash over him—because here was the explanation for that enormous thaumic spike.

Gerald, Gerald. What have you done?

Because it had to be Gerald. It couldn't be anyone else.

"Oy. Madam," said Reg, perched piratically on his shoulder. "You know who that's supposed to be, don't you?"

"Yes," Melissande whispered, with tears in her voice. "Grimthak."

"Grimthak?" he said. He couldn't tear his gaze from Gerald's impossible creation. "And who the bloody hell is Grimthak?"

"A Kallarapi god," said Melissande. "Monk—Mr. Markham—get us out of here. Now."

With Gerald's location set into the portable portal's destination node, there came one nasty moment when he thought he wouldn't be able to adjust the device's parameters to accept simultaneous travel by two adults and a bird.

Come on, come on, Markham, you pillocking plonker. Are you a genius or aren't you? Pull your finger out. Get it done.

"Ha!" said Reg, as his rejigging of the portal's matrix finally took and a pinpoint of light in the air before them began to blossom. "About time, sunshine. What took you so long?"

Bloody hell, Gerald. How do you stand it?

"Sorry," he said curtly. "But I assumed you'd want to reach the other side in one piece."

Perched on Melissande's shoulder now, the bird sniffed. "Let's leave the witty banter for when we don't have a dragon on top of us, shall we?" She bounced a little. "Come on, Your Highness. Giddyup. Let's go."

"Don't look at me," he told Melissande. "I'm not the one who rescued her from the wilderness." Then he held out his hand. "To be on the safe side."

Her lips twitched, just a little. "All right. Provided you don't try making a habit of it." Her fingers closed around his, cool and ever so slightly trembling. "On three?"

The brilliant portal shimmered like a lake in bright sunshine. He nodded. "Why not? On three. One—two—"

They leaped through it on three.

A dizzying rush . . . a wrenching unreality . . . and then they ripped through the air on the other side of the thaumaturgical conduit and landed with a bone-rattling thud onto cold dirt in the sudden dark.

"*Ow!* That's my *face!*"

Hastily he snatched his hand away. "Sorry, Melissande. Gerald, are you in here?" And then he winced and froze. "Um, Your Highness, not to complain or anything but your elbow's in a very precarious part of my anato—"

"Monk?" said a disbelieving voice. It sounded small and frightened. "Is that you?"

Gerald? Since when was Gerald small and frightened? But before he could speak, the bird rattled her tail. "Oh, yes, fine, ask about Markham first why don't you? When I'm the one sitting here faded to a mere shadow of my former glory after flying *and* hitching from here to Ottosland then convincing Markham and his idiot colleagues that your life was in danger and then risking my life *again* to get back to this ether-forsaken kingdom using Markham's highly illegal and practically untested portable portal! And why is it so *dark* in here? Why doesn't somebody turn on the lights?"

Oh. Right. He snapped his fingers. "*Illuminato.*"

And just like that, there was light.

"Reg!" cried Gerald, and fell to his knees. "Oh my God, *Reg*, you're *alive*!"

And then Reg was saying something, scolding again, she was always scolding. But Monk didn't pay any attention. He could hardly make sense of the words. Because Gerald—Gerald—

Bloody hell. Gerald. What happened to you?

There wasn't a mark on him. Not a scrape. Not a bruise. But his face had gone so *thin* and there were smeared shadows beneath his eyes and his eyes— his *eyes*—

Oh, Gerald. What have you seen?

His friend was clutching Reg so tightly the bird could hardly breathe. "Lional said you were dead, he said he'd killed you!" He was practically babbling. But Gerald *never* babbled. "He *did* kill you, *look*, there's your body! Over there!"

Feeling sick again, Monk stared as Gerald and Reg fussed at each other over some trick with a dead chicken. He could feel his heatbeat's dull thudding in his ears.

This is bad. This is very bad. Something very bad's happened to Gerald.

"Mr. Markham?"

He turned at the light touch on his arm. "Your Highness?"

"What's wrong?"

So she'd been watching him. She could feel his dismay.

I wonder if that means she's ass over teakettle too?

It'd be nice if it did. He was feeling horribly alone.

"Nothing," he said, because whatever Gerald

had been through her brother was behind it and he wanted to spare her that pain for as long as he could. "Sorry. I just—"

And then Gerald was asking him about how they'd found him and the portable portal. He explained everything, quickly, but instead of being pleased about it Gerald suddenly looked sick. Said something about a lodestone and how he'd forgotten Lional didn't reactivate it but before they could sort that out—and before he could stop her—the love of his life was shouting at his horribly altered best friend.

"What the hell were you *thinking*, Gerald? Making a *dragon*?"

Gerald flinched. "I'm sorry."

But Melissande wasn't in the mood for apologies—and it seemed that Gerald had no intention of defending himself. So he tried to stop her—and the look she gave him was like being stabbed.

Reg flapped from the cave floor to his shoulder. "Don't," she said softly. "With Lional off his rocker and the Butterfly Prince disqualified on grounds of mental health, as in not having any, she's New Ottosland's ruler now. She's got a right to ask."

Maybe she did, but he didn't have to like it. Gerald's face was scaring him.

"So what did Lional promise you in return for his dragon?" Her Royal Highness demanded, magnificent in her anger. "Gold? Jewels? Land? *What did he promise you*?"

Silence. And then Gerald lifted his sad, shadowed eyes. "You don't want to know what he promised me, Melissande."

Oh God. Oh God. Here it comes. This is the bad part. This is the part I don't want to know.

Except he couldn't turn away from it. Gerald was his best friend. Gerald was here because he'd shown him that advertisement. Whatever had happened, he was partly to blame. So he couldn't stay silent. He had to speak up.

"Lional tortured you, Gerald. Didn't he?"

On his shoulder, Reg gasped.

And Melissande, oh Melissande, she didn't want to hear it either. She didn't want to be the sister of a man who could do something like that. So she tried to blame Gerald and even though it had been love at first sight he was angry with her, so angry, because Gerald didn't lie. Was she *blind*, not to see it? Couldn't she see he'd been hurt? But when he tried to defend his best friend she turned on him. It was all a mess, such a terrible mess, and he had no idea how to clean any of it up.

And then he heard—really heard—what Gerald was saying. Like a coward, he wanted to run.

No. No. I don't want to hear this.

But how could he not hear it, after Gerald had lived it?

Eventually the sickening tale of cruelty and suffering came to an end. Melissande, the love of his life, stood like a weeping marble statue and on his shoulder Reg felt turned to stone.

He looked at Gerald, and Gerald looked back. The cost of that confession was etched in his face. The price of his endurance—the finding of his limit—was etched deeper still. "There's something else," Gerald said tiredly. "Lional's controlling the dragon using the *Tantigliani sympathetico*."

Melissande smeared a dirty sleeve across her wet face. "What does that mean?"

So Gerald explained. Melissande swayed, close to folding to the cave's dirt floor. But she didn't, because she was Melissande. He wanted to hold her—and kept his hands to himself. She'd never forgive him if he made her look weak.

Feeling bludgeoned, he shook his head. "Bloody hell, Gerald. Every wizard who's ever tried that incant has gone mad. Even Tantigliani in the end. You say Lional's lost himself inside the dragon's mind? Does that mean . . ."

Gerald was like a man cut out of paper. Like a man mere heartbeats from crumbling to ash. "Yes." He glanced at Melissande. "I'm sorry, Your Highness. I'm pretty sure it's too late for Lional."

Stirring at last, Reg rattled her tail feathers. "Then the only way to stop the dragon is by capturing the king."

Monk touched a fingertip to her wing. "He's as good as half a dragon himself now."

"Fine," she said, shrugging. "Then we don't capture him. We kill him."

And because there hadn't been enough raw emotion already, her blunt assessment sparked another passionate row. Melissande wept again and this time he did touch her. He put his arms around her—and she didn't push him away.

Reg flapped over to Gerald, who cradled her against his chest. "Honestly, Reg. Have you *heard* of being tactful?"

"If being tactful will kill that torturing bastard, Gerald, I'll tact up a storm," she said grimly. "You see if I don't."

Gerald dropped a kiss to the top of her head, then looked up. "She is right, Monk. Lional and his dragon have to be stopped."

Well, yes, obviously, but—

"I know you want to be the one to stop them, Gerald," said Melissande. Stepping away, she smoothed her hands down the front of her shirt, putting her armor back in place. "But Lional broke you once. He could break you again."

Gerald's flinch was like a sword running through his own body. "*Melissande.*"

She turned on him. "I'm sorry, Mr. Markham, but I can't afford kindness just now. My kingdom's at stake. Or are you going to tell me *you* think he's up to it?"

Damn. *Damn.* She had to ask him that, didn't she? With Gerald standing there, after everything he'd just said . . . after everything he'd endured. Days and days of unspeakable torment. Gerald, the Third Grade wizard who could turn lizards into dragons. Who'd tried and tried not to . . .

And who did break. He did.

With an effort Monk met his best friend's sad, quiet gaze. "I don't think we can decide anything stuck in this cave," he said, his voice rough. "I think we need to portal out of here and see what's happening back at the palace."

Reg nodded. "Good idea, sunshine. And then we can—"

"No," said Gerald. "Reg and I can portal to the palace. You and Melissande should go back to Ottosland, to the Department. Corner your Uncle Ralph, Monk, and kick up the biggest stink the place has ever seen until those hidebound bureaucrats get off their asses and send some help."

"Absolutely not," Melissande snapped. "I'm staying here. I have to be *seen*. The people *need* me. I won't be the second person in my family to let them down on the same damned day!"

"No—Melissande—the only hope your people have is if you stay safe!" Gerald insisted. "Let Rupert fly the family flag, he—"

Her expression changed. "Oh, lord. *Rupert*. I forgot about Rupert! I have to find him, he'll be terrified. And if *Lional* finds him . . ." She spun around. "Well, Monk, don't just stand there. Get that portable portal of yours working and take us out of here! *Now!*"

By a minor miracle he managed to get them onto the palace's roof. The dragon was nowhere in sight. Neither was Lional. But what they could see struck them all to grieving silence.

In every direction distant pillars of black smoke churned into the sky. Closer to the palace, outbuildings not reduced to mounds of rubble smoldered and burned; the greedy crackling of flames reached them in fits and starts on the erratic, smoke-laden breeze. Staring over the roof's balustrade they saw great burned patches in the gravel and on the grass edging the palace forecourt, as though someone had upended huge barrels of acid onto them. Even at this height they could smell the acrid stench of the dragon's poison. See the remains of what once had been people, laughing living New Ottoslanders, reduced to charred and stinking carcasses.

There were fresh tears on Melissande's cheeks.

"Is one of them Rupert? One of them could be Rupert, he could be dead down there, or in his butterfly house. I have to go and—"

Monk reached for her, but Gerald grabbed her first. "No, Melissande, *think*. If Rupert is dead there's nothing you can do for him. And if he isn't that means he's hiding. Either way you've got a lot more to worry about than the fate of one man."

A creak and flap of wings and Reg landed on the balustrade beside distraught Melissande. "He's right, ducky," she said sternly. "The only man you need to be thinking about is Lional. Because strictly speaking he's not a man any more. He's an abomination. And abominations have to be destroyed."

Oh God. Reg, you really need to learn tact.

Melissande walked away and he went after her, leaving Gerald and Reg to do what they liked. "Your Highness—Melissande—*please*, Melissande. Wait."

She slowed, then stopped. Turned. Not weeping now, but white-faced beneath her scattered freckles and shivering with distress. *"What?"*

Helpless, he looked at her. Spread his hands wide, then let them fall. "I don't know. I don't know. Just . . . don't walk away."

"From you?" she said, incredulous. "Monk Markham, I barely know you. Why do you *care*?"

If I tell her I love her she'll pitch me off this roof. Or she'll laugh in my face, and then I'll have to jump.

"I don't know," he said again, shrugging. "I just do." He tried to smile. "Do you mind?"

Behind him, Reg and Gerald were arguing. Snatches of pain blowing fitful in the breeze. Something about stopping Lional. Fighting fire with fire.

Reg was furious. Gerald sounded despairing. This was turning into one hell of a day.

Now Melissande looked helpless. "Do I *mind*?" she muttered, harassed, pressing a hand to her forehead. "I don't know. I suppose not. I mean, all right, strictly speaking, it's presumptuous and a terrible breach of royal etiquette and protocol and—"

"Does all that claptrap really matter?"

She opened her mouth, then closed it again. "No. Not really. But if I *am* going to be queen then I should at least notice it. You know. In passing."

The breeze swirled again, laden with more painful argument and the raw stench of death. Flinching, Melissande closed her eyes.

"I don't know how this happened," she whispered. "How did this happen?"

To hell with protocol and etiquette. Monk wrapped his arms around her and let her hold on tight.

"I'm sorry," he said, rocking her. "But we'll fix this, Melissande. All right? We'll fix it."

With a shuddering sigh she relaxed against him. "You promise?"

"I promise."

She tipped her head back. Looked up. Beneath her shock he caught a glimpse of humor and breathtaking strength. "You realize I've no sane reason to believe that?"

"In my line of work, Your Highness, sanity is overrated," he said . . . and would've said something else, something truly crazy, only Reg's sharply raised voice stopped him.

"—Lional dead, Gerald, *you'd* be the danger. And whoever tried to stop you, well, they'd need to read the *Lexicon* too. And it wouldn't end there, I promise you that. Say this hypothetical wizard succeeded and managed to kill you. All it means is there'd be *another* rotten wizard who'd have to die . . . and so the *Lexicon* would be used again . . . and again . . . and again. Is that what you want, sunshine? Every last good wizard in the world dead because of you?"

His altered face still chalky-white, fired up with an awful, unfamiliar desperation, Gerald turned on her. "What else can I do? The magic I know doesn't have teeth, it doesn't have talons, it can't kill Lional *or* his damned dragon! I *have* to use the *Lexicon*, Reg!"

"*No!*" Wings wildly flapping she launched herself into the air to hover furiously above him. "I'd rather see you dead—I'd rather kill you *myself* than see you—"

Now what? With a chill of foreboding, Monk followed interrupted Reg's outraged stare. *What the hell?* Camels? Were those camels? And those glinting things—were they *swords?*

"Oh *blimey!*" Reg groaned. "That's *all* we need!" Dropping back to the balustrade she glared at Melissande. "Oy! You! Madam-Queen-in-Waiting! Front and center, ducky, New Ottosland's got visitors!"

CHAPTER TWO

Monk stared at the mighty army of Kallarap, gathered in the grounds of Melissande's palace. Then he glanced at Gerald, unnervingly calm and silent beside him.

"You know—that's a lot of camels."

Perched on Gerald's shoulder, Reg snorted. "And warriors. And swords. And spears."

True. But that wasn't the most disturbing thing. The Kallarapi holy man was making his skin crawl. Power roiled off him like heat from the sun. The sultan was powerful too. An absolute ruler, comfortable with his authority and not afraid to use it. Growing up a Markham meant he could spot the genuine article with both eyes closed.

Be careful, Melissande. If you let them, these men will swallow you alive.

"Don't worry," said Gerald. "She'll be fine."

Melissande—*his* Melissande—was giving Zazoor a piece of her mind. Small and vulnerable and so very badly dressed, she was staring down Shugat and Zazoor like a warrior queen from the mythic past.

Of course she'll be fine. I'm an idiot to doubt her.

He glanced again at Gerald. "I know. But what about you?"

Pale and tired, Gerald pulled a face. "What about me?"

How could he answer that? What could he say? They needed a bathtub full of brandy and two straws for that conversation. "Gerald . . ."

"Never mind," said Gerald, so remote. So changed. "It doesn't matter. Now shut up, would you? I want to hear what they're saying."

Yes, well, what they were *saying* was good old diplomatic double-speak as Melissande, Zazoor and Shugat quickstepped around the mess Melissande's mad brother had made. Like fencers testing for a likely opening, they parried words and dodged lunges and sought for a face-saving way to retreat from the brink.

When they got to the bit about Melissande marrying Zazoor he came damned close to swallowing his tongue.

"Settle down, sunshine," said Reg, leaning close. "Zazoor's safe. Not even the Kallarapi are that desperate."

"Reg!" he said. "How can you—"

And then he forgot what he was going to say, because Zazoor was smiling.

It wasn't a good smile.

"Highness," the sultan said, silky with polite menace. "The payment of debt is a good thing, but Kallarap will not starve without your pennies. I am sent to you by my gods, who would have me speak with you of sacrilege. And treachery. And yes, indeed: of *honesty*."

Oh, damn. Damn, damn, damn.

But before he could leap to the rescue Gerald shoved Reg at him and marched into the fray. "Sultan Zazoor, your quarrel is with me."

"What? What?" Reg thrashed in his grasp, trying to get free. "What is that idiot boy doing now?"

Monk felt an unfamiliar sting in his eyes. Had to clear his throat before he could speak. "What does it look like, Reg? He's being Gerald."

Abruptly still, Reg moaned softly, the smallest sound of distress. "I want to bloody *kill* that Lional."

"You and me both, ducky," he said, close to snarling. "You and me both."

Heartsick, they watched Gerald throw himself on the mercy of the merciless Kallarapi. Confess his sins and take all the blame, not a word in his own defense, no attempt to explain. "I made the dragon because I'm weak."

"All right, that's *it!*" Reg shrieked, and in a wild flurry of wings and tail feathers flailed her furious way to Gerald's shoulder. "Weak my granny's bunions! Now you listen to me, Zazoor! If you knew what that bastard Lional did to my Gerald to get that dragon you'd—"

"The bird?" Zazoor said to Shugat.

Shugat nodded. "The bird."

Zazoor considered her. "*Not*, I think, trained."

"Trained?" screeched Reg. "What do you think I am, a bloody circus act?"

Monk kept out of it. Not even he could defend Gerald the way Reg could. And she was defending him, fearlessly tongue-lashing Zazoor and the holy man. Interestingly they let her, indulging her tirade without interruption. Melissande glanced at him once, eyebrows raised. *Should I chime in, do you think?* He shook his head. Reg was doing just fine on her own.

But then Shugat climbed down off his camel and pressed his gnarled hand over Gerald's heart. His own heart stopped beating. If this was retribution there was nothing he could do . . .

It wasn't. With a great burst of light from the crystal in his forehead the Kallarapi holy man stepped back. "The bird does not lie, my sultan. The wizard has suffered. His blood still stinks of foul enchantments."

His heart started beating again and he was able to breathe—until Zazoor's dark gaze stabbed him, one hand beckoning.

Bloody hell. This'll teach me to poke my nose outside R&D.

Zazoor wasn't smiling now. "And who are you? Another wizard?"

"Yes, Magnificence. I'm—"

"A friend," said Gerald, and burned him silent with a look. "Innocent of these doings. He's not to be harmed."

Zazoor almost laughed. "You would stop me?"

"I'd try."

The sultan's flickering glance indicated his army, and Shugat. "You would fail."

Monk held his breath. Was he the only one who could tell just how shaken Gerald really was? How close he'd been pushed to losing his mind?

Back down, mate. Back down. I can take care of myself.

Gerald's attention was focused solely on Zazoor. "Yes. I might fail. But not before I'd tried."

Zazoor laughed. "Holy Shugat. This wizard asks us to help him destroy the dragon. What is our answer?"

As it turned out, not the one they were hoping for. Outright rejection. A refusal of aid. To be honest he wasn't surprised—but Melissande was. She raged, she argued, she threw herself against Kallarap's indifference. Gerald threw himself after her, but it was no use.

"He who made the dragon must now unmake it," Shugat pronounced, eyes rolled to slivered white crescents. "So say The Three, whose words are holy and cannot be denied."

And then Gerald, the mad bastard, the crazy fool, the damned hero, shrugged Reg off his shoulder and dropped to his knees. Offered himself to the Kallarapi in exchange for Melissande's kingdom kept safe.

Holding Reg again, standing with Melissande, the world shifted and smeared as his eyes filled with proud grief.

Bloody hell, Gerald. Oh, bloody bloody hell.

Then two things happened and everything changed. Melissande's loopy brother Rupert burst among them, covered in dead butterflies, making her cry . . .

. . . and one of Zazoor's warriors pointed a finger and shouted.

"Draconi! Draconi!"

Lional's dragon was coming, its emerald and crimson savagery blazing in the sun. For a moment, just a moment, Monk found himself transfixed. *Damn. That thing's beautiful.* And then sanity returned.

Over the Kallarapi hubbub: "Monk—*Monk*—"

Gerald, tugging on his arm. Tugging him to privacy. Still holding Reg, he wrenched himself away from the glory of the dragon. "What?"

"You've got to get out of here," said Gerald, his voice low and his face worryingly intent. "Take Melissande and Rupert with you. Monk—"

He yanked his arm free. "Forget it. I'm not leaving you here to face that thing on your own!"

Something dreadful shifted behind Gerald's eyes. "Why? Because you don't trust me? Because you think Melissande's right? I broke, so I'm broken?"

The sharp shift in Gerald's expression told him he'd answered before he could speak a word.

Damn. "Gerald—"

With a terrible smile, Gerald shook his head. "Don't. You're probably right. What Lional did to me . . . what *I* did . . ." His lips pressed to a thin line. "It's my mess, Monk. I have to clean it up."

"Yeah, okay, but you don't have to clean it up *alone.*"

"If you prod the Department off its ass I won't be alone, will I?" Then Gerald sighed. "Please, Monk?" He glanced at the royal siblings, who were clutching each other like children. "I can't do this if I'm scared something might happen to them. Or to you."

God. How was he supposed to argue with that? He couldn't. And when Melissande and Rupert tried to argue Gerald froze them with an *impedimentia*. Then he looked at Reg.

"I want you to go, too."

"What?" the bird squawked. "Don't be ridiculous, Gerald. I'm staying."

But Gerald wouldn't hear of it . . . and nothing Reg said could change his stubborn mind.

Dry-mouthed, defeated, Monk dragged the portable portal from his pocket, flicked it on and set the destination coordinates. "For the record, mate, I think this is a bad idea."

"Probably." Gerald smiled again. It was still ghastly. "Thanks, Monk."

"Yeah, well, you want to thank me?" he retorted, scowling. "Don't do anything stupid."

Like die. D'you hear me, Gerald? Don't you dare bloody die.

Gerald kissed Reg, handed her over, then stepped back. With a soft *whoosh* the portal opened. On a deep breath Monk grabbed Melissande's arm, then Rupert's. Reg's claws were sunk deep in his shoulder. For once the bird had nothing to say.

"All right. I'm ready."

The dragon was much closer. They could hear its lazy wings beating the air. The Kallarapi had fallen silent. He couldn't bring himself to look.

"Monk, Reg," said Gerald, so calmly. "Take care of each other—and our royal friends. Don't let them boss you. And Monk?"

Oh God, oh God. Gerald didn't think he was going to survive. The world smeared again. "Yes?"

Another smile, a proper smile. For a moment, a heartbeat, he looked like himself. "Good luck with the princess. You're going to need it."

Then Gerald released the *impedimentia* . . . and the portal swallowed them in one gulp.

Zazoor said, "Wizard, that was honorably done."

Light-headed with relief, Gerald stared at the point where the portal had opened, swallowed his friends, then vanished. Whatever life was left to him now, be it hours or minutes or scant swift seconds, at least he could face it with some kind of peace. They were safe.

I failed them in the cave. I let Lional break me. But now I've got a second chance—I won't fail them again.

He turned and looked at Kallarap's sultan. "You think I'm the kind of man who'd let one more innocent life be lost if he could prevent it?"

Shugat fingered his staff. "The kind of man you are is yet to be revealed," he said before Zazoor could reply.

The dragon was almost on top of them now, flames and smoke billowing in its wake. The clear air trembled.

He sneered. "What's that, Shugat? More of your gods' *wisdom*?"

"Yes."

Damn the holy man and his cryptic utterances. He took a step towards Zazoor. "Magnificence, don't listen to him. That dragon's dangerous, you—"

"Oh *look!*" cried a lilting voice. "It's a party and we weren't invited. Do you know, we think our feelings are *hurt*."

Lional.

Cold with inevitability, Gerald looked to Shugat and the sultan. Unmoved, they watched Lional make his suave, insinuating way through the ruined flowerbeds to the edge of the carriageway where grass met gravel.

He turned to Zazoar, the blood pounding in his head. "It isn't too late. Help me. *Please.*"

Unmoved, unmoving, Zazoor sat on his ebony war

camel and stared down at his holy man. Shugat inspected the tip of his staff, leathered face creased in thought, then glanced up at Zazoor. After a moment of silent communion they closed their eyes.

So. I'm alone.

Something . . . some hope or belief or faith in the ultimate goodness of man . . . broke inside him. Bled swiftly, quietly, flooding all the cracks and chasms of his soul.

Lional laughed. "Gerald, Gerald. Why are you surprised? Didn't we tell you they're a dreadful bunch?"

He snapped his fingers . . . and in a beating of wings, with a hissing song of welcome, the dragon touched lightly to the ground at his side. Sunlight trembled on its scarlet and emerald scales, striking sparks from the diamond-bright sheen of its spines. Poison, green and glowing, oozed from each razor-sharp tip. Dripped harmlessly down the dragon's brilliant striped hide and Lional's green silk arm. Fell to the ground . . . which at its touch dissolved in a cloud of noxious smoke.

Kissing his palm to the dragon's cheek, Lional sighed. Some subtle flow of flesh and bone rippled beneath his skin. Seemed to elongate his skull and dagger his teeth. Gerald thought he saw a shimmer of crimson scale, swift as fish-scales in a river.

"We were hunting," said Lional in a soft and singsong voice, subtly not his own. "The sheep, the boar, the bullock, the stag . . . blood like crimson nectar . . . but before we'd killed our fill we felt the air change. Smelled the rank unwelcome coming of the nasty little man with his stone of power and we thought . . ."

Abruptly, Lional blinked. The dragon blinked. They stirred as though waking from a dream. Two creatures, one mind. Their living connection absolute. It was terrible . . . and beautiful. Then Lional smiled, a bright flashing of teeth, and the shadows beneath his skin sank from sight.

"Well, well, well," he drawled. He sounded himself again. "Hello, Zazoor. What brings you and your holy lapdog to my kingdom? *And* without an invitation. So *rude!*"

If Zazoor was unnerved by the ravening beast just feet away he gave no sign. He might have been attending a tedious tea party or receiving a tiresome guest in his own home. "What brings us here, Lional? Fate. Destiny. The will of the Three."

Lional's smile widened. "Can't you make up your mind? Well, it's nice to see some things never change."

Zazoor's answering smile was deadly. "When we were at school, Lional, I knew you for a cowardly boy who bullied and cheated to get his way. Now you are a man grown and you resort to torture when bullying and cheating no longer suffice. Indeed you have the right of it, my old school chum: truly, some things never change."

Lional's smile vanished. His caressing fingers—with nails longer and thicker than they'd been just yesterday—dropped from the dragon's face and his blue eyes darkened, the flickering red flame in their depths leaping high.

"*Burn them*, my darling. Burn them to *ash*."

The dragon roared, its lower jaw unhinging to reveal a cauldron of fire. Flames writhing green and scarlet burst from its dagger-toothed mouth. Swift as a striking snake Shugat snatched the stone from his forehead and held out his hand. A bolt of blue-white light collided with the gushing fire. There was a hissing of steam and stinking smoke like hot lava striking an arctic sea. The dragon screamed, rearing on its hind legs, wings thrashing. Lional, fingers clawing desperately at his mouth, screamed with it.

Gerald turned on Shugat. "See? You can hurt them! For God's sake, Shugat, you *have* to help me!"

Shugat glared, his eyes like the heart of a distant sun. He opened his mouth as if to speak . . . then froze. His eyes rolled back in his head, his arm flung wide and his tight-clutched staff began to shiver and twist.

The stone he held exploded into life.

Its surge of power drove Gerald to his knees. As he struggled to breathe he heard Lional, shrieking, and the dragon's echoing roar. He looked up.

Lional's fingernails had gouged deep furrows in his face; blood flowed from his cheeks, his lips, his chin. The dragon was wounded too, its scales cracked and blackened, thick gore bubbled and stinking. But within moments the scales healed, and with them Lional's wounds. His hands came up, fingers curved into talons, and his eyes were soaked in scarlet.

Shugat moved in a blur of speed. As a stream of foul curses spewed from Lional's lips he swept staff and stone in an arc that encompassed himself, his sultan and the entire Kallarapi army. In its wake sprang a translucent domed barrier; motionless within, Shugat and Zazoor and the warriors of Kallarap waited.

Stranded, unprotected, Gerald watched Lional and his dragon throw flame and vitriol and the worst curses in history at the holy man's shimmering shield. Spittle flew from Lional's mouth and green poison poured down the dragon's teeth, turning the ground beneath their feet to acid mud as the attack went on and on.

Still the shield held.

Exhausted, half-fainting, Lional fell back, one hand grasping at his dragon's spines to stop himself from falling. Equally spent, the dragon lowered its head and panted, wings limp and splayed upon the ruined grass.

Inside the barrier Shugat's eyes unrolled. He sighed, arms falling to his sides. Looked at Gerald, one wild eyebrow lifting in sarcastic invitation.

Oh. Right. Gerald ran.

The flowerbeds at the far edge of the palace gardens had somehow escaped untouched, with unburned blossoms rising rank upon perfumed, bee-buzzed rank. With the last of his strength he dived headfirst into a cloying collection of hollyhocks, daisies and snapdragons.

Ha.

Panting, he snatched up his arms and legs thinking: *hedgehog.* This far from the palace, to his shamed relief, he couldn't smell the stench of the dragon's kill. Thank God. Images of Lional and the dragon rose like flames before him.

Kill *them?* He'd *never* kill them.

Oh God. I really am going to die.

Some six inches from his nose a rustling of leaf litter. He sucked in moist, compost-rich air, unmoving. Another rustle. And then a lizard, a skink, skinny and brown with only one good eye, darted out from under a leaf and stopped, nervously scenting the air with its tiny tongue.

Gerald held his breath. Memory replayed recent, desperate words.

"I'm the only wizard with a hope against Lional. But only if I fight with the same weapons he's got!"

When he'd said it he was convinced that meant using Lional's stolen copy of *Grummen's Lexicon*. But what if . . . what if . . .

You know what they say. Fight fire with fire. Or . . . dragon with dragon?

His stunned mind reeled. No. He was mad. How the hell could it possibly *work*? As lizards went this one was pathetic. With its left eye shriveled, practically *crippled*. Its matrix would make a piss-poor dragon; even with the strongest magic this little skink could never hope to match the brute muscularity and mindless viciousness of the Bearded Spitting lizard Bondaningo Greenfeather had found for Lional. The dragons would never be equal: magic could only do so much. And that meant . . .

I'm sorry, Reg. I'm sorry, Monk. I don't have a choice. Lional has to be stopped.

At all costs, the monster had to be stopped. And this weak, tiny, half-blind lizard wasn't the answer.

I'm not the answer. I'm not good enough. Whatever tricks I've done here, I did by luck and accident. I have no idea what I'm doing. And when push came to shove . . . when I needed to be strong?

He'd seen the truth in Melissande's eyes. Worse— in Monk's. They didn't think he could defeat Lional . . . and they were right. He couldn't. Not without a special kind of help. And if Shugat wouldn't give it to him then his only sure chance of saving New Ottosland from its insane king was with *Grummen's*

Lexicon—and any other handy texts Lional might've left lying around.

And when it's over, and that mad bastard's finished, the Department can de-incant me. They must have some kind of top secret apparatus for stunts like that. And if they don't, well, Monk can invent one. After the portable portal he should be able to take care of that little problem in his sleep.

With another rustle of leaf litter, the tiny half-blind lizard turned tail and scuttled back under cover. Feeling sick, Gerald hoisted himself onto his elbows and risked a look around the gardens then up at the sky No sign of Lional or his hideously beautiful dragon. So he'd best make a run back to the palace now because there was no way of knowing how long this sliver of luck would last.

Probably Lional and his dragon will broil me alive as my fingers touch the handle on the palace's back door . . . and who's to say it wouldn't serve me right?

But that kind of thinking wasn't helpful. If Reg could hear him she'd be severely unimpressed. On a deep breath he rose to a crouch, got his bearings on the palace—and ran.

Breath rasping in his throat, elbows flapping, knees pumping—he'd never been one for sports, not even at small school—he sprinted, more or less, towards the nearest bit of palace he could reach. Every gasp of death-tainted air churned his belly. He caught a smeary glimpse of Shugat and Zazoor and their camel army, serenely safe within their milky shield.

Miserable bastards.

There was still no sign of Lional or the dragon. But even as he ran he could feel the lick of flames, the burn of acid poison, and hear the ominous slapping of wings.

Miraculously he reached the palace in one piece and started looking for a way inside. Forget the enormous front doors. An obvious entrance like that, in full view of any dragons that happened to be strolling past, would be asking for trouble. Instead, skin crawling, he jittered his way along a blank section of wall—what, not even any windows to clamber through?—until he stumbled around a cornery bit—

—and over another body.

Damn.

It was Reggie, Melissande's sort-of boyhood chum and erstwhile house arrest guard, tumbled out of an inconspicuous side-door at the foot of a long, steep staircase. Some kind of special secret palace guard in-and-out, perhaps. From the ugly angle of Reggie's crooked head it seemed the fall had broken his loyal neck. There wasn't time to feel grief or guilt, to kneel and press the young man's eyelids down over his clouding, sightless eyes. To shed a tear. Lional and his dragon were coming.

"Sorry, Reggie," he said, gingerly stepping over the sprawled corpse. "Sorry."

Somewhere deep inside himself someone was screaming. It was the old Gerald, the Gerald he'd been before the cave. Before he surrendered to Lional, to cowardice, and created that glorious, murderous dragon.

No. Stop. Reg was right, you can't do this. Those grimoires are poison. Stop right now, Dunnywood, before it's too late.

But he couldn't afford to listen to his ghost. These

drastic times were his doing and only drastic action could undo them.

The secret guard staircase took him up and up and at last to an open doorway. Stepping through it into a deserted corridor, he realized from the painting on the wall in front of him—a particularly memorable flock of bilious-looking geese—that he wasn't far from Melissande's apartments. But did that mean Lional's kingly suite was close by? He'd never been given an actual top-to-bottom palace tour. He had no idea where the bastard put his head down at night . . . and he didn't have time to waste searching this antiquated rabbit-warren. There had to be a faster way of finding that *Lexicon*.

Frustrated, uncertain, Gerald banged a fist hard against the corridor wall beside him. That small pain woke lightly sleeping memories of his recent, harsher sufferings—and he abruptly straightened. Really? Was it possible? It should be. Shugat had tasted Lional in his blood. And if Shugat could, then surely so could he. And *if* he could then that meant . . .

Closing his eyes, he sank himself deep within. Sent his *potentia* questing. When it found Lional's lingering, filthy fingerprints he shuddered. So. He was marked for life, then. The foul incants Lional breathed into his mouth were become a part of him, part of his matrix, flesh, blood and bone. The notion was horrifying. Almost as horrifying as what he contemplated doing now.

Maybe Reg was right. Maybe there was another way to—

Stop it, Dunwoody. Stop trying to wriggle out of this. You know you have to. There's no other way.

So. He'd found Lional's mark. Now to use the mad king's foulness to track down his private suite in the palace.

Shuddering anew, Gerald wrapped a thread of *potentia* around Lional's hideous echo. Then he turned the rest of his magical self outwards and sought for the echo's counterpart—memories of Lional—contained within the confines of the palace.

No, not there. That's the dining room. Not there either, that's the Large Audience Chamber. And that's the Small one. Come on, come on. I want his bolt hole. I want his lair.

He was being tugged to the easiest places, the public places, where he'd already been. And why was that? Because, Tavistock or not, the glorious dragon or not, he was still at heart a Third Grade wizard with a Third Grade wizard's grasp of magic? Or was it Lional being crafty? Even in his own kingdom was he protecting himself?

Of course he is. Lional's mad and dangerous but he's not an idiot. With a succession of First Grade wizards on the loose of course he'd protect himself.

So. Don't look for Lional's echo. Look for his fingerprints, on carpet and brick.

Straight away, because it was close, he stumbled across the incant Lional had used to keep Melissande locked behind her own doors. Very nasty. Brilliant, but nasty. It was nothing short of a miracle that Monk had been able to break it. Briefly he felt a burst of pride in his friend. Crazy Monk Markham, the metaphysical genius. On the heels of pride, sorrow.

He's going to be so angry when he finds out what I've done.

With a grunt he wrenched himself away from that

profitless line of thinking. It didn't matter how Monk felt, or Reg, or Melissande. Or at least he couldn't let it matter. He let himself sink more deeply into that dark place Lional had hollowed out inside him.

Sentiment is weakness.

Eyes still closed, leaning against the corridor wall now, his body shaking, he pushed further and harder. Stirred up in his blood, the remains of Lional's curses started screaming. Or were they his own screams? Either way, it didn't matter. The only important thing now was finding the *Lexicon.*

A tug on his *potentia.* A sharp rebound. A sudden burning conviction. *That way.* On a deep breath he opened his eyes, pushed off the wall and started walking. Instinct dragged him along, dragged him almost to jogging, down corridor after corridor, up staircase after staircase, heading for the palace's highest floor. The closer he got to Lional's domain the harder his *potentia* tugged at him, so tuned now was it to Lional's caustic thaumic signature.

He didn't encounter another soul. Every last servant had fled, every single government lackey had deserted his or her post. With their sleepy little kingdom turned on its head, with a dragon raining acid and fire from the sky and their sovereign hunting them instead of protecting them, what could they do except run? But how many had run only to die anyway, in the palace gardens or on its carriageways or down in the city?

And is Zazoor feeling proud of himself, sitting there safe in his little bubble? Is his Holy Shugat pleased? What kind of gods does the old man serve, that he could sit there with all his power and not lift a finger to help the innocent?

Resentful anger simmering, warming him, helping to keep his fears at bay, Gerald kept on through the eerily empty palace. His heart thumped and his breath whistled as he climbed yet another daunting flight of stairs. The next opened door he fell through would take him into the attics or onto the roof, wouldn't it?

But no. The next door he eased open showed him an opulent corridor—where Lional's thaumic presence shouted loud enough to send him deaf, dumb and blind. Shouted so cruelly he staggered and dropped to his knees, one hand still clutching the door knob, the other fisting to his head. Lional, ever prudent, had warded the corridor with a brutal keep-your-distance hex. Snarling the hallway in thaumic barbed wire, armed with teeth and talons and a bloody minded ferocity, it tore at his *potentia* until he was whimpering in his throat.

I can't break through that. How can I break through that? I'm only as good as the incants I know right now, and I don't know any incant that could dismantle this hex. Not even Reg taught me an incant strong enough for this.

So—was that it? Had he been defeated before he ever really started? Looked like it. Looked like Lional's native cunning had beaten him without so much as raising a sweat. For all the good he could do here he might as well have stayed in the cave, in the dark, and starved slowly to death. Letting go of the door knob he folded to the floor and rolled himself into a tight ball, battered by Lional's inimical magics.

Gerald Dunwoody, what are you doing? Stop being such a pathetic tosser!

Startled, he unrolled himself and sat up. "Reg?"

But he was alone. That was just Reg's voice, the voice of his conscience, kicking him in the pants. Ashamed, he scrubbed his hands across his face. Oh, lord, he *was* pathetic, wasn't he?

If I don't get back on my feet and finish what I started then I'm no better than Shugat and Zazoor, hiding behind their precious, indolent gods.

Through slitted eyes he stared the length of the gilded, plushly carpeted corridor. Saw, at its far end, Lional's hexed double doors. Beyond that flimsy barrier lay *Grummen's Lexicon* and Saint Snodgrass alone knew what other proscribed texts. He was yards, mere yards, from laying his hands on the weapons he needed to defeat Lional, save New Ottosland—and possibly the rest of the world. And the only thing standing between him and victory over New Ottosland's mad king was this one measly, wicked, obliterating hex—which he didn't have the first notion how to dismantle.

But I made a dragon, so I can bloody well do this.

Grimly determined, goaded—and he knew it—by an unaccustomed but undeniable sense of competition with the Department of Thaumaturgy's one and only Monk Markham—he faced his fears. Faced Lional's hexed doors. Braced himself—feet wide, shoulders thrown back, head lifted, teeth gritted—and opened himself fully to the worst of Lional's magic.

CHAPTER THREE

It was like throwing himself into a writhing pit of insane vipers, or diving headfirst into a vat of boiling acid, or trying to ride a hundred wild horses bareback, all at once. The hex took him and shook him and tried to tear him apart. Flogged him and crushed him and threatened to splinter his bones.

Every instinct he possessed was screaming *get out, run away* but grimly he fought that cowardly impulse as hard and as bitterly as he fought Lional's hex. His heart was drubbing so hard he was afraid it might burst—or that his eyeballs would explode or his jaw crack into pieces. He could feel a howl building in his throat. Prying his teeth apart he let it out and heard it bounce back and forth between the walls of the corridor, a skin-crawling cry of pain and near-insanity.

Lost within Lional's merciless attack he flailed and thrashed, dimly aware of his battered *potentia* as it grappled with the onslaught of dark magic. He didn't know how to help his strange powers, or control them, had no idea how to harness their strength to his need.

If there was an elegant, subtle way to dismantle Lional's incant, well, he had no idea what that was. And he didn't have the time to work it out, either. Because time was precious and it was fast running out.

Oh, Saint Snodgrass. I could use some help about now . . .

Howling again, Gerald pulled his *potentia* back inside himself. Poured every last skerrick of his strength into crushing it small, then smaller, compressing it until it too was howling. He felt like he'd plucked the sun from the sky and was trying to stuff it into an egg cup—and the sun, his *potentia*, was fighting back. Rivers of sweat poured down his face, down his back. He could feel his spine bowing, his knees bending, could feel his heart trying to batter its way right through his ribs. His unremarkable body couldn't take much more of this. Punished by Lional and by himself it was threatening to fly apart, to escape this unending torment in death.

No—no—just a little more—a little longer—

And on the screaming brink of self-destruction he let himself fly free.

Like molten fire his power poured out of him, angry and indiscriminate, to smash the bindings of Lional's warding hex and obliterate its fabric. The keep-your-distance incant went up in flames and greasy smoke, stinking, unwholesome. Reeking of every foul enchantment Lional had so eagerly embraced.

Sobbing, Gerald fell forward onto his face, unable to save himself. The corridor's plush carpeting saved him from a broken nose or worse. Gasping he lay there, excoriated, waiting for the flames and agony to subside. When he thought he could feel his bones whole within him, when he thought he could trust himself to sit up in one piece, he pushed himself off the carpet and looked around at the scorch marks on the gilded walls and the expensive carpet. Stared, astonished, at the smoking doors to Lional's private apartments, drunkenly hanging from their half-melted hinges.

"Gosh," he said, his voice a thin, surprised croak. "How about that, Reg? I did it."

And surely Lional would know he'd done it, too. So what little time he had left, he'd be a fool to waste it. Wincing, he staggered back onto his feet, made his way along the unimpeded corridor—and crossed the threshold into Lional's private domain.

It stank of dark magic.

Standing just inside the open doorway, one hand braced against its almost too hot to touch frame, Gerald fought to keep his stomach from turning itself inside out. Every breath sucked the stench of corrupted power into his lungs, sent it flooding through his veins. Was it his overworked imagination or did even his sweaty skin feel sticky and fouled with it?

I don't understand. This entire palace reeks of Lional. How did none of the other court wizards not notice what was going on right under their noses? And what about Shugat and his gods? Am I supposed to think Lional just—what? Slipped their minds?

Possibly that was the most terrifying thing of all— that Lional possessed such strength, such mastery, that he could hide himself and his workings from the keen senses of a holy man like Shugat. That he could hide from the world-class First Grade metaphysical experts he'd hired to serve him. To die for him.

But then . . . who am I to talk? I didn't notice, did I? If I'm so special, if I can do things that make a man like Monk panic, how come I didn't realize the truth the moment I stepped out of the portal?

The unpalatable answer stared him rudely in the face. Because Lional was unique—and unthinkable. What Melissande's brother had done was so heinous, so appalling, that nobody thought it could—or would—be done. Or had realized that not only did Lional have the twisted imagination, and the will, to conceive of this plan, but that he also had the means to make his demented dream come true.

Bloody Pomodoro Uffitzi. This is all his fault. If he hadn't hoarded those grimoires . . . There's always one who thinks the rules don't apply to him. Why does there always have to be one?

And so now, because Uffitzi had been an arrogant plonker, two nations and countless innocents stood on the brink of destruction.

"Unless that ratty old holy man changes his mind and does something before it's too late," he muttered, suddenly needing to hear a friendly voice. No matter he was talking to himself—even that was better than the resounding silence of Lional's apartments.

Shugat. Mighty and mysterious and downright terrifying. Powerful enough to withstand the worst of Lional's foul magics—yet unwilling to help the helpless people of New Ottosland.

And why is that? Why won't he lift a finger? I don't understand.

Unless . . .

Chilled with fresh horror, Gerald swiped stinging sweat from his eyes. Could Shugat *want* this? Could

Kallarap's holy man and its sultan and its gods *want* Lional to run the length of his madness unchecked? Were silence and inaction their way of ending New Ottosland without a single scimitar drawing blood? Of putting an end to their tariff payment problem without directly getting involved?

Or are they convinced that I can handle Lional without their assistance?

Either way, he was in trouble. New Ottosland was in trouble. Because here he stood, a Third Grade wizard—sort of, technically—with extra powers he didn't begin to understand or control, who'd never so much as set foot in a proper wizarding academy, who'd received his barely adequate qualifications from a modest correspondence course that important wizards like Errol Haythwaite pretended didn't even exist.

And somewhere not far enough away was Lional, who'd left mere metaphysics behind some four dead wizards ago and had transformed himself into something the world of thaumaturgy had never seen.

Oh, lord. If I don't stop him here, today—if he gets past me and leaves New Ottosland—then he'll just keep killing First Grade wizards and taking their potentias.

The thought of Lional, twinned with his dragon and wielding the power of ten First Grade wizards, or twenty, or more, weakened his knees so he nearly dropped back to the carpet. Squeezing his eyes tight shut he gritted his teeth to keep an unmanly whimper trapped in his throat.

I can't do this. Dragon or no dragon I'm not good enough. Lional with a mere five potentias *is more than I can handle. Come back, Reg. I need you. Tell me what to do.*

Except—he already knew what to do. And he'd come here to do it. And if Reg *were* here she'd only try to stop him, so it was best she wasn't. Because if anyone could talk him out of this crazy plan it was Reg.

"Stop bloody stalling, Dunnywood, you tosser," he told himself savagely. "You've got no choice. Thousands of lives are depending on you—so get on with it."

The burning tide of fear receded and a little strength returned to his numbed limbs. Swiping sweat again, he straightened out of his slump, took several deep breaths, ignoring the taint in the air, and for the first time looked at his surroundings properly. Lional's apartments were dim, their curtains drawn and no lamps lit. The light from the corridor behind him barely washed over the threshold, as though the darkness of Lional's soul were soaking it up, like a sponge.

Letting go of the door frame he snapped his fingers, hoping to ignite whatever candles or lamps might be usefully lying about the place. Incant accomplished he stared, blinking in the sudden illumination, expecting to see—

Well. Not this.

"Blimey, Reg," he said, looking around. "I thought at least there'd be a cauldron or a skull. Something arcane and sinister and suitably repellent. Not to mention a few bucket loads of gilt and an ocean of velvet."

But no. The room he stood in wasn't plush or opulent or arcanely sinister. It was the antithesis of plush and opulent, every unadorned surface a stark black and white. No chairs, sofas, fountains or froufrous. One spindle-legged desk with a lone burning lamp on it. And not a single darkly arcane artifact in sight. If he hadn't known without a doubt that this was Lional's lair he'd never have believed it.

"Mind you," he added. "This is only the foyer."

Like his own royal apartments there were three doors leading out of the suite's severely restrained entrance hall. So if the similarity of design continued, that meant Lional's bedroom—and *Grummen's Lexicon* and whatever other revolting books he kept handy—lay behind that door *there*. On a deep breath Gerald took a step towards it, then hesitated. *Wait a minute, Dunwoody. Just wait.* This was Lional's private domain. No matter the ferocious keep-your-distance hex guarding the corridor, that didn't mean the place was safe. If he rushed in willy nilly now like some over-excited First Year student he might well trigger another guarding hex and get himself killed before he could do anybody any good.

Remember Reg's rule: look before you leap. It prevents a lot of unnecessary bleeding.

Thrusting aside his growing sense of urgency he closed his eyes and pushed his *potentia* through the curdled ether, seeking danger.

And found it, of course.

All three doors in Lional's apartment were hexed. And not singly hexed either, no. They were link-hexed, which meant that to get into Lional's bedroom he'd have to unbarricade all three in the correct sequence or risk—well, something disgusting. Wonderful. Clearly today *nothing* was going to be simple, or straightforward, or quick.

Heart thudding hard again he approached the doors, step by cautious step, reaching out both hands in the hope that he'd be able to sense something to help him proceed. He could feel his *potentia* quivering, reacting to the incants sunk into the aged oak. Not dark magic this time, not exactly. Just Lional's twisted thaumic fingerprints leaving a tainted smear in the ether, the multiplicity of stolen *potentias* garbled and gross. He felt his belly heave, protesting as again he heard the anguished screams of his predecessors . . . and felt their agony as they went up in flames . . .

Stop it, you idiot. Don't think about that. They're long dead, past helping. All you can do now is avenge them.

Shuddering, he wiped a clammy hand down his face. This wretched place was getting to him. He couldn't let it. He had to concentrate.

"Come on, Dunnywood." Alarmingly, his voice sounded thin and lost. "It's nearly over."

At least the door hexes were nowhere near as ferocious as the keep-your-distance hex. Lional felt himself safe here, in his private domain. But his unbearable arrogance was neatly tempered with caution. New Ottosland's mad king wasn't leaving anything to chance. The triple-hex was convoluted, tangling itself in complex loops and knots, and tugging on the wrong bit would doubtless unleash disaster.

Daunted, Gerald pinched the bridge of his nose between thumb and forefinger. He had *such* a headache brewing. But he couldn't afford to dwell on that either. Pain was just another distraction. Besides, if he didn't make it past those hexes a headache would be the least of his worries. Blinking hard to clear his blurry vision, he stared at the three doors. He could sense nothing, *nothing*, to suggest the order in which he needed to clear Lional's wickedly clever incants. He could stand here for hours, days, *weeks*, and be no closer to the answer. The hexes were clear and slippery like rain-washed glass. His *potentia* slid over them, unable to get a purchase. Unable to feel anything, sense any order or echo or hint of how to unlock them.

He turned aside, frustrated, feeling that tide of fear rising. There was no *time* for this nonsense. Lional would be coming. He could be inside the palace even now, snarling his way upwards, ready to rip intruding Gerald Dunwoody to bloody shreds. Without the protection of *Grummen's Lexicon* he didn't stand a chance against New Ottosland's mad king.

"So bugger *this* for a boatload of monkeys!" he shouted. Raised clenched fists over his head, summoned his *potentia*—and unleashed it on the barricaded doors.

They exploded in a storm of splinters.

Without even thinking he whipped his *potentia* around himself like a cloak, a flexible shield. The released energies from the destroyed hexes billowed harmlessly about him, dirty smoke and spitting sparks. Bits and pieces of ruined doors bounced off his etheretic armor and tumbled to the black-and-white marble floor, some of them burning.

Stunned, he stared at the gaping holes in the wall that used to be three doorways, then carefully eased his tight grip on his *potentia*. Like a sword gliding back into an oiled scabbard it slid back inside him, out of sight.

"Gosh," he said. "That was—different."

And terrifying. Because he'd no idea what he was

doing. Not consciously, anyway. Temper and desperation had combined in a single hammering heartbeat and suddenly he was smashing powerful hexes as easily as Reg snapped flies in mid-air.

Lional's bedroom suite lay beyond the middle doorway. With a single word and a hand wave he banished the lingering smoke then marched through the empty doorway into the private parlor beyond. His earlier incant had lit every lamp and candle in here, too. Again, to his surprise, he found no overwrought opulence. Oh, there was a certain sumptuosity to the sitting room, silk curtains and velvet upholstery and plush carpets underfoot. Beneath the poisonous dark magics the air smelled sweet. There were fresh flowers in crystal vases. Ebony chairs and a low table inlaid with mother of pearl. No gilding. Rich forest green and midnight blue were the dominant colors— and crimson, too, splashed here and there like drops of blood from a wound.

No books of magic in here.

A single door in the back wall led out of the private parlor. Gerald tested it, but at last found no hex. So he took the door by its handle, twisted it, pushed— and walked into the room beyond just like an ordinary, everyday man.

And here was Lional's bedroom, almost as austere as the rest of his apartments. Dull bronze walls, plush black carpet—and an enormous four-poster bed. Its drapings were bold crimson, as though Lional felt the need to sleep in blood. Tavistock cowered on the red velvet spread, topaz eyes slitted, fangs bared in a terrified snarl.

Gerald sighed. "Bugger."

He stared at the lion and the lion stared back. On the nightstand on the right-hand side of the bed, a tower of ancient texts. The stench of unwholesome incantations was so oppressive he could practically taste the dark magics contained between their covers. The ether shivered with them, a subliminal note of evil on the very edge of sensation. He could feel his *potentia* shrivel like a garden slug sprinkled with salt.

And here's me, come to take that evil into myself. Come to let it devour me alive . . .

Stranded on the bed, the lion rumbled in its throat.

"Poor old Tavistock," he said, pity stirring for the cat he'd so carelessly sported with to further his own petty ambitions. "Doesn't look like you're having much fun."

The lion rumbled again—agreement, or a warning of imminent attack?

"I've got some bad news for you," he added, taking a prudent half-step back. "Lional's found a new pet. I'm afraid you're going to have to shift for yourself."

Except—how could it? This was a lion, with an appetite to match. And with the palace deserted . . . nobody to feed the wretched thing . . . either it would starve to death or start eating people.

Oh, just what my conscience needs. A man-eating lion on the loose, courtesy of me.

"Tavistock," he said. "I think it's time for a change."

The words of the transmog reversal incant were buried in his memory somewhere, courtesy of Reg. But he knew, without knowing precisely how he knew, that he didn't need the words. Not any more. His *potentia*, woken to full life by the accident at Stuttley's staff factory, bubbled inside him like a hot spring. He could feel it expanding within the confines of its mortal prison, his body, shimmering his blood and vibrating his bones. Every time he'd used it since arriving in New Ottosland, whether he meant to or not, in the strangest way it felt like he'd been feeding that power. Giving it what it needed to grow.

So that all he needed to do now was *look* at Tavistock and see the cat held captive within the lion. See Tavistock as he'd been before, on the audience chamber dais, in Lional's lap, just a cat, just a fluffy cat, no more dangerous or disturbing than that . . .

"Tavistock," he whispered, and held out his hand. "Go back now. Go back. Be a cat again."

The thaumically-charged ether crackled. On Lional's enormous bed Tavistock twitched, tail lashing, and lumbered to his feet. Threw back his vast, maned head and roared, saliva-slicked fangs dripping. Around him the air curdled, tinting bluish orange. Then a crack of sound and a flash of light. A thunderstorm roaring through the ether. Gerald grunted, an echoing tempest raging through his unquiet blood as his *potentia* obeyed his command.

"Reversato!"

Another flash of light and crack of sound and the lion was gone. Instead, a bemused cat sat blinking in the middle of Lional's bed. Long marmalade coat wildly ruffled, whiskers bristling, eyes like saucers, Lional's abandoned pet took one look around the room, let out a loud, indignant wail and bolted.

One word, that's all it took, one word and a thought and I reversed a Level Twelve transmog. Who am I? What am I?

"Good luck, Tavistock," he murmured. "And good riddance."

Staring after the cat, he wondered if he could undo the dragon the same way. But no. Not with Lional linked to it by the *Tantigliani sympathetico*. His strength fed their bond beyond any easy breaking.

More's the pity.

Now that it felt safe to move about Lional's bedchamber he crossed to the nearest window and tugged its bronze silk curtain aside. Stared through the glittering glass at the palace gardens beyond, then up at the sky. Both were empty. No sign of Lional or his dragon. No sign of life at all. There were two more curtained windows and he looked through both of them, just to make sure. The third window afforded him a glimpse of the palace forecourt, where he'd left Shugat and Zazoor and the Kallarapi army.

They were gone. Holy man, sultan and every last camel. Vanished as though they'd never existed.

"And good riddance to you too," he added, feeling bitter. Feeling betrayed. *Idiot.* "You'd only have ended up getting in my way."

So. Lional and his dragon. If they weren't hanging around the palace, where could they be? Off terrorizing the countryside some more? Probably. Lional did enjoy his little amusements. And he believed himself invulnerable, facing no kind of danger from the likes of Gerald Dunwoody. Which was bad luck for the countryside—but a stroke of good luck for him. It was a reprieve, of sorts. A mistake on Lional's part. Perhaps the only one the mad king was likely to make.

Letting the curtain fall back across the window, he

turned to stare again at the vast crimson bed. Towering on the nightstand, Lional's stolen grimoires beckoned. Five—no, six ancient volumes. So many. So much evil. Palms sweaty, breathing uneven, his throat suddenly hot and tight, Gerald pushed through the bedroom's still-thickened etheretic atmosphere until he was standing so close to those terrible books that all he had to do was uncrook his elbow and he'd be touching them.

Or they'd be touching him.

"I'd rather see you dead here and now—I'd rather kill you myself than see you—"

"Oh, Reg," he whispered, the memory of her terror for him like acid in his veins. "I'm sorry, but I don't have a choice. You saw what Lional's turned into. Whatever's inside me won't be enough."

He cried out as his fingers closed on the first grimoire. Such a shock of latent power searing through him. A dark voice whispering, full of malice and glee. His knees had gone weak again, threatening to buckle. Still clutching the grimoire he sank to the edge of Lional's bed. The feather mattress gave way beneath him with an almost-silent sigh. With a heart-thumping effort he forced his eyes open, made himself look down and read the title of the book in his sweaty, trembling hands. The damn thing was so heavy he had to rest it on his thighs.

Grummen's Lexicon.

Of course. Start with the best.

The *Lexicon* was bound in brass and black leather, its title embossed on cover and spine in faded gold lettering. The rich binding was scarred with age. Wrinkled here and there. On the top right-hand corner, a single fingerprint, scorched scarlet. Holding his breath Gerald touched his own finger lightly to it, and heard in his mind the lingering echoes of a scream.

He snatched his hand back. Then, though he wasn't what anyone would call a religious man, church being one of those things he almost never bothered with, even though it meant disappointing his mother, he looked up. Who knew? Maybe the gods of Kallarap were listening.

"I'm doing this because I have to, all right? Just— please. Please, whatever happens to me, whatever happens once I'm done—if Reg is right—don't let them send Monk to hunt me down. I couldn't bear that. Send anyone else—Errol Haythwaite, for example. But please, not Monk."

Silence. Not so much as the smallest hint that a deity of any kind was listening, or in the mood to grant his despairing request.

Oh well. I can't say I really expected a reply.

Mouth dry, rivulets of sweat burning his ribs and spine, he stared at the *Lexicon*. Once he opened the wretched thing, once he exposed himself to the first of its foul incants, there'd be no going back. This new Gerald Dunwoody would cease to exist, almost before the old one's corpse had grown cold.

And who—or what—would take his place was anyone's guess.

Before he could change his mind, before he let the gibbering fear take over his body, make it throw down the *Lexicon* and run him screaming from Lional's chamber—

Just do it, Dunnywood. Do it. Do it.

—he opened the book. Recited the handy little

incant Reg had taught him, way back in the early days of his wizarding correspondence course, the learn-it-fast hex that made the dullest man a speed-reading, incant-absorbing machine.

With a spark and a sizzle, the incant ignited. Dimly he felt himself turning page after page with fingers that belonged to someone else. He didn't understand how, but his unnatural *potentia* was enhancing Reg's quick-learn hex. Like a thirsty flower his mind absorbed Grummen's collection of fetid magics faster than he could make sense of the words. He heard himself breathing like a runner in a race. Felt his heart crashing from rib to rib. Tasted the foulness of Grummen's hexes and incants, coating his throat and the inside of his mouth with bile. His fingertips burned, and his bleary eyes. His vision was smearing, blurring as crimson as Lional's vast bed. He was roasting, he was freezing, he was losing himself. Someone had turned his bones to lead. They were so heavy in his flesh now he thought any moment they'd tear free.

And then he turned the *Lexicon*'s last page. Read the incant inscribed upon it—*Regarding the Extraction of Knowledge from the Recently Dead*—and felt the necrothaumic compulsion incant's power sink inexorably into his grossly overfed mind.

With a strangled groan Gerald lost his grip on the heavy grimoire. Heard it thud to the plush black carpet and a heartbeat later thudded beside it. A windstorm was howling inside his skull, scouring the confines of its bony bowl like a banshee trapped in a bubble. Little trickles of its fury dribbled between his parted lips. For one terrible moment he thought he was back in the cave, at the mercy of Lional's merciless curses. With a louder groan he rolled onto his back and stared at the ceiling of Lional's self-restrained chamber. Painted black, it was daubed with eye-searing sigils that in another lifetime he'd never have understood.

But he understood them now, and what they meant made him weep. Or perhaps he wept because they were no longer a mystery. Because the howling in his head wasn't a banshee at all, but the last raging cries of a dying Gerald. Because rising from the ashes of *that* Gerald was *this* one.

A Gerald with the power to make the dead speak. To kill with a thought. To fashion mud into a man. A copy of a man. A wicked shambling pretense of a man. Who could boil a woman's blood in her veins without fire, blind a disobedient child, reduce a village to cinders and a cow to blood and hide . . . all with a small and simple word.

His heart was beating sluggishly now, his blood thick and dark with Grummen's terrible knowledge. With a struggling effort he pushed to his feet. He was a newborn necromancer, learning how to walk.

With a sigh of relief he collapsed onto Lional's bed. Pressed the heels of his hands against his hot eyes, willing his red, smeared vision to clear. When he let his hands drop his gaze shifted to the other books on the nightstand, tugged there as though by some thaumaturgic force. He tried to resist—he didn't need to know any more. He was burdened enough with the contents of *Grummen's Lexicon*. But he couldn't fight the compulsion to reach out to that tower of books and take the next one into his hands.

Pygram's Pestilences.

A slim little volume, this. Clothbound in eggshell blue. So harmless looking, like a nice lady's diary. Before he could stop himself—try to stop himself—the book was open in his lap and he was devouring each hex. Even though he knew firsthand how evil, how despicable, these magics were. Even though he'd unspeakably suffered through each and every one during his time of torment in Lional's cave. The notion of learning them, of perhaps using them on another living being—he should be revolted, repulsed, he should destroy the text with a look—and yet he couldn't. He didn't. Instead he opened himself to Pygram's curses and let the words and the sigils engrave themselves on his bones.

I'll be all right. I'm a good man. I won't use them. This is just a precaution. It's like I told Reg: I have to know how to fight fire with fire.

With the last curse absorbed, the book joined *Grummen's Lexicon* on the carpet.

So. That was two down and four to go. There was no point in turning back now, no point at all in trying to resist. Whatever Lional knew *he* had to know, or he'd have done this for nothing. Killed the other Gerald for nothing. And he'd stand no chance of killing Lional in revenge.

One by one, dear Reg's learn-it-fast hex sped up to the point where he'd stopped seeing the actual words, he read the rest of Lional's forbidden library. *A Compendium of Curses.* Charming. *Foyle's Foilers.* Wittily barbaric, that one. Who'd have thought a mass murderer would have such a sense of humor? *Madam Bartholomew's Little Surprise.* A hex in forty-six parts, each one more horrible than the last. And finally, sickeningly, a grimoire almost as appalling as the *Lexicon*: Jonker Trinauld's *Guide to the Unnatural*.

Bloated beyond bearing with the filthiest incants ever devised by witch or wizard, Gerald tossed Trinauld's dreadful leatherbound observations aside and slid from Lional's bed onto the floor. He had a headache like a railway spike driving into each temple, pain so powerful and purposeful he couldn't see straight. Exploding behind his closed eyelids bright starbursts of agony, exquisitely timed with the hammer beats of his heart.

And beneath the pain, beneath the starbursts, his *potentia* seethed and bubbled.

No wonder Lional had gone mad. No man was meant to contain these kinds of magics. Not all at once. He was coming apart at the seams himself, all those dark magics prisoned inside him, boiling and bubbling and yearning to be free. If he opened his eyes would he see his skin, fissuring? Would he see cracks appearing and glimpse the evil within? His *potentia* had been force-fed full to vomiting, was crammed to its limits with incants and hexes that should never have been born. And now it seethed and surged the hot blood in his veins, demanding expression. Screaming to be heard.

On his hands and knees, fingers tangled in the black carpet's deep pile, Gerald opened his eyes. Felt the pain behind them. Heard the roaring in his skull. A storm was building inside him, strong enough to smash his bones and spill his blood. Strong enough to kill him if he didn't let it out.

The carpet beneath his hands was starting to smoke.

Lurching to his feet he threw back his head and let out a howling shriek. The ether erupted—and he erupted with it. In a burst of blue flames, the curtains caught fire. The carpet caught fire. Lional's vast crimson bed went up in smoke and sparks. Behind the burning curtains the windows exploded.

He watched as the blue flames fed greedily on Lional's private chamber. Smiled, and snapped his fingers, and turned the flying shards of glass to ice. The ice melted, steaming. The fire continued to burn. In his veins, in his arteries, his newly blackened blood burned wildly with it. Now he stood at the heart of a thaumaturgical conflagration—sublimely untouched and untouchable as the blue flames roared his delight.

"Good," he said, nodding. "That's good. That feels right."

Smiling, he went in search of Lional.

CHAPTER FOUR

The other Ottosland, the same day

"Right," said Melissande. "I've had just about *enough* of this."

Monk sighed. "I did warn you. Look, Melissande, they'll get to us when they get to us so there's no point—"

"No, Mr. Markham, there is *every* point! Because at the rate your precious Department's going I'll have qualified for the pension before they come to a decision!"

And stop calling me Melissande. Just because in a moment of weakness I sniveled all over you, that doesn't mean you get to take liberties.

Except apparently it did, because she couldn't quite bring herself to reprimand him out loud.

Squatting between them, Reg refluffed all her feathers and said, "Oh, give it a *rest*, you two, or I'll do *both* of you a mischief."

They were sitting uncomfortably side by side by side in a drab gray waiting room outside some official chamber or other in Ottosland's antiquated Department of Thaumaturgy building. Apart from the back-breaking chairs there wasn't a stick of furniture. Neither were there windows to look out of or any tedious old magazines to read. The room was cold and stuffy and not designed to succor its occupants.

Oh lord. I wish I knew what was happening to Gerald.

Shivering, she glanced through the open door to the drab gray corridor beyond. "Where the hell has Rupert got to? It doesn't take *this* long to use the lavatory."

"Ha," said Reg. "He's probably been side-tracked by a moth."

"That's not funny! Whatever you may think of him he really *loved* his butterflies, you horrible bird! And Lional killed them and now he's *grieving* for them. He's probably got his head buried in a towel right now, crying his heart out for those stupid, *stupid* insects!"

Monk, carelessly presumptuous and dangerously attractive, gave Reg a look. "You know, you're really not helping."

With an effort Melissande pulled herself back from the brink of embarrassment . . . and didn't object when Monk took her hand in his. Even though she should. Even though public displays of affection were highly irregular. It was a wonder the bird wasn't screeching about that, along with everything else.

"Nobody's *helping*," she muttered. "It was stupid to come here. Gerald had *no business* forcing me to come here. I should be at home, fighting for New Ottosland. After all, I'm prime minister and practically the queen!"

Not that she wanted to be. She couldn't think of anything worse. *I wonder if I'll have to change my name to Lional . . .*

Reg roused out of her slump. "Don't you worry about New Ottosland, ducky. Gerald's taking care of it. He's a wizarding prodigy, he is. And we'll be hearing from him any moment. You'll see."

She exchanged a mordant glance with Monk over the top of Reg's head. Clearly the bird didn't believe her own pep talk. *I don't believe it either. It'll take more than a prodigy to beat Lional and his dragon. It'll take a miracle . . . and I'm not sure they exist.*

Monk tightened his fingers. "Don't give up, Meli—I mean, Your Highness. The Department will come through for us. It's just going to take a little time. It's all such a bloody mess. At last count we've got five different nations involved and three of them aren't officially talking to each other."

Ah, politics. *I am sick to death of politics. I think I'll ban it when I'm queen.* She pulled a face at him. "I'm not giving up. And call me Melissande."

Despite his own imperfectly concealed worry, Monk's lips quirked in a brief grin. "Thought you'd never ask. Look, do you want me to go hunting for Rupert while—"

The main chamber's large double doors opened. "Come in, please," said a discreet secretarial type dressed in sober black. "Lord Attaby will see you now."

Abruptly aware of appearing less than her best, Melissande slid off the chair and lifted her chin, defiant. "And not a moment too soon. I was just about to make a Scene."

As Reg hopped onto Monk's waiting shoulder

she marched past the discreet secretary and into the chamber. Stalked across the room's dingy carpet, Monk and Reg at her heels, and halted in front of the long polished oak conference table on the far side of the room. There was a click behind her as the secretary closed the double doors.

To her fury she saw the Ottosland officials at the table had been drinking tea and eating biscuits. *Tea and biscuits while my kingdom is dragged to hell in a hand-basket. How dare they?* "Right," she said, glaring at the three men ranged before her. "Which one of you is Lord bloody Attaby?"

The man in the middle, reeking of affluence and self-importance, inclined his head fractionally. His thinning silver hair was slicked to his skull with something smelly and expensive. "I am Lord Attaby, Minister of Thaumaturgy for the Ottosland government."

She looked left then right at his silent bookends. "And these two?"

"My colleagues," said Lord Attaby blandly.

"I see. And do they have names?"

"None that are relevant to these proceedings," said Lord Attaby. "Madam."

She snorted. "I'm not madam, I'm Her Royal Highness Princess Melissande, Prime Minister of New Ottosland and—and—Queen Presumptive."

Lord Attaby laced his fingers before him, frowning. "Or so you claim."

"*Claim?*" she demanded. "What, you think I'm *lying?*"

"I think you are a young foreign woman lacking both identification and requisite travel documentation who has entered this country by dubious and possibly illegal means," said Lord Attaby, looking down his nose at her. "And who, it would appear, has suborned one of its citizens into breaking some very, *very* serious laws."

Monk stepped forward. "No, she hasn't, Lord Attaby. That's all on me. And she is who she says she is, I can vouch for that. Unless you think I'm lying too."

Lord Attaby's chilly expression plummeted below freezing. "It would appear, Mr. Markham, you have been laboring under the mistaken apprehension that your illustrious family name would afford you unlimited protection in this matter. Allow me to disabuse you of this naïve—"

The man on Lord Attaby's right lowered his almost-imperceptibly raised hand. Melissande looked at him more closely; anyone who could halt an aristocrat mid-tirade was worth examining. He was extremely . . . nondescript. Unlike Lord Attaby, whose shirt was silk, he wore plain cotton. His watchband was leather, not gold, and he altogether lacked a pampered air. His hooded gray eyes were years older than his round, faintly lined face and short, mousy brown hair suggested. He didn't look like an enemy. He didn't look like a friend. More than anything he looked like a greengrocer, or some other kind of inoffensive shopkeeper.

How very odd, she thought. *I wonder who he is?*

The man on Lord Attaby's left took advantage of the silence and said, "Your part in this, Monk, will be dealt with in due course. For now let us focus on the reason for Her Highness's unorthodox appearance in the country."

Melissande glanced at Monk. He was subdued now and ever-so-slightly pink around the edges. "Yes, Unc—Sir Ralph."

"Lord Attaby," said Monk's important relative, properly deferring. "Do continue, sir. I believe time is a commodity in short supply."

"Time, Lord Attaby, has pretty well run out!" she said hotly. "At least for your citizen Professor Gerald Dunwoody! I'm assuming you *do* care about him at least, even if you couldn't give a toss about the five dead wizards or the people of Kallarap or *my* people, in New Ottosland, some of whom are already dead because of this string of disasters! You know, none of this would ever have happened if people like you hadn't failed to monitor Pomodoro Uffitzi more carefully! If *he* hadn't got his hands on those dreadful grimoires *I* wouldn't be standing here thaumaturgically related to a dragon!" She tilted her chin at him. "Now what have you to say about *that*?"

Lord Attaby sat back, thinly smiling. "A great deal, as it happens." His fingers drummed the table, making his teaspoon dance on its saucer. "Am I to understand, Your Highness, that you . . . and your government . . . accept no responsibility for recent events? Are you claiming that your brother King Lional bears no culpability whatsoever for the murder of five wizards, one of whom was an Ottoslander, or the deaths of your unfortunate citizens and his intended invasion of your peaceful neighbor?"

Melissande felt herself turn red. "No," she said curtly. "Of course Lional's culpable. He's also crazy. I'm not making excuses, I'm just giving you the facts."

Lord Attaby's smile was remarkably unpleasant.

"In my experience, *Prime Minister*, facts are malleable things. They can be massaged to fit any number of scenarios depending upon a variety of preferred outcomes."

"Really?" she said, seething.

He nodded. "Really."

"How very interesting. Because in *my* experience that's known as falsifying evidence. Manipulating the truth. To be blunt, Lord Attaby, it's known as *lying*. Also *covering your ass*."

The nondescript man on Lord Attaby's right looked down, lips twitching. Monk's illustrious relative frowned disapprovingly. Lord Attaby scowled, his pouchy face burnished dull crimson. "Young woman—"

"No, *not* 'young woman,'" she snapped. "You were right the first time. Do at least try to keep the protocol intact." Leaning her fists on the oak conference table she thrust her face into his. "Now let's get something straight, *my lord*. As far as I'm concerned there's plenty of blame to go around for this fiasco. And when it's over by all means, let's sit down with tea and biscuits and parcel it out like lumps of sugar. But before that, if it's not too much to ask, could you and your hoity-toity Departmental chums here *stop* pointing fingers for five seconds and do something constructive?" She raked them with a furious gaze. "Because in case you've forgotten, gentlemen, people are *dying*! And in light of that, how I got here and so on and so forth is just a steaming pile of bollocks!"

"I'm so sorry, gentlemen," said a brisk voice from the doorway. "You mustn't be offended. My sister has a temper but her heart is in the right place. And as it happens this time I agree with her. We don't have time for recriminations."

Melissand spun around. "*Rupert*? Rupert, where the hell have you been?"

As the discreet secretary closed the doors again Rupert walked towards her, one hand outstretched. "Darling Melly." He still looked ridiculous in his ruined blue velvet knickerbockers and orange silk shirt but even so . . . something was different. He'd *changed*. The way he carried himself, the look in his eyes. Even the sound of his voice was different. No longer shrinkingly apologetic, but sure and strong. Reaching her, he took her hand and kissed her cheek. "I've been sorting out a few things. Lord Attaby?"

Horrible Lord Attaby was on his feet. So were his bookends. "Your Majesty," he murmured. "I take it you and the Prime Minister have reached an agreement?"

"We have," said Rupert. "Everything's arranged."

Dumbfounded, Melissande stared at Monk then Reg then back at Rupert. "I'm sorry," she said, and pulled her hand free. "*What's* arranged? Rupert, what are you—"

He kissed her cheek again. "I'll explain everything later. You have my word. But right now you need to come with me, all of you. We don't have much time if we're going to save Gerald."

Folding her arms, she shook her head. "Sorry, Rupert, but I'm not going anywhere until you tell me what's going on. This has been a very long, very *bad* day, and I'm just about ready to—"

Without even so much as a courteous knock the drab chamber's doors banged open again and an alarmingly flustered minion scuttled in, a piece of paper clutched in one hand. Lord Attaby, freshly crimson, thumped a fist on the table. This time all three teaspoons, and the teacups, leaped and rattled in their saucers.

"Juby! What is the meaning of this? We are in private session! Have you taken leave of your few paltry senses, man, barging in here when—"

"I'm sorry, my lord. I'm terribly sorry," the minion wailed. He had an odd, squarish-shaped face and every inch of it was sweating. "But this couldn't wait." He thrust the piece of paper at outraged Lord Attaby. "From Priority Monitoring, my lord."

Lord Attaby flicked a glance left and right at his silently concerned bookends then took the piece of paper from Juby. Melissande heard an odd little sound beside her and turned, to see Monk easing a finger between throat and shirt collar. His eyes were wide and glassy with concern.

"What?" she murmured. "Monk, what's going on?"

"Dunno," he murmured back. "But it won't be good."

"Priority Monitoring means trouble?"

He nodded. "Big trouble."

"What kind?"

"Sorry. No idea."

"Reg?"

Still firmly ensconced on Monk's shoulder, the dratted bird ruffled her feathers and shrugged. "Don't ask me, ducky. Bang their snooty heads together if you want some answers."

Actually, that wasn't a bad idea. "Lord Attaby, what—"

"Hush, Mel," said her strangely altered brother,

with an authority she'd never before heard in his voice. "Wait."

Lord Attaby was rereading the urgent note with a look on his face that said he hadn't believed it the first time and didn't want to believe it now. Was it a trick of the chamber's lighting or could she see sweat on his brow? Silently the minister pushed the note towards Monk's important uncle, who pulled a pair of wire-rimmed spectacles from his inside coat pocket, placed them precisely on his nose and read the minion's urgent missive.

Monk's important uncle stopped breathing, just for a moment.

"If I may?" the nondescript third man at the table said quietly, and held out his hand. Without bothering to ask Lord Attaby's permission Monk's uncle passed the note to him. The nondescript man read it, just the once. When he was finished he closed his eyes. Melissande, watching him, thought it the most alarming thing she'd ever seen. Because in his eyes, before he'd hidden them . . .

Oh lord. Oh Saint Snodgrass. This is bad, isn't it?

"All right," she said, heedless of good manners and international protocol. "What exactly is going on? What's this Priority Monitoring station, and what's it monitored that's put all three of you terribly self-contained gentlemen into a tizzy?"

As the minion Juby's eyes bugged nearly out of his head at her tone, and Rupert touched warning fingers to her arm, and Lord Attaby sucked in a swift, offended breath, the nondescript man flicked the piece of paper across the table towards her.

"See for yourself, Your Highness."

"*Sir Alec!* I have not—"

"We can't hide it from them, my lord," said the mysterious Sir Alec, who looked like a greengrocer but clearly wasn't. "We might not like it but they are involved."

Before Rupert could take the note she snatched it off the table and scanned the scribbled message. "*An unprecedented thaumaturgical event.* What's that when it's at home?" She glanced at the note again. "Or in this case New Ottosland."

"Show me," said Monk, and plucked the note from her suddenly cold fingers. He read it quickly then looked up, every last skerrick of color drained from his cheeks. "Are you sure about this, Jubes? Somebody's not playing a practical joke?"

"Of course I'm sure!" said the minion Juby, his voice shaking. "I was bloody there, wasn't I, when the alarms went off. The gauges *melted*, Monk. They're nothing but etheretic *goo*. I'm telling you—" And then he choked to a halt as Lord Attaby thumped the table again. "I'm sorry, my lord. It's just—I never—"

"You're dismissed, Juby," said Lord Attaby coldly. "Get back to your post. And not a word about this to anyone who wasn't present at the time, is that clear?"

Juby nodded so hard and fast his neck almost snapped. "My lord," he squeaked, and fled.

"I think, Lord Attaby," Rupert said in the same mild voice Lional used just before somebody was made very sorry for something, "that you need to explain what's going on."

His expression horribly grim, Lord Attaby folded

his hands neatly on the table. "I can't do that, Your Majesty."

"Oh, I think you can," said Rupert. Never in his whole life had he sounded so dangerous. "And I think you *will*. This business touches upon my kingdom and its welfare. Therefore you *will* tell me—"

"He can't," said Sir Alec, the deceptive greengrocer. "Because he doesn't know. None of us knows precisely what has happened in your kingdom, Your Majesty. Only that it's catastrophic."

"Yes, but what does that *mean* exactly?" Melissande demanded. "Are you saying that between them Gerald and Lional have—have—that somehow they've managed to destroy the whole place?"

"That's—unlikely," said Sir Alec. "But something has definitely occurred, something—"

"If you say *catastrophic* one more time," she said crossly, "I will give you *such* a smack."

He blinked at her, once. "Something we are currently unable to quantify," he said at last, "beyond the fact that the event is unprecedented."

"And what does *that* mean?"

"It means Gerald's in even more trouble than he was when we left," said Monk, furious. "I'm a blithering idiot. I *never* should have let him—"

"Please, Mr. Markham," said Rupert, "let's not. I'm sure once the dust has settled there'll be plenty of blame to go around. Now. This unprecedented thaumaturgical event. It seems obvious to me that either Gerald or my unfortunate brother Lional is behind it. If it's Gerald then I venture we have cause for optimism. But if it's *Lional*—"

Melissande flinched. Found herself wishing

quite desperately that she could take hold of Monk Markham's hand. "Please don't say that, Rupes. I don't think I could bear it if—" She couldn't even bring herself to say the words out loud. "Sir Alec, can't you tell who's behind what's happened?"

Sir Alec shook his head. "I'm afraid not."

"I'm sorry," said Rupert, very clipped. "But I find that hard to believe. It's my understanding Ottosland's Department of Thaumaturgy prides itself on being the most comprehensive establishment of its kind in the world. And yet there you sit claiming *you can't tell* who has triggered this unprecedented thaumaturgic event?"

As the three men at the table exchanged inscrutable looks, Monk cleared his throat. "Actually, Your Highness, it's true. We can't. Our international monitoring stations aren't calibrated that way. Not for individual thaumic signatures. Sorry."

Rupert stared at Monk, and Monk stared at Rupert. Then Rupes nodded, apparently satisfied.

Struck again by how *different* her brother was, Melissande touched Monk's sleeve. "Can't you work out what's happened? I mean, you were able to find Bondaningo's thaumic signature in the hex Lional put on my doors and . . . well . . . Gerald's your best friend. If anyone can work out if he's the one behind this thaumaturgical event, surely it's you."

Painful shadows shifted in Monk's eyes. "Melissande—Your Highness—I would if I could, believe me. But it doesn't work like that. I don't think anyone's been able to read a thaumaturgic event long-distance. At least not *this* kind of long-distance."

"True," said Sir Alec, suspiciously mild. "But to

my knowledge, Mr. Markham, nobody has ever invented a portable portal before, either. So perhaps Her Highness's suggestion isn't—"

"Now you wait a moment, Alec," said Monk's uncle. "That's *my* reprobate of a nephew you're enticing into yet more unsanctioned, unpalatable and patently unsafe thaumaturgic shenanigans and I don't appreciate you meddling in my family's—"

"Thank you, Sir Ralph," Lord Attaby snapped. "Your sentiments are understandable but irrelevant. This is a crisis and in a crisis it's a case of all hands on deck. Mr. Markham—"

Monk jumped, then yelped as Reg dug all her claws through his coat to stop herself from falling off his shoulder. "My lord?"

"Can you do it?" said Lord Attaby, leaning across the polished oak conference table toward him. "Are you able to ascertain which wizard is behind this unprecedented thaumaturgic event?"

"Um," said Monk, his voice strangled. "I don't know. Maybe."

"How, Monk?" said his uncle, incredulous. "You've no reference points, no thaumic signature on record for comparisons, no—"

"Oh dear," said Lord Attaby, all his teeth on show in a deeply unamused smile. "And would that be guilt plastered across your face, Mr. Markham?" He looked at Sir Ralph. "I think there's something your enterprising nephew has neglected to tell us, Sir Ralph."

Sir Ralph covered his face with one hand. "When this is over, I am going to kill him."

"Certainly that would be one way of solving the

problem," Lord Attaby agreed. "But if we could for the moment stay focused on our more immediate concerns?" Sitting back, he laced his fingers across his middle. "Come now, Mr. Markham. Those of a religious persuasion tell us confession is good for the soul. If I were you I'd start confessing, for I suspect your soul needs all the help it can get."

Melissande tightened her fingers on Monk's arm. "Please? You might be New Ottosland's only hope. And whatever trouble you get into afterwards, Rupert and I will help you out of it. My promise as a princess and a prime minister and an almost-queen."

With a groan, his face milky pale, Monk nodded. Then he looked at his three superiors, grimly entrenched behind the oak conference table. "I covered up for Gerald when he transmogged King Lional's cat into a lion."

"I'm sorry?" said Lord Attaby, after a moment. His ferocious smile had vanished behind a frown. "Did I hear you aright? You falsified official Department records?"

"No!" said Monk, alarmed. "No, of course not, Lord Attaby. I just—I turned off the monitoring alarm before anyone else heard it and reset the etheretic calibrators. The information should still be there. All I did was . . . gloss over it."

"All you did," his appalled uncle moaned. "Nephew, I swear—"

"So what you're saying," said Sir Alec, before Monk's uncle made good on his murderous threat, "is that we have a captured sample of Mr. Dunwoody's enhanced thaumic signature?"

Monk nodded. "Provided nobody's accidentally purged the records, yes."

"And you're confident you can use this sample to establish the cause of our monitoring meltdown?"

"Confident, sir?" Monk swallowed. "Well, I don't know about confident but I'll give it my best shot."

Lord Attaby pushed his heavy oak chair back from the table and stood. "Then I suggest we waste no more time on recriminations and expostulations and instead get on down to Priority Monitoring. Your Majesty, I'll have you and your—er—your prime minister escorted to a more comfortable chamber where you can—"

Melissande gave him a look worthy of Lional. "Oh no, you won't. This is our kingdom you're talking about, my lord. We're coming down to Priority Monitoring with you. Aren't we, Rupert?"

"Why yes, Melissande," Rupert drawled. "I rather think we are."

For the briefest moment she thought Lord Attaby might argue the point—but then he gave up. Smart man. "Very well," he sighed. "Upon the understanding, Your Majesty, that you will be under the *strictest* code of confidentiality. Whatever you see or hear cannot be discussed with anyone not currently in this chamber. And frankly, after today, I'd rather it were never discussed again. Do I have your word on that?"

"You do, Lord Attaby," said Rupert, with the most regal nod. "Mine and my sister's."

Lord Attaby heaved another sigh. "Fine. Mr. Markham, find somewhere to put that ridiculous bird, will you? This is the Ottosland Department of

Thaumaturgy, not a zoological garden. And if you can't procure a cage you can stuff it in a cupboard!"

"I beg your bloody pardon?" said Reg, tail feathers rattling. "Stuff yourself in a cupboard, you silly old goat!"

A paralyzed silence. And then Monk plucked Reg off his shoulder and held her up to his face, nose-to-beak. "You had to do it, didn't you?" he said, sounding desperate. "You had to mouth off and make everything worse. You couldn't just—just sit in a cage for an hour until I worked out how to help Gerald, could you?"

"Oh, *please!*" Reg retorted. "As if Gerald's getting out of this pickle without *my* help! This pickle *you* landed him in, sunshine, when you showed him madam's *stupid* Position Vacant advertisement without waiting to consult *me* on whether—"

"Oh for the love of Saint Snodgrass, would the pair of you *shut up?*" Melissande shouted, and fetched Monk a resounding clout on the back of his head. "What's *wrong* with you? Carping and bickering while Gerald's in trouble!"

"Hey!" said Monk, turning on her. "D'you mind? That hurt!"

"Really?" she retorted. "I find that hard to believe, seeing as how your head's a solid block of wood!"

Reg rattled her tail even harder than before. "Ha! You tell him, ducky!"

"Shut up, Reg, or I'll clout you too," she said, glaring. "Monk's right, *ducky*. You should've kept your beak shut. I was just about to tell Lord Attaby that you had to come with us because you're a beloved childhood pet but *now*—"

"Now," said Lord Attaby, his expression forbidding, "I can see we have yet another crisis to contain. I take it this isn't a mere trained talking bird?"

"Far from it," said Sir Alec. His voice and face were impassive but there was a definite gleam in his chilly gray eyes. "In fact, my lord, upon a closer examination, I think you'll find this isn't a bird at all."

Lord Attaby stared at him. "Not a bird? What are you talking about man, it's got feathers. And a beak."

"True," said Sir Alec. "But appearances can be deceiving—can't they, Your Majesty?"

With a puffing effort Reg wrenched herself free of Monk's grip and flapped onto the oak conference table. Head tipped to one side, she gazed gimlet-eyed at him.

"Speaking from experience, are we, sunshine?"

"Something like that," said Sir Alec, dry as a desert. "And when this current crisis is resolved I'm sure it will be most edifying to compare notes. But in the meantime—" He turned. "My lord, the bird might well prove useful to our cause. I suggest it accompanies us down to Priority Monitoring."

Lord Attaby's jaw dropped. "You suggest—" And then he shook his head. "Very well, Sir Alec. There's no time for a lengthy debate—and Saint Snodgrass knows your instincts have proven sound in the past. But you can stand surety for its trustworthiness."

Melissande held out her arm. "Come on, Reg. Let's go."

So Reg hopped onto her arm and from there to her shoulder and they all trooped down into the bowels of the Department of Thaumaturgy building, a stiff-backed Lord Attaby leading the way. The Priority Monitoring station was a small, windowless cubbyhole buried beneath floors and floors of less-secret government divisions. Almost every square foot was crammed full of cluttered desks and rickety chairs and extraordinary machines sprouting gauges and thaumostats and wiggly, jiggly thaumatographs. Some of them had indeed melted to goo.

"Everybody out," Lord Attaby ordered, sweeping his goggle-eyed minions with a glare guaranteed to petrify wood. "In fact, go home. You're relieved of duty until tomorrow. And not a word about any of this, do I make myself clear? Consider yourselves bound by the Official Secrets Act."

A chorus of obedient *Yes, sirs*, and then the four astonished wizards, including Juby, departed before their superior could change his mind about the early mark.

"Right then," said Lord Attaby, once they were alone. "Get on with it, Mr. Markham."

As Monk stripped off his coat and rolled up his sleeves, and Lord Attaby withdrew to quietly confer with Sir Alec and Sir Ralph, Melissande let Rupert tug her sideways for their own private conference.

"Are you all right?" he asked softly, smoothing a lock of hair behind her ear.

"No, of course I'm not," she said, feeling snappish. Refusing to be charmed by his sweet, caring gesture. "Rupert, what's going on? What's *happened* to you?"

Rupert looked at Reg. "Do you mind?"

"Huh," Reg said, sniffing. "All these public displays of affection. Not what *I'd* call royal, ducky."

"Nobody asked you, Reg," she said, and twitched her shoulder. "Get off. I want to hug my brother."

"I don't know," Reg grumbled, and hopped onto the back of the nearest empty chair. "No decorum. That's your problem, ducky. You've got no bloody decorum."

Folded hard to Rupert's skinny chest, surprised by the sudden wiry strength in his arms, she rested her cheek against his velvet coat and sighed.

"You knew all along there was something the matter with Lional, didn't you?"

"I'm afraid I did, yes, Melly," said Rupert, his voice aching with regret. "Since I was a boy. Sorry. It wasn't safe to tell you."

There was so much she could have said. But what was the point? It wouldn't change a single thing that had happened.

"Oh, Mel," Rupert sighed. "I knew he was bad, and probably mad, but I never *dreamed* about the wizards."

She tightened her embrace. "Oh, Rupes. None of this is your fault. And it's not mine, either. This is Lional's doing, all of it."

"Mel . . ."

She could feel the tears crowding thickly in her throat. "I know," she said, choking. "He has to be stopped. And if he won't surrender willingly—"

"Let's hope it doesn't come to that."

Of course they could hope—but hope wasn't exactly a fearsome weapon, was it? "What d'you suppose has happened back home?" she whispered. "D'you think it's possible Gerald's managed to—to kill him?"

Rupert shook his head. "I don't know. Is Gerald the kind of chap who could bring himself to kill?"

Shamelessly eavesdropping, Reg snorted. "Blimey bloody Charlie. You won't last five minutes as king with *that* kind of noddy thinking, Butterfly Boy. Every man jack in the world has got at least one murder in him. Justified or not, in cold blood or in hot. And after what your charming brother did to my Gerald—"

Melissande pulled out of her brother's arms. Felt herself shudder, remembering what Gerald had told them in the cave. Seeing Rupert's confusion, she patted his cheek.

"I'll explain later, Rupes."

Over at one of the terribly complicated thaumaturgical monitoring stations that hadn't melted to goo, Monk sat back with a relieved sigh. "All right. The information's still here." He held up a small crystal. "I've copied it."

"Very well," said Lord Attaby, tight-lipped and tense. "What now?"

"Now, sir?" Monk wiped a shirt-sleeve across his sweaty face. "Now I figure out what the hell is going on in New Ottosland. I hope."

CHAPTER FIVE

They were all staring at him: Melissande, Reg, New Ottosland's unlikely-looking next king, Uncle Ralph, Lord Attaby—and Sir Alec.

Of them all, Sir Alec's stare was the worst.

Sir Alec was one of those wizards often whispered about in dark corridors. Lots of rumor, very little fact. Once or twice Uncle Ralph, after partaking of his brother's fine post-prandial brandy, had dropped mildly inebriated hints about the man's secret, shadowy doings. Alluded to feats of thaumaturgical espionage and derring-do that could never be discussed in the cold light of day.

"There are some things, Monk my boy, you'll be happier not knowing," Uncle Ralph liked to say, waving a fat, confiding cigar for emphasis. *"Truth be told, I wish I didn't know 'em. Truth be told, between you and me, I don't know how Alec sleeps at night."*

Because he was a Markham on his father's side and a Thackeray on his mother's he'd long ago lost count of how many pies his family's fingers dabbled in, one way or another, but the upshot was that he knew a little something about the seamy underbelly of wizarding. He didn't need details to guess the kind of nastiness his uncle hinted at. Especially if he let himself meet Sir Alec's measured, steady gaze.

Which he didn't. The man's guarded gray eyes were *far* too disconcerting. Especially now, watching him prepare for a little thaumaturgical sleight-of-hand which—in theory—shouldn't be possible.

But that's what I do, isn't it? I turn theory into fact. Even when—especially when—I'm not supposed to.

And to think his family had found it amusing when he was a child.

Feeling the wintry weight of Sir Alec's regard, he tucked the small crystal containing an imprint of Gerald's unauthorized Level Twelve transmog into his pocket and looked up.

"I know what you're thinking."

Sir Alec's light brown eyebrows lifted. "I doubt it."

Yeah? Well, Sir Alec, how's this for size? "You're thinking—the government's thinking—that Gerald's some kind of loose cannon. That he's a menace. A danger to society—or even the world." He scowled. "But you're wrong. Gerald Dunwoody's the most harmless wizard I ever knew. *And* the most decent."

"In my experience," said Sir Alec, not arguing, just observational, "decent, harmless wizards don't turn lizards into dragons at the behest of insanely despotic tyrants."

Bastard. "That isn't what happened!"

Mysterious Sir Alec breathed out a whispery sigh. "Your loyalty is admirable, Mr. Markham, but we both know it's precisely what happened."

With an effort he kept his fingers from fisting. Made

himself not look at Melissande and Reg. "There were mitigating circumstances."

"Which will be discussed in full once Mr. Dunwoody has returned to Ottosland," said Lord Attaby, at his most repressive. "And most likely taken into account. But that is a discussion for another day, Mr. Markham."

Yes. Right. In other words *Get on with it.*

And Lord Attaby had a point. Even now Gerald could be locked in a desperate battle for his life. Waiting for him. Relying on him.

I never should've let him talk me into leaving.

Standing adrift amidst the Department's sea of thaumaturgical monitoring equipment, he took a deep breath to steady his thumping heart. "Have we got a recording of the event on a machine that hasn't been melted?"

Sir Alec swept his keen gaze around the cramped, crowded room then nodded. "Try that one."

That one was probably the oldest thaumatograph still in use anywhere in the Department—or possibly the civilized wizarding world. Oversized and clunky, its plain copper wiring antiquated, it hulked in the corner, largely overlooked these days. The latest-model thaumatographs employed wiring composed mostly of brinbindium, newly discovered in the darkest jungles of Ramatoosh. Highly etheretically conductive, a little temperamental, prone to spontaneous reverse thaumaturgic fluctuations, yes—but terrifically sensitive to the most minuscule of etheretic fluctuations.

Which is possibly why the new monitors tossed in the towel once they picked up the goings-on in New Ottosland.

"Well, Mr. Markham?" said Lord Attaby, shifted

from repressive to impatient. "Can you do this or can't you? Time is fast slipping through our fingers, you know!"

"Sorry, sorry, my lord, yes, I do know," he muttered, and wriggled his way between the crammed-in desks and gooified modern thaumatographs to the aged pile of copper wiring, circuits and gears that was the Abercrombie Eleven Etheretic Thaumatograph (1843 Patent Pending). "If you'd give me a moment—"

"There are no moments remaining, Monk," said Uncle Ralph, sounding tense. "Now prove yourself a Markham and get the job done! We need to know what's going on in New Ottosland!"

He risked a single glance at Melissande, defiantly ramrod straight beside her odd brother. She slayed him. Tart-tongued and bossy and horrifyingly self-sufficient. Everything a well-bred girl wasn't supposed to be. Her eyes met his and his heart banged like a hammer.

I'm going to save her kingdom for her.

With a loud flustering of wings Reg joined him at the thaumatograph. "So, Mr. Clever Clogs, can you really do this or are you just flapping your lips for the exercise?"

Offended, he looked down his nose at her. "What do you think?"

"I think we're all going to get terminal indigestion if you've bitten off more than you can chew, sunshine."

Bloody hell. How did Gerald *stand* it? "D'you mind? I'm Monk Markham."

"Oh, really?" Reg fixed him with a glittering stare.

"And what else would you like engraved on your headstone if this doesn't work and my Gerald ends up paying the price for your thoughtless meddling in his life?"

Oh, God. *Gerald.* He had to look away. Pretend interest in the old monitor before him. "He's my best friend too, Reg. Don't you know there's nothing I won't do to save him?"

Reg sniffed. "I never said your heart wasn't in the right place, sunshine. But this?" She shook her head. "It's never been done."

"Well, you know what they say, Reg," he retorted, flicking the Abercrombie's switches to stand-by. "There's a first time for everything."

"And that includes blowing yourself to smithereens!" the dreadful bird retorted. "Which is a first *and* last time event, my boy." She tipped her head and glared at him, dark eyes bright with irritated frustration. "Or hadn't you thought of that, Mr. Genius?"

A betraying bead of sweat trickled down his temple. "Of course I've bloody thought of it, Reg. Now would you please be quiet? I need to concentrate."

"Need your head examined's more like it," she snapped. "Now what can I do to help?"

He stared at her. "Gosh, Reg. I don't know. Let me think. Hey, here's an idea. Maybe you could *shut up*?"

"Mr. Markham . . ."

And that was Sir Alec, using his voice like a cattle prod.

"*Please*, Reg," he muttered. "Gerald's life depends on me getting this right."

And those were the magic words. The bloody bird shut up.

Everybody was staring at him again, waiting for him to pull a thaumaturgical miracle out of his . . . hat. The air in the small, closed room trembled with tension, the atmosphere taut like a thunderstorm waiting to break. *Bloody hell, Dunnywood. The things I do for you.* Willing his hand steady he selected an empty recording crystal from a tray on the table beside the Abercrombie and slotted it into place. The old thaumatograph beeped once and started to hum. That was his cue to bang his fist on the replay button, pass his hand over the recording crystal to activate it and then monitor the readout closely for signs of brewing trouble. Close to holding his breath, he watched the etheretic gauge's needles jump and the ink squiggle on the paper and the etheretic transducer crystals flash orange, then red, then a brighter red until they glowed like the heart of an overheated sun. The 'graph's blank and colorless recording crystal began to shimmer, then blush. Pale pink. Dark pink. Now shading to bright red. To crimson.

He could feel the build up of energy within the crystal's confines, feel the rising stresses on its matrix. The Department used only the best recording crystals, but even so . . .

His long hair started to stir, prickles of thaumic energy nipping over his skin. Deep in his bones he felt an answering thrum. In his blood, a growing incandescence.

"Oy," said Reg, feathers nervously rustling. "Mr. Clever Clogs. I don't like this. I don't like this at *all*."

And neither did he, but there was no turning back. The air around the old thaumatograph shivered as the invisible ether started to dance. Then the recording crystal began to vibrate, protesting the speed and density of information being funneled into it. He heard a thin high note of stress, a diamond chip scraping glass.

"Mr. Markham—"

"Almost there, Lord Attaby," he said, lifting one hand. "Just a few more seconds."

"We might not have a few more seconds, Monk!" Uncle Ralph retorted. "Now shut the damn thing off before—"

"I can't," he said, as the recording crystal continued to protest. "I need every scrap of information on the event that the monitor captured."

"But—"

"It's all right, Uncle Ralph. Don't lose your nerve now."

Uncle Ralph spluttered. "Lose my nerve? Lose my *nerve?* You arrogant young whippersnapper, who d'you think you are, talking to me like I'm some—"

"Mr. Markham."

He nearly leaped clean out of his shoes. How did Sir Alec *do* that? Creep so close without so much as stirring the air? What was it, some kind of secret thaumaturgical stealth enhancement?

And where can I get one? Or maybe I could whip up a version of it for myself . . .

"Oy, bugalugs," said Reg, always so helpful. "Don't look now but your recording crystal's about to go kablooey."

Ignoring the bird and the disconcerting Sir Alec, he turned back to the thaumatograph. Reg was right, damn her eyes. The recording crystal was edging towards black now, rattling in its slot on the shuddering machine. The etheretic gauge's inky needles skewed wildly across the unspooling paper, scrawling a terrifying warning of things gone madly awry half way around the world.

Bloody hell, Gerald. What did you do?

"Shut it down, Mr. Markham," Sir Alec said quietly. "It's an old machine, and right now it's the only reliable long distance thaumatograph we've got."

"Yeah—yeah—in a second," he said, not taking his eyes off the recording crystal. He was pushing, he knew he was pushing, but a partial recording of what had just happened in New Ottosland wasn't enough. He needed to know the whole story. Without the whole story he might not be able to help Gerald. Besides, the recording was nearly finished. Just a bit more—a *bit* more—

"Mr. Markham."

"Nearly, Sir Alec. Nearly. If I can just—"

But no, he couldn't just. With a snap and a sizzle and a belch of choking smoke the Abercrombie Eleven Etheretic Thaumatograph (1843 Patent Pending) emitted a grinding groan and started dripping melted copper onto the floor.

Reg flapped cursing into the air. "You stark raving nutter, Monk! *Now* look what you've done!"

Oh bugger bugger bugger bugger—

Heedless of the gut-churning agitated ether, of splattering copper and acrid smoke and the risk of imminent explosion, of Lord Attaby's protests and Uncle Ralph's incoherent fury, seeing only the fleeting look of despair on Melissande's face in the heartbeat before she managed to regain her self-control, he flung himself at the dangerously overburdened thaumatograph.

Sir Alec stared at him from the other side of the monitor, his nondescript face calm, his eyes narrowed and cold as mid-winter.

"We have less than two minutes in which to balance the etheretic energies, Mr. Markham," he said, as though he was commenting on the weather. "And then there's going to be a rather large explosion. So let's not dally, shall we?"

Monk nodded. "Right. After you, Sir Alec."

And on a blind leap of faith they plunged their *potentias* into the etheretic maelstrom engulfing the thaumatograph.

Heat and cold and bright, bright colors. The stink of burned ether and the emptiness of freezing thaumic particles. Dimly he felt Sir Alec's presence as the senior wizard wrestled with the monitor's etheretic balances, thrown so far off-kilter by whatever had happened in distant New Ottosland. Recognizing a superior discipline, if not exactly a superior *potentia*, he followed Sir Alec's disciplined lead.

"*Ease back on the throttle a trifle, Mr. Markham,*" Sir Alec's ghostly voice whispered. "*Just because you have it is no reason to use it.*"

What? And then he realized he was pouring all of his *potentia* at the problem. Letting his fears overtake his good judgment.

"*Sorry,*" he said, his own voice ghostly, and hastily readjusted his response.

"*Good,*" said Sir Alec. "*Now let's make a cradle, shall we?*"

It felt damn peculiar, linking his *potentia* with that

of a wizard he knew only by mysterious reputation and had never even spoken to before today. This kind of intricate, complicated thaumic working was usually reserved for wizards who'd had time to familiarize themselves with the quirks and foibles of a colleague's thaumic signature. Incautious collaborations could—and often did—lead to nasty accidents.

But he and Sir Alec didn't have time for the thaumaturgic niceties.

A small, observing part of himself marveled at the other man's icy control. He'd never felt anything like it. The precision of application, the razor-keen mastery of thaumic energies, the deftness of his touch as he honed and narrowed his focus, imposing his implacable will upon the machine that with luck held the key to the conundrum that was Gerald Dunwoody.

Mysterious Sir Alec had just become a whole lot mysteriouser.

With their *potentias* neatly melded, not a hint of incipient collapse or rejection, they eased the thaumic cradle they'd created around the damaged thaumatograph. Used their blended etheretic energies like glue, sealing the breaches that threatened to explode the vitally important monitor. Its copper wires stopped melting. Its innards stopped belching noxious smoke. The hysterical inked needles ceased their flailing and the recording crystal, undamaged, settled back in its slot.

With a final mechanical groan and a cooling *plink plink plink*, with scant seconds remaining, the roiled etheretic energies within and surrounding the thaumatograph smoothed out. A heartbeat later came an odd pulling sensation, like a knot coming untied, and their two linked *potentias* slithered apart.

Very slowly, panting, Monk unscrunched his eyes. "Did we do it? I think we did it. Didn't we?"

"It would appear so," said Sir Alec. The only hint that he'd just exerted himself was a slight roughness around the edges of his voice. He cleared his throat. "Nicely done, Mr. Markham."

"Blimey bloody Charlie!" said Reg, perched on top of a nearby newer-fangled and now defunct monitor. "You cut that a bit close, didn't you? What were you trying to do, give me a conniption?"

Ignoring the damn bird—how was it Gerald hadn't throttled her by now?—Monk shook his head. "I think you did most if it, Sir Alec. I was pretty much just along for the ride."

"Humility, Mr. Markham?" Sir Alec's thin lips curved in the faintest of smiles. "You surprise me. I wasn't under the impression you possessed any."

Oh ha very ha. Fishing in his pocket for the recording of Gerald's Level Twelve transmog, he risked a glance at Melissande. She was so pale all her freckles stood out like fallen leaves on a snowfield. Even without a magnifying glass he thought he could count every last one of them. Her peculiar brother had his arm about her shoulders, holding on tight. Another risky glance, this time at Uncle Ralph and Lord Attaby, made his heart thud uncomfortably hard. Identical frowns and clenched jaws held the promise of much astringent lecturing in his immediate future.

Not wanting to think about *that* he hurriedly paid attention to the old thaumatograph. Chancing burned fingers he plucked the recording crystal out of its slot. Ouch, yes, it was hot, but since he wasn't bursting into flames . . . He closed his grip around it and took a quick surface reading. Oh yes, there was Gerald and his oddly altered thaumic signature.

How about that? I did it. The entire unprecedented catastrophic thaumaturgic event safely recorded for posterity. Ha! Monk Markham strikes again.

But his pleasure didn't last long.

Bloody hell, Gerald. What did you do?

"Well?" Reg demanded. "What's it say? Don't just stand there gawping, sunshine! What's Gerald done now?"

"*Reg*—" He pulled a face at her. "I don't know yet. I don't even know if Gerald's behind what's gone wrong."

The lie was told before he knew it—but it didn't much matter. The truth couldn't be hidden. It was a stopgap. A way of catching his breath. Of giving him time to figure a way to save Gerald from the fallout. Or as much of the fallout as he could manage. He could feel Sir Alec and Uncle Ralph and Lord Attaby, all three of them sharply staring. Did they believe him?

Somehow . . . I think not.

"What do you mean, you don't know?" Reg squawked, tail feathers rattling. "*Find out*, you wretched boy!"

"I can't believe I'm saying this," said Melissande, "but I agree with the bird. Stop congratulating yourself, Mr. Markham, and read that bloody crystal! Or I swear I'll forget I'm *not* the new Queen of New Ottosland and send out for an ax!"

Startled, he stared at her. Flinched and stepped back as insane King Lional's sister, the unexpected love of his life, glared at him with the heat of a thousand newborn suns.

Oh. Right. So she's not joking. Fine. I can take a hint when it's threatening to cut my head off.

Feeling a colder regard, he shifted his gaze to Sir Alec. "What?"

Sir Alec came around the monitor to stand uncomfortably close. "Let's stop this juvenile pretending, shall we, Mr. Markham? Either your friend has caused this catastrophic event or he's been caught up in it. Either way he's in dire trouble. Your friend, Mr. Markham, is what you might call an untidiness. A *dangerous* untidiness. I wonder—are you ready for what will likely happen next?"

Mouth dry, throat closing, he took another step back. "Next? What are you talking about? Are you implying Gerald's in—that the government might—that *he* might—" Suddenly he remembered Uncle Ralph's inebriated ramblings. *I don't know how Alec sleeps at night.* And then, feeling sick, he wondered if he understood anything at all. "Just what is it that you do for the government, exactly, Sir Alec?"

This time Sir Alec's chilly smile was frightening. "I keep things tidy, Mr. Markham. I clean up other people's mess."

Clean up. Now there was a terrifying euphemism. He made himself meet Sir Alec's intimidating gaze. Summoned a little intimidation of his own.

"Well, you're not cleaning up Gerald," he said, his voice low. Painfully aware of Melissande, almost within earshot. "None of this is his fault. Give me your word you'll leave him alone or—"

"Or what?" said Sir Alec, so impersonally

polite. "What is it you imagine you can do, Mr. Markham?"

How odd, that he could go from admiring to hating someone in such a short space of time. "Sir Alec, this isn't Gerald's fault," he said, sounding anything but impersonal. *But I don't care. I don't.* "Something happened to him when Stuttley's factory went up. Something nobody was expecting, or could have foreseen. In the name of all things thaumaturgical, when he left here for New Ottosland he was rated a piss poor Third Grade wizard! And the next thing he knew he was turning cats into lions. That's—that's—"

"Unprecedented. I know," said Sir Alec, watching him closely. "A word I suspect will be quite worn out before this is over."

"Please," he said, and heard the catch in his voice. "*Please.* At least say that any *cleaning up* will be a last resort."

"I'm not a wasteful man, Mr. Markham," Sir Alec replied after an awful pause. "I don't throw anything away if I don't have to."

It was the only assurance he was going to get— and it wasn't anywhere near good enough. Still feeling sick, he glanced at silent Reg. "Well? Come on. I can't believe *you* don't have an opinion."

Reg chattered her beak, dark brown eyes glittering. "You want my opinion? *First* we find out what's happened in madam's back yard. And then if this government plonker starts waving a dustpan and brush around I think *you* should knit his intestines into a throw rug while *I* pluck out his eyeballs and use them for marbles. *That's* my opinion. Care to second it?"

He grinned. "Hear, hear."

"Monk—" Uncle Ralph joined them. "*Enough*. If you can read those damn recording crystals then stop messing about and *read* them. Otherwise—"

"Sorry," he said. Glanced over at Melissande. "Sorry. All right. Here I go . . ."

With the original cat-into-lion transmog recording clutched tight in his right hand and the Abercrombie recording crystal folded hard in his left, he closed his eyes to block out extraneous distractions—like the hint of tears in Melissande's green eyes—and reached out with his *potentia*.

The vibrations from the transmog set his bones humming anew. He was astonished all over again, recognizing that this was the new Gerald. Before the accident at Stuttley's his friend had been a tentative, almost apologetic wizard. A man who found it hard to believe he'd earned the right to wield his cherry-wood staff and expected at any moment to have it taken away. And no amount of cheerleading from the sidelines—from himself *and* Reg—had made a difference. In his heart that Gerald had thought of himself as a wizard by mistake. A tailor's son from Nether Wallop who'd be unmasked as an impostor any tick of the clock.

But now? After his catastrophic thaumic accident? *This* Gerald felt as confident as—as Errol Haythwaite, and that was saying something.

I don't understand how nobody saw this coming. He worked for the Department of Thaumaturgy, for crying out loud. Why didn't they see it?

Then again . . . why didn't he?

It was a question he'd been asking himself ever since Gerald had tripped the monitors with that first

Level Twelve trick—and he was nowhere near close to any kind of answer.

Some bloody friend I am. Some genius. A genuine thaumaturgic marvel right under my nose and I couldn't smell it. I'm a bloody disgrace.

"Mr. Markham . . ."

And that was Sir Alec, playing cattle prod again.

"Nearly done," he muttered. "Don't fuss at me."

With Gerald's remade thaumic signature fresh in his mind, he focused his attention on the Abercrombie's recording crystal. Packed full of energy and imagery, the first touch of his *potentia* to its contents sent him staggering sideways. He heard Reg say something, steady on, something like that, but her words were muffled by the cold and heat and breath-stealing power surging through him.

Suddenly his mind was filled with a darkness he was frightened to touch.

But I have to. I have to know—

Except he knew already. A single glance had told him. He was a genius, after all. That darkness was familiar, its thaumic fingerprints belonging to his kind and gentle friend. Sort of belonging. A version of his friend. Because what he could feel, what his *potentia* showed him, was a gentle power warped and twisted into something no longer itself. Something hungry and brutal and unfamiliar with loving care. Reeling with shock, he collapsed against a handy desk.

Bloody hell, Gerald. What have you done?

A wind was blowing in his face, through his hair. Shrieking. What the—

No. It was Reg. He opened his eyes.

"*—going on, Monk Markham! You tell me right this*

instant or I'll be using your eyeballs for marbles, just you see if I don't!"

She was flapping hysterically in front of him, loosened feathers floating free to drift haphazard into piles of melted copper and goo.

Then someone's hands seized his shoulders and started shaking him. Started shouting, sounding as upset as Reg.

"Monk! Monk, what did you see? What's happened? *Tell us!"*

Melissande.

He let her shake him. He couldn't pull away, couldn't argue or complain.

Gerald, you stonking idiot. What have you done?

Letting go of his shoulders, Melissande slapped him hard across the face. "*Mr. Markham!* For the love of Saint Snodgrass *pull yourself together!"*

"Steady on there, Your Highness! There's no need for that!"

Uncle Ralph, coming to the rescue? That was one for the books. His father would need a stiff drink and a lie down when he heard.

"Sir Ralph is right, Melly," said New Ottosland's unlikely king. "You really mustn't slap Mr. Markham, you know. I'm sure he's doing his very best to help."

Ignoring them both, Melissande slammed her fists against his chest, leaning into him until her nose and his were practically touching. Her lovely green eyes were terrified, and desperate.

"What did you see, Monk? *What did you see?"*

He couldn't keep it a secret. But instead of looking at Melissande he turned his head and looked at Reg, who'd subsided, exhausted, on a cluttered, report-covered desk.

"Go on," the bird said, her voice ragged. "I can take it. What's that fool boy gone and done now?"

She might be able to take it, but he couldn't. His eyes were burning, hot tears blurring his vision. He could feel Sir Alec's cold gaze on him, waiting for an excuse to start *cleaning up*.

"What do you think, Reg?" he said dully. "He's done what he wanted to do in the first place. What we thought you'd talked him out of doing."

"But—what? No," said Melissande, uncertain, as Reg covered her face with one wing. "No—no, he couldn't have. Not when he knew—not after the cave—no, Monk. You're wrong. You've made a mistake. He *wouldn't*."

"What are you talking about?" demanded Lord Attaby. "What is it you think Mr. Dunwoody has done?"

Sir Alec held out his hand. "May I, Mr. Markham?"

There was no hope of protecting Gerald now. Barely able to meet Sir Alec's almost compassionate gaze, he handed over the recording of New Ottosland's unprecedented thaumaturgic event. Watched Sir Alec close his fingers around the crystal, close his eyes and open himself to the images and impressions contained within it. Watched the shock shudder through him, and the pain, and the horror.

And then he watched the color drain from Uncle Ralph's face as his father's unsympathetic brother saw the impact strike deep in the heart of his formidable, enigmatic colleague.

"Alec?" Uncle Ralph whispered. "Alec, what—"

Sir Alec dropped the recording crystal as though

it were a live coal. "What texts did he have access to, Mr. Markham?" he said, ignoring Uncle Ralph. "Do you know?"

"*Grummen's Lexicon*." His voice was so husky he had to clear his throat. "And—and *Pygram's Pestilences*. For starters."

Briefly, so briefly, Sir Alec's hard gaze eased. "I'm sorry. And what other grimoires are we dealing with? How many?"

He shook his head. "I don't know."

"Your Highness—" Sir Alec turned on Melissande. "Have you any idea what—"

"No," whispered Melissande. "I wasn't even aware those awful books had been brought into the kingdom. Not until Gerald told me in the cave. After Lional—after he—"

"Forgive me," said Rupert, "but I don't have the foggiest idea what you're talking about."

"We're talking about disaster," said Reg, pulling her head out from under her wing. Her voice was soft and unsteady, sodden with grief. "Mayhem and calamity and catastrophe and woe. My Gerald's done a foolish thing, Butterfly Boy. He's sacrificed himself to try and stop your wicked brother."

Rupert's mouth dropped open. "*What?* You mean he's *dead?*"

When Reg didn't answer, Monk looked at Melissande's ridiculously-clothed brother. "No, Your Highness. It'd be easier for everyone if he was."

Bloody hell, Gerald. What were you thinking?

"I'm afraid, sir, that in a misguided attempt to defeat your magically enhanced brother," said Sir Alec, his voice as gray and chilly as his eyes, that brief compassion fled, "Mr. Dunwoody has followed him down a most unfortunate path. He has taken upon himself aspects of the worst kinds of thaumaturgy. Illegal incantations, perverted and vile."

"He said the only way he could beat Lional was to fight fire with fire," said Melissande, her voice unsteady. "He must've found where Lional kept Pomodoro Uffitzi's filthy library and—and—"

"*Grummen's Lexicon?*" Shaken to his bootstraps, Lord Attaby groped for the nearest chair and sat down. "God help us. You're quite certain of this? There's absolutely no chance you've misread the situation?"

Stooping, Monk retrieved the recording crystal Sir Alec had dropped. Then, biting his lip, flinching in anticipation of what he was about to feel, he sank his mind back inside it. This time he didn't try to fight the recorded impressions, the series of explosions in the ether as the foulest dark magics known to wizardry ignited Gerald's untapped, unexplored *potentia* and sent shockwaves surging through the etheretic plane. Alchemied his desperate friend into something new and terrible.

When he'd felt it all, when he felt as empty as a tomb from which the quiet dead had been stolen, he opened his eyes and looked at Attaby. "No, my lord. We're not wrong. Whoever Gerald was—I fear that man is gone. And I don't have the first idea who—or what—has taken his place."

"Is that all you felt, Monk?" asked Uncle Ralph, breaking the dreadful silence. "It doesn't seem like enough to melt most of our best equipment. I mean, the long range monitors didn't pick up on King Lional's taking in these dark magics, did they? So perhaps something else has happened. Perhaps—perhaps Mr. Dunwoody and King Lional met in a cataclysmic battle and *that's* the unprecedented thaumaturgical event our monitoring station recorded."

"Monk?" said Melissande in a small voice. "Could that be true?"

Helpless, he shrugged. "I don't know."

"What d'you mean, you don't know? How can you not *know*?" she demanded. "Are you a genius or aren't you?"

"Melissande—" He dragged his fingers through his hair. "It's not that simple! I mean, we're calling this *unprecedented* for a reason!"

"And—and what about Gerald? Could he still be alive?"

"Don't ask stupid questions, ducky," said Reg, her eyes gleaming. "How's this ridiculous Markham boy supposed to know the answer to that, standing here half a world away from your wretched little kingdom? There's only one way we're going to find out exactly what's happened. We've got to go back to New Ottosland—and save that boy from himself before it's too late."

CHAPTER SIX

Standing in the palace's fragrant, lovingly tended gardens, bathed in gentle sunshine and the fires of his reforging, Gerald tipped back his head and searched the sky for Lional's dragon.

Well. My dragon, really. After all, I made it. That makes it mine.

He smiled.

A rising breeze wafted the unpleasantness of charred bodies towards him. All those unfortunates who'd fallen foul of Lional's indiscriminate wrath. So many little people in the world, unable to defend themselves against evil men like Melissande's demented brother. Remembering the loyal guardsman Reggie, vaguely recalling a sense of impotent grief, he snapped his fingers and sprang flowers into life where, throughout the kingdom, those poor souls had collapsed to embers and ash. Every last dead man, woman and child now a rose or a pansy or a searingly sweet freesia.

There. That's a fitting memorial, I think. Beauty from ugliness. Could there be a better legacy?

That small distraction dealt with, he returned his attention to the question of his dragon. And Lional. He mustn't forget Lional. A pestilent flea to be cracked between two fingernails. New Ottosland's mad king had outstayed his welcome. This tiny nation would be well rid of him.

I have so much work to do. So much good. With great power comes great responsibility . . . and I have more power than any man alive.

The pale blue sky was empty of dragon—and he had no sense of the marvelous creature or Lional in the gardens or nearby. They'd taken themselves off somewhere . . .

But now it's time to return.

With as much effort as a hurricane blowing out a candle he sent a thread of his *potentia* spearing through the ether. His power cleaved the thaumic veil like that well-known hot knife through butter. So easy, so effortless. He felt like a dam with all its confining banks sundered, his undreamt-of powers flowing and flooding through him. Set free at last.

This is me. The true me. Won't Reg be surprised?

Within heartbeats he'd found both king and dragon, harrying a herd of milch cows on the rural outskirts of the kingdom's capital. The beasts floundered and foundered and sprawled in bloody death, carcasses littering the green field with profligate abandon. How typically Lional, to take out his frustrated spite on dumb animals who couldn't fight back.

Really and truly, he's got to go.

The dragon's mind was a cauldron roaring with flame. Chained to Lional by inimical magics, it writhed in heartbreaking pain and confusion. With a thought he eased its suffering. Weakened the *Tantigliani* bond. Recognizing his touch the dragon threw back its scaled head and kissed the sky with fire. Furious, Lional tried to overthrow him. The feeble attempt made him laugh.

Come to me, sweet one, he crooned to the glorious crimson and emerald dragon. *I'll set you free.*

While he waited he searched idly for Shugat and Zazoor and their impotent army . . . and was stung with surprise when he couldn't find them.

So their silly gods shield them from me, do they? Oh well. It hardly matters. I don't want their sand and their stupid jeweled tears. And I've certainly got no interest in their smelly, uncomfortable camels. If they don't interfere with me I'll likely leave them alone.

A shiver in the ether heralded his dragon's eager approach. Smiling, filled with the kind of excitement that used to fizz him as a boy, when it was his birthday and he was staring at his unwrapped presents on the breakfast table, he watched the empty sky and looked for it to fill.

And there it was, the dragon. His miracle. His gift. Heart lifting, throat tightening, he watched the magnificent creature tread the air lightly towards him. Its vast wings were dulcet, caressing the sunlight like a shy lover's kiss. Spoiling the picture, Lional—his beautiful face ugly with temper, perched behind the dragon's wings and clutching its elegant neck like a bully holding onto some stolen trifle.

"What are you doing, Gerald?" Lional shouted as the dragon settled sweetly on the grass. "What are you playing at?"

"Playing?" He frowned, reproving. "I'm not playing, Lional, I'm perfectly serious. Can't you tell?"

There were blotches of cow's blood on the dragon's iridescent hide. Horrible. With a wave of his hand he removed them. Removed Lional while he was at it, tumbling Melissande's mad brother off the dragon's back into an ungainly sprawl on the ground. The dragon lowered its head and looked at him, crimson eyes banked with fire.

Lional scrambled awkwardly to his feet. There was cow's blood on him too. It could stay there. And if he wasn't very careful his own would soon be joining it.

"*Dunwoody—*"

Puzzled, Gerald stared at him.

I was afraid of him once. Not so long ago he made me soil myself with fear. How odd. And what a relief, to be done with that Gerald.

"It's over, Lional," he said quietly. Men of power had no need to shout. "Your reign is at an end. If you surrender yourself peacefully I'll see you come to no harm. You'll be imprisoned, of course, but you'll still be alive. But if you *don't* surrender peacefully—" He shrugged. "Well. Then life will become rather unpleasant and you'll only have yourself to blame."

"*What?*" Lional laughed, incredulous. Beneath his smooth, pale skin a ripple of crimson scales. The *Tantigliani* still held. "Gerald, have you gone mad?"

He shrugged again. "Not at all. That's what you did, Lional. What I've done is . . . find myself."

Lional stared at him, ferociously silent. And then he reached out with his stolen *potentias*, with the magic that would never truly be his no matter how hard he tried to pretend.

"*Tagruknik!*" he swore in a tongue that wasn't his,

either. What a thief he was, this mad king of New Ottosland. "Gerald—what the hell have you done?"

Oh and it was sweet, it was *delightful*, tasting Lional's stark fear. The dragon, still chained to him, poor thing, lashed its tail and roared in frightened sympathy, flame shriveling the flower beds, poison dripping to corrode and char the clipped grass.

He rolled his eyes. "Oh come on, Lional. You know bloody well."

The healthy color drained from Lional's beautiful face, leaving it gray and sickly. "You can't have. It's not possible."

"Not for the old Gerald, no," he agreed. "But thanks to you and the cave I'm not the old Gerald any more. Thanks to you and the cave I'm an entirely new man. With your help I've found a fresh focus." He smiled. "New purpose."

Another ripple in the ether as Lional pushed with his *potentias*. Pushed to no avail. He really was wasting his time. Eyes wide, his breathing harsh, he stared. "No. It's not *possible*. I left those grimoires guarded. Warded beyond any hope of breaching. No wizard could—"

"No ordinary wizard, true," he said, and shoved his hands in his trouser pockets. "But come on, Lional. You've known since your failure in the woods that I'm anything but an *ordinary* wizard."

Sweating, Lional stepped back. The dragon hesitated, then echoed him. "No," he said, shaking his head. "This is a trick."

Gerald sighed. "Lional, Lional. Tell me, what did you *think* you were doing when you were torturing me in that cave of yours?"

Lional didn't answer. Just stared at him, his sky blue eyes narrowed. One hand reached out to touch the dragon's breathing side. As though touch confirmed ownership. As though he had the right.

He raised an eyebrow. "You don't know? Or is it you just can't bring yourself to admit it? Never mind. I'll admit it for you. What you did, Lional, old chum, was murder me. The old me, that is. And the Gerald you replaced him with, you made *that* Gerald into a murderer—like you. And—well—the thing is, you see, I couldn't live with that. I couldn't live with *being* that. Being you. So now there's me, Lional. A third Gerald. A Gerald who's going to put a stop to your nonsense once and for all."

"You think so?" said Lional, teeth bared in a feral smile. "Then you're an idiot, Gerald. A doltard, like Rupert. You're no match for me and my dragon."

"Actually, Lional?" He pulled his right hand from his pocket and held it up, fingers spread wide. "It's *my* dragon. And I'd like it back now, if you don't mind."

He clenched his fingers hard and fast, wrapping his *potentia* around the *Tantigliani*'s tight strands. Shrieking, Lional dropped to his knees. Beside him the dragon roared, fresh flame burning the flower-scented air, head thrashing in wild protest as the binding incant cut deep.

He winced. "Sorry, my beauty. Sorry. Be strong. It'll be over soon, I promise."

Teeth gritted, blood trickling from both nostrils, Lional fought back. His magic may have been stolen but that didn't mean it wasn't formidable.

"No—you can't have her—you *won't* have her—we won't let you—we are *one*!"

The punch of Lional's resistance was hard enough to rock him on his heels. Bones thrumming, blood surging, he punched back. Felt a sizzle of pleasure as Lional cried out and fell onto his hands and knees. Felt a trickle of guilt as the dragon's roar echoed his pain.

"It'll only hurt worse if you resist me, Lional," he warned. "Let go. Stop fighting. I won't tell you again."

But of course Lional didn't listen. He was mad, after all. With an outraged howl he lurched back to his feet and spat out a slew of filthy curses. So foul were the incants that the air between them caught fire, drowning the scent of flowers with the stench of putrid death.

Gerald extinguished the hexes with three unbinding words.

"I swear, Lional, you're the doltard," he said, as Lional recoiled in shock. "Compared to you Rupert's a bloody genius. Now for the love of Saint Snodgrass, you fool, stop this nonsense and—"

With another furious howl Lional launched a fresh attack. This time the dragon attacked with him, teeth and claws and flame and poison unleashed.

No time for kindness or a delicate touch. With both fists clenched now, with a word and a vicious push of his *potentia*, he severed the unnatural bonds of the *Tantigliani sympathetico*. Severed Lional from the dragon and set the beautiful creature free.

Lional collapsed, screaming as though he'd just been eviscerated. Half his face and his right arm were turned to blackened lizard scales. The dragon screamed with him, lethal tail lashing, thrashing the surrounding flower beds to shreds.

Gerald leaped forward. "No! No! It's all right! It's all right! He can't hurt you now! I've saved you!"

Dazed and confused, the dragon swung its head side to side, looking first at himself and then at screaming Lional. One luminous crimson eye was clouded gray and weeping blood. Blood dripped from its wide nostrils and fell scorching on the ground.

Hating himself for hurting the creature, Lional's victim like so many others, heedless of the green poison oozing from its mouth, he risked a hand to the dragon's shoulder. Wrapped its pain in a soothing hex and forced it to calm.

"There, there," he crooned. "Stand still. Stand quiet. You'll be all right soon, I promise."

The dragon looked at him with its one good eye, tail continuing to thrash. The flower beds Lional's father had so lovingly cultivated were ruined, reduced to churned dirt and torn foliage. Bits and pieces of blossom. All that diligent work, destroyed in scant heartbeats.

Well, it serves him right for raising such a horrible son.

Slowly, slowly, the dragon's tail ceased its thrashing. Its head lowered, drooping groundwards, as its anger surrendered to magic.

"That's better," he told it. "Poor thing. You be quiet now. I'm your friend. I won't hurt you."

"But I will, you treacherous bitch!"

And too quickly for stopping, Lional blasted the dragon with a *mordicanto majora* from Stanza Seventeen of *Madam Bartholomew's Little Surprise.*

The dragon shrieked once and fell dead at his feet.

Gerald spun around. "*Lional*! What the *hell* did you do that for?"

Lional rolled over and sat up. His right eye was burst and bubbled in its socket, the lizard scales where his cheek had been now dribbled with gore. His left eye was turned dragonfire crimson, glaring with a rage as hot as the sun.

"The dragon was mine," he growled. "You had no right to touch it."

Poor thing, poor thing. I should've known. I should've saved it. "No, it was mine, Lional," he said, shaking. "I *made* it. You only stole it. You steal everything. You're just a petty thief."

Lional got his feet under him and stood, drunkenly swaying. "I am a *king*. The King of New Ottosland. Everything contained within this kingdom is mine—including *you*, Professor. To do with as I will."

Gerald sucked in a deep breath to stop the shaking. *He killed my dragon. He's going to pay for that.* "I'll give you this, Lional. You're stronger than I thought. Anyone else would've died with the breaking of that *sympathetico*."

Lional's hideously deformed face twisted in a smile. "I'm not anyone else."

He nodded. "That's true. You're one for the books all right, Lional. But now it's time for this chapter to end."

"I don't think so," said Lional. "I write my own story, Gerald. And in *my* story you're not even a *footnote!*"

Killing hex met killing hex in cacophonous mutual obliteration. For all his unique *potentia* and the dark magics he'd absorbed, Gerald felt himself fly through the air like so much leaf litter caught in a high wind. He struck the ground hard, the breath driven from his lungs in a grunting whoosh. Bouncing to his feet, blinking to clear his spotty vision, he saw where Lional had landed, clear across the far side of the gardens near the convoluted, meticulously maintained hedge-maze that led to the rear of the palace.

"Right," he said, scrambling to his feet and dusting himself off. *Ow.* He had bruises. Lional was going to pay for them too, along with everything else. "Time to finish this."

Lional was up again and raggedly running. Towards him, not away.

"The fool must want to die, Reg." He shrugged. "Oh, well. It's his choice. I don't care one way or the other."

But that wasn't true, and he knew it. He wanted Lional dead.

Strolling, not running, he crossed the undamaged grass to meet Lional's oncoming rush. With his one good eye Lional saw him and bared his bloodied teeth in a snarl. Came faster, shouting foul incantations between wet, panting breaths.

He snapped his fingers. *"Stop."*

Like running face-first into a stone wall, Lional slammed to a halt.

"Lional, Lional, Lional . . ." Still strolling, he joined Melissande's motionless brother. Looked all that ruined beauty up and down and sadly shook his head. "Well, you can't say I didn't warn you. I did try to resolve this reasonably . . . but I suppose that was foolish. After all, who can reason with a madman? Not me, apparently." He frowned. "You shouldn't have killed the dragon, Lional. That was the proverbial last straw, I'm afraid. One innocent victim too many, old chap. I simply have to draw the line."

Silenced as well as halted, Lional impotently glared.

"And now I'm going to punish you," he added. "Because if anyone deserves to feel sorry for himself, Lional, it's you."

With a flick of his finger, a push of his *potentia*, he tipped Lional over backwards to thud onto the grass. Hexed immobile, Lional could do nothing but glare and breathe. His one good eye rolled wildly, trying to focus.

Gerald looked to the dead dragon, some fifteen paces distant. *Poor thing.* Wings splayed pathetically, its body sprawled like a giant's abandoned toy. Anger and power simmered inside him, each feeding the other. Growing fat and impatient. Longing to be let loose to wreak vengeance. Justice. Lional had caused so much pain . . .

Time for him to feel a little, I think. For some people there's just no learning without doing.

"I'm sorry. Please forgive me," he said, and meant it. Feeling Lional's panic he glanced down. "No, not you, Lional. The dragon."

Hoping there was forgiveness, somewhere, for what he'd done—what he'd let be done—he snapped his fingers twice. His *potentia*, answering, wrenched the two largest teeth from the dragon's massive mouth. Another finger snap saw Lional's arms stretched out wide, bared palms to the cloudless sky. A garbled sound vibrated in Lional's straining throat.

"Pin him," he said. "Make our Lional the Butterfly King."

In a blur of magicked motion the dragon's teeth flew through the air and plunged one each point-first through Lional's waiting palms, sinking deep into the earth beneath him.

"You can scream if you like," he said. "If it helps. I don't mind."

Released from the holding hex Lional opened his mouth and shrieked, heels drumming his agony against the close-mown grass.

"Hmm. You know, that's interesting," he said, head tipped to one side. "I was right. The dragon's poison isn't affecting you. Must be a leftover advantage from the *sympathetico*."

Lips flecked with bloodied spittle, Lional tried to lift his head. "I'm going to kill you, Dunwoody. I'm going to—"

He smiled. "No, you're not, Lional. You're going to lie there and cry."

Eyes slitted Lional twisted, gathering his stolen *potentias* into a tight fist. "Oh, yes. I am going to kill you. But first I'm going to hurt you, Gerald, I'm going to make what I did to you in the cave feel like a slap and a tickle, I swear. You'll *beg* me to—"

"Oh, shut up, Lional," he said—and took back all those thieved magics. Gathered them into a single pulsing, diseased mass and wrenched them without pity from the blood and bones of the wicked man who'd stolen them.

Lional's scream was beyond agony. Beyond anything human, or even animal.

As Melissande's brother writhed and gobbled on the grass, spitting blood and bile and vomit, Gerald watched the pulsing mass of power bob in the afternoon sunshine like an obscene, distorted balloon. Tears pricked his eyes. Five wizards killed for those *potentias*. Five good men destroyed. There was only one thing he could do for them now. He clenched his fist. Breathed a single word: *Dissipato*. And watched the stolen *potentias* spread and thin like smoke, thin and thin and thin and vanish into thin air.

Lional was shuddering at his feet. He looked down. "Ah ah, Lional, I said *cry*, not *die*."

It was nothing, *nothing*, to steady Lional's laboring heart. To restore his violated body's equilibrium. To keep him alive. Magic was effortless, his *potentia* so instantly responsive to his will. He hardly needed the words, a simple thought was enough. It was marvelous.

I'm a new kind of wizard. I am unique.

The thought pleased him, enormously.

Eat your hearts out, Haythwaite and Co.

He looked down again. "All right, Lional. Now we've got *that* settled, let's move this along, shall we? There's a debt you need to repay and we've barely touched upon it. Trust me, one little scream hardly balances the scales."

His good eye tear-filled and bloodshot, Lional stared up at him. "And you call me mad."

"Oh yes," he said, cheerful. "You're stark staring bonkers, old chap."

"And what kind of justice is it that tortures a man lacking his wits?"

"Ordinarily no kind," he said. "But the thing is, Lional, you're a special case. You sent yourself mad. You did it on purpose, murdering those wizards for their *potentias*. So as far as I'm concerned that exempts you from any kind of compassionate consideration." Dropping to one knee, he leaned close. "Or, to put it another way, I'm about to show you all the mercy you showed them. And me. I think that's only fair, don't you?"

A pulse beat in the hollow of Lional's elegant throat. Fueled by terror it pumped and pumped. How *satisfying* it felt, to know that Lional could feel terror.

"You do know *you've* gone mad .don't you, Gerald?" Lional whispered. "Madder than I ever was. I can see it in your eyes. And they're going to hunt you down like a rabid dog when they realize. All those wizards in Ottosland's famed Department of Thaumaturgy? Men you think are your friends? They'll take one look at you and—*oh*."

Mildly curious, Gerald watched as one by one the lizard scales peeled off Lional's cheek, revealing the glistening and greenish-pink suppurating flesh beneath. The pulse in his throat beat harder, echoing his incoherent pain.

"I'd rather you didn't talk about my friends," he said. "I'd rather you didn't do anything but scream."

Which is what Lional did. Such a lovely, lovely sound.

It was truly extraordinary, what he could do now. How with a mere thought he could manipulate sinew and muscle. Spring blood free of its conduits. Crack bone. Twist nerves. Lional shrieked like a girl. Remembering those long days in the cave, the filth and the stink and the utter degradations, he spiced up *Pygram's Pestilences* with a few neat quirks of his own. Remembering Reggie and all the other palace staff, those poor people in the capital and all of Rupert's harmless butterflies, he honed his *potentia* like a sword-blade and blunted it on Lional's soul. Remembering the trick with the hexed chicken, those terrible hours he'd believed Reg was dead, he scaled new heights of invention and was rewarded with Lional's desperate tears.

After some time had passed, and Lional had pretty much lost his voice, he pushed to his feet and stretched, unkinking his spine. Breathed deeply of the fresh garden air, absently listening to Lional's whimpering sighs. The afternoon was waning, dusk waiting in the wings.

"You know Lional, it's a great shame," he said, glancing down. "If you'd not gone mad you might have made a halfway decent king. You're certainly handsome enough. Or you were. I don't know why it is, but people like their kings to be handsome. Their prime ministers too. Leaders in general. As though a pretty face were *any* kind of measure of worth. It's not, of course. I mean, look at Melissande. Even after I'd tarted her up, underneath the polish she was still—well—*plain*. But you'd be hard pressed to find anyone better at her job. Don't you agree?"

Lional moaned, barely conscious. His thrashing heels had battered quite deep holes in the soft ground.

"Why, if you hadn't gone mad you could've followed your father's example," he said, untucking his shirt-tail and wiping smears of blood from his fingers. "Found something to amuse yourself with and left all the real ruling to Melissande, behind the scenes. But you didn't. You had to go and get all obsessed with being a wizard. As obsessed as Rupert is with his wretched butterflies. Which only goes to show you two have far more in common than you might think." He glanced down again. "Lional? Are you listening?"

Stirring, Lional dragged open his eyes. The one that had burst when the *sympathetico* was severed looked painful. But then, so did the ruptured lizard scales on his cheek and arm, and the bruises and lesions and pustules and boils, and the splintered ribs and shins and sliced wounds in his chest and belly and thighs.

"Bastard," Lional muttered. "Kill me."

"Oh no," he said, cheerful. "I couldn't do that, Lional. I mean, you spared my life after the cave, didn't you? Returning the favor is the least I can do."

A crimson tear rolled down Lional's ravaged cheek. "Illegal."

"Yes, I know," he said, dropping back to one knee beside Melissande's brother. "Stealing a wizard's *potentia* is *terribly* illegal—and for very good reason. What a blessing it turned out you couldn't steal mine, eh? I mean, now that we know I'm a once-in-a-lifetime kind of wizard. *Think* of the mischief you'd have got up to . . ."

The holes in Lional's palms had widened considerably, what with all his thrashing about. But the dragon's teeth kept him safely pinned in place, secure as one of Rupert's dead butterflies on public display. Kindly, Gerald brushed a fingertip across Lional's sweaty brow. Smiled to see the mad king shudder and try to turn aside.

"Now, I know you think you've been punished enough," he said softly. "But actually, Lional, I'm not sure you're the best judge of that. I mean, admit it—you are just the teeniest bit biased, aren't you? But I will admit there should be some kind of rhyme or reason to our proceedings. So how does this sound? Let's say we assign an amount of time for each of your dastardly crimes, say, one hour of suffering—just one little hour—set against every life you've taken so far. Does that sound fair? I think that sounds fair."

For once in his glib life, Lional had nothing to say.

"So if we use that as a yardstick, Lional, I think you'd agree that we've barely begun. I mean, only today you must've killed over a hundred people. So that's at least one hundred hours of suffering you owe this kingdom, Your Majesty. And it doesn't include the five wizards you murdered. Now, by my reckoning you've been screaming for two hours. Well, two and a bit. Which means—"

A ripping in the ether. A stirring of new *potentias*. A familiar, unwelcome flapping of wings. And then he and Lional were no longer alone.

"Gerald Dunwoody!" cried Reg. "What's the meaning of this?"

It took Monk a moment to make sense of what he was looking at. And then, when he did, he wanted to close his eyes. Or run away. Or possibly throw up what little food he had in his stomach.

Bloody hell, Gerald. Have you gone mad?

Beside him, Melissande clutched at his coat sleeve, making soft little sounds of distress. It was taking everything he had not to echo her. Beside her Rupert breathed harshly, close to groaning. And then there was Sir Alec, who—

"Wait," he said, his voice low, grabbing hold of the government man's elbow, keeping him back. The portable portal had spat them out a long stone's throw past the stricken dragon. In other words, uncomfortably close to Gerald and the half-butchered man on the ground. "Just wait, Sir Alec. Let Reg handle it. He won't lash out at her."

"Are you sure?" Sir Alec murmured, then glanced pointedly at the hand restraining him.

Oh. He let go. "Yes."

Sir Alec wasn't convinced. "Look at his eyes, Mr. Markham. I don't think you can say with any authority what your friend—your former friend—is likely to do."

He didn't want to, but he looked at Gerald's eyes. The last time he'd seen them they were a nice, ordinary brown. And now—*now*—

"I don't care," he said, dogged, his stomach heaving in protest. "I know Gerald. No matter what he's done, no matter what—what kind of magics he's mucking around with, he would *never* hurt Reg."

Sir Alec snorted. "Well, for the bird's sake, Mr. Markham, I hope you're right."

Yeah, well, so do I. He glanced down at Melissande. "Is that Lional?"

Shivering, she nodded. "Please, Monk. We have to do something. I know Lional's awful but—"

"But he doesn't deserve that," said Rupert. "Melissande's right, we have to—"

"*Wait,*" he said sharply. "Because I'm telling you, right now Reg is our best hope of this mess not blowing up in our faces."

Landed safely on the bright green grass—well, green where it wasn't splattered with blood—Reg was marching to and fro like a sergeant major at mess-time inspection. Ignoring Lional, Gerald had dropped to a crouch and was watching her closely, his lips twisted in a faint, almost amused smile.

"—don't believe this, Gerald," Reg was saying,

her voice unusually high-pitched. "I mean, not that I care a fat rat's ass about *this* tosser—" she flipped a contemptuous wing at Gerald's prisoner and kept on truculently marching, "—but even if you are giving him a taste of his own medicine—and I don't blame you for that, nobody would, he did you *such* a mischief—I *do* take exception to you ignoring my excellent advice and dabbling your fingers in those mucky grimoire pies!"

Sighing, Gerald shook his head. "Reg, honestly. I'm fine."

"Fine? *Fine?*" she demanded, and bounced up and down. "Gerald Dunwoody, have you looked in a *mirror?* You are *not fine.* Your eyes would give a *ghost* nightmares!"

"My eyes?" said Gerald, puzzled. "What are you talking about? What's wrong with my eyes?"

"They've gone *crimson*, you tosser!" Reg shouted, tail rattling fiercely. "Like someone's stuck two live coals in your daft head!"

"Oh," said Gerald, after a moment. "Oh, well. It could be worse, Reg. They could have exploded, like Lional's eye."

Bloody hell. Monk exchanged a glance with Sir Alec, whose carefully blank expression gave nothing away. And then, before he or anyone else could stop her, Melissande abandoned the sensible *wait and see* approach and launched herself at Gerald.

"Professor Dunwoody! As New Ottosland's former prime minister I *demand* to know what you're doing!"

Gerald rose out of his crouch, that still not-quite-amused smile curving his lips. Shoving his hands in his pockets he rocked a little on his heels.

"What does it look like I'm doing, Melissande? I'm making Lional sorry."

To her credit, Melissande looked at her oldest brother without throwing up all over him. "And I'm sure he is sorry," she said, her voice almost steady. "I'm sure he's *very* sorry. But I think you've made your point, Gerald. I think it's time to stop."

"Stop?" said Gerald. "Oh no. I don't think so. I've hardly begun."

Melissande tilted her chin at him. "I'm afraid I'll have to insist, Professor. I appreciate the sentiment behind your actions but we have our own judicial system here in New Ottosland. You have to let *our* laws deal with Lional, and what he's done."

Gerald shook his head. "There are no laws to cover the crimes Lional's committed, Melissande. Not even the international wizarding community has a statute to fit him."

"Then we'll write one," said Sir Alec, following Melissande's lead. "I'll see that an emergency sitting of the United Magical Nations is convened, so contingency charges can be drawn up to deal with these extraordinary events."

Hanging back, Monk watched Gerald watch Sir Alec approach, an unsettling, detached curiosity lighting his altered face. "Really? And who are you? I don't think we've met."

Halting a pace away, Sir Alec nodded a wary greeting. "We haven't, Mr. Dunwoody. My name is Sir Alec . . . and we have to talk."

CHAPTER SEVEN

Gerald's unnerving smile didn't waver. "Ah. I take it you're from the Department of Thaumaturgy?"

Sir Alec nodded. "That's right."

"Which division?"

"Special Operations," said Sir Alec, after the briefest hesitation.

"Never heard of it."

"I'd be alarmed if you had, Mr. Dunwoody," said Sir Alec. "Now, if I might suggest—"

"No, you might not," said Gerald, with a bite in his voice that hadn't been there before. "You and I, Sir Alec, have nothing to talk about. This isn't Ottosland. You have no jurisdiction here."

And now it was Rupert's turn to join the fray. "Sir Alec has whatever jurisdiction I choose to grant him," he said, joining Melissande. "Professor—"

Gerald turned. Eyebrows lifting, he ran his dreadfully altered gaze up and down Melissande's other brother. On the ground beside him, amidst the beds of hollyhocks, pansies and snapdragons, Lional trickled blood and moaned.

"Why, Rupert. You look . . . different."

"Not as different as you," said Rupert, standing his ground despite all the changes in New Ottosland's royal court wizard. Impressed, Monk wished he could tell him to shut up before he talked himself into trouble. "Gerald—is it true? What they're saying? Did you—have you—"

"Stuffed a few new tricks down my shorts?" Gerald grinned. In that swift moment he *almost* looked like himself. "Yes, Rupert. It's true."

Rupert shook his head. "That was very brave of you. And very, *very* foolish. I wish you hadn't."

"And I wish I hadn't had to," said Gerald, shrugging. "But the thing is, Rupert, life can be a bugger that way. Now—what about you? What's your explanation? Because right now, old chap, I'd have to say that despite the unfortunate plus-fours you're looking positively *kingly*. As though you wouldn't know the difference between a Dumb Cluck and a donkey."

And the notion didn't seem to amuse him at all. His etheretic aura was electric. Feeling it, Monk didn't know whether to laugh or scream. Stand Gerald near a thaumatograph now and he'd melt it to slag.

Oh, Saint Snodgrass's bunions. I'm good, but if it comes right down to it I don't think I can take him. I don't think I can take him even if Sir Alec lends a hand. I don't even know if that's Gerald any more.

The notion was so appalling he was hard put to keep his dismay a secret. He could feel fear and a terrible grief building in his throat.

God, Gerald. Please. Let's stop this before it's too late.

Rupert was dithering, uncertain how to answer

this new and not-so-improved Professor Dunwoody. Even Melissande seemed shocked to uncertainty.

"I think," said Sir Alec, with a sharp look at the royal siblings beside him, "that this might not be the best venue for our discussion. King Lional requires medical attention—and rigorous incarceration, given—"

"No, he doesn't," said Gerald. Despite his dangerous aura he sounded positively cheerful. "Lional's perfectly harmless now. Couldn't hurt a butterfly. Not any more." He nudged Lional's flaccid left arm with his foot. "Could you, Your Majesty? And you wouldn't want to either, would you? You've been a very bad boy but you've learned your lesson, haven't you?"

Bloodied eyes closed, his ribs hardly moving as he breathed, Lional didn't respond.

But Reg did. Having abandoned her sergeant-majorish struttings and tail-rattlings, now she sat on the grass with her feathers fluffed out like a hen ready to roost.

"*Harmless?*" she hooted, monumentally disbelieving. "That deranged tosser? That'll be the day! You need a cool drink and a lie down, Gerald, all this excitement has gone to your—"

Gerald's dreadful crimson eyes flared. "*I said I've taken care of it.*"

Monk felt the power behind the words sear the air and scorch his skin. He heard Melissande's little gasp. Rupert's, too. Saw Sir Alec fail to hide a flinch. On the grass, Reg opened her beak in shock, all her feathers abruptly flattened.

"Now, now," she said, rallying. "I'm sure there's no need to take *that* tone of voice."

"Sorry," said Gerald—but any sorrow was perfunctory. There radiated from him now the most obliterating sense of power, as though a candle had been transmogged into a blast furnace. "I just—I don't like it when people doubt me. You know that, Reg. It hurts my feelings."

"Oh, stop being so sensitive," she snapped. "This isn't about your feelings, sunshine, it's about you having taken leave of your senses. And another thing—why are you talking like a third-rate mustache-twirling villain all of a sudden? It's not *like* you, Gerald. *None* of this is."

"No?" Gerald's slow smile was chilling. "What if you're wrong, Reg? What if this is the most like me I've ever been?"

Monk swallowed. Never in a million years would he have believed he'd ever have to treat carefully around Gerald Dunwoody. But this was like balancing polarity-opposed tetrathaumicles in an etheretic combustion chamber.

He took a cautious step forward. "That sounds . . . wonderful, mate. I'm pleased for you. Honest. But if you don't mind me asking—when you say you've *taken care of it*—you're talking about King Lional, right? You've—you've—" He tried not to look at the bloodied, stuporous, half-blind man at his friend's feet. "You've rapped him over the knuckles, let's say, and—"

"I mean I've sorted him out," Gerald said, impatient. "For good. I've defanged him, Monk. No more magic. I took back the *potentias* he stole. Thanks to me Lional can't hurt anyone ever again."

He'd done *what*? "But—but—" He beat down

the urge to stagger about clutching at his hair. "Gerald—"

"Oh, come on, Monk," said Gerald. Smiling again, but not nicely. Not like the Gerald he used to know. The Gerald he'd bullied and cajoled into answering Melissande's desperate job advertisement. "I thought you of all people would understand."

He stared, his heart painfully pounding. *Understand what, mate? That Reg and I are right and you've gone around the bend?* "Am I being thick? Sorry. It's only— well—this is all a bit much to take in, y'know?"

"It's not *that* much," said Gerald. Impatient again, with a nasty undertone of arrogance.

But Gerald's not arrogant. That's not who he is.

Or—who he was.

And that's the question, isn't it? How much of this man is still Gerald? My friend. The stubbornly conscientious wizard I left behind.

From the looks of things . . . not enough.

"If I might inquire," said Sir Alec, breaking the taut silence. "Once you removed the stolen *potentias*, Mr. Dunwoody, what did you do with them?"

Gerald shrugged. "I got rid of them."

"You didn't—" Sir Alec hesitated, "—make use of them yourself?"

"*No!*" said Gerald. Now he looked genuinely shocked. "What do you take me for? A ghoul, like Lional? I dissipated them into the ether. It was the least I could do."

"I see," said Sir Alec. He was very quiet, and so watchful. "That's impressive, Mr. Dunwoody. Really. But it's not what one might call *orthodox* incanting. So I take it that means—"

"Oh, come *on*, man!" said Gerald. "Stop being coy. *Yes*, I made use of the proscribed texts Lional took from Pomodoro Uffitzi. Enhanced my natural thaumaturgic abilities—which as it turns out are a lot more impressive than I'd been led to believe. But don't tell me that's news to you. I'll bet when I activated all those interesting incants the etheretic surge blew up half the DoT's monitoring equipment."

Sir Alec risked a swift, wintry smile. "As it happens we did notice some unusual thaumaturgic activity. *And* we assumed it had something to do with you. But it never hurts to have one's theory confirmed."

"Of course it doesn't," said Gerald, choosing to be amused. "Especially since someone somewhere is expecting a report about this. Am I right?"

"Well . . ." Sir Alec flicked a speck of lint from his sleeve. "I do serve a bureaucracy, which would grind to a halt without regular reports."

Gerald pulled a rueful face—and for a split second he looked like his old self. "I know. I used to be a probationary compliance officer. Practically gave myself arthritis, writing reports."

"I'm gratified you understand, Mr. Dunwoody."

"Oh, I do, Sir Alec," said Gerald, as earnest as ever he used to be. Only now his sincerity struck a sour, false note. Hearing it, Reg rattled her tail.

Monk managed to catch her eye. *Don't. Don't. It's too dangerous. Don't.* But Reg, being Reg, ignored him.

"So let me get this straight, sunshine," she said. "Just so there aren't any misunderstandings. Even though I told you not to, you barged right in and mucked about with those filthy grimoires."

Haughtily surprised, Gerald looked down at her.

"That's right. Because the last time I looked, Reg, you weren't my mother. I did what had to be done. What you and Monk were too frightened to do. What Shugat was too selfish to do, and Melissande and Rupert here were too incompetent to do. *I stopped Lional.* I saved New Ottosland. And I think it'd be nice if you just said *thank you* and left it at that."

Monk blinked, the blood thundering in his ears. *Oh, no. Oh, no.* The heartbreak in Reg's eyes as she stared at Gerald was breaking *his* heart . . .

Dammit, mate. You bloody fool. You didn't have to do this. We'd have found a way to stop Lional without this.

Melissande and Rupert were staring too, in guilty dismay. As for Sir Alec, his face was glass-smooth, revealing nothing of his thoughts or feelings. The silence surrounding them seemed to deepen. Grow cold. Even the palace garden birds were hushed.

"Now I realize," said Gerald, turning to Sir Alec, "that what I've done is a violation of the Official Code of Conduct but I'm sure you'll agree I didn't have a choice." He spread his empty hands wide and smiled, one bureaucrat to another. "Exigent circumstances. I was saving a kingdom."

Sir Alec nodded, still giving nothing away. "Certainly that's a legal argument, Mr. Dunwoody. One I'll be sure to mention in my report to the Ministry."

As Gerald and Sir Alec stared at each other like fencers over their crossed, unbuttoned blades, Monk cleared his throat. "So, Gerald—exactly how much of those proscribed thaumaturgics did you take on board? Was it just *Grummen's Lexicon,* or—"

"No," said Gerald, his voice edged, his gaze still locked with Sir Alec's. "I took them all."

"And when you say *all*," said Sir Alec, glacially calm, "what exactly do you mean?"

Gerald's face tightened. "You're being coy again, Sir Alec. I don't like it."

Reg rattled her tail feathers. "Never mind what you do and don't like, sunshine. Just answer the bloody question."

And that earned *her* a hot look, nastily annoyed and so not-Gerald. Suddenly afraid—*bloody hell, I'm afraid if Gerald Dunwoody*—Monk took another step forward, seeking to distract him. Because if Gerald lost his temper and did something awful to Reg—

"I know it's a nuisance, mate," he said, trying to sound helpful and unafraid, "but probably we should know what texts Uffitzi was hiding. Probably there'll be forms to fill out about them, once we get back to—"

"I like *patronizing* even less than *coy*, Monk," said Gerald, his dreadful crimson gaze narrow. "Do you mind?"

And maybe Reg was right. Maybe the time had come for a little pushing back and bugger the danger. "Actually I do, yeah," he retorted. "You're the one being coy here, Gerald. Not us. So come clean and be done with it. What other grimoires did Lional have stashed away besides the *Lexicon*?"

Gerald seemed genuinely shocked by that. "*Come clean?* You make it sound like I'm a criminal, Monk, instead of—"

Of what. A hero? His gaze flickered to Lional. *What kind of hero does that to a man?* "That's not what I mean."

"Oh, all right," said Gerald, with a theatrical

sigh. "If you *must* know, New Ottosland's former king had six grimoires in total." He held up his fingers and started counting them off. "The *Lexicon*, a *Pygram's*, a *Foyle's Foilers*, a *Compendium of Curses*, *Madam Bartholomew's Little Surprise* and—oh, yes. Trinauld's *Guide to the Unnatural*. All in all a really fascinating collection." He smiled. It was horrible. "I can personally vouch for the *Pygram's*. Lional used every last hex on me in the cave, y'know."

Turning to Sir Alec, feeling sicker than ever, Monk saw that his uncle's mysterious colleague had paled. *Oh, no. This can't be good.* "Sir Alec?"

"Every one of those texts is on the international proscribed list," Sir Alec said, his voice harsh with revulsion. "Arguably they are the six most feared grimoires in the history of thaumaturgy. Not to put too fine a point on it, they are *notorious*."

"Notorious, eh?" said Gerald, obscenely cheerful. "Well, I can't say I'm surprised. Bloody awful, some of those incants. Enough to turn your stomach inside out—and I'm *not* talking metaphorically."

"Although—" Sir Alec was watching Gerald closely. "I was under the impression that both the *Bartholomew* and the *Guide* were no longer extant."

"Were you?" said Gerald, one eyebrow raised. "Oh. Then somebody in Records needs their wrist slapped, don't they?" Then he frowned. "Mind you, now that I think about it—" He looked down at Reg again, lips pursed. "D'you know, it occurs to me that in between all that nagging you might have had a point."

"Oh, yes?" Reg said warily. "And I'm supposed to be flattered now, am I?"

"Keep on like that and you'll be better off silent," Gerald retorted.

"Can you be a bit more specific, mate?" Monk said. *Bloody hell, when this is over I should find work as a lion tamer.* "I mean, Reg spends half her time nagging, doesn't she?"

And that made Gerald laugh. "Too bloody true, Monk!"

"So—"

"I'm referring to what she said about those texts falling into the wrong hands," said Gerald. "Which they did. First Pomodoro Uffitzi's and then Lional's, here. Two complete scoundrels. It's obvious the Ottosland Department of Thaumaturgy and the United Magical Nations between them aren't up to the task of protecting the world from grimoires like the *Lexicon* and the rest."

Sir Alec cleared his throat delicately. "And you are?"

"Who better?" said Gerald, and clenched his right fist. Closed his eyes. Whispered something under his breath.

The shock that roared through the ether then knocked Monk to the grass. Sir Alec, too. Even Melissande and Rupert staggered, though they were hardly what anyone would call thaumaturgically gifted. And Reg let out a shriek as though someone had set her feathers on fire.

Tasting blood, Monk shoved himself, shuddering, to hands and knees. *Dammit, Gerald.* He looked at Sir Alec, just as stunned beside him. "It's not possible, is it?" he said through gritted teeth. "Not just like that. Not with one word and a *thought*. He hasn't just—"

Even Sir Alec's ironclad composure wasn't proof against this. "What do you think, Mr. Markham?"

I think we're neck deep in trouble, sir. That's what I think.

With an almost-groan Sir Alec found his feet, then held out a helping hand. Monk took it, was hauled upright, and found himself standing shoulder to shoulder with Uncle Ralph's colleague, who stared at Gerald as though he were facing a firing squad.

"That was unwise, Mr. Dunwoody."

"Really? You think so?" said Gerald. He hadn't even broken a sweat. Didn't look the least bit exerted, even though what he'd just done—what he shouldn't have been able to do, what no wizard living should be able to do—was momentous. "I don't."

Pale as freshly skimmed milk, Melissande stepped forward, shaking off Rupert's restraining hand. "What's unwise? What just happened? Gerald, what did you do?"

With a flapping effort Reg took to the cooling afternoon air and landed on Melissande's shoulder. "I'll tell you what he did, ducky. He got rid of those manky grimoires. Burned them to a crisp."

"Really?" said Melissande. "From here? Without even seeing them? Or touching them? How is that possible?"

Gerald laughed again, so pleased with himself. "Anything's possible, Melissande. All you need is the power—and the will."

"So those horrible grimoires are destroyed?" She looked around their small, silent group. "Well—that's a good thing, isn't it?"

"I should think so," said Rupert. "Those filthy

books Uffitzi brought into this kingdom have caused nothing but misery. I for one am glad Gerald's rid us of them."

"*Thank you*, Rupert," said Gerald, theatrical again. "It's good to know *someone's* on my side."

Sir Alec frowned. "It's not a question of sides, Mr. Dunwoody. Our concerns—"

"Don't concern me, actually," said Gerald, waving a dismissive hand. "I'm more interested in what's happened to Rupert. You've gone all assertive and opinionated all of a sudden, Your Highness. Or should that be *Your Majesty*?" He smiled. "Being sneaky, were you? Hiding from Lional? I like it." He glanced down at the stuporous king. "Pity he'll never know how you deceived him. He'd feel like an idiot, and it'd serve him right." His crimson gaze shifted to Melissande. "Did you know? Or did Rupes here play you for a fool too?"

"Hey," Monk protested. "She's not a fool."

And that got Gerald staring at him. "You mean I was right? You've gone ass over teakettle for Lional's bossy sister? Oh, *Monk*." Another smile, dazzling and dangerous. "That's so sweet."

He felt his blood freeze. "Ah—yeah. Thanks."

"Have you set a date yet?"

What? "No. Not exactly. Look, Gerald—"

Ignoring him, Gerald turned to Rupert. "So, Rupes. Given how you New Ottoslanders feel about Tradition—note I used the capital T—would it help if I vouched for Mr. Markham, here? He's clean, he's sober—most of the time—and he's not a half-bad wizard to boot. And really, you're all in his debt because he's the one who pointed out that Lional was shopping for another court wizard. You could call him our matchmaker, really. So it only seems fair that I return the favor, don't you think?"

Monk felt Melissande's fingers fumble for his hand. He tightened his grasp. *Stay calm. Don't say anything. We need to get out of here and decide what to do.* Her fingers squeezed his, and he felt a rush of relief.

Rupert's smile was careful. "Yes. Well, Professor, any friend of yours must be a friend of mine, obviously. But I don't think I dare cast myself in the role of Melly's matchmaker. You know how independent she is. She'd smack me."

Gerald laughed and laughed. "You're right, Rupert. She bloody well would. I mean, you should've heard what she said about Lional for trying to fix her up with Sultan Zazoor!"

"Yes," said Rupert, smile fading. "I can imagine. And look—Gerald—speaking of Lional . . ."

"Yes?" Gerald spared his bloodied victim an indifferent glance. "What about him?" And then he sighed. "Oh, come on, Rupert. Don't tell me you feel *sorry* for him? Don't tell me he's just been *misunderstood*? Did you *see* all the bodies? He's killed hundreds of your subjects! I'm sorry, but your precious brother's a mass murderer, Your Highness."

A light breeze ruffled Rupert's lank, dullish brown hair, rousing the faded stench of fire and death. "I promise you, Gerald, there's no need to remind me of that. In fact, I've known for many years, since I was a boy, that Lional wasn't . . . right. It grieves me beyond words that I wasn't able to prevent today's tragedies." His faded blue gaze flickered to his tormented brother, then back to Gerald. "And I do understand why you felt the need to—to punish him. He hurt you dreadfully. He's hurt everyone dreadfully. But if what you say is true, if his magic's gone—"

Gerald was smiling again, but his eyes were cold. "It's gone. And it won't be coming back."

Rupert nodded. "I see. Then please—in that case—show mercy now. Let Melissande and me take him into the palace. Let us find a physician to treat his wounds. He yet must answer for his crimes—but not to you. Not after this. He must answer to the people of the kingdom he so wantonly betrayed."

"Ha." Gerald stared down at bloody, half-butchered Lional. "Mercy? After what he's done?"

"Perhaps you're right," said Rupert. "Perhaps he deserves more and worse than this for the misery he's caused. Probably he does. Probably you could make his suffering last another ten years."

A glint in Gerald's blood-red eyes. "Twenty. At least."

"But it wouldn't undo what he's done," Rupert said gently. "It wouldn't bring the dead back to life or wipe away your terrible suffering. Nothing can do that. If you go on tormenting him, Gerald, all you'll do is tarnish your soul."

Silence, as Gerald brooded on the body of his erstwhile torturer.

"Butterfly Boy's right, sunshine," Reg said at last. "You've made your point. You've made Lional scream. Forget about him. You've got bigger things to worry about now."

"Oh, yes?" said Gerald, cocking an eyebrow. "And what would they be, Reg?"

"Well for starters, my boy, we can talk about how your eyes have—"

A flash of blinding white light. A rumbling, like distant thunder. And then an old man in a ratty robe and sandals appeared out of nowhere, leaning his bent weight on a gnarled wooden staff. A jagged piece of crystal glowed between his eyes.

Shugat.

Gerald heaved a great sigh, unimpressed. "Come to save the day after all, Mr. Holy Man? Well, you needn't have bothered. You're too late. *I've* saved it—so why don't you bugger off back home while you still can?"

The old man thumped his staff into the soft grass. "What you have done, wizard, is an offense against all men!"

"And what *you* did was hide behind your gods' skirts and then run away!" Gerald retorted, his etheretic aura flaring. "So don't think you can poke your nose in now, with your flash and dazzle parlor tricks and your silly bit of stone. I asked you, Shugat—no, I *begged* you—to help me. You wouldn't. So I helped myself."

"Foolish boy, you have *destroyed* yourself," Shugat declared hotly. Another thump of his staff echoed the cooling air with more thunderous rumbles. "In a moment of weakness you have changed your destiny. You have changed the world—and not for the better."

"So *you* say," said Gerald, scathing. "But why should I care for what you say, Shugat? *Go home.* And if they're still hanging around here somewhere like a bad smell, make sure you take Zazoor and your silly camel army with you."

"Now wait just a minute, Gerald," said Melissande, her cheeks flushed pink with crossness. "I'm sure we're all very grateful that you stopped Lional. And I suppose you are still New Ottosland's Royal Court Wizard. For the moment, anyway. But that doesn't mean you get to—"

Gerald turned on her. She stepped back, quickly, paling again. "Shut up, Melissande," he hissed. "Without me you'd be wading armpit-deep in blood by now. Your precious little kingdom would be reduced to smoking cinders. So like I said, I think it's about time you showed me a little genuine gratitude. A little *respect*."

"Or what?" asked Sir Alec, breaking his watchful silence. "We'll end up like King Lional? Pinioned, spread-eagled and tortured nearly to death?"

Gerald's eyes shone like wet blood. "If you're asking whether I'm prepared to defend myself, Sir Alec, the answer is *yes*. Do you think I'm stupid? Do you think I don't know why you were sent here? You're not a paper-pusher, you're a spy for the Department. A shill. A *stooge*. Well, let's get one thing straight, shall we? I care as much for the vaunted Department of Thaumaturgy as I do for Holy Shugat and his stupid gods! Where was the Department when I saved the day at Stuttley's? I'll tell you where it was, Sir Alec. It was standing behind me kicking me in the ass. Washing its hands of me. And what—now you think I'm going to bow and scrape and hope I'm forgiven for doing what needed to be done here? For saving thousands of lives? Think again. Because the days of kicking Gerald Dunwoody's ass are *over*."

Shocked, Monk stepped forward. "Gerald—mate—"

"Don't *you* bloody start, Monk!" Gerald said viciously. "What would you know about it? The Department's golden-haired R&D boy. Its resident genius. Born into the right family, with the right connections. You were never *not* going to be asked to join the Worshipful Company, were you?"

What? "Now hang on a minute," he said, feeling his own temper stir. "Since when did I ever rub your nose in any of that? It's not *my* fault who my family is, Gerald. I never asked to be born a Markham, did I?"

"Maybe not," said Gerald, his crimson eyes hateful. "But you never stopped to ask yourself what you were getting out of it, either. All the little lurks and perks of being in the right clan."

He could feel the others holding their breaths, willing him to back down, to go along, to let it be. But he couldn't. He couldn't stand here and let the man wearing his best friend's face spout this kind of claptrap and get away with it. Not without being challenged, at least.

And who knows? I might get through to him. Gerald's still in there somewhere. I know he is. And if I can just get him to hear me . . .

He shook his head. "That's not true, mate. I've always known I've had advantages other wizards never got. The best tutors. The best equipment. A ride to the top in the fast lane. I've always known it, and I've never been comfortable with it."

"Oh, Monk, I don't think you're that uncomfortable," said Gerald. "You never looked that uncomfortable from where I was sitting. But I'll grant you—yes, sometimes I think you felt a *tiny* twinge of guilt." He shrugged. "But hey, that's easily fixed, isn't it? All you have to do is make friends with the pathetic Third Grader. That way you can pat yourself on the back for not being a bigoted plonker like Errol bloody Haythwaite."

He heard Reg sigh, brokenly. *"Oh, sunshine . . ."*

"And that's your theory on why we're friends, is it?" he said, keeping his voice steady with enormous effort. "That's how much—how little—you really think of me?"

Gerald's expression twisted. "Yes, it bloody well is! You don't understand, Monk. You'll *never* understand. You can do what you like and get away with all of it. Because you're a Markham. Because you're *special*. Well it turns out *I'm* special too, *mate*. So watch yourself. I'm not going to be patronized by anyone ever again. Not even you. *Especially* not *you*."

The words were like punches from a clenched fist. Swallowing the pain, closing his eyes to the raw antagonism in Gerald's face, which was worse than the crimson eyes, he took a deep, steadying breath. He could feel Melissande beside him, horrified, and Reg's dumbstruck distress. Even Sir Alec was taken aback. Even the old man Shugat who'd appeared out of nowhere.

Another deep breath, and he looked at his friend. "I'm sorry, Gerald," he said, very quietly. "If I made you feel—inadequate—I'm sorry. I never meant to. And I'm not your friend so I can feel superior to a tosser like Errol. I'm your friend because I like you. Because you're a good, decent man."

"He *was* a good, decent man," said Reg, still slumped on Melissande's shoulder. Her voice trembled. "Before he mucked about with those grimoires. But now he's—he's—"

"Don't," he said, turning, and touched a fingertip to her wing. "You'll only make things worse, Reg. He can't hear us. What's happened to him—it's too new. Too overwhelming. Just—don't take any of it to heart. He's not himself. He's not thinking straight. He doesn't mean any of it."

"You fool," said the old man Shugat, and bowed his bald head. "He means every word. Woe to the wizard who has lost his way."

"*Lost* it?" said Gerald, incredulous. "You're the fool, old fool. I've *found* my way. After bumbling in the dark for years I finally know who I am. *What* I am."

Sir Alec cleared his throat. "And what would that be, Mr. Dunwoody?"

"The best damn wizard *you're* ever likely to meet!" said Gerald, and laughed.

"No," said Shugat heavily. "Not the best. The worst. Boy, you have become an abomination. The bird warned you. Woe to the world that you did not heed its advice."

Gerald spat on the grass. "If I'd heeded her advice, Shugat, you'd most likely be inside that dragon's belly right now. You and Zazoor and your silly camel army. Are they still here, by the way? Hiding? That's wise, if they are. Trust me, if they know what's good for them they'll bloody well stay hidden. And if *you* know which side your bread's buttered on—"

Shugat stabbed the ground with his staff, and the ether trembled. "Think not to threaten a man who talks to the gods!"

"I'm not," said Gerald, chin lifted, eyes glittering. "I think Lional was right about you, Shugat. You're a man who *claims* to talk to the gods. You're a man who claims the gods exist. But I don't see them anywhere. If I'm so bad, so dangerous, an abomination, why haven't they stopped me? Why didn't they stop Lional?" Another laugh, sneering and contemptuous. "I'll tell you why. Because they don't exist. It's all a flim-flam, Shugat. And you're a holy flimflam man."

The rough crystal in Shugat's forehead flared once. Monk winced, feeling the power roil through him. "A sad day, this is," said the old man. "A day to make the gods weep. Turn back, young wizard. Turn back if you can. For if you do not you will live to see your name a curse."

Melissande leaped forward as the old man raised his staff. "No—wait—you're not *leaving*? Shugat, please, you can't leave. We need you. We need Kallarap's help. *Stay*."

Shugat shook his head. "Kallarap is Kallarap, Highness. We dwell in our desert and the world wanders its own way."

"But—"

Another blinding flash of light and she was talking to herself. Shugat had vanished.

"Silly old fart," said Gerald, still sneering. "If he and Zazoor think they're getting those back-tariffs now they're sorely mistaken. And if they try anything funny you refer them to me, Rupert. I'll sort them out for you."

"Thank you, Gerald," said Rupert faintly. "I'm sure that's very kind."

Gerald smoothed his sleeve. "Well, it is, actually. But that's the whole point, which I rather think you're all missing. I *am* kind. And I'm generous—at least to my friends." He looked around at all their faces. "You are my friends, aren't you? I'm not mistaken in that?"

Monk swallowed the bile that rose into his throat. *God help us.* "Of course we are, mate."

Gerald nodded, pleased. "Good. Because you know, you really don't want to be my enemy. Just ask Lional." Then he sighed. "And since we're back speaking of Lional again—and of friendship—" He snapped his fingers once and the long, daggerish teeth piercing Lional's palms, keeping the unconscious former king pinned to the ground, pulled free and tumbled to the grass. Lional moaned but didn't open his eyes. "He's all yours, Rupert. And while I just know you're going to have a physician look at him, I'll tell you this for nothing. You'll be wasting your time. The bastard's too far gone. Me taking back those stolen *potentias* didn't agree with him at *all*."

Rupert, his face ashen, turned to Melissande. "Stay with him, Melly. I'll go and fetch a handcart or a wheelbarrow or something."

"All right," she said, almost tearful. "But hurry."

"Perhaps you'd care for some assistance, Your Majesty?" said Sir Alec.

"What?" said Rupert, startled. "Oh—yes—er, why not? You can help, if you like."

Gerald watched them head back to the palace, his crimson gaze amused. "So funny," he murmured.

"What is?" said Melissande, crouched beside Lional and dabbing his forehead with a surprisingly frilly, feminine hanky.

"Sir Alec, of course," said Gerald, his eyes wide. "Thinking that I don't know he's going to try and contact the Department. Warn them about me." He pretended to shiver with fear. *"Take precautions."*

Monk exchanged a look with Reg, who raised one wing in a tiny, tiny shrug. The gesture was eloquent. *You fix this, sunshine. I'm all out of ideas.*

"I don't know, Gerald," he said, trying to sound nonchalant. "I mean—"

"I do," said Gerald, the contemptuous amusement dying out of his face, leaving it cold and remote, the face of a stranger. "But that's all right. Trust me, I have *everything* under control. You've got nothing to worry about, Monk. The world will never have to fear a Lional of New Ottosland again."

CHAPTER EIGHT

Ottosland, nearly three months after the
Wycliffe Airship Company affair

"Come *on*, Reg, flap *harder!*"

"Harder? *Harder?* If I flap any harder my bloody wings are going to fall off!"

"Then I'll hex them back on again, all right? Just *flap!*"

"Y'know," Melissande said to Bibbie, leaning sideways on her stationary pushbike, "this would actually be funny if it wasn't so ridiculous."

"Hey!" said Monk, turning on her. "If you've got breath to talk you're not pedaling fast enough! *Mush!*"

She glared at her improbable and wild-eyed young man, beads of unladylike sweat dripping off her nose and chin. "I beg your pardon? *What* did you say?"

"You heard me!" Monk retorted, dancing around the experiment-crowded attic like a demented dervish with ants in his pants. "Come on, Mel, this is important. *Pedal!*"

"Why don't *you* pedal, you lazy plonker!" panted Bibbie, madly pumping the pedals of her own stationary bike. "Why are *we* the ones doing all the work?"

"Good question," said Gerald, who was busily plunging an etheretic agitator up and down in its housing, by hand. "I wouldn't mind an answer to that myself."

Monk dashed along the row of thaumatic containers that he'd crammed up against the attic's windowless wall, checking each one's fluctuating capacity gauge.

"You know why! Come on everyone, this is *important*."

It was Gerald's turn to mop sweat from his face. "Well, yes, Monk, we know it's important to *you*. But explain again why it's important to *us*?"

"*Why*?" Abandoning the slowly-filling containers, Monk gaped at him. "Well—because it's important to *me*, of course! Gerald, how can you even *ask* me that?"

"He can ask," said Bibbie, only half-heartedly pedaling now, "because if anyone finds out about this it'll be our necks in the noose alongside yours!"

"Oh, Bibbie, stop being such an alarmist," said Monk, and held up an etheretic pressure gauge to the attic's fitful light. "Nobody's going to find out."

Still flapping in front of the pedestal fan Monk had converted into a thaumaturgic generator, Reg hooted breathlessly. "You keep saying that, sunshine," she panted, "but so far your Department watchdogs have found out about the portable portal, the tetrathaumic compressor, the etheretic particle slicer *and* the go-lightly hex."

"Yes, but *not* the interdimensional portal opener!"

said Monk, triumphant. "Or the bits and pieces I've got going in here. So you see? We're all perfectly safe."

"From everything except heart failure," said Bibbie, and collapsed over the handlebars of her pushbike. "That's it. I'm done."

"And so am I," added Reg. She swooped away from the fan, landed heavily on the nearest thaumic container and skewered Monk with a smoldering glare. "Flapped to skin and bone, I am. So mark my words, you bloody young reprobate. There'd better be some prime beef mince in my very near future or there'll be prime trouble. Savvy?"

Monk ran at her, hands waving. "Reg, Reg, what are you *doing*? Get off there, get *off*! I've nearly killed myself building up enough thaumic charge to last the week and you're going to tip that container over and waste it!"

"*You've* nearly—*you* have—" Reg gobbled incoherently, tail rattling. "Right. That's it. Gerald Dunwoody, get him out of my sight, quick, before I forget I'm a lady!"

"Now, now, everybody, just calm down," said Gerald, abandoning the agitator and staggering between Reg and Monk, both arms outstretched. "There's no need for violence."

"Speak for yourself, sunshine!" Reg screeched. "Right now my need is bloody overwhelming!"

"*Reg* . . ." He wiped his shirt-sleeve across his sweating face. "Look, I know he's irritating but fair's fair. I mean, we did agree to this, didn't we? We did promise we'd help him out of his temporary difficulty. So I don't think it's right to start complaining now."

"When it comes to difficulties there's nothing

temporary about your muggins of a friend!" Reg retorted. "He lurches from one crisis to the next dragging us in his wake! And don't try to deny it because we both know it's true!"

"Well, sometimes it's true," said Gerald, fighting a grin. "But then you could say the same about me, couldn't you? In fact, I seem to recall that you do. Quite often."

"That's different," said Reg, sniffing.

Aggrieved, Monk stared at her. "Why?"

"Because he's my Gerald, that's why. And *you*, Monk Markham, are trouble with a capital T on two bandy legs!"

Melissande sighed and let her feet slip off her own pushbike's pedals. *Time for the voice of reason to speak up.* "I'm not going to say he isn't, Reg, but he's *my* trouble on two legs. Which aren't bandy at all, if you don't mind. So leave him alone."

"And get off that container, Reg, *please*," Monk added. "It's not designed to take your weight."

Gerald snatched her up before she could launch herself at Monk with beak and talons. "Settle down, Reg. He didn't mean it that way."

"I'm parched," said Bibbie, still draped over her handlebars. Still managing to look beautiful, of course, even when pink-cheeked from exertion and damp with perspiration. "And famished. What's in the pantry?"

"Don't ask me," said Monk, eagerly rechecking the thaumatic containers capacity gauges. "When did you last go shopping?"

"When did *I*—" Bibbie straightened, her vivid blue eyes lighting up with temper. "It's *your* turn this week. It was your turn *last* week, too, *and* the week before that but you never go. You've always got some pathetic excuse. Monk—"

"Gotcha," said Monk, with his crazy, anarchic grin. "Honestly, Bibbie. It's like stealing sweeties from a baby."

Bibbie glowered. "Monk Markham, I loathe you."

"No, you don't," he said cheerfully. "You love me."

"Believe me, Monk, I *loathe* you," she retorted. "Reg is right. You're nothing but a walking talking disaster, brother of mine. If you hadn't gone and upset Uncle Ralph—*again*—we wouldn't have to be panicking about the levels of ambient thaumic energy usage around here and *that* means we wouldn't be nearly *killing* ourselves trying to generate enough of it to store and power your *ridiculous* experiments."

"Hey!" said Monk. "Do you mind? They're your ridiculous experiments too!"

Bibbie slid off her stationary pushbike and marched towards him, hands fisted on her slender, muslin-swathed hips. "For your information, Monk, *my* experiments aren't ridiculous," she said, halting in front of him. "*My* experiments are adding invaluable knowledge to the field of sympathetic ethergenics. And *most* importantly, Monk, *my* experiments are sanctioned, which is more than we can say for *yours*!"

"Sympathetic ethergenics," Monk muttered. "Hocus bloody pocus, you mean."

Melissande exchanged an alarmed look with Gerald, who tucked Reg into the crook of his arm and raised a warning finger at his friend. "Hey! Remember the house rule? No disparaging witchcraft!"

"I don't see why I can't disparage it if I want to," said Monk, truculent. "I mean, it's my bloody house."

Bibbie stamped her stylishly-shod foot. "Oh fine, yes, rub it in, why don't you? Honestly, Monk, why is it you *never* pass up the chance to remind me that I'm only living here out of charity and—and your insatiable need to feel superior? *And* your inability to keep a housekeeper for longer than five minutes?"

Sighing, Melissande rolled her eyes. *Truly, I might as well hobnob with the inmates of the Ott Insane Asylum. I mean, it's not like there's any appreciable difference.* She looked at Gerald again.

"Feel free to hex the pair of them, Mr. Dunwoody. I won't object."

"No," he said, grinning, "but Sir Alec probably would."

"Oh, who cares about him?" said Reg, hopping onto his shoulder. "That tight-lipped, dictatorial, secret Department stooge."

Gerald flicked her wing with his fingertip, still grinning. "As it happens, I care. You know, seeing how he's my boss. In fact, seeing how he's everyone's boss, at least in a roundabout way, I'd say we should all care." Then he turned back to squabbling Monk and Bibbie. "That's *enough*, you two! *Monk*—"

"I know, I know," Monk groaned, and flicked his exasperated sister a grudgingly apologetic look. "Sorry, Bibs. It's just—I'm going spare here, not being able to work at full capacity." He dragged his fingers through his floppy dark hair. It needed cutting. Monk's hair almost always needed cutting. "Honestly, I don't know how much longer I can stand it."

Bibbie's crossness collapsed into heartfelt sympathy. "Oh, Monk." She smothered him in an enthusiastic hug. "I know. It's awful. But it won't be forever. At least, it won't be forever if you manage not to tip off Uncle Ralph. Are you sure you're not doing anything up here that's going to trigger one of his stupid alarms?"

"Of course I'm sure," said Monk. Then he frowned. "Well. You know. Pretty sure."

"You need to be more than pretty sure," she said, leaning away from him. "I mean, those alarms of his are dreadfully sensitive."

Monk wriggled free of her. "I know, Bibbie. I'm the one he tricked into souping them up, remember?"

Bibbie giggled. "I still can't believe you fell for that, you silly goose. The whole family knows you never trust a *thing* Uncle Ralph says."

"Yeah, well," Monk muttered. "I won't be trusting him again any time soon."

"So," said Gerald brightly. "Are we done now? Have we generated enough thaumic energy to keep you experimenting for a couple of days at least?"

Monk checked the monitors on his row of thaumatic containers. "I think so," he said at last. "Mainly it depends on what happens with the multidimensional etheretic wavelength expander."

Melissande looked at the expander, Monk's latest pride and joy, which was the most convoluted contraption she'd ever laid eyes on. Taking up a full third of the large attic's floor, a complex, confusing tangle of wiring and prisms and conductive coils and strange, disconcerting bits and bobs of questionably borrowed Department equipment, it had the alarming habit of drifting in and out of dimensional phase. The thaumic dampeners he'd set up to contain its etheretic undulations were supposed to prevent that, but the restrictions his incensed uncle Ralph had placed on his thaumic usage meant that the contraption's containment was sporadic, at best.

She jumped as Monk put his hand on her shoulder. "How many times do you need me to say it?" he murmured. "I promise, Mel. It's perfectly safe."

"I'm sorry," she said, with a little shudder. "I can't help it. I don't mean to doubt you, it's just I wish it *looked* safe."

Even as they stared at the expander it began another dimensional slide. Shimmering like a mirage, random sections of its convoluted construction started fading then pulsing back into brief visibility.

"Dammit!" said Monk, and leaped for the contraption's control box. "Why does it keep *doing* that?"

"Um," said Gerald, diffident behind them. "I can take a gander at it, if you like."

Melissande watched Monk hesitate. Not because he didn't trust Gerald's thaumaturgic abilities, but because the only thing in the world he was possessive about was his experiments. Generous to a fault, willing to strip himself naked to clothe someone less fortunate, when it came to his experiments he was the most miserly man she knew.

"Ah," said Monk, his gaze sliding sideways to his precious interdimensional expander. "Well—"

Gerald sighed. "Sorry. I should know better than to—"

"No, no, it's me, mate," said Monk, hair flopping into his face the way it tended to when he was annoyed. "Not you. I'm a pillock and a plonker." He waved an inviting hand and retreated. "Go on. Have at it. Lord knows I've tried a dozen times to stop its bloody shenanigans."

Melissande looked at the bird, still perched on Gerald's shoulder. "Come sit on me, Reg. Just in case."

Reg hopped across, and with an almost shy smile Gerald hunkered down beside the fluctuating expander. Held his right hand out over the bit nearest him, fingers spread, and closed his eyes.

"What's he doing?" Bibbie whispered, joining them. "Saying a prayer? Gosh. I didn't realize it was that far gone."

"No, he's *not* saying a bloody prayer," Monk whispered back. "I don't know what he's doing, exactly. He's—he's pulling a Dunnywood."

Reg looked down at her beak at him. "I beg your pardon?"

"That's what we call it down at the Department," said Monk, half-amused, half-sheepish. "Nobody understands what he does, you see. Or how he does it. According to everything we thought we knew about thaumaturgics what Gerald can do isn't supposed to be possible. Mind you, *Gerald's* not supposed to be possible." He shrugged. "And yet there he is, large as life and twice as tricky."

"Oy," said Reg. "Mind your language, sunshine. My Gerald's not *tricky*."

"Well, Reg, he's something," said Bibbie, and whistled. "Phew! Feel those etheretic particles dance, Monk!"

Not for the first time, and definitely not the last either, she knew it, Melissande felt a sharp twinge of regret as her erratic young man and his scatty sister marveled in low voices at something she'd never be able to feel. Very nearly a year now she'd had to get used to the knowledge that whatever else she was destined to be in this world, a dazzlingly stupendous witch wasn't part of the picture.

Almost a year. Shouldn't it have stopped hurting by now?

Startled, she felt Reg's beak brush swiftly and lightly against her braided hair. "Takes all kinds, ducky," the bird said softly. "Flash and fireworks are all fine and dandy provided someone's remembered to stock the pantry—and don't you forget it."

Oh, yes. The pantry. "I didn't know you knew about that."

"Ha," Reg snorted. "Bugger all escapes these beady eyes, madam. And if that young man of yours starts making a habit of taking credit where it's not due I shall definitely be poking him in the unmentionables." Another snort. "I must say I'm surprised at you for letting him get away with it."

"Oh well," she said, resigned. "It's just this once. I mean, he's been so terribly depressed about having his thaumaturgic usage curtailed. You know what he's like, Reg. Without his experiments and inventions I think he'd curl up and die."

"Who'd curl up and die?" said Monk, turning aside from Bibbie. "What are you going on about?"

She smiled at him. "Nothing. What's happening now?"

"Your guess is as good as ours," said Bibbie. "Gerald, what are you doing?"

But Gerald didn't answer. Still hunkered down

beside Monk's wonky contraption, his pleasantly plain face was oddly serene. His outstretched hand moved gently, waving above the dimensionally-sliding equipment.

And then he nodded, sharply. "Right. I see it. That's your trouble, Monk." He opened his eyes. "You've got an inherently unstable connection between the dimensional phase inducer and the etheretic sub-stabilizer. They're like you and Bibbie—put them side by side and they can't stop themselves from squabbling."

"Huh," said Monk, frowning. "So are we talking fatal or fixable?"

Gerald straightened out of his crouch. "Oh, fixable," he said confidently. "Completely."

"Yeah, but by whose standards?" Monk said, his smile wry. "I mean, I'm only a genius. You're the freak of thaumaturgics, mate."

Reg rattled her tail feathers so hard she nearly overbalanced. "Right. That's *it*. Call him a freak *one more time*, my boy, and I really will poke you in your unmentionables!"

"Reg . . ." Gerald shook his head. "Honestly. What have I told you?"

"Bugger all worth listening to when it comes to Monk bloody Markham!"

Melissande dug her elbows into Monk's ribs. "For the love of Saint Snodgrass just apologize, would you?" she muttered. "Or Reg'll go on about this until the end of next week and *I'm* the one who has to live with her."

"Sorry, Reg," said Monk, rubbing his side. "Sorry, Gerald. Just kidding. No harm meant."

"Ha!" said Reg, and chattered her beak. "I'll remember that sincere apology for when I poke you in your—"

"Reg, give over, would you?" said Gerald. "We both know you're not poking him anywhere."

"You don't know anything of the sort," Reg said darkly. "Because there's a great deal you don't know about *me*. I may be a sweet and harmless bird these days, sunshine, but when I was a queen I did more with men's unmentionables than poke them!"

"*Anyway*," said Monk, breaking the hotly embarrassed silence, "about my wonky wavelength expander . . ."

Gerald cleared his throat. "Yes. Right. Well, as I was saying, the problem's fixable. I mean, I could fix it right now if you like, only—"

"Only no thanks," said Monk, alarmed. "With my luck Uncle Ralph's got a whole roomful of monitors trained on the house and with your screwball thaumic signature you'd set off an alarm, sure as shooting. Besides. It's my mistake. I want to fix it. And I will fix it once I've got unlimited thaumaturgic power at my disposal again. But in the meantime . . ."

"Never mind," said Bibbie, as her brother returned to the expander's control panel and began to shut down his wonky contraption. "You'll get it to work eventually, Monk. You always do."

Monk flashed her a small smile. "Bloody oath."

"So are we done here?" said Bibbie. "Or are you expecting me and Mel to climb back on those stupid pushbikes and pedal until our feet spontaneously combust?"

With a final shimmer and a series of clicks and

groans, Monk's expander deactivated. He closed the control panel, gave the contraption a last, regretful look, then frowned. "Sorry? What did you say?"

"Never mind," his sister groaned. "Is there really food in the pantry or was that a lie to keep my bum on that bike seat?"

Melissande caught Monk's guilty eye and smiled, with faint menace. "No, there's food, Bibbie. What say we go downstairs and I make us all pancakes?"

"Pancakes?" Bibbie clapped her hands. "Really? With lemon and sugar and whipped butter and maple syrup?"

"And castor oil for afters," she said. "Yes. Why not?"

"Oh Melly, I do *love* you," said Bibbie, beaming. "Come on! I'm *famished*."

She had to smile. Sometimes, for all that Bibbie was a breathtakingly beautiful young woman and a devastatingly powerful witch to boot, more often than not Monk's little sister was hardly more than a child.

"Go ahead and fire up the stove, why don't you?" she suggested. "Tell Gerald about what happened today with Mr. Frobisher. Monk and I will be right behind you."

Taking the hint, for once, Reg flapped over to Gerald's shoulder. "Mr. Frobisher," she said, witheringly scornful. "That soggy old noodle! Didn't I say he'd give us a headache, eh? Didn't I? I swear, the next time that manky Sir Alec sticks his nose into the office I'm going to give him *such* a piece of my mind! Who cares if Frobisher is that Department stooge's friend? Ha! Forget about caring. Who *believes* it? Friends? Sir Alec? Don't make me laugh!"

"Hey," said Melissande, as Gerald, Reg and Bibbie

made their way downstairs, Reg's ongoing outrage echoing in the stairwell. "Monk. Are you all right?"

Monk shrugged, not looking at her. "I'm fine."

"Monk . . ."

With a heavy sigh he shoved his hands into the pockets of his threadbare jacket. "No. I am. Really. It's just . . ."

She slipped her hand through his arm and leaned her head on his shoulder. She could feel his unhappiness like a small, damp cloud. "I know."

His cheek came to rest on her newly-washed hair. "It's not that I don't understand that we need rules and regulations. Thaumaturgics are dangerous. Without rules and regulations, all those tedious checks and balances, well—"

"You get something like Lional," she said quietly. "It's all right. You can say it."

"You never talk about him, Mel."

"What is there to say? Lional's the past. I'd rather think about the present." And the future.

Specifically our future, as in—do we have one?

Except the time never seemed right to have that conversation. And while she was perfectly confident running Witches Incorporated, either on its own or as a disguise for Sir Alec's mysterious Department, when it came to matters of the heart—when it came to her and Monk—all of a sudden she felt ridiculously shy and totally tongue-tied.

"Hah," said Monk gloomily. "If I think about the present I get a nosebleed. I mean, for all anyone knows, Mel, I could be on the brink of a thaumaturgical breakthrough that will change the world as we know it. But Uncle Ralph—all of them—they insist on playing it safe to a ridiculous degree. I don't understand it. What's thaumaturgy for if not to make progress?"

Instead of answering him straight away, she looked around his crowded attic. Aside from the unreliable multi-dimensional expander she could count seven other experiments and inventions in various stages of completion. Everything from a scaled-down thaumic combustion engine to a funny little contraption he swore blind would brew tea without the need for human intervention.

"Maybe," she said, her gaze inexorably drawn back to the deactivated expander, with its faintly ominous implications, "it's that they feel Ottosland's progressed far enough for the moment."

"But—but that's ridiculous!" he protested. "Thaumaturgy's like a shark, Melissande. If it doesn't keep swimming it'll die. We can never stop challenging the limits of our understanding, if for no other reason than to make sure we don't get left behind and some other country, like Jandria, say, a country without our conscience, gets ahead of us in the thaumaturgical race. Because if that should happen . . ." He shook his head. "Well. I dread to think."

"I'm not saying I agree with your uncle, or the rest of those Ministry dodderers," she said. "I don't. If it was up to me I'd hand you a big bag of money and say have at it! Invent me something to make the world a better, safer place!"

He slid his arm free of hers and walked away a few paces. Shoved his hands back in his pockets and brooded down at a portable thaumic cauldron he'd said was cooking up a new and improved hex to keep Gerald's silvery eye brown. Then he glanced at her.

"But?"

"But you're forgetting about the politics of the situation," she said gently. "And politics—"

He pulled a face. "I hate bloody politics."

"I know you do, but so what? Politics is the sinew of our society, Monk. And like it or not you have to take that into account. You can't just—"

"No, Mel. What I *can't*," he said, turning on her, his eyes wide and full of turmoil, "is stomach this constant interference. You know, they take my work, my inventions, the ones they find out about, anyway, or that I tell them about, and the ones I'm working on down at R&D, and once they're out of my hands I don't know what happens to them. I don't know what they're doing with them. I don't know if they've been stuck on a shelf in a warehouse somewhere, or if they've handed them over to some other wizard to—to fiddle with—or—" He folded his arms over his head and stamped his haphazard way around the attic, neatly avoiding his various works-in-progress. "At least I know what happens to the work I do here, Mel."

She'd never seen him so upset. "I don't understand," she said, after a moment. "Monk, are you saying you don't—you don't trust the people you're working with? That you don't trust the *government*?"

With a heavy sigh he slumped against the pushbike she'd pedaled so hard. "No, I'm not saying that," he muttered. "I just wish I had more control over what I do. Over what gets done with what I do. That's all. Especially now, with me answering to Uncle Ralph *and* Sir Alec."

"I thought you said the arrangement wasn't working out too badly."

"It's not," he said, and heaved another sigh. "Sir Alec says I'm making an important difference, even though he won't go into detail. I mean, he's a sneaky, secretive, unscrupulous bastard but funnily enough I do trust *him*."

Oh, dear. "But not your Uncle Ralph?"

"No," he said, grudging. "I trust him too, even though *he's* an interfering, self-righteous prig. But the thing is he doesn't work alone, does he? Neither of them does."

"Monk . . ." Stepping carefully, mindful of what her young man would say if she so much as nudged one experiment a hair's-width out of place, she joined him at the dratted pushbike and took his hands in hers. Squeezed lightly, reassuringly. "I think you're worrying for no good reason. You're letting your imagination run away with you because you're tired and crotchety and you don't like being bossed."

He managed a small grin. "Well—that's not entirely true. I mean, it depends on who's doing the bossing, doesn't it?"

"Oh," she said, feeling her cheeks heat. "Well—"

His fingers tightened around hers. "Melly, I do wish you'd reconsider. Things are different now. With Bibbie moved in here, and Gerald, nobody could accuse you—accuse us—of doing anything improper. I'm the owner of the establishment, my sister's the housekeeper and Gerald's a lodger. You could be a lodger too. It's all perfectly respectable. And there are so many empty rooms in this old pile I'd hardly notice you were here. Seriously, how much longer can you keep on living in that horrible little cubbyhole at the office?"

I'd hardly notice you were here. Now there was a romantic invitation . . . "It's respectable to have a male lodger and a relative for a housekeeper, yes," she said, shaking her head. Pretending his careless comment didn't hurt. "But that's as far as it goes, Monk. Especially since I'm not like other people."

He groaned. "Oh come on, Mel, don't start with all that *I'm a princess* malarkey again. This is Ottosland, we don't believe in roy—"

"Not constitutionally perhaps, but the social pages of the *Times* believe in it with a passion," she retorted. "And I am not about to do anything that will reflect poorly on Rupert. Besides, I like my little cubbyhole. It's peaceful, it's private, and it's very economical. I'm particularly fond of the walk to work."

Now it was Monk's turn to shake his head. "I just don't understand how you can bear to be cooped up in that little box. After growing up in a palace? It makes no sense to me."

And it makes no sense to me why you'll ask me to move in here like a lodger but you won't suggest a—a formal arrangement.

But she couldn't bring herself to say those terrible words out loud. For all that she'd railed against tradition back home, there were some time-honored practices she was happy to support. Like being the marriage propose*e*, and not the propose*r*. Because there was bossy and then there was overbearing and she had no desire to cross that particular line.

"Yes, well, you don't have to understand it," she said. "All you have to do is accept it."

Monk grumbled something under his breath, then shrugged. "Fine."

They were still holding hands. That was something, wasn't it? That was—was encouraging. A sign. Wasn't it?

I wonder, is it being overbearing if I try to—I don't know—nudge things along a bit? Drop a not-so-subtle hint?

"Monk, I—"

A flapping of wings, and then Reg was perched on top of the half-open attic door. "Oy, you two, that's quite enough surreptitious canoodling to be going on with, thank you. Mad Miss Markham says to tell you that she's finished telling Gerald all about Mr. Frobisher and she's so famished now she's beginning to feel faint, so if you don't come downstairs this instant and start cooking her those promised pancakes then she's going to start cooking them herself."

"God, no," said Monk, paling, and let go of her hands. "She'll have the whole kitchen on fire. Come on, Mel. Quick. Before the house goes up in flames around our ears and I'm out on the street looking for a cubbyhole of my own."

So they trooped on down to the cozy kitchen and she made what felt like hundreds of pancakes, each one crisp and light and flavored with laughter and friendship. Monk had abandoned the notion of keeping on a full-time staff after his late Great-uncle Throgmorton's people refused to return to Chatterly Crescent, even though the sprite that chased them away had been sent packing to its home dimension. But it didn't matter. He and Bibbie and Gerald managed between them, more or less, and if sometimes little chores like pantry-stocking got left up to her, well, she didn't mind. It made her feel . . . needed.

At last even Bibbie pushed her plate away. "If I eat

another bite I'm going to explode," she announced. "That was wonderful, Mel. Y'know, if the agency does end up going ass over eyebrows you can always hire yourself out as a cook."

"Hear, hear," said Gerald, around his own last mouthful.

Monk was grinning. "And you can count on us for references."

"Thank you so much," she said with a sarcastic curtsey. "Truly, I'm touched." She glanced at the kitchen clock, quietly ticking. "Golly. Look at the time." A tug and a twitch had her apron strings untying. "I'll have to head home. I've still got some *I*'s to dot and some *T*'s to cross with the Frobisher business."

"So don't you sit there like a rabbit in the headlights, Mr. Markham," said Reg, with a rattle of tail feathers. "Go fire up your jalopy so you can drive us back to Witches Inc."

"Oh," said Monk, whose grin had faded. Now there was an all-too-familiar glazed look on his face. "Yes. Um—"

Gerald shook his head. "Bloody hell, Markham. You're hopeless, you know that, right?"

"Don't tell me, let me guess," Melissande said, resigned. "You've been struck by a thaumaturgical thought and you need to follow through on it without delay."

At least Monk had the grace to be embarrassed. "Ah—"

"It's all right," said Gerald. "I'll drive you and Reg home."

"What?" said Bibbie. "No. *I* can drive—"

"No, Emmerabiblia, you bloody well can't!"

The chorus of refusal was deafening. Bibbie stared back at them, offended. "Honestly, you lot. I fixed the mangled fenders, didn't I? What more do you want?"

"I want back the ten years you scared off my life, ducky," said Reg. "That's what *I* want."

As Bibbie lapsed into sulky silence, Gerald picked up the jalopy keys from the bench. "All set?"

Monk slid off the kitchen stool. "I'll—ah—I'll walk you to the front door."

Melissande lifted her hand to him. "That's all right. I'm tolerably sure I can remember the way by now. Reg?"

Quietly snickering, Reg jumped onto her shoulder.

"Good night, Monk," she said, with all the dignity she could muster, and hung her apron on the back of the kitchen door. "Bibbie, I'll see you in the morning. Please don't be late, and *don't* forget the post."

Gerald opened the kitchen door for her and she walked out, her head high . . . even as her heart broke, just a little.

CHAPTER NINE

Y ou see," said Gerald carefully, as he backed the jalopy out of Monk's dilapidated garage, "the thing is, when it comes to thaumaturgics he just can't help himself. He's always been like that, ever since I've known him. Well. According to Bibbie, ever since he was born, practically. So . . ."

"I'm sorry, Gerald, but I'm not entirely sure what it is you're trying to say," Melissande replied in absolutely her snootiest princess voice ever. And that meant her feelings really were hurt. *Dammit, Monk. Sometimes I really could kick your skinny ass.* "And by the way, if you don't steer to the left," she added, still snooty, "you're going to undo all of Bibbie's work on the fenders."

He bit off a curse and wrenched the old jalopy's wheel hard to the right, swinging its rump just in time to clear the converted stable yard's crumbling brick gatepost.

"Ha," said Reg, perched on the back of the jalopy's rear passenger seat. "And you've got the nerve to call Madam Scatterbrain cockeyed."

Ignoring Reg he slowed, shifted the jalopy out of reverse then swung its long, blunt nose to follow the narrow driveway out to Chatterly Crescent, where he rolled to a stop. The autumn night was cool and damp, a drizzle misting before the vehicle's bug-eyed headlamps. Thanks to the lateness of the hour the sweepingly curved street was quiet, muted lights shining cozily behind every curtained window. All those nice ordinary people, living their nice, ordinary lives. And to think he used to be one of them . . . those days seemed a long way off now. Another lifetime. Another Gerald Dunwoody. Abruptly melancholy, he breathed out a sigh.

But would I go back? if there was a way, would I undo Stuttley's and the rest of it? Wipe my life clean and go back to being that Gerald? Apologetic . . . marginally competent . . . longing for more and so afraid I'd never get it.

The thought made him shudder. No, he was thrilled he'd left that Gerald behind. But then, remembering the price others had paid for his transformation, for his secret dreams of greatness spectacularly coming true, all pleasure died . . . and he felt nothing but a drowning guilt.

"Oy," said Reg from the back seat. "Bugalugs. Have you fallen asleep?"

He shook himself out of pointless regret. He was who he was now. Nothing could change what was done to him. What he'd done. The only thing that mattered was what he did next.

Chatterly Crescent remained empty of traffic. Over to the right the looming bulk of the Old Barracks cast shadows across the uneven cobblestones. The drizzle, thickening towards rain, dripped with rising determination down the windshield so he activated the wipers as he eased the jalopy into the street.

"No, Gerald, that's the horn," Reg said helpfully, as an ear-splitting caterwaul shattered the peaceful night.

"Really?" he shouted, and tried one of the dashboard's other buttons. "I would never have guessed." He glanced at Melissande again, hoping to surprise a smile, but no. She was still frowning. Still regally distant. Brooding over Markham, though she'd never admit it.

Bloody hell, Monk. Have you got rocks in your head? Are you besotted with Her Royal Highness or aren't you?

The answer, of course, was yes. Monk adored Melissande. So it was an absolute mystery to him why his friend was holding back, why he hadn't come right out and unequivocally declared himself. Sure, things had been a bit tricky lately, what with him being tugged to and fro between the demands of his superiors in Research and Development and Sir Alec. And then of course there was the latest unpleasantness over his extra-curricular experiments—but what did any of that have to do with romance?

Nothing. And it's not like he's an idiot, or completely inexperienced. There have been other young ladies. Not many and not for long, but still.

Which perhaps meant that this was the first time Monk had been genuinely . . . smitten. And perhaps that was the explanation for his reticence in a nutshell.

Sleepy Chatterly Crescent came to an end, which meant they had the choice of turning left or right onto The Old Parade. Hitting the right indicator button, which produced an orange hand on a long lever, its fingers making a singularly impolite gesture—*bloody hell, Monk!*—he eased the jalopy into the sporadic westwards traffic flow. And that gave him an excuse to glance at Melissande. No two ways about it, she was definitely fed up—and quite possibly on the brink of tears. Which was so unlike her that he felt his stomach sink.

I'm no good at this. I think it's time to change the subject.

"So, Melissande, I was wondering," he said after a few moments of frantic brain-racking, as the jalopy chugged along with its narrow tires hissing on the wet road. He had to be a bit careful along here, they needed to turn off The Old Parade any tick of the clock. Easing back on the accelerator, he leaned over the steering wheel and peered through the windshield. Drat it, where was the turn-off? The night's mizzling rain was making the world all smeary . . .

Melissande shifted in the passenger seat to stare at him. "Yes? Wondering what, Gerald?"

Hitting the indicator button again then changing down gears, he eased the jalopy to a grumbling idle and waited for an oncoming horse-and-carriage to pass. The horse was soaked, its ears pinned back to show its lack of enthusiasm.

Poor thing, and on a horrible night like this, too.

"Gerald!" Melissande said sharply. "Wondering what?"

He blinked at her. "What? Oh—yes—sorry—about this problematical Frobisher person." The hard done-by horse trotted sullenly by, carriage in tow, and he made the turn across The Old Parade. "Will you be all right dealing with him or would you like me to—"

"Thank you, Gerald," said Melissande icily, "but I'm perfectly capable of handling one dyspeptic senior citizen without a man's assistance. Or a wizard's, for that matter. In case you hadn't noticed we are living in the modern era. It's amazing what women can do these days without the help of men. Or wizards."

"Although the same can't be said for vice versa," added Reg. "You do know you've just gone the wrong way down a one-way street, Gerald?"

Bugger. He'd turned too soon. It was all Monk's fault.

There was nobody coming towards them and nowhere to turn around anyway so he took a deep breath, put his foot down on the soggy accelerator and nudged the jalopy along a bit faster with the merest hint of a speed-em-up hex. Nipping out of the entrance to the one-way street, barely avoiding an unfortunate encounter with a cab that was traveling *far* too fast for the prevailing conditions, he eased back on the jalopy's accelerator and the thaumaturgic rev-up and settled into the fitful traffic bowling along Central Ott Way, which would take them in more or less the direction of Witches Incorporated's modest office.

Melissande was so *quiet.* He glanced at her sidelong. Lord, she really was upset—and some instinct told him it was about more than just Monk and their unromantic romantic entanglement. So what else could it be?

"How's Rupert?" he asked casually. "Have you

heard from him lately? Everything going all right back home?"

"Rupert's fine," she said, distant, staring through the rain-speckled passenger window. "He's very busy, working on his modernization program. Not everyone's as enthusiastic about it as he is."

"Tradition with a capital T digging its heels in?"

She shrugged. "Something like that."

"You're not wishing you were back there, giving him a hand?"

"*Lord*, no," she said. "And anyway, Rupert doesn't want me involved. He says the *idea* of me in trousers and business is one thing but the *fact* of it just now would make his job harder, not easier."

Right. So probably she wasn't homesick. What did that leave? He could feel Reg settled on the back seat, loudly not saying any number of things.

Thanks, ducky. You're a bloody big help, you are. The one time I could use some unsolicited advice . . .

Really, though, there was only one other explanation for Melissande's glum mood. He glanced at her sidelong again. From the look on her face there was a very good chance she'd bite his head off for asking . . .

But she's my friend and she's miserable. And if I'm right it's partly my fault.

In which case he owed her the chance to do some biting.

"So, Melissande, I suppose it's time we talked about the agency. You know, how this new arrangement of ours is working out."

Behind them Reg snorted, softly. Melissande stiffened as though he'd stuck her with a pin. Ah-hah. In his new line of work that was called a *clue*.

They hadn't talked about it since he'd joined the girls at Witches Inc., but he strongly suspected that she still hadn't come to terms with the agency's new and unusual circumstances. Even though Sir Alec had kept his word—at least so far—which meant there'd been no government interference with how the agency was run—well, unless you counted clients like Arnold Frobisher—still . . . he thought she was unhappy. He thought she was resenting the loss of her autonomy.

And that is my fault. I got her and Bibbie and Reg caught up in the Wycliffe affair. Exposed them to secrets they weren't meant to know. And that gave Sir Alec no choice. Gave Melissande no choice. It was surrender independence to the Department or be closed down altogether. Damn. Why is it that every time I try to do the right thing it seems I help things go more wrong instead?

Melissande continued to gaze at the passing street. "You don't need to worry about Witches Inc., Gerald. That's my job. It's my agency."

"Oy! And mine," said Reg, annoyed. "And Madam Scatterbrain's, though probably it's better if we don't say *that* aloud too often. We don't want to give the little horror ideas."

"Hey," he said, casting her a look over his shoulder. "Scatterbrained I'll grant you. Plus she's impetuous and careless and far too brave for her own good, but Bibs is no horror. So you can take that back, thank you."

Reg sniffed. "Make me."

Bloody hell. Ignoring Reg, he focused on Melissande. "Look, I know it's your agency and I'm just the ring-in," he said, slowing the jalopy for the left-hand turn that would take them off Central Ott Way and into the outskirts of the shabby genteel business district where the agency lived. "But, Mel, that doesn't mean I don't have a stake in Witches Inc. For all our sakes I want it to succeed."

"I know you do," said Melissande as they swung neatly around the corner, splashing through puddles and startling some scavenging rats.

"Well then, in that spirit," he continued, "I'd like to suggest that in the future somebody who isn't Bibbie should deal with any susceptible old men who come to us for help, no matter how they found their way to the door. I mean, honestly, we're lucky the old boy didn't drop dead from a heart attack. Just *looking* at Bibbie tends to increase the blood pressure."

Melissande considered him. "It doesn't increase mine."

"It does when you're looking at her floating on a dustbin lid on the other side of the open office window," said Reg, ever helpful. "Or when she's forgotten to bring in the post *again*. Or when she's—"

"Thank you, Reg," said Melissande, back to snooty. "I think we both know what Gerald's referring to."

Another tail-rattle from the back seat. "Oh. You mean the fact he's ass over teakettle about the girl and can't bring himself to say anything to her?"

This time he gave her a scorching glare. "*Reg!* Do you *mind*?"

"Just stating the bleeding obvious, sunshine," said Reg. "Or did you think neither of the very intelligent women in this jalopy had noticed?"

He swallowed. And what did that mean? Did it mean *Bibbie* knew that he had feelings for her? And if she did know was she wondering why he'd not declared himself? Was he hurting her the way Monk was hurting Melissande?

Oh, blimey. Why wasn't I born a turnip?

"It's all right, Gerald," said Melissande. "Your not terribly secret secret's safe." She glanced at Reg. "Well. With me, anyway."

Bloody Reg. "All I meant," he said, in a valiant attempt to get the conversation back on track, "is that there are some clients who might best be dealt with by a man. Nothing to do with competence, just—"

"Don't," said Melissande. "Really, Gerald? Just *don't*. Because if you think I'm in the mood to be told that women can't do the job like a man then you're nowhere near as clever as you look."

"Um—" All of a sudden it was very important to concentrate on the rainy street in front of them. "Yes. All right."

"And speaking of Arnold Frobisher," Melissande added, still snippy, "just how many of our clients *are* Sir Alec's fault?"

He shook his head. "Sorry. I don't have a clue. Sir Alec doesn't tend to confide."

And if that's not an understatement, I don't know what is.

As he slowed them down again, getting ready for the awkward dog-leg turn that would put them onto Tapster Street which would then lead them circuitously to Daffydown Lane, Melissande folded her arms in that particular way she had.

"I'm sure he doesn't," she said sourly. "However, be that as it may, leaving Sir Alec's procurations aside—and no matter how troublesome the inconveniently concupiscent Mr. Frobisher has proven to be—we needed his business. In case you've not noticed, Gerald, being taken over by the government hasn't precisely made us *rich*. We're still scrambling, and as far as I can tell we're going to keep on scrambling for the foreseeable future."

"Yes, I know, only . . ." He cleared his throat, feeling fresh guilt. "It's all part of our cover story, remember? Sir Alec did explain."

"Yes, and now *I'm* explaining," Melissande retorted, a positively martial light in her eye, "since it seems to have escaped your keen wizardly observational skills, that like it or not Bibbie's blood-pressure raising attributes are an asset to the establishment. Just like me being related to a king is an asset. And assets exist to be exploited."

"Oy!" said Reg, and she sounded offended. "What about me? I'm the third witch of Witches Incorporated. Technically. I'm the technical advisor. I'm an asset too, ducky, and don't you forget it!"

"That's true," Melissande admitted. "You're cheap to feed."

This time Reg's silence lasted all the way to the end of Tapster Street, into Daffydown Lane and to Witches Incorporated's front door.

Relieved, Gerald pulled the jalopy over to the pavement and shifted the gearstick into neutral so the engine could idle. If he was smart he'd bid the girls good night right now and pretend he'd never noticed the tension between Melissande and Monk.

But then nobody ever accused me of being smart, did they?

Besides. They were his friends, and in his line of work friends were hard—if not impossible—to come by. *And* he'd introduced them. It was his fault they'd met. So he had a vested interest in making sure things worked out, didn't he?

He cleared his throat again. "Look. Melissande. About you and Monk . . ."

"Oh, Gerald," she groaned. "Please, can't you—"

"I know, I know," he said hastily. "It's none of my business. Except that it *is* my business because I care about both of you a great deal and I want you to be happy. So if it would help for me to talk to Monk then—"

"Don't you *dare!*" she gasped, horrified. "How would you like it if I took Bibbie aside and nattered to her about *you*?"

Despite all the reasons why that was a terrible idea he nearly said, *Oh, would you?*—but he managed to bite his tongue. Reg was aching for an excuse to poke her beak in and the thought of her giving Bibbie romantic advice about him . . .

I'd be better off sticking hot needles in my eyes.

"Then let me say this, Melissande, and then I promise I'll shut up," he said. "Whatever's going on with Monk—whatever the reason is that he hasn't—that he's not—it isn't because he doesn't care. He really does care. But this business with his uncle—"

Sighing, Melissande tugged on her long, rust-red plait. "It's all right, Gerald. There's no need to fuss— or defend him, either. Monk's old enough to do his own talking. As for me, I'm a big girl now too, which means I can fight my own battles. So if you don't mind I'd rather not talk about it any more. Or about Mr. Frobisher, the old coot. I'll handle him."

He patted her hand. "I know you will, Your Highness. You're brilliant."

There was enough street-light filtering through the windshield for him to see that she was blushing. "Yes. Well." She shoved her spectacles back up her nose. "As it happens, Gerald, since we're talking agency business, there is a question I've been meaning to ask you."

His fingers tightened on the steering wheel. A note in her voice. An ominous undertone. "Yes?" he said, wary.

"When does Sir Alec intend sending you on another janitorial assignment? I mean, he bullied Witches Inc. into becoming part of his wretched Department and now here we are, nearly three months later, and you're *still* pretending to be a Third Grade wizard. I was under the impression you were supposed to be an occasional thaumaturgical contributor, not a permanent fixture. So what's going on?"

It was a very good question—and he had no answer. "Tired of having me around, are you? Eager to see me off the premises for a while?"

"Don't be silly," she snapped. "Even pretending to be a common or garden not terribly special locum you're as much an asset to the firm as Bibbie's blue eyes or my soppy brother."

"I am? You mean as a mere male I'm good for something after all? Aside from taking out the rubbish, I mean."

"Target practice, if you're not careful," Reg muttered from the back seat.

Melissande tossed her plait off her shoulder with an impatient shrug. "Of course you are. Because even though it pains me to admit it, you're right. Sometimes the best woman for the job is a man. Mr. Arfenbacher's little embarrassment, remember? He was never going to talk to a witch about that. And Lady Grune? A total stranger to the concept of sisterhood, that bloody woman. You saved the day there too, Gerald."

"Oh," he said, and was surprised to find himself ridiculously pleased. "Well. You know. Just doing my bit."

"And that's the problem, isn't it?" said Melissande. "Because the more you keep *doing your bit* the more clients are going to ask for you to work on their case. You'll turn into your own walking billboard and we won't need to mention you in our advertising even as a footnote. Which is going to make running the agency that much harder, if I can't say for certain whether you're going to be available. What if I give you a terribly important job and then in the middle of it Sir Alec whisks you away? What happens to us then? To our reputation?"

"You'd manage," he said. "And Melissande, Sir Alec did explain that—"

She slapped the jalopy's dashboard. "Yes, Gerald, I *know* what he explained. I was there, remember? I signed the paperwork. In triplicate. But the plain unvarnished truth is that we're a better agency *with* you than *without* you so just answer the question, would you? Please? *When* are you likely to be sent away on Department business?"

He shrugged. "Honestly, Melissande, I don't know."

"Well, that's not good enough!"

"I'm afraid it'll have to be. Sorry."

She snatched up her plait and bit the end of it, savagely. "Well, it's *not*. I've a good mind to make an appointment with your precious Sir Alec and—"

"No! No! Melissande, you can't!" Horrified, he

stared at her. "Really, you can't. You promised you'd stay out of Department business, remember? Don't you know how close-run a thing it was, you and Reg and Bibbie and Monk getting mixed up with the Wycliffe affair? The favors Sir Alec called in to protect all of us—to keep the agency open and you from being sent home to Rupert in disgrace—Melissande, *please*. You can't."

"I didn't know there'd been that kind of trouble," she said after a long silence. Then she tilted her chin, and behind her spectacles her eyes glittered dangerously. "Why didn't you tell me there'd been that kind of trouble? Is that why you've not been sent on an assignment yet? Are you being punished because of what happened with Wycliffe's?"

"No, of course not," he said, even though there were moments when he had his suspicions. "It's just the way things go in the janitor business. The right kind of assignment hasn't come along, that's all."

"Good," said Melissande. Then she frowned at her lap. "Although, to be honest, Gerald, I hope it never does. I don't want you disappearing into the underworld of black market thaumaturgics or international skullduggery or whatever catastrophe comes along next."

"But that's my job, Melissande," he said gently. "My *real* job. The agency—it's just camouflage."

Staring out of the passenger window, she sighed. "I know."

"And when that Sir Alec does get around to sending you on another mission, even if you could turn him down you wouldn't," said Reg. "Would you?"

"Is she right?" said Melissande, when he didn't answer.

Reg hopped from the back seat onto the back of the driver's seat, behind his left shoulder. "Don't be a tosser, madam. Of course I'm right. Our Gerald's getting antsy—aren't you, Gerald? You're starting to feel cooped up. *Bored.* And even though that Sir Alec's got you jumping through hoops once a week out at Nettleworth, it's not the same. It's not enough. You're as bad as that Markham boy, drat you. You don't like having your wings clipped any more than he does. You, Gerald Dunwoody, are pining for action."

Melissande raised an eyebrow at him. "Exactly. What she said."

Rats. "Well, *she* happens to be wrong," he retorted. "I'm not pining for anything and I don't have wings, clipped or otherwise."

"Oh, pishwash, Gerald," said Reg. "Pull the other one. With any luck it'll come off and then I can smack you over the head with it."

Scowling, he let himself slump until his knees hit the dashboard. "Fine. So you're right. But what difference does it make? I can't *force* Sir Alec to send me out on assignment, can I? And anyway . . ."

This time it was Melissande's turn to prompt. "Yes? And anyway what?"

At this time of night Daffydown Lane was as silent as the grave. As he stared out at the darkness the drifting drizzle hardened, turning into proper rain. The sound of it drumming on the jalopy roof and the lane's cobbles was oddly comforting. A childhood sound of warm blankets and steaming hot cocoa and his mother tucking him in with a kiss.

"The problem is," he said at last, "that I'm neither fish nor fowl. I never have been, really. When I was a Third Grader I scraped by as a compliance officer, just, but I was never going to climb the ladder of bureaucratic success. And then came Stuttley's, and New Ottosland, and suddenly I'm the most powerful wizard in the world, apparently, which means I'm too dangerous to be let loose without supervision. The thing is, I'm starting to suspect it's not that there *aren't* any missions Sir Alec could send me on. There are. The problem *is* he's afraid to."

"Sir Alec? Afraid?" Melissande shook her head. "Sorry, but he doesn't strike me as the fearful type."

"Fine. Then not Sir Alec, but the men he answers to. He's got clout, a lot of it, but he's not autonomous."

"Told you that, did he?" said Reg. "Over crumpets and a nice cup of tea?"

Not in so many words. Sir Alec had turned being cryptically circumspect into an art form. But there had been some hints, since the Wycliffe affair—some gaps in the conversation he'd been able to fill. And once or twice Mr. Dalby had given away more than he realized.

And then of course there's how the other janitors look at me, when they think I'm not looking. The truth is I don't bloody well belong anywhere.

"Something like that, Reg," he said, shrugging. "The point is they really don't know what to do with me. I *think* if I accidentally fell under a bus tomorrow there'd be a lovely funeral and sighs of relief all around."

"Oh, Gerald, *surely* not!" said Melissande, genuinely shocked. "*Surely* they appreciate your immense value to Ottosland. To the world. Certainly to thaumaturgics. They *can't* be so short-sighted as to let their fear of the unknown override what they've got in you?"

Reg cackled. "Of course they can, ducky. They're politicians, aren't they? *And* bureaucrats. The most dangerous combination of criminals in the world."

"Do you mind?" he said, glancing over his shoulder. "*I* was a bureaucrat, remember?"

"And *I* was a politician," added Melissande.

"Ha," said Reg smugly. "And so I rest my case."

Melissande pulled a horrible face at her, then gave up. "So what are you saying, Gerald? That this whole idea of seconding Witches Incorporated into his Department was a ruse? Sir Alec's way of—of—hobbling you? Containing you? Keeping you out of mischief?"

"I don't know," he muttered. "I didn't think so at first, but every time I turn around lately someone else is on a job and I'm still here."

She chewed at her lip. "Well—what does Monk think?"

"I haven't talked it over with him."

"Why not?"

He gave her a look. "Why do you think? Because he's got his own problems to worry about. And because if I did, and if he even halfway agreed with me, he'd be off shouting at his Uncle Ralph—or maybe even Sir Alec—and what he needs to do in the next little while is keep his head down and *not* draw any more attention to himself. At least, not for the wrong reasons."

"Oh," said Melissande, subdued. "So—he really is in hot water then? I mean, he laughs it off and tells me not to worry, but—"

"Um—well—" he prevaricated. Then Reg whacked

him on the back of the head with her wing. "*Ow!* Reg, don't *do* that!"

"If you'd answer the question, sunshine, I wouldn't have to!" she retorted. "Is that Markham boy in trouble or isn't he?"

Damn. Me and my big mouth. "He's under scrutiny," he said. "It's complicated. Not everyone in the government likes the Markhams. There are people—a few people—important, influential people—who wouldn't sob themselves to sleep at night if Monk had a spectacular fall from grace and maybe took Sir Ralph and a few more of the family down with him."

"And how do you know this?" said Melissande. Not in her snooty princess voice this time, but the voice that reminded him that for a while, and under impossible pressures, she'd single-handedly run an entire kingdom.

He made himself meet her steady, serious gaze. "Sir Alec told me," he said. "Over crumpets and tea."

It had by far been the most frightening conversation of his alarming career. Sir Alec's curt advice had burned itself into his memory.

"Take heed of your incorrigible friend, Mr. Dunwoody. There are those around him who are less than friendly. He would be wise to curtail his exuberance—and you would be wise to encourage him in that pursuit."

"And you're only mentioning it *now*?" Reg demanded, and hit him again. "Gerald Dunwoody, what's the *matter* with you?"

"I'm thinking concussion," he snapped. "Now lay off me, Reg. As it happens I've been waiting for the right time to say something to him. But there hasn't been a right time. He's been too busy climbing the walls."

"That's true," said Melissande, after another silence. "And *I've* been too busy *pouting* to notice. Gerald—"

"Yes. Of course I'll look out for him. Trust me, Melissande, no matter what it takes I'll always protect Monk—even from himself." He snorted. "*Especially* from himself."

"Thank you," she whispered, then kissed his cheek. "And good night."

"Good night, sunshine," said Reg, getting ready to flap after Melissande. "See you in the morning."

Bugger. He couldn't stay cross with her for more than five minutes. "Night, Reg. Sleep tight."

She looked down her beak at him. "And while you're busy worrying about that Markham boy," she added, "spare a frown for yourself, Gerald. Because I've got a nasty feeling in my water things are about to hot up around here."

Oh, Reg. Shaking his head, he watched her join Melissande at the front door of the old building that housed the Witches Inc. office.

Ignore her, Dunnywood. She only says things like that to make you hop.

But still . . . as he put the jalopy into gear and pulled away from the pavement, he couldn't ignore the nasty tickle in the back of his mind that said maybe, just this once, Reg wasn't wrong.

CHAPTER TEN

By the time he got back to Chatterly Crescent, Bibbie was nowhere to be seen and Monk was in the parlor brooding into a glass of finest aged Broadbent brandy and poking at the pine branches burning cheerfully in the fireplace.

"She's barricaded herself in her workroom so she can play with her ridiculous ethergenics," his friend said, not turning away from the crackling flames.

Damn. Am I that bloody obvious? "What? What are you talking about?"

Monk gave the burning logs one last good shove then leaned the poker against the hearth. "Come on, Gerald. I know you're keen on her. And I don't want to insult you. But—"

Suddenly cautious, he headed for the drinks trolley and poured three fingers of brandy for himself "But if you lay a hand on my sister it'll be pistols at dawn? Monk—"

Brooding into the leaping flames now, Monk hunched one shoulder. "Don't *Monk* me, mate. You think I like having to say it? You think I think you're not good enough? If you think that you're an idiot. Bibs could travel the whole world and she'd not find a better man."

He swallowed half his brandy in one gulp, poured himself a generous finger more, then retreated to an armchair.

I was wondering when we'd get around to this conversation. Funny, how when it comes to tricky things to say we always seem to find ourselves in the parlor, with the brandy.

"It's all right," he said, even though it wasn't, really. Even though a tight knot had formed under his ribs. "She's your sister. Your only sister. You love her. You want to protect her. And when you look at me all you can see is danger."

Monk swung around to face him. "So. You do understand."

"Don't you be an idiot, Monk," he said tiredly. "Why the devil do you think I've not breathed a word to her?"

"Oh," said Monk, after a moment, and retreated to the other armchair. "Right. Sorry. I should've realized—"

"Yes, you bloody should've." He tipped the rest of the expensive Broadbent down his throat. Probably not a good idea, given that the pancakes he'd had for supper weren't noted for their alcohol absorption properties, but in that moment it was hard to care.

"I mean," said Monk, determined to flog the expired equine, "let's face it, Gerald. In your line of work you've got old agents and bold agents but no old, bold agents. At least none that I've seen. And you're pretty bloody bold, mate. And come to think of it, as far as your Department's concerned *old* is something of a relative notion. Sir Alec's what—in his fifties? And he's the oldest fogey you've got."

Sadly, that was true. "I'm not arguing with you, Monk."

Monk swallowed more of his own brandy. "Bibbie's still practically a girl. And the bald truth of it is that I don't want her widowed before she's grown her first gray hair."

"Neither do I."

"It's just—you need to understand a brother's position, mate," said Monk, waving his almost-empty glass for emphasis. "I don't want Bibbie's heart ripped out of her chest and thrown onto the ground and—and stomped to mush. I mean—I mean—what if there were *sprogs*, Gerald? What if you and my little sister fell all the way in love, and you got married, and you had a baby, and—and then that bloody icicle Sir Alec sent you off to somewhere like—like Tarikstan, say, some thaumaturgical hellhole, anyway, and you got yourself killed and there's Bibbie with a baby and no husband and what kind of a brother would I be, eh, what kind of a loving brother would I be if I stood back and let that happen? I ask you?"

Gerald looked at him. "Um—just how much brandy have you had?"

"That's not the point," said Monk, jabbing a finger at him. "The point, my friend, is—"

"Yes, I know what the bloody point is," he snapped. "So long as I'm a janitor I can't afford to get myself tangled up in petticoats."

"Hmmm," said Monk, and leaned back in his

chair. "Don't think Bibs wears petticoats, actually. Something about suffrage—although I couldn't say for certain. I wasn't really paying attention at the time. You know what she's like. Once she gets on a hobbyhorse she tends to ride it to death."

"A Markham family trait, it would seem," he murmured. Then he sighed, and put his empty glass down on the small table beside him. "Look. Monk. I'm not about to pretend I'm not fond of Bibbie, because you're my friend and I owe you the truth. So. The truth is I'm very fond of her. And if circumstances were different I'd throw my hat in the ring, petticoats or no petticoats. But as you say, my circumstances are precarious and I don't want Bibbie's life ruined or her heart stomped to mush any more than *you* do."

"Good," said Monk. "I'm happy to hear it."

"Really?" he said, considering his friend closely. "Because you don't look happy. You look like a cat that lost the canary. You're not still bothered about the thaumaturgic limit, are you? Because that'll be lifted in no time, Monk. The whole bloody thing's a storm in a teacup anyway. It's politics. Face-saving. If you weren't a Markham I'll bet nobody would've said boo."

"I know," said Monk. "It's not that. And anyway, I've fiddled a way around the bloody limiting, haven't I? Because I *am* a Markham and we never say die." He pulled a face. "We might say *ouch* a lot while they're trying to beat us to a bloody pulp but the fateful word *die* doth never pass our lips."

"Then what is it?" he asked. "If it's not the bureaucrats playing silly buggers—what's the matter?"

Monk rolled his head on the armchair and stared

into the fireplace. The flames' warm, reddish glow cast deep shadows and remolded his face. He looked much older all of a sudden, solemn and serious and nothing like himself.

"Plummer wants me to make him a new shadbolt-breaker."

Odd. Given Monk's work in R&D, that didn't seem to be an unreasonable or even an unusual request. At least not unreasonable or unusual enough to explain his friend's out-of-character low spirits.

He frowned. "Plummer?"

"You don't know him?" said Monk, eyebrows lifting. "Huh. I thought you knew him. He's Errol's new boss."

Errol. Gerald felt his nerves twitch. *Bloody Errol Haythwaite. I could live the rest of my life quite happily never hearing that name again.* "We don't mix with the domestic agency, you know that. Besides, I'm under strict instructions to stay well away from him. As far as I'm concerned, Errol Haythwaite's dead."

"I know," said Monk, and shifted his somber gaze back to the flames. "Still. I thought you might've—ah—"

"What? Ignored a point-blank order and be keeping tabs on him under the table?" He shook his head. "No, Monk. *You're* the one who likes living dangerously. *I'm* the one trying to keep his nose clean."

Monk's half-smile acknowledged the hit. "He's doing pretty well, actually. Our old chum Errol. Flying through the domestic agency's training program like a witch on a broom."

And that made him smile. "I wouldn't use language like that where Melissande or Reg can hear you. Not unless you want to get poked in the unmentionables. And what the devil are you doing, Monk, spying on Errol? Are you a glutton for punishment? Do you *want* to get suspended, or worse?"

"Hey," said Monk, with a trace of his usual energy. "Nobody ordered *me* to pretend Errol's dead. And I don't trust that smarmy bugger. The way he weaseled out of what happened with the portal network—"

Oh lord, not again. "Monk, he wasn't responsible for what happened with the portal network."

Monk stared in outraged disbelief. "How can you say that, Gerald? He practically colluded with that bastard Haf Rottlezinder!"

"No, he didn't. And can we please change the subject? Defending Errol Haythwaite makes me want to throw up."

"Ha! Then don't defend him!"

"*Monk . . .*"

"Fine, all right, sorry," Monk muttered, slumping again. "But you're bloody unbelievable, Dunnywood. Is there a vacancy in the Pantheon of Saints or something?"

"Not that I'm aware of. Now, about this Plummer and the shadbolt-breaker he wants you to whip up for him. What's that about? I was under the impression the Department's awash with shadbolt-breaking incants."

Monk nodded, morose. "It is. At least, we have plenty that'll break an ordinary shadbolt. But—"

"I won't breathe a word," he said, as Monk hesitated. "If this is classified. But if you'd rather not risk it that's fine. No offense taken."

"Idiot," said Monk, giving him a look. "I'm

just . . . ordering my thoughts. The thing is, Plummer's people brought someone in for questioning but he's shadbolted to the eyebrows and they can't unbind the bloody thing without killing him. Everybody who's anybody in Plummer's outfit has had a crack at it—and they've all failed. Seems the wizard who designed it is the same nasty bastard who helped Permelia Wycliffe with *her* black market magics. The wizard in custody's one of his minions. And since Permelia's completely off her trolley and there's no sign of her climbing back onto it any time soon, that means she can't tell us anything about him. *And* since Plummer's only lead to him is this shadbolted lackey, well—they're in a pickle."

"And they want you to unpickle them? Well. It's a compliment, I suppose."

Monk snorted. "Some compliment." With a flourish he finished his brandy. "You won't have heard, Plummer and his lot are playing their cards close to their chests, but whoever this black market wizard is? Seems he's not pussyfooting around. That tycoon the other day—Manizetto?"

He had to think for a moment. "I don't—no, wait. Yes, I do. The man who tripped and fell in front of the bus in Central Ott?"

"The man who *appeared* to trip," Monk said darkly. "Turns out he was hexed, courtesy of our mystery wizard—and you did *not* hear that from me. I'm telling you, mate, whoever this bastard is he's got to be stopped. Which means *I've* got to unbind the shadbolt on Plummer's prisoner without harming a greasy hair on his head."

Gerald whistled. "You're right. I take it back. It wasn't a compliment. What are you going to do?"

"Well . . ." Monk tossed his emptied brandy glass from hand to hand, frowning. "As luck would have it the weasely little minion was carrying a spare shadbolt on him—of course, he won't say why—but the only way to unravel the incant's matrix is to muck about with it while it's active. And as hard as this might be to believe, I couldn't find anyone who was willing to let me shadbolt them so I could play."

Even though this wasn't funny, he still had to chuckle. "No, really? Mr. Markham, I'm shocked, I tell you. *Shocked.*"

"Yeah, well," said Monk, and pulled a face. "Smart ass."

They grinned at each other, and for a moment the shadows seemed to lift.

"So," he said, spuriously casual, "I don't suppose you brought the spare shadbolt home with you?"

Monk contrived to look outraged. "Mr. Dunwoody, how can you even *suggest* such a thing? Removing a sensitive piece of evidence from Department premises would be against the *rules!*" He put down the empty glass and slid out of the chair. "Don't move. I'll just nip upstairs and fetch it."

But he did move, to the drinks trolley, and splashed a little more brandy into each of their glasses. Monk returned to the parlor soon after, carrying a small, innocuous-looking wooden box.

"Blimey," he said, still holding the brandy glasses, as Monk unlocked and opened it. A sick, protesting surge in the ether churned echoes in his gut. "That's *nasty.*"

"Told you," said Monk, staring at the shadbolt-crystal nestled in a cradle of old lamb's wool. "Have a read of it, Gerald, and tell me what you think."

But before he could put down the glasses and take the small box, the parlor door flew open and Bibbie rushed in. "What *is* that? Monk, what the devil are you playing with?"

"Oh," said Monk, blankly. "Bibbie. I thought you were mucking about with your silly ethergenics."

Bibbie had changed out of her lovely peach-colored muslin day dress into a shapeless green cotton shirt and baggy tweed trews—*curse you, Melissande*—and had covered up most of both with a stained and slightly charred thaumaturgist's apron. Her long golden hair was bundled haphazardly into a scarf.

"Forget it, Monk," she snapped, her glorious sapphire eyes alight with temper. "You're not going to distract me with a cheap shot like that." She pointed at the hex box. "Powerful witch, remember? Etheretic sensitivity rating right off the charts? Now *what* is that abomination doing in this house?"

Monk dragged his fingers through his floppy hair. "Rats," he muttered. "Bibbie—go back upstairs, would you? Please? And forget you ever saw this."

"No, I don't think I will," she said, folding her arms. "Perhaps if you'd been a *little* less sarky about my ethergenics—"

"*Please*, Bibbie!" said Monk, alarmingly close to desperate. "This isn't a joke. It's bloody dangerous. I can't have you—"

"You're telling *me* it's bloody dangerous," Bibbie snapped. Nose delightfully wrinkled, she stepped closer to the hex-box and stared at the hazelnut-sized black crystal inside it. "And more than *that* it's familiar." She looked up. "This was made by the same wizard who made Permelia Wycliffe those fake jewels *and* the hex she used to kill her horrible brother."

"Come on, Monk," said Gerald, as Monk gaped at his sister. "Did you really think she wouldn't make the connection?"

"I was hoping all those ethergenics had scrambled her brain!"

"Well, that was ridiculously optimistic of you, wasn't it?" said Bibbie, poisonously sweet. "If eleven months of Reg's lectures haven't sent me doolally then what makes you think ethergenics could make a dent? Now, Monk, for the last time—*what is going on?*"

She even had a beautiful scowl. Watching her as Monk quickly explained his dilemma, Gerald felt his heart thud painfully against his ribs. It wasn't only her beauty, though that tended to strike him dumb. No, it was her wit and her audacity and her brilliance that seduced, leaving him weak at the knees and struggling for breath.

Cold, damp misery settled over him like a cloud.

Forget it, Dunwoody. You and Bibbie can never work out. Not unless someone finds a cure for being a rogue wizard.

"Right," said Bibbie, when Monk finished his tale. "So let me see if I've got this straight. In order to catch the black-hearted wizard behind all kinds of nefarious, murderous and wicked skulduggery, you need to find out how to unbind *that* shadbolt. Yes?"

"Yes," said Monk, nodding. He looked distinctly harassed. "But you can't help me, Bibbie. This is supposed to be a secret. I'm not supposed to have this hex. I'm not even supposed to have told Gerald about it, and *he's* a government secret all by himself. If anyone finds out I've told *you* then trust me, my head will not only roll, it'll get stuck on a pike and paraded through Central Ott."

Bibbie smiled at him brightly. "Don't be silly, Monk. Of course I can help."

And before they could stop her she snatched up the shadbolt-crystal and popped it in her mouth.

"Oh, Saint Snodgrass," Monk said, breathless. "Emmerabiblia Markham, what the hell have you done?"

Ignoring him, Bibbie pulled a face and flapped her hands. "Ew—ew—it tastes *disgusting*!"

"Bibbie," Gerald whispered. Mouth dry, heart thundering, he took a step towards Monk's crazy sister then stopped. "Bibbie, what's happening?"

"Nothing yet," she said. "The wretched thing's still dissolving." She pressed a shaking hand to her middle. Beneath the bravado she was horribly afraid, he could see it. Feel it. *Bibbie.* "Honestly, boys, when you catch this dreadful man can you take a moment to explain to him the many and varied uses of sugar?"

Monk was standing so still he might've been nailed to the floor. Looking at him, Gerald realized this was the first time he'd ever seen his friend terrified.

"Monk," he said urgently. "*Monk.* It's all right. We'll get her out of this. She'll be fine."

Slowly, painfully, Monk dragged his agonized stare away from Bibbie. "You don't know that."

He grabbed Monk's arm and shook it. "Yes, I do. *I do.* Now pull yourself together, Mr. Blue-Eyed Boy Genius of the R&D Department! You want to waste the chance Bibbie's given us? That shadbolt's going to activate any moment so bloody well *get focused.*"

Bibbie nodded, her face still twisted with revulsion. "He's right, Monk. It's starting to unfurl. I can feel it. So get cracking on a way to release me once it does, otherwise I'm going to be late to the office in the morning and I'll be stonkered if I have to put up with a lecture from Melissande *and* Reg!"

"Right," Monk muttered. "Right." He shook his arm free. "Gerald—we'll read it together. Compare notes afterwards. On three. One—two—*three*."

In the weeks since he'd moved into the old house in Chatterly Crescent, he and Monk had spent quite a bit of time in thaumaturgical tandem, cautiously testing the ether and each other to see what was what. They weren't evenly matched; his transformation into a First Grade wizard with extra oomph meant he out-powered even the renowned Monk Markham. But even so they'd managed to pull off some impressive feats of metaphysics—and that now proved to have been most serendipitous, because their mucking about had shown him how to comfortably adjust his own thaumaturgic intensity to match his friend's impressive but still lighter punch.

Eyes closed as he navigated the agitated ether, he was acutely aware of Monk and Bibbie and the imminently-activating shadbolt. Its incant was foul, corrosive, blooming like a rancid rose.

Nearly . . . nearly . . . hold on, Bibbie. Hold on.

The incant ignited and Bibbie screamed.

"No, don't touch her!" Gerald said, holding Monk back. "You might contaminate its thaumic signature."

Monk's breathing was harsh and ragged, like sobs. "Bloody hell, Bibbie," he said, his voice strangled. "When this is over I'm going to bloody kill you."

"Provided one of you doesn't kill me sooner," said Bibbie, through clenched teeth. There were tears in her eyes. "Just—hurry up, will you? Please? This thing is horrid."

"Come on, Monk, concentrate," he said. "Our window of opportunity's slamming shut."

Linking *potentias* for the second time, he and Monk plunged themselves into the etheretic maelstrom surrounding Bibbie. Tainted by the fast-maturing shadbolt, it seethed and surged, protesting against the dark magics Bibbie had unleashed in the parlor.

Bloody hell, I hope this doesn't set off an alarm somewhere in the Department.

His belly churned frantically, the brandy he'd drunk fighting to come back up again. Grimly he fought just as hard to keep it down.

Beside him, Monk grunted. "I can see it. Can you see it, Gerald? What do you think?"

I think that shadbolt's a bloody monstrosity.

Unshackled, Bibbie's etheretic aura was pure and clean and colored a faint golden-rose, like fresh snow at sunrise. Looking at it now, though, all he could see was a filthy, festering tangle of corrupted magic that strangled Bibbie's aura like diseased barbed wire. The worst of it was centered around her head, her face, the shadbolt's purpose to keep her mouth shut, her mind imprisoned. To keep all her secrets from spilling into ears not meant to hear them.

As though a giant fist punched him, he remembered the dream—the illusion—created for him by Monk's *delerioso* incant. Remembered that wizard who'd never existed—what was his name? William?— and the shadbolt he'd been asked to break as part of his final janitor's exam, and how it had felt to smash the binding hex. Pretend-William had howled like a dying dog.

But lord, this is real. And I hate it.

Even as he railed against the horror smothering Bibbie, a part of his mind, the detached, wizardly, rogue agent part, was admiring the shadbolt's ruthless complexity. Was memorizing its blueprint, the way its confining strands thickened and twisted and looped themselves in such knots . . .

Monk's furious distress was growing, reverberating through their linked *potentias*. Any minute now it would be a real problem because that distress was threatening to disrupt any useful reading of the shadbolt—and without an accurate reading, without discovering the key to its disarticulation, Bibbie would remain trapped within it as securely as Mr. Plummer's prisoner was trapped.

"Monk!" he said. "Don't you *dare* fall apart on me now. Come on, get a grip. If a slip of a girl can stand this, so can you!"

With an effort that sent waves of pain rippling through the ether, Monk throttled his anguish and regained his balance. Their thaumic link held. Breathing hard, they continued to examine the cruelly constricting shadbolt.

"Gerald—Monk—not to be a nag, but would you mind getting a move on?" Bibbie whispered, her voice small and close to breaking. "Only this isn't quite as much fun as I thought it would be."

Choking, Monk let out a long, shaky breath. "Gerald—can you break this damned thing?"

He felt his heart sink. *Yes, Monk, of course I can.*

But what use would that be? He couldn't march into Mr. Plummer's office and break the one on his prisoner, could he? Monk had to do that. And he had to do it without help. No one could know about Gerald Dunwoody's unauthorized, unsanctioned thaumaturgical assistance.

"Gerald!"

He eased himself out of the ether, drawing Monk with him. Drained and shaky they looked at each other. Monk's face was chalk-white and sweating, the habitual manic amusement in his eyes chased away by stark fear.

As for what Monk could see in his eyes, he didn't want to know.

They looked at Bibbie, transfixed before them. She was chalk-white too, tears trickling down her cheeks. But as they turned to her she smiled. She was so brave. So wonderful.

"You can do this," she said, her hands clenched to fists by her sides. The pain of the shadbolt shuddered through her. "You're the best wizards in Ottosland. In the world. When you two work together there's nothing you can't achieve. All right? Do you believe me?"

Gerald nodded. "Of course. Only—" He turned back to Monk. "Look—"

"I know," Monk said, grim. And of course he did. He was a very, very smart man. "So what are we going to do?"

"Take it step by step," he said. "Slowly. Did you see the incant's central helix?"

"Yes," said Monk, his mouth pinched at the corners. "It's the same as the other one. A triple-chained reversing skeleton. Quadruple-linked through the spinal hex into the outlying semi-cants. It's a bastard, Gerald. A thaumaturgical minefield."

"Yes, but we'll defuse it. You heard what Bibbie said—we're the best in the business." Somehow he managed to make himself smile. "Okay. So. The key to dismantling the shadbolt lies in the outlying semi-cants."

Monk frowned. "It does? Are you sure? I didn't see—"

"Yes, you did. You just didn't realize what you were looking at. Look again. Go on."

This time Monk sank his senses into the ether alone. Staying unsubmerged, Gerald watched Bibbie's face as her brother cautiously poked and prodded his way around the shadbolt. The lightest touch pained her. More tears brimmed in her eyes and her teeth sank into her lower lip, threatening to draw blood.

"It's okay, Bibbie," he said softly, not daring to touch her. "I'm here. You can do this. It'll be over soon. You're all right."

Blinking rapidly, she nodded. "I know. Oh, Gerald . . ." Her voice broke. "It hurts."

Bibbie.

It nearly killed him not to hold her, not to crush her to his chest. She was so brave, and he loved her, and barring a miracle—or a disaster—she could never be his.

With a gasp Monk pulled himself out of the ether. "I saw it! I saw what you mean. And you're right. But there's a trick to it. A nasty one. The bloody things are sequenced. Trip them out of order and—"

"And what?" said Bibbie. "Monk? And what?"

"You'll die," he said flatly. "It's a failsafe." He glanced sideways. "That isn't in the other shadbolt."

"Which is why you weren't expecting it," he said. "Monk, settle down."

But Monk was nowhere near to settling. "One mistake, Gerald. One mistake and I'll kill her."

Bibbie tilted her chin, just like Melissande. "Well, then, big brother. Don't make a mistake."

Groaning, hands pressed flat to his face, Monk turned away. "I can't. It's not just the sequence, Bibs, there's some kind of timing involved on top of it. Did you feel that too, Gerald?"

"I did," he said. *Bugger it.* "And that's not something I can help you with, Monk. I mean, I can—I will, if you want—tell you in which order to trip the semi-cants. But you're the only one who can judge the timing."

Monk let his hands drop. "I *can't*," he said, with a terrible intensity. "You do it. You do it all. You won't make a mistake, but I might."

"No, you won't," Bibbie protested. "Monk, you won't."

He turned on her, savagely. "You don't bloody know that!"

"Yes, I do," she said. "I do, because I'm your little sister and you love me and you know bloody well I'll come back and haunt you if you get it wrong. And if you *don't* do it, Monk, then you won't be able to remove the shadbolt from the man Plummer has in custody which means I did this for nothing. And then I'll hate you, Monk. D'you hear me? I'll *hate* you. Forever!"

"Which'll make us even, won't it?" Monk retorted. "Because I already hate you for doing this, you stupid, *stupid* girl!"

"Fine, then, hate me!" she shouted. "See if I care! So long as you get this horrible thing off me you can hate me all you like!"

"Hey, hey," said Gerald, catching Monk by the shoulder. "Bibbie's right. You have to be the one who does this. For once you need to take all the credit. The slightest whiff that I'm involved and we'd both be finished and—" He swallowed, hard. "It might be selfish to say it, but I need to stay a janitor. The only reason I'm breathing free air is because of Sir Alec. Right now, if I didn't have him to hide behind— well—I'd be in a spot of trouble."

Monk shook his head, his face taut with distress. "In other words you're asking me to choose between my best friend and my sister."

It sounded awful when he put it like that. "I'm asking you to trust yourself. You always have before."

"Yeah, well, *before* you were a clumsy Third Grade wizard, weren't you? And now—"

He took Monk by the shoulders. "And now I'm telling you that you can *do* this. *I* might have changed but you haven't. You're the great Monk Markham, the terror of R&D."

"God," said Monk, shivering. "I think I'd rather be a tailor."

"No, you wouldn't. Trust me." He spun Monk around and gave him a little push. "Now go on. It's not polite to keep a lady waiting."

"Ha," said Monk. "That's no lady. That's my sister."

But he walked back to Bibbie, and stood before her, and smiled. "Are you ready, Emmerabiblia?"

Her chin tilted again. "Don't call me that. I hate it."

Monk's hesitant smile quirked briefly into a grin. "I know." And then he flicked a glance over his shoulder. "So what's the order of the semi-cants, Professor Dunwoody?"

Gerald closed his eyes and summoned to mind the shape of the shadbolt. "Tero, duo, quadro, une. Canti, sexto, octo, sept."

Monk muttered the sequence under his breath, then nodded. "All right then. Hold down your petticoats, Bibs. This could get a little bumpy."

A deep breath, a whispered prayer—and Monk dived back into the ether. More than anything Gerald wanted to dive back in there with him, but he didn't dare risk it. Monk couldn't afford even the slightest distraction. And anyway, Bibbie shouldn't have to go through this alone.

"I'm holding your hand, Bibs. Can you feel it?"

She nodded, her eyes so bright and brilliant. "Yes. Yes. It's all right, Gerald. Don't worry. I'm not afraid."

Maybe not. But I am. Bloody hell. We're all mad.

He felt the first semi-cant surrender to Monk's command. Felt time tick by, each second like a blow from a sledgehammer. Then the second semi-cant collapsed, followed almost immediately by the third. The ether was writhing, thrashing at the release of dark powers. The fourth surrendered. The fifth. More waiting, and then the sixth. The seventh. And then he waited again . . . and he kept on waiting . . . and the sledgehammer seconds threatened to smash him to the floor.

"What's happening?" Bibbie whispered. "Is something wrong? What's taking so long? Gerald—"

"Don't—don't—" he croaked. "Bibbie, don't move."

The eighth and final semi-cant disintegrated in a soft thaumic explosion which tossed Bibbie backwards until she struck the parlor wall. Monk crashed to his knees, retching, bringing up brandy and blood.

"Bibbie!" Gerald shouted, and leaped for her. "Bibbie, are you all right?"

She was retching too but there was no blood, Saint Snodgrass be praised. The smothering shadbolt was gone, her aura untrammeled now and shining. She pushed him aside.

"Monk!" she said. "Monk, are you all right? *Monk!*"

Superfluous to requirements, Gerald watched as his best friend and the woman he shouldn't—couldn't—love fell into each other's arms.

"You did it, you did it, Monk," Bibbie sobbed. "I knew you could. I told you. And now you'll help Plummer catch that murdering black market wizard and that'll shut Uncle Ralph's bloody trap for good!"

"What?" Monk demanded, and wrenched himself free of her desperate embrace. "Bibbie—is *that* why you did it? To put paid to Uncle Ralph?"

Her old scarf had come undone, and her glorious golden hair tumbled free around her face and shoulders. "Why else, you idiot?" she said, and punched his chest. "I mean, I had to do *something*, didn't I? Or you'll have me pedaling that stupid stationary bike of yours until my feet really *do* spontaneously combust!"

CHAPTER ELEVEN

Arms folded, kid-booted toes tapping, Melissande stood on the front steps of the Witches Incorporated office building and waited for Gerald and Bibbie to arrive. The previous night's miserable drizzle had cleared just after dawn, leaving the sky washed clean and the sun with its work cut out to dry up the generously scattered puddles. Boris, fastidious as ever, was seated on the front steps beside her, washing his face and whiskers and refusing to set so much as a toe onto the pavement until all the nasty water was gone.

"It's a quarter past nine, Boris," she announced, after glancing at the watch pinned to her sensible blouse. "And they're still not here. I'm at my wits' end, I tell you. In fact I'm starting to think that dreadful Miss Petterly had the right idea. As of today tardiness is going to be rewarded by salary deductions, no ifs, ands or buts. Unless that scatterbrained girl and the lovestruck idiot we got foisted on us without so much as a by-your-leave are here in the next five minutes I am keeping back a full ten percent of this week's wage. I'm putting my foot down, Boris. Hard. Move your tail."

It wasn't fair. It was rude and inconsiderate and—and unkind. And as if her colleagues' lack of punctuality wasn't enough to bring her out in hives, there was that singularly unnerving Sir Alec to deal with.

"Why me, Boris?" she said, peering along depressingly empty Daffydown Lane. Clients, clients, where were all the *clients*? "What did I ever do to deserve this?"

Boris, his tail now wrapped neatly around his haunches, dabbed a damp paw behind his ears and declined to answer.

She nodded. "Exactly. *Nothing*. I've done *nothing* to deserve this disrespectful treatment. Maybe I should stop being plain Miss Cadwallader and go back to being a Royal Highness. Maybe then I won't get treated like—a—a *coat-stand*. A rickety one, moreover, that's been shoved in a corner and left for the woodlice!"

Boris stopped washing his face and sat up a little straighter, ears pointing towards the end of Daffydown Lane. A moment later Monk's mud-splashed jalopy chugged into view.

"At last," she said, and marched down the pathway to greet them.

"Sorry, sorry," said Gerald, climbing out from behind the jalopy's wheel. He'd parked right behind Sir Alec, but didn't seem to realize. "It's my fault. I overslept."

"Really?" she said as he ducked around to open the front passenger door for Bibbie. "I find that hard to believe, Professor Dunwoody. In fact, as Reg would say, do pull the other one so I can—"

Bibbie clambered out of the jalopy. For once she didn't look cool and calm and elegant. Well, at least, she did on the surface. But underneath the usual polish—

"Please, Mel, don't go on at Gerald," she said wanly. "It's my fault. I'm the one who overslept. I wasn't feeling well."

Gerald was hovering in a far more obvious fashion than usual. And Bibbie had faint purple shadows beneath her eyes. Her eyes met his once, briefly, then she quickly turned away.

Melissande glared at them, her temper rising anew. "Oh, *wonderful*. Reg could be playing marbles with *both* of my eyes and I'd still be able to read *that* look. Come on. Spill the beans. What's gone wrong now?"

"Wrong?" said Gerald. His voice was very nearly a squeak. "Sorry, Melissande. I don't know what you're talking about."

"Oh, yes you do," she retorted. "You both have *I've got a big fat guilty secret* written all over you—in capital letters!"

"No, we haven't," almost-squeaked Gerald.

Bibbie sighed. "Yes, we have. Come on, Gerald, we knew we'd probably never fool her. Mel—I'm sorry. But it's best if you don't know."

Hurt battled with outrage. *Excuse me? What am I? A bloody big mushroom?* "Really? And why would that be, pray tell?"

"Because *if* we explain then your blood pressure will shoot so high every last one of your arteries will explode."

"For once," Gerald added, terribly apologetic, "she's not exaggerating."

Oh—oh—*buttocks*. "Fine," she snapped. "Don't tell me. See if I care." *I'll just get it out of Monk.* "I don't have time for your silly games, anyway. As it happens we have a *real* crisis on our hands."

"Already?" said Bibbie plaintively. "But it's only twenty minutes past nine!"

"Don't remind me," she said, still snappish. "Or I really will dock your salary this week. Now pay attention, both of you. That wretched Sir Alec's here."

Gerald turned the color of week-old skimmed milk. "What?"

"You heard me. He's here." She pointed. "See? That's his car. And *he's* up in the office right now, drinking tea. Reg is keeping an eye on him."

"But why?" said Bibbie, as unattractively pale as Gerald. Did she realize she was clutching at his wool-coated arm? "Why is he here? Did he say? What does he want?"

"A word with Gerald."

"But—but—" Gerald waved his arms around, heedless of Bibbie's femininely clutching fingers. Which meant that whatever the two of them had done it was *seriously* serious. Something they couldn't afford for Sir Alec to find out about.

Wonderful. At this rate I'll have to move in to Chatterly Crescent, the proprieties go hang, or one of these geniuses is going to do someone else a great big mischief.

"I don't understand," said Gerald, staring over their heads to Witches Incorporated's blind-shrouded front window. "If he needs to talk to me he summons me to Nettleworth. Did he say he'd tried to reach me? My crystal ball's not on the blink. At least I don't think it is. Did he say if—"

"No, Gerald, the subject of your crystal ball did not arise," she snapped. And then, mortifyingly aware of the unfortunate entendre, felt herself blush in blotchy embarrassment. "So I can only assume he avoided regular communications. Which probably means that whatever he's got to say he's not keen for your colleagues at Nettleworth to overhear it."

Bibbie turned to Gerald. "Or else he knows," she whispered. "And he's decided to handle it under the table. I mean, he's not you or Monk but he is a powerful wizard, Gerald. Maybe he—"

"No," said Gerald, shaking his head. "They'd have sent your Uncle Ralph to the house if that were the case."

"You think so? Really?" Bibbie's tired eyes shone with hope. "Because otherwise—" She blinked back tears. And tears most definitely weren't like Bibbie. "Oh, Gerald."

Melissande felt her insides go cold. *Saint Snodgrass preserve me, what did they get up to last night?* "Gerald, are you quite sure you've no idea what he's doing here?"

"None," said Gerald. "He hasn't explained himself at all?"

She looked at him. "Suffering from a mild concussion, are we?"

"Sorry," he said, wincing. "What's his mood like? Could you tell?"

"Well, when I came downstairs *almost half an hour ago* he was perfectly polite," she replied, feeling newly waspish and not inclined to spare their feelings. "But now he's had almost half an hour of Reg making pointed remarks, so—"

"Bloody hell," Gerald groaned. "Did you have to leave him with Reg?"

"I had to leave him with someone, Gerald! I couldn't just abandon him alone in the office, could I?" she retorted, perilously close to unladylike shouting. "Now please go upstairs, find out what he wants and then get rid of him so we can get to work! Arnold Frobisher is due here at ten, if you recall, and it's going to take me nearly every minute I can lay my hands on to calm myself enough to make sure I don't kill *him* in lieu of *you!*"

Gerald took a prudent step back. "Right. Yes. I can do that. And while I'm doing that, ah, why don't you and Bibbie and Boris enjoy the sunshine? I won't take long. Two shakes of a lamb's tail, I promise."

"Are you out of your mind?" she said, glaring. "Whatever he's got to say to you he can say to me and Bibbie at the same time. We are Witches Incorporated and we are a team."

"Oh. Um." Gerald rubbed his nose. "Look. I know you and Bibbie signed various Secret Acts and so forth, Melissande, but given the lengths Sir Alec's gone to for a private conversation I'm pretty sure he won't want an audience for this."

She spread her hands wide. "And behold me, Gerald, once again not caring." She turned on her heel. "Now come on. I want this over with. *Some* of us have *proper* work to do."

"It's all right," said Reg from her ram skull, as they marched into the main office. "All the teaspoons are accounted for. I haven't took my eyes off him once."

"Sir Alec," said Gerald, very cautious, closing the office door. "Good morning."

Sir Alec, neatly seated in the best client chair, nondescript as ever in his ordinary brown suit, slipped the notes he'd been reading back into his shabby leather briefcase.

"Good morning, Mr. Dunwoody. I wasn't aware you kept bankers' hours at Witches Inc."

"No, no, that was me," said Bibbie, her cheeks pinking. "My fault. Don't blame him. Gerald's always on time when I'm not around."

"I see," said Sir Alec. His cool gray eyes lost a little of their chill. "You and your brother. So much alike."

"Thank you," Bibbie said faintly. "I think."

"Ah, Sir Alec, don't take this the wrong way," said Gerald, stiff and formal beside Bibbie's desk, "but what are you doing here?"

"Have a seat, Mr. Dunwoody," Sir Alec replied, as though these were *his* premises and he was in charge. "And I'll explain. You too, Miss Cadwallader, and you, Miss Markham.

Surprised, Melissande looked at him. "You're inviting us to stay?"

"Yes," said Sir Alec, resigned. "Since I'm sure Mr. Dunwoody will only share with you what I tell him the moment I depart."

Reg chattered her beak. "Saint Snodgrass's bunions, you're a sarky bugger, sunshine."

"Really?" said Sir Alec, one pale brown eyebrow

lifting. "Well, far be it from me to contradict such a renowned exponent of the art."

Melissande choked back a laugh at the look on Reg's face.

But Gerald wasn't amused. A deep line was creased between his brows. "Sir Alec—"

"Relax, Mr. Dunwoody," his formidable superior said, sounding bored. "When you cross the line you may believe I'll tell you."

"I'd rather you told us what's going on," said Bibbie, and dropped herself into the chair behind her desk. "This is all terribly mysterious, Sir Alec." Elegant chin propped winsomely on her interlaced fingers, all her earlier distress carefully hidden, she fluttered her outrageously long eyelashes at him. "Have you a very special assignment for the team at Witches Inc.?"

"I'm afraid not," said Sir Alec, spuriously apologetic. "But I do have a task for Mr. Dunwoody."

Gerald was still standing at ramrod attention, more like a lance-corporal than a secret government agent. "A task, sir?"

"What kind of task?" said Melissande, and shifted sideways until she could rest her elbow on the top of the filing cabinet, where Reg brooded on her skull like a shag on a rock. Absolutely she wasn't sitting down, on principle alone. "And how long will it take? Gerald's got jobs booked, I'll have you know. Secret government department front or not, Sir Alec, we do still operate as a legitimate business and I don't take kindly to abruptly disappearing staff."

Sir Alec raised that lethal eyebrow again. "I happen to know, Miss Cadwallader, that Mr. Dunwoody is not currently engaged on any jobs for this agency—but even if he were, my needs take precedence. Also, I feel compelled to note—in the interests of veracity—that since joining your intrepid band of investigators that this is the first time I've approached him on a matter of janitorial business, and so the term 'abruptly disappearing staff' does not in this case apply. At least, not to Mr. Dunwoody. Given the Markham family propensity for unauthorized thaumaturgics, I'm not prepared to speak for Miss Markham."

"Well, that's a relief," said Bibbie, her cheeks becomingly flushed with temper. "Because I'm perfectly capable of speaking for myself!"

"I'm sure you are, Miss Markham, but I'd appreciate it if you'd refrain," said Sir Alec. "Just this once. So we can conclude our meeting in a timely fashion. I'm sure you don't want to keep Mr. Frobisher waiting."

As Reg muttered crossly under her breath, Melissande lifted her chin at Gerald's aggravating superior. "And if someone does call expressly requesting Gerald's services?"

Sir Alec shrugged "Then you'll tell them, with regret, that he is otherwise engaged."

"Doing what?" said Gerald. "Or can't you say in mixed company?"

"I can't say with complete abandon," Sir Alec replied after a moment, "but I can assuage your colleagues' curiosity this much, Mr. Dunwoody: you'll be taking a short trip out of the country. Having a quiet word with someone who knows someone who knows something about something about which *I* would like to know."

Melissande scowled. *Honestly,* all this ridiculous secret agent doublespeak. But Gerald was nodding as though Sir Alec's gobbledegook made perfect sense. And perhaps it did, to him. He was the government agent, after all.

"Right, sir," Gerald said, with a glint in his eye. "And you need me for this task because . . . ?"

Up went Sir Alec's eyebrow again. "I'm sorry. Am I required to justify myself to you, Mr. Dunwoody?"

"Oh, stop being so bloody starchy," said Reg. "It's a fair question and you know it. Want me to answer it? I'll bet you five field mice I can."

"Alas," said Sir Alec, not even pretending to be sorry this time. "I'm bereft of field mice. But let that not stop us, Reg. By all means—answer the question. And if you get it wrong I'll think of another forfeit."

"Don't, Reg," said Bibbie, still rankled. "You don't know what he's got up his unfashionable sleeve."

"Actually, I do," said Reg. "A stringy white arm with not enough bicep on it."

Sir Alec smiled, but his eyes didn't lose any of their gray chill. "Stalling for time, Dulcetta?"

Reg stretched one wing above her head and yawned. "You're sending Gerald because when he plays his cards right he's no more of a head-turner than a genuine Ottish street sweeper and you don't want him and your chatty friend getting themselves noticed while they're chatting."

"Exactly," said Sir Alec, with a small nod, one fencer to another acknowledging a hit. "Even in our small world Mr. Dunwoody remains an unknown quantity. He's the perfect candidate to slip in and out unobserved."

Melissande drummed her short, blunt finger-nails on the side of the filing cabinet. "In and out of where?"

"None of your business, Miss Cadwallader," said Sir Alec.

Bloody secret government departments. With an effort she unclenched her jaw. "Fine. But I do need to know how long he'll be gone. So that when prospective customers call wanting his help I can tell them how long they'll have to wait for it."

"I'm afraid I have no idea."

"And how are we supposed to run a business when—"

Sir Alec stood, economically athletic. "That's not my concern, Miss Cadwallader. My concern is with the security of this country. Our arrangement guarantees that Witches Inc. will remain solvent. I advise you to take comfort from that, and adjust your business ambitions accordingly."

"Ha!" said Reg. "I'll adjust your bloody ambitions, sunshine. In case you haven't noticed I've got a long beak and I'm not afraid to use it!"

Gerald lifted his hand. "*Reg.*"

"What?" Reg complained, her feathers ruffled. "He marches in here and starts bossing us around, says he's dragging you off by the scruff of your neck without so much as a d'you mind, thanks ever so, and here's us being left behind and—"With a timely gasp for air, she fixed Sir Alec with a gimlet gaze. "Mind you—"

"*No*, Reg," said Sir Alec. "Under *no* circumstances are you accompanying Mr. Dunwoody. And make no mistake—if you try I will have you restrained."

"Fine," Reg muttered sulkily. "Have it your way. But if anything happens to him because I wasn't there . . ."

Gerald spared her an affectionate glance, then focused his attention on Sir Alec. Melissande, watching him, saw the chilling, subtle shift from sweet, thoughtful, slightly harassed Gerald to the terrifyingly powerful wizard who'd created two dragons and defeated mad, misguided Lional.

She felt her heart thud harder. In their daily Ottish life—at Chatterly Crescent, here at the agency, and on those days when they took a little time to have some fun—it was possible to forget that this darker Gerald even existed. She knew Gerald worked very hard to forget him. Though they'd never talked about it, she knew he'd still not come to grips with the man he was now. Just as she was sure he'd still not found his wizarding limit. And that frightened him. It frightened Monk, too. He'd never said it aloud, but she'd caught him looking at his best friend once or twice . . . and in his guarded eyes there'd been a deep unease.

But it's the hidden, dangerous part of him that Sir Alec wants. He needs it. And he has no compunction about using it, either. Not when lives and secrets are at stake.

More than anything, she wished she could dislike the man for that. But she couldn't. Because once upon a time she'd had a brother called Lional.

Cool and remote, almost a stranger, Gerald nodded at his boss. "You want me to come now?"

"There's no time like the present."

"Do I need to go home and pack?"

Sir Alec shook his head. "There's a bag in the car for you."

"Large or small?"

"Sufficient," said Sir Alec, a sardonically appreciative glint in his eyes. "I'll give you a moment to make your farewells. But only a moment. Time is a factor."

"Thank you," said Gerald. "I'll see you downstairs."

Sir Alec picked up his briefcase and offered the smallest of bows. "Ladies. Always a pleasure."

"Ha," said Reg, staring down her beak at him. "Speak for yourself, sunshine."

At the door, Sir Alec hesitated and turned back. Looked at Bibbie, no warmth at all in his eyes. "Miss Markham, a word to the wise which you might like to pass along to your brother."

Bibbie's bright smile was the equivalent of a cocked pistol. "Which one?"

Sir Alec's answering smile was razor-thin. "Guess. Then tell him this: bravado is an admirable trait on the sporting field. Elsewhere, however, it more often than not backfires. Tell him he might like to practice discretion for a change. Doubtless it will have all the charm of novelty."

"You know, Gerald," said Bibbie thoughtfully, as the door closed behind him, "I could probably dislike your boss without much effort at all."

"Don't be silly, Bibs," Gerald said, surprisingly sharp. "He's the best friend we've got."

Bibbie lowered her gaze, looking hurt.

"Reg," said Gerald, and crossed to the filing cabinet. "Stay out of trouble, will you? At least till I get back?"

"*Me*?" said Reg, with a valiant attempt at outrage. "That's rich, that is, coming from you."

Reaching up, he dropped a brief kiss on the top of her head. "I'll be fine. Home by tomorrow night, I'll bet you five field mice."

She sniffed. "You know perfectly well I hate field mice, Gerald. They taste like cow poop. I was just twisting his tail."

"And a champion tail-twister you are, ducky," he said. "Melissande—"

She wasn't going to cry. She *wasn't*. Gerald Dunwoody was a trained secret agent with more wizarding power in his crooked little finger than any other First Grader in the world. There was *nothing* to worry about. He was going to be *fine*.

"Good luck with Mr. Frobisher," he said, and brushed his fingers down her arm. "Don't take any nonsense from the silly old fart, even if he is an old family friend of Sir Alec's."

She tilted her chin at him. "As if I would. After a lifetime of Lord Billingsley? Arnold Frobisher doesn't scare me."

He kissed her cheek. "I'll see you soon."

"Good luck, Gerald," said Bibbie, admirably composed. "Bring us back a souvenir."

Gerald's smile wasn't quite steady. "I'll do my best, Bibbie. Tell Monk to keep his nose clean or I'll kick his ass when I get back."

The door closed behind him and immediately the sunlit, crowded office felt cold and empty.

Bibbie fished a hanky out of her pretty new reticule and savagely blew her nose. "I have an influenza," she said, stabbing Reg with a baleful glare.

"Did I say you didn't?" Reg protested. "Blimey. Don't take my head off, ducky, it's not *my* fault he's gone."

Melissande finished blinking back her own tears and pushed away from the filing cabinet. "It's not anyone's fault," she said, going to her desk. "He works for Sir Alec. He only pretends to work here. And since that was never a secret we can't moan about it now."

Reg heaved a sigh. "His first assignment without us. You realize he's going to go ass right over elbows."

"He'll do no such thing, you revolting old hag!" Bibbie snapped. "He's Gerald Dunwoody."

"Yes, ducky, I know," said Reg, giving her a look. "Which means on the way home one of us better light a candle to Saint Snodgrass."

"*Anyway*," said Melissande, before the feathers started flying. "We've got horrible Arnold Frobisher arriving any tick of the clock. And then what do we do with ourselves for the rest of the day?"

"Mount a prayer vigil at the church," said Reg. "That boy's going to need all the help he can get."

"*Once*, Mel," said Bibbie, her perfect teeth bared in a snarl. "Let me hit her just *once*. She'll only be unconscious for a minute. I promise."

"No!" she said, and banged her fist on the desk. "The only person doing any hitting around here will be *me*, and that's only if Arnold Frobisher pinches my behind again."

"Now, now," said Reg, scolding. "Hitting's hardly royal behavior."

Melissande rolled her eyes. "Don't tell me, let me guess. You want to poke him in the unmentionables. And I suppose poking men in the unmentionables is royal, is it?"

"Ha," said Reg, her dark eyes wickedly gleaming. "Royal? Bugger that. It's the most fun you can have with your clothes on, ducky!"

Sir Alec handled his government-issue car with a quiet efficiency that wasn't the least bit surprising. The shock would have been if he'd driven any other way.

"So, Mr. Dunwoody," he said, as they reached the lightly populated outskirts of Central Ott and turned onto Greater Flushcombe Road. "Any questions?"

Gerald looked out of the window at the passing semi-rural countryside. Wherever they were headed, he'd not been there before. In fact, this was his first trip out of the city in months.

"No, Sir Alec. I think I'm clear. Once I reach my destination I'm to take a room in the Grande Splotze Inn, using the name Barlowe. As soon as the dining room opens I'm to take the small table under the stuffed moose head with the chipped left antler, making sure to wear the yellow cravat that's been provided for me, and wait until my contact stops to tell me I should really try the elk stew. Overcome by his kindness I'm to invite him to join me for supper, over which he will—if we're very lucky—tell me some interesting things about a certain black market wizard we're anxious to meet."

Sir Alec nodded. "Exactly." Then, glancing sideways, he added, "And if you're going to snigger I suggest you do it now. Sniggering in Grande Splotze might easily get you killed."

Damn. "I'm sorry, sir. But honestly—it is rather like something out of a bad cloak-and-dagger novel."

"I don't read bad cloak-and-dagger novels, Mr. Dunwoody," Sir Alec said coolly, "so I'll have to take your word on that. As for your arrangements, they were made by the man you'll be meeting over the elk stew. Given the risks he's taking I'm not inclined to criticize. Are you?"

"No, sir," he muttered, and hunched a little in the uncomfortable passenger seat. Nobody could make him feel small the way Sir Alec could. "Sir—"

"When you come back," said Sir Alec, slowing the car to take a sharp left-hand turn onto a road that looked to be taking them into deep rural territory, "and you've been fully debriefed, I suggest you take a day for yourself and catch a train to the seaside. Alone. It's my experience that fresh salt air and solitude do wonders for one's perspective."

This was about Monk again. He knew it. "Sir—"

"I'm doing my best, Mr. Dunwoody," said Sir Alec. "And so is Sir Ralph. But unless your clever young friend starts helping himself not even his uncle and I will be able to save him."

Stupid bloody politics. Stupid old men. "Sir—Monk's a genius."

"I know, Mr. Dunwoody. That would be the problem."

They drove some twenty-five more miles in

silence. Around them the countryside grew markedly more full of sheep. At last Sir Alec slowed almost to stopping, then guided the car down a long narrow private road. It took them all the way around to the back of a seemingly deserted farmhouse, where a straggle of outbuildings sagged under the sunny sky. The surrounding silence was profound.

"Right," said Sir Alec, and stopped the car. "Here we are."

And *here* was in the middle of nowhere. Clambering out of the car, overnight bag clutched in one hand, Gerald looked around, perplexed. "Ah—Sir Alec? What—"

"With me," said Sir Alec, infuriatingly calm, and led the way into the nearest slatternly barn.

Instead of cows, or even sheep, the barn contained a portal.

"It's unregistered," said Sir Alec, answering his unspoken question. "One of a handful we use for little jobs like this. Perfectly safe, of course. Just—off the national grid. All right, in you hop."

Secret portals? The Department operated *secret portals*? What else didn't he know? Feeling stupid, Gerald stared at his superior. "You're a licensed portal operator?"

For once, Sir Alec's brief smile was almost warm. "Mr. Dunwoody, over time you'll find I'm licensed for a great many things." He reached into his pocket, pulled out a small copper disc and tossed it. "Use that for your return journey. It'll shoot you through to a different unregistered portal. We don't like to use the same one twice in any mission. There'll be a phone so you can call the Department for a lift back to Nettleworth. And don't worry. The travel token has a falsified destination signature. The Grande Splotze portal operator will be none the wiser. Now—have a safe trip and I'll see you again soon."

Gerald slipped the return travel token into his pocket. "Yes, sir."

And with nothing else to say, he stepped into the portal and vanished.

"Y'know," said Reg, "I wouldn't do that if I were you, sunshine."

Holding a finger steady on a precariously balanced thaumic constrictor, Monk blew his hair out of his eyes. "Well, you're not me, are you, Reg?"

Reg cackled. "And if you think I don't give daily thanks for that, Mr. Markham, you've got cockroaches in your undershorts."

He looked at Melissande. "Have I told you today how grateful I am that you took her with you so she's not living with me?"

"I wouldn't live with you if you paid me in rubies," said Reg, offended. "Cheeky bugger."

They were up in the attic, fiddling with experimental thaumaturgics. Well. Drinking brandy and fiddling. And more the former than the latter. Sort of. What he *really* wanted to do was have at his multi-dimensional etheretic wavelength expander, except . . . well, it was still pretty unstable and Gerald wasn't here. So instead, he and Bibbie were working on her ridiculous ethergenics project with Melissande taking copious notes and Reg making a nuisance of herself on one of the stationary push-bikes. It was all terribly *domestic*.

"I *think*," said Bibbie slowly, emerging from one of her trances, "that what we need to do next is cross-wire the thaumic constrictor with the etheretic enhancer, and feed the feedback pulse back through a compromising subharmonic Bodley prism."

"Say that again, ducky," said Reg. "Backwards. I dare you."

Bibbie flapped a hand at her. "Shut up, you silly woman. Monk, what do you think?"

I think Melissande looks adorable with ink smudges on her nose. "Um—really? A Bodley prism? You don't want to use a Crumpshott?"

"No," said Bibbie, decisively. "Any fool can split the harmonics with a Crumpshott."

"And by any fool," said Reg, amused, "she means Demelza Sopwith."

"Hey!" said Bibbie. "I thought we agreed that name was never to be spoken."

Reg rattled her tail feathers. "Sorry. Perhaps if I had some brandy I could remember things like that."

"*Forget it!*" Melissande and Bibbie shouted together.

"Remember what happened the last time you got your beak into brandy?" Melissande added. "I refuse to go through that again."

Reg subsided, sulky. "Well, at least I didn't climb into a fountain and crush innocent goldfish to death down my décolletage."

"You don't have a décolletage, Reg," said Melissande, teeth gritted. "Not any more. But I do. So shut up or I'll pretend *you're* a goldfish."

"I need more brandy," Monk announced, and scrambled to his feet. "Lots of it." The girls ignored him, they were too busy squabbling. Leaving them to it, he took the stairs two at a time down to the parlor where the drinks trolley lived. Suitably fortified he headed back upstairs, only to be halted midway by a banging on the front door.

"What the hell?"

It was late. They weren't expecting anyone. And if it was Gerald returned from his mission he'd let himself in. Bugger. He didn't want visitors. Mildly grumpy, he turned around, thudded back down the stairs and padded along the hallway to the hexed front door. Tucked the bottle of Broadbent under his arm, canceled the hex and swung the door wide.

"Yes? What is it? What do you—"

The man on the doorstep wore the same face he looked at in the mirror every morning.

"Markham!" the man gasped. "Monk Markham! Let me in, for God's sake! We have to talk!"

Monk banged the door shut in the man's face—his face—reset the hex and climbed back up to the attic.

"Um—girls?" he said, halting in the doorway, and was amazed he sounded so unperturbed. "If I could just have your attention?"

They looked at him inquiringly: Melissande, Bibbie and Reg.

"Um—girls—am I drunk?"

"Well, drunk's a relative term when it comes to

you," said Bibbie, considering him. "But on balance no. I wouldn't say so. Why?"

He cleared his throat. "Because I just answered the front door and I'm standing on the doorstep. I don't suppose you'd like to come downstairs and see?"

CHAPTER TWELVE

"Bloody hell," said Reg, peering down from Melissande's shoulder at the figure collapsed on their doorstep. "I thought you were joking."

Monk spared her a look. "About something like *this*?"

"Oh, for the love of Saint Snodgrass, don't you two start," said Bibbie, and shoved everyone aside. "Whoever he is, however he got here, he's in trouble, can't you see? Help me get him inside. Monk— *Monk*—don't just *stand* there, you idiot. *Help*."

"The parlor's probably the best place for now," said Melissande. She sounded terribly self-contained, and looking at her face he couldn't tell what she was thinking or feeling. "I'll jolly up the fire."

"Good idea," he said. "Ah—Melissande—"

She waved aside his concern. "I'm fine. Bibbie's right. We should get him inside before somebody sees him."

As she and Reg retreated, he helped his sister haul—haul—

*Me? Can I say me? Or is it not-me? I must be drunk.
Or dreaming. Is this real? It can't be real. Can it?*

—*him* over the threshold and into the house. The
man was a dead weight, stuporous and groaning. No
luggage. No handy name tag. No anything to suggest
who he was, where he'd come from or what the devil
he was doing here in Ott. In Chatterly Crescent.

On my doorstep.

"Get the door," Bibbie grunted, the man half-
draped over her shoulder. "And double-hex it. No,
better make that a triple. The last thing we need tonight is any more visitors."

Blimey, had his little sister always been this
bossy? Or were Reg and Melissande starting to rub
off on her?

*Great. That's all I need . . . another bossy female in
my life.*

"Yes, Your Majesty," he muttered, and took care
of the front door. Then he helped Bibbie get—get—
not-me—all the way down the hall and into the parlor, where Melissande had indeed jollied up the fire
and even managed to shove the arm chairs out of the
way and heave the old sofa in front of the warmly
dancing flames.

Reg was perched suggestively on the edge of
the drinks trolley. "Really, now, under the circumstances, don't you think I *deserve* a brandy?"

"I'll bloody flambé you in the stuff if you don't
give over, Reg," Bibbie said, close to snarling.
"Come on, Melissande. Don't just stand there, grab
his ankles. We need to get him lying flat."

With much huffing and puffing and muttered

cursing they got—got—not-him—laid out on the sofa like a not-quite-dead corpse.

Reg flapped over from the drinks trolley to land on the sofa's back. "Hmm," she said, head tilted, considering their unexpected guest. "Hope you've got some shovels somewhere, Mr. Markham. Because from where I'm sitting it looks like curtains for you."

Strategically retreating, Monk shoved his hands in his pockets. "That's *not me*, Reg," he snapped, feeling a violent shiver run through him. "Don't call him *me*."

She sniggered. "Well, if that's not you, sunshine, he's doing a bloody good imitation."

"Where did you put that bottle of brandy, Monk?" Bibbie demanded, looking around. "He could probably do with a nip."

"Oh, fine, yes," said Reg, all her feathers fluffing. "Waste perfectly good brandy on a man with both feet in the grave all the way up to his armpits, why don't you, but deny *me* the solace! After a shock like this, and me with all those years in my dish! Blimey! There's no justice in the world."

"Well, Reg, you're right about that much," Bibbie retorted. "Because if there was any justice in the world you'd have talked yourself into asphyxiation a few centuries back! *Monk*. Where's that *brandy*?"

Bugger the brandy. He couldn't tear his gaze away from the shoes on not-him's feet. Shoes were good. Shoes were safe. Except—except—

I bought those shoes last year. From Mr. Chokati's Famous Shoe Emporium. In the big sale. I know for a fact they're upstairs in my closet. So what are they doing on this impostor's feet?

"Never mind, Bibbie," said Melissande, so quietly he could hardly hear her. "I'll fetch the brandy."

The brandy. Yes. He'd put the bottle down somewhere, hadn't he? Mel would find it. She was good at things like that. Being organized. Being tidy. Efficient. He had to stay here and not think about shoes.

The man on the sofa, who wore dark trousers and a pale shirt and a slightly tired three-quarter length blue coat that looked horribly familiar—*but I am not not not going to think about that*—stirred and started muttering. Nothing intelligible, just nonsense words laced with pain. Monk felt another violent shiver run through him. That was *his* voice. That was the way he sounded when *he* was in pain. He kept staring at the shoes. It seemed safer that way.

Bibbie was crouched beside their completely unnecessary visitor, holding his hand in a firm but gentle grasp. "Hush," she said softly. "It's all right, Monk. You're safe."

Monk? Monk? Bibbie, what are you doing? You can't call him that! He's not Monk, I am.

As though she could hear his thoughts, his little sister turned and skewered him with a glare. "I don't begin to know how this is possible but this man is you, Monk. He is. *Look* at him. Look at his face and tell me he's not you."

Oh, Saint Snodgrass and her forty-seven descendants. Feeling sick, feeling dizzy, he dragged his gaze away from the shoes he'd bought seven months ago and looked at the face of the man on the sofa.

Made himself take a few steps towards him and look again.

Bloody hell. That's me.

Although . . . now that he came to actually pay attention . . . it wasn't *exactly* him. Not the him living this life, at any rate. The face of the man on the sofa was thinner. Oddly older. And it had lines in it . . . deep lines . . . that only suffering could carve. The Gerald they'd found in the cave, his face had been lined the same way after that mad bastard Lional had spent days playing with him—but eventually those lines had smoothed and then, praise Saint Snodgrass, they'd disappeared, leaving only occasional blank looks and patches of silence in their wake.

Whoever had been playing with *this* man—this not-him—they were still playing. But where? And how?

Melissande returned with the brandy and an empty glass. Bibbie poured a little into it, slipped an arm around the man's—the other Monk's—shoulders and helped him sit up a bit.

"Here," she said, with a small, encouraging smile. "It's all right. It's just brandy."

He heard a rattle of tail feathers and looked at Reg, still perched on the back of the sofa. The wretched bird was giving him a meaningful look. Then she looked at Melissande, head tipped to one side again. His heart banged like a drum.

Oh, lord. Mel.

She was so pale all her freckles stood out like fallen leaves on a snowfield. Even without a magnifying glass he thought he could count every last one of them. Not even in the middle of the Lional-crisis or the Wycliffe-kerfuffle had he seen her looking so shaken and unsure.

Gingerly he joined her and wrapped his fingers around hers. Her skin was icy. "Hey. You know that's not me, right? *This* is me. I'm holding your hand."

"I know," she said, and slipped free of him. "But if he's *not* you, Monk . . ."

Exactly. Then who is he?

Beside them, Reg snorted. "Well, if I didn't know better, sunshine, I'd say he was your evil twin. But since I *do* know better I'm going to say you're his."

He didn't even bother to glance at her. "Thank you, Reg. That's terribly helpful."

"I don't know," Reg added, huffy. "That poker-assed Sir Alec picked a fine time to whisk Gerald off in a cloud of secrecy, I must say. We could do with his nattering around about now."

The man on the sofa flinched and jerked his head away. Brandy spilled down his chin and the front of his coat.

The coat Bibbie gave me three Solstices ago.

Saint Snodgrass's bunions, this really was insane.

Bibbie held out an impatient hand, fingers snapping. Straight away Melissande took a plain, unfrilly hanky from her tweed trousers' pocket and passed it over.

"There you are," said Bibbie, dabbing the man dry. "All better. Can you talk sensibly now?"

"Not if he's anything like our Monk Markham, he can't," said Reg. "Honestly, ducky. Do remember who you're dealing with."

"*Melissande . . .*"

"Please, Reg," Mel said, her voice low and not quite steady. "You really aren't helping."

Reg chattered her beak. "Don't be ridiculous. Of course I'm helping. If you're flapping at me you're not going into hysterics, are you? That's called keeping up morale, that is."

Mel turned to him. "Monk, he didn't like it when Reg mentioned Gerald. How can he know Gerald? And why would mentioning his name upset him?"

"*Why*?" said the man on the sofa, his eyes dragging open. "How can you even *ask* me that, Melissande? How can you—" He pressed trembling fingers to his chapped lips. "Oh. Sorry. I keep forgetting. I'm all over the place from the transition. And—and—" A terrible shudder racked him head to toe. "And then there's the shadbolt."

"*Shadbolt?*" said Bibbie, and leapt to her feet. "What shadbolt?" Closing her eyes she reached out with her *potentia*, then after a moment pulled back again. Her eyes were wide and brimful of shock. "I don't understand. How can that even be poss—"

Alarmed, Monk abandoned Melissande and went to his little sister. "Bibbie, what is it? What did you feel?"

"I don't know," she whispered, wrapping her arms around her ribs. "I'm not sure."

"Well, is he shadbolted or isn't he?"

"I just said I don't *know*," she snapped. "Why don't you look, Monk, instead of asking stupid questions. Have a poke around in his aura and—and tell me what you feel."

What? Poke around in the etheretic wrapping of a man wearing his face? And his shoes? Not to mention his coat. But that was the *last* thing he wanted to do.

"Well?" said Bibbie. "What are you waiting for?"

"It's all right, Bibs-and-bobs," the man on the sofa whispered. "I knew this was going to be difficult. He just needs some time. You all do."

Bibbie dropped the hanky. "Bibs-and-bobs? Only Monk calls me that. And he hasn't called me that in *years*. How could you *possibly*—"

"Because I know you," said the man on the sofa. "I know all of you. Sort of."

"Bibbie," said Monk, jerking his head. "A word? You too, Mel. And you, Reg."

"But Monk—"

"He's not going anywhere, Bibbie," he said sharply. "Please?"

Reg hopped onto Melissande's shoulder, Bibbie reluctantly retreated from the sofa, and the four of them huddled like conspirators on the other side of the room. Their unexpected and mysterious guest closed his eyes, his right hand folded protectively over his coat pocket.

"Mel?" Monk said, keeping his voice down. "Are you sure you're all right?"

She'd regained a little of her color, but still she was disturbingly unbossy. She nodded. "I'm fine. It's just like—he—said . . . this is a shock."

"I suppose we really are awake," said Bibbie. Whatever she'd sensed, looking for the shadbolt, she had herself in hand again. "I mean, there's no chance this is one of your stupid practical jokes, Monk? A dream-hex gone bonkers?"

"Cross my heart," he said fervently, and swiped a finger twice across his chest. "No chance at all."

"Fair enough," said Bibbie, frowning. "But it could still be a hex, couldn't it? Some kind of disguise incant, to make one person look like another? An alive person, I mean. Dead is easy."

Monk chewed at his lip. "I doubt it. We've been trying to come up with one for over a year now and—what?" he said, when all three girls stared at him. "What?"

Bibbie was giving him her best gimlet glare. "You never said anything about working on *that* kind of project, Monk Markham. That kind of project's a bit risky, isn't it? Not to mention illegal."

"Of course it's risky," he said, impatient. "But you can bet every government in the world has got someone like me working on it. And technically it's not illegal if the government's doing it. You know, as an anti-criminal preventive measure. Or something."

Reg snorted. "Political hypocrisy. Got a lovely smell, hasn't it?"

"Look, forget about this being any kind of doppler hex," he said. "*And* forget I mentioned I was working on one, would you? I've been sworn upside down and inside out to secrecy."

Rolling her eyes, Bibbie sighed. "So in other words whoever this man is it's unlikely he's someone hexed to look like you."

"Exactly. And anyway, a hex wouldn't explain how he knows us," said Melissande. "Or our nursery nicknames."

He nodded. "Or how he's wearing my coat and my shoes."

"So him practically having a heart attack when I mentioned Gerald," said Reg. "What do we think that was about?"

"You mentioned Sir Alec, too," said Bibbie. "Maybe that's what upset him. I mean, Reg, you practically have a brainstorm every time his name's mentioned." She snuck a quick look over her shoulder. "What if this is some dastardly plot against Monk, and Sir Alec's a part of it?"

He blinked at her. "Dastardly plot? Bibbie, have you been reading Gerald's awful cloak-and-dagger novels again?"

"It's no secret you've got enemies," she retorted. "So he could be one of them. Or—or—he could be some dreadful thaumaturgical experiment gone wrong! What if he's been a prisoner somewhere in the Department of Thaumaturgy building—or maybe out at Nettleworth—and he's escaped and come to us for help?"

Reg looked down her beak at her. "Forget the sensational novels, ducky. How much brandy have *you* had this evening?"

"Fine," said Bibbie. "Then you explain him, Queen Smarty-pants."

"Obviously none of us can explain him," said Melissande. "The only person who can explain him is *him*. But first—" She folded her arms. "About this shadbolt he claims to have. Would someone care to explain what that is? Nothing so simple as an embarrassing skin condition, I suppose?"

"Sadly, no," he said, and fought the urge to look at Bibbie. "It's like a pair of thaumaturgical handcuffs, only it fits around your head. There are lots of different kinds, some more severe than others."

"They bind a witch or wizard's etheretic aura," Bibbie added. "Shackle their *potentia*. Criminals often use them to stop themselves—or others—from talking if they get arrested and questioned."

Melissande grimaced. "Sounds positively barbaric."

"Um," said Bibbie, staring at the carpet. "Yes. You could say that."

"But useful," added Reg. "And not just to the crims. With a little bit of tweaking you'd be surprised what information a shadbolt'll get you out of the nasty little spy who's been impersonating a diplomat."

They stared at her.

"Oh, please," she said. "You think being a queen in the olden days was easy? Try it sometime. You'll be ordering shadbolts by the gross."

"So, these shadbolts," said Melissande, heroically ignoring her. "Why is it I've not heard of them?"

Monk shrugged. "They're not common knowledge. Not beyond official circles—and the criminal classes, of course."

"Really?" said Melissande, eyes narrowed with suspicion. "Bibbie seems pretty well-informed."

"One of the drawbacks of being a Markham," Bibbie told her. "I grew up hearing things I wasn't meant to know."

He managed a smile for her. "Only because you used to listen at keyholes."

"And only *then* when your eavesdropper hex stopped working."

"Blimey," said Reg. "Talk about the criminal classes."

Bibbie poked her tongue out. "And you of course would be speaking from personal experience."

"So these shadbolts," Melissande murmured, frowning, one finger pointedly raised to keep Reg quiet. Amazingly, it worked. "You can feel them?"

"Yes," said Bibbie, nodding. "They leave a distinct imprint in the etheretic aura of whoever's wearing one."

"But you couldn't sense one shackling him?"

"No," said Bibbie, after the briefest pause.

Monk looked at her closely. *All right, Bibs, my girl. What is it you're not telling us?* But before he could ask, Melissande said, "Are you saying he's lying?"

"About wearing a shadbolt? I don't see why he would."

"No, no, why would he lie?" said Reg, and chattered her beak. "Because there's nothing the least bit hinky about any of this at all."

"She's got a point," Monk said. "Much as I hate to admit it. Bibbie—"

"No, Monk, I wasn't mistaken," his sister snapped. "I should think if anyone knows what a shadbolt feels like, it's me."

Behind her perfectly polished spectacles, Melissande's green eyes were narrowed again in a look that boded no good. "And if that wasn't a loaded comment then I'm a giraffe. *Shut up*, Reg. Bibbie—"

Bibbie touched Melissande's arm lightly. "Not now, Mel. This isn't the time. We've got far more important things to worry about."

"Don't call me Mel."

Bugger. She really was cross. "Bibbie's right, Melissande," he said, strategically apologetic. "It's a conversation for another time, when there's only one of me in the room."

"Fine," said Melissande, and belligerently folded her arms. "But don't imagine that conversation won't be taking place."

Gosh. To think he'd thought his heart couldn't sink any lower. *Melissande on the warpath. Just what we need.* "Bibbie, when you looked for the shadbolt, what did you feel?"

To his dismay, Bibbie's blue eyes flooded with tears. "I told you, I don't *know*," she said, her voice a broken little whisper. "I was imagining things. I had to be. It was a trick. He's hexed. He must be. This *can't* be real."

"Hey, hey," he said, sliding his arm around her shoulders. She was trembling. *Bibbie.* Shocked, he pulled her close. "It's all right, Bibs. Come on, now. It's all right."

"No, it's *not* all right, Monk," she said, and wrenched herself out of his hold. "And do you know why? Because I felt *you*. I felt your *potentia*. And since that can't be possible, I must be going mad!"

"No, you're not, Bibbie," said the man on the sofa. "You're perfectly sane. You *did* feel his *potentia*. Because he's me . . . and I'm him."

"Don't be ridiculous," said Bibbie, glaring. "There's only one Monk Markham and I'm standing beside him."

The man on the sofa nodded painfully. "You're almost right. There's only one Monk Markham in every world. But you see . . . this isn't my world, Bibbie. My world's next door."

"Next door?" said Melissande, breaking the heavy silence.

"In a manner of speaking," said the man on the sofa. "At least, that's the easiest way to explain it."

Bibbie took a hesitant step towards him. "You're not making this up?"

"Bibbie . . ." The man managed a smile. "When it comes to metaphysics when did I ever make things up?" His voice cracked on the last word, and his haunted, horribly familiar eyes filled with tears. "Oh, Bibs. It's really you. I'd forgotten how you used to be. It's been so long and—oh—damn—*damn*—"

"Monk? Monk, what's the matter?" cried Bibbie, and dashed to the sofa.

Dazed, Monk watched his sister hold the man—another Monk—against the shudders of pain running through him without relief. They seemed to go on and on forever. But at last, just when he thought he couldn't stand it any more, the man on the sofa let out a sobbing sigh and relaxed.

"What was that?" Bibbie demanded, easing back to a crouch. "Monk, what's been done to you?"

The Monk from next door wiped a shaking hand across his face. "It's the shadbolt," he muttered. "He doesn't like it when I talk out of turn."

"Who?" said Bibbie fiercely. "Who put the shadbolt on you, Monk? And what kind of shadbolt is it that can stay hidden like that?"

"A special one," said the Monk from next door, then winced and gasped. "Please—don't ask me to explain—it hurts too much—it hurts—"

"Sorry, sorry," Bibbie whispered. "Look, obviously you need help. Tell us how we can help you."

"You can get it off me," said the Monk from next door. "*Please*. Monk?"

"What? No," said Monk, feeling sick. Feeling his other self's desperate stare punch him in the gut. "I can't. Are you bonkers, mate? *No*."

The Monk from next door's face had drained to a sickly, sweaty gray. It was scarred, too. He'd not noticed that before. A cut along the left cheekbone, the kind of mark left behind by a blow from a fist made of fingers heavy with rings. Seeing that scar, knowing that if he looked in a mirror he wouldn't see it reflected back at him, he felt a dreadful premonition whip through his blood like roaring flames of ice.

He's a me from somewhere else not far enough away— and wherever that is, it's got big problems. And now he's brought those problems with him. Here. To me.

Oh, bloody hell.

"Look," he said tightly. "Mate. I'm sorry, but you've made a mistake. Go home. We can't help you."

Shocked, Bibbie turned to him. "*What?* No— Monk—listen, we can't just—"

"No, Bibbie, *you* listen!" he retorted. "Don't you see this is wrong? He's not meant to be here. Saint Snodgrass alone knows what damage he's doing to our etheretic integrity. He could be putting our whole world at risk."

"You don't know that!" said Bibbie hotly "You could be wrong!"

"And what if I'm right?" he said. "Are you willing to take that risk? Bibbie, we don't even know how he *got* here!"

The Monk from next door laughed, a rusty, unused sound. "Yes, you do, Monk. You bloody well do. You stare at the ceiling at night when you're meant to be asleep, wondering. Thinking, *Is it even possible? I bet it is. I bet I could . . .* We both know you do, *mate.* You can't lie to me."

He nearly jumped out of his socks when Melissande took hold of his arm. "Monk, what is he talking about?"

"Mel . . ." It was hard, it was so hard, but he made himself look at her. Princess Melissande of New Ottosland, short and stocky and bossy and brave. Ethics like armor. A sense of justice like a sword. The woman he loved, but wasn't sure he could marry.

Me and Gerald, eh? What a bloody pair.

"Monk," said Melissande, insistent, and tightened her grasp. "Do you know how he got here or don't you?"

He looked across at the man on the couch. *Of course I know. Because he's me, and I'm him, and there's precious bloody little we won't try once.* Their eyes met, and he felt the most peculiar jolt: recognition and fear and a terrible sorrow.

He sighed. "You brought it with you?"

"I had to," said the other Monk. "I have to go back."

"Then show them," he said, and sighed again, because it was too late for all of them now.

The Monk from next door reached into his pocket and took out a small, rough, insignificant-looking stone.

"Hey!" said Bibbie. "That's your portable portal.

The—the Mark B prototype. The one you acciden-tally turned into an interdimensional—*oh*."

"Blimey bloody Charlie," said Reg, disgusted, breaking the stunned silence. "Oy. Mr. Twin. Did you jigger that thing to do what I think it's done? And if you did, sunshine, then how many *more* of you idiots are running loose, d'you think?"

Reprehensibly, unforgivably, Monk felt a pang of pure jealousy shoot through him.

Bugger. He really did it. Does that mean I could do it too?

And then he yelled in pain as Reg leaned side-ways on Melissande's shoulder and yanked hard on a beakful of his hair. "Forget it, you raving lunatic!" she shrieked, slightly muffled. "Are you out of your brandy-pickled *mind*?"

"I'm sorry," said Melissande, icy as winter, let-ting go of his hand completely and stepping aside. Reg squawked a protest as she was nearly pulled off her shoulder-perch. "Just let me see if I've under-stood this correctly. This *other* Monk Markham—to all intents and purposes *you,* Monk—took what he—*you*—freely admitted was a dangerously un-predictable accidental invention, namely the inter-dimensional portal opener—and—and *twiddled* it until he—*you*—could get it to open a portal into—into—*what*, exactly?"

"A parallel world," said Monk, in perfect unison with himself from next door.

The look in Melissande's eyes was lethal. "I see. Well, now. Ah—Reg?"

"Yes, ducky?"

"Do you know what I think?"

Reg's eyes were gleaming too. "I think I can hazard a guess."

"I think that if ever there was a time a man deserved a good poking in his unmentionables then—"

"Hey!" he said, backing up. "Don't look at *me*, Melissande. *I* didn't do it. *He* did. Poke *him*."

Melissande wasn't beautiful when she was angry. She was *angry* when she was angry. Practically breathing fire. "You heard what he said, Monk! You've been bloody thinking it! It was only ever a matter of time!"

The man on the sofa—Monk from next door—gasped a little, then started laughing. "Oh, Saint Snodgrass," he wheezed. "I have missed this so much." And then, quite dreadfully, he started weeping.

"Stop it," said Bibbie, close to tears again herself. "All of you, just stop it. We're in real trouble here and all you can do is *squabble*. Shame on you. We're going to help him and that's all there is to it."

"But Bibbie—"

"*Fine*," she shouted. "Then *I* will. Don't you see, Monk? I have to. This man is my *brother!*"

Silenced, he stared at her. "No, he's not," he said at last. "I am."

"You *both* are, you blithering idiot. And I can no more turn *him* away than I could abandon *you*."

"Bibbie's right," said Melissande, temper under control now, brisk and royal as only she could be. "We've got no choice. We have to help."

"But we don't even know what he's doing here!"

And we don't want to know, Mel. We really, really don't. Trust me.

"Then why don't we ask?" she said. "Nicely. Without shouting."

The Monk from next door let the portable portal drop to his side, coughing weakly, then shook his head. "You can ask, Mel, but I can't answer. Not with this bloody shadbolt in place. I'll tell you everything, I promise, but only after Monk gets the wretched thing off me."

Furious, resentful, he took a step closer to the sofa. "And how the hell am I supposed to remove an invisible shadbolt, genius?"

"Trust me," said the Monk from next door. The misery in his eyes was awful. "It won't be invisible to you."

In other words he was going to have to go looking for it. He was going to have to paddle around in this man's etheretic aura—in his own etheretic aura, as good as—searching for a shadbolt not even Bibbie could find.

Bloody hell, Gerald. Where are you when I need you?

"Monk," said Melissande. "Do we really have a choice?"

For the first time since meeting her, he wished she'd shut up. "No."

"Is there anything we can do to—"

"You can back off," he said curtly. "Stand well away. And don't any of you breathe so much as one word."

"Right," said Bibbie. "The floor is yours, Professor Markham."

As she joined Melissande and Reg in moving to

the furthest corner of the parlor, he dropped cross-legged to the carpet beside the sofa. Took a deep, deep breath and made himself look into the face of the Monk from next door.

What else was different, apart from the scar? They had the same lanky dark hair, in need of a cut. The same thinly-bridged nose that his mother liked to call aristocratic. The same quizzically-arched eyebrows. The same lopsided mouth. Their prominent cheekbones were identical. They shared a pointed chin. They had the same crooked eye-tooth, thanks to Aylesbury's bad temper.

But our eyes . . . good God, our eyes . . .

The eyes he was looking into had looked into hell.

"I knew you'd help me," his unwanted twin whispered. "Knew it was worth it. You're the only one I can trust."

He knew the answer but he asked the question anyway. "Is this going to hurt?"

His other self smiled. "It doesn't matter, Monk. You have to."

For one bad moment he thought his courage was going to fail, that he was going to let himself down, let the girls down. Let down this man who looked— almost—like him.

One last glance behind him, at Bibbie. At Melissande. At Reg. All three girls were gravely silent, urging him on. He loved them so much. How could he not do this?

Hesitant, feeling far shakier than he'd ever admit, he took the Monk from next door's hand in his own. Waited to feel some strong shock of recognition. Waited to see if this would make him wake up. No such luck. The fingers in his—*my fingers*—were long and thin and cool. Strong fingers. Clever fingers. Fingers used to playing with thaumaturgical fire.

He closed his eyes and stared into the ether, into the aura he'd never once seen from the outside. Searched for the shadbolt hiding within it like a lethally-honed knife sleeping silent in its sheath.

Oh, he thought, wondering. *Oh. Is that what I look like?*

Monk Markham's aura was royal blue shot through with gold. At least, the parts of it that weren't distorted and twisted were royal blue and threads of gold. He couldn't bring himself to look at the ruined bits, not yet, so instead he concentrated on the remnants of beauty still untouched.

Unlike Gerald, he'd known from childhood he was special. Born with metaphysical talents few others would ever know. But even though he'd been tested so many times and in so many different ways that he'd long since lost count, had stopped keeping track even, not *once* had he ever been shown himself like this.

Because they didn't think it mattered? Or because they were afraid it might matter too much?

Growing up with Aylesbury, he'd promised himself he would *never* let magic go to his head. Thaumaturgical power was not the measure of a man. No matter what he invented, it could never be more important than being a decent human being. But since he'd never actually come right out and said that, perhaps it wasn't surprising his family—and the Department of Thaumaturgy—would err on the side of caution.

And I do have a habit of ignoring the rules.

But that was different. That wasn't about being better. It was only ever about the work.

The man on the sofa, the Monk from next door, stirred a little—and he remembered what it was he was meant to be doing.

An invisible shadbolt? Bloody hell. Who has the power to make a shadbolt invisible? It's a major feat of thaumaturgics to put a normal one together.

To find the answer he had to look deeper into this Monk's damaged aura. He had to forget about the beauty and confront the pain instead.

Do I really want to do this? No, I bloody well don't.

Steeling himself, he inched his *potentia* deeper and closer to the dark, distorted patterns in the aura that suggested, like shadows on water, the presence of something dangerous beneath. He could see the patterns quite clearly. Thought it was odd that Bibbie couldn't. She was one of the best witches of her generation.

He felt the other Monk flinch. Felt himself flinch with him. And then felt a teasing, taunting hint of something familiar. Or almost familiar. Something that should be familiar—and yet was somehow not *right*.

Gathering his *potentia*, he plunged his awareness into the heart of his unlikely twin's aura, tearing it wider, baring it to his eyes. He saw the shadbolt in all its vicious, strangling glory, felt its thaumic signature . . . and heard himself cry out. Felt himself spiraling downwards, falling backwards, falling apart.

Because this was impossible. This had to be a mistake. He knew who'd made that shadbolt . . . and he knew he had to be wrong.

Gerald.

CHAPTER THIRTEEN

Seated at his dusted and neatly ordered desk, Sir Alec stared at the open folder in front of him. Re-reading it was pointless. He knew that. He'd read the report four times and none of the words had changed. The truth hadn't changed. His agent was dead. One moment's inattention. One heartbeat of distraction. That was all it ever took. Just one. Not that the eye-witnesses put it that way, of course. The eyewitnesses, being ignorant, had seen what they were meant to see: a horrible shooting accident. One of those things that regrettably happened, sometimes, when a bunch of jolly chaps got together and went after grouse.

But he knew different. Saltman had gotten too close, too fast. He'd spooked his quarry and his quarry, instead of bolting, had turned to fight.

Damn you, Felix. What were you thinking? You should've known better. I thought you did.

Not an inexperienced janitor, Saltman. This had been his ninth assignment. Sloppiness like this was simply unacceptable. And now months of painstaking work had all been for nothing. Their quarry was on his guard now. Who knew how long it would take for him to relax his stirred defenses? This had been their chance, perhaps their only chance, of nipping Grantham Farnsworth's activities in, as they said, the bud.

Beneath the anger he did feel grief. As hard as he tried he could never quite keep himself from forming a sympathetic attachment to the men he moved about the international stage like breathing chess pieces. Perhaps if he'd never been a janitor himself. Perhaps if he had no idea what it was like to risk life and sanity to keep the innocent masses safe. Perhaps then he'd be able to maintain a prudent distance. But he'd long since abandoned any hope of achieving it. His only hope was that no man whose life ultimately depended on him would ever know the depths of his feelings. Would know that he had feelings at all.

The second-to-bottom right hand drawer of his desk contained a heavy, official stamp and a stamp pad soaked in blood-red ink. Ralph said that was gaudy and ostentatious but he felt it was important not to pretend in black. Death wasn't black, at least not until the funeral. Before then it was crimson.

Neatly, precisely, he stamped Felix Saltman's file. A single word: *Inactive*. So circumspect. So polite.

The loss of an agent never failed to complicate his life, but at least it had been quite some time between drinks. And seeing, thanks to Saltman, that the pursuit of Farnsworth must for the next while be abandoned, his Department retained its precarious equilibrium.

Which was a slight and stinging consolation.

He slotted Saltman's folder in the cabinet reserved for inactive files. That cabinet had been around for years, put to use long before he'd begun his tenure as head of the Department. He'd known perhaps a quarter of the men whose lives were interred within it, and of that quarter about one third had died on his watch.

He never allowed himself to wonder what the final tally would be.

His office wall-clock sounded softly, ticking towards nine. Slicing through time. He often worked late. Fewer distractions. A world deceptively at peace. The office's heavy curtains were drawn and a small fire burned merrily, but the dancing flames failed to lift his mood.

Gerald should have returned from Grande Splotze by now. At the very least he should have made contact, if there were problems. If the man he was meeting had failed to show up.

He nearly succumbed to the lure of good malt whiskey. Felix Saltman was dead. Careless or not he deserved one small toast. But he left the bottle of aged Loriner unopened. Instinct was stirring and he'd long since learned to trust it.

Something's not right. There's another shoe somewhere, wanting to drop.

He had plenty with which to occupy himself while he was waiting. His in-tray overflowed with notes and observations and reports. So he returned to his desk and stifled instinct with work. Sat on the corner of his desk, a small, innocuous sphere of crystal. More a marble than a ball. Its vibration was known to very few. He'd trusted Gerald with it, though. He'd trusted Gerald with many things.

I don't care what Ralph says. He'll not let me down.

He looked up as someone tapped on the closed office door. "Come."

"Sir," said Dalby, ghosting in. He had the softest tread of any agent in Nettleworth—or out of it, for that matter. "Sorry to disturb you."

Frowning, Sir Alec returned his pen to its holder and sat back. "You're still here?"

He could always trust Frank Dalby to answer the unasked question. "Got a bloke who knows a bloke," he said, ever the laconic. "Chance of a tip. Worth losing some sleep on."

In another lifetime he and Frank had both been janitors. They were of an age. Had shared experiences. If Frank resented answering to him now he'd never shown it. But it was doubtful. Frank Dalby was born to hide in the shadows. The glare of politics would kill him inside a week.

Comfortably at ease on the other side of the desk, Frank gave the tip of his nose a thoughtful rub. "Bloody fool, that Saltman."

He felt his lips twitch. To say that Frank was unforgiving was like saying water was wet. "We all make mistakes."

Frank snorted. "Felix bloody did, and all." He let his disinterested gaze slide around the room. "You got anything brewing in Splotze?"

The other shoe dropped, a soft sounding of doom. "Why do you ask?"

"Nothing on the duty board about Splotze," said Frank, his gaze upcast at the firelit ceiling. "And everyone's accounted for." His gaze dropped. "Everyone based here."

It was an invitation to a confidence which he

wasn't inclined to share. With a flick of his fingers he indicated his work-covered desk. "If there's a point, Dalby, you might consider reaching it."

Indifferent to rebuff, Frank fished in his pocket and pulled out a folded note. "Back-channel squawk," he said, handing it over. "Didn't make much sense but I wrote it down just in case."

He took the note. "I see." As far as he knew, his labyrinth of informants didn't include a detour via Frank Dalby. "Back-channel how?"

"Remember Scrubby Yates?"

Scrubby Yates, in a roundabout way, had once nearly and spectacularly cost them their lives. Ah yes, indeed, the good old days. "Vaguely."

"Turns out Scrubby still keeps half an ear to the ground," said Frank, a sardonic glint in his eye. "One toe in the water. A couple of fingers in a few pies. Someone reached out to him. He wouldn't say who. I pushed, but he said he's grown attached to his head."

"And what has that to do with Splotze?"

"How should I know?" said Frank. "All I know is Scrubby moaned about the accent. And then he clammed up. I said I'd send him some ale."

The folded note was burning his fingers like a brand. "Fine. Half a case and not one bottle more. I'd rather not encourage him. Scrubby Yates's time has both come and gone."

Frank didn't often grin, but he was grinning now. "Half a case it is." And then his amusement died, as though an internal switch had flipped. "I'm here if you need me, Ace. Just say the word."

Frank Dalby would never have made the mistake

Felix Saltman made. "It's doubtful," he said. "But I'll certainly bear it in mind. Thank you, Mr. Dalby."

As soon as the office door clicked shut behind his former colleague, he unfolded the note and read it. One sentence. Eight words.

Didn't he want to wear a yellow cravat?

Cryptic for some. Clear as glass for him.

Gerald Dunwoody had never arrived.

"*Gerald?*" said Reg, shocked. "*Gerald* put a shadbolt on him? *My* Gerald?"

Monk scowled at her. "No, Reg, *his* Gerald. I thought you were paying attention."

Inconveniently close on Melissande's shoulder, she whacked him with her wing. "I *am* paying attention. And mind how you speak to your elders, sunshine. *You're* not too old for a thrashing and *I'm* not too old to give you one."

Rubbing at his arm, he sighed. "Sorry."

"I should bloody think so," said Reg. "Because we've just got through establishing that muggins over there is you, haven't we? Which means *his* Gerald is *my* Gerald and I can't see *my* Gerald doing something like that. Can you?"

They'd retreated to the parlor's furthest corner again, the better to have a quiet conniption. The Monk from next door had lapsed into a doze, worn out by the effort of getting here and having his etheretic aura rummaged through like a bargain bin at a market stall and whatever else he'd been enduring up till now, that made him look like—*that.*

"Are you all right?" Melissande asked quietly.

"Because you look like you've got the most fearful headache."

"I have," he admitted. "But never mind. Let's concentrate on the shadbolt for now."

"The shadbolt *my* Gerald—or *any* Gerald—couldn't possibly inflict on *anyone*," said Reg, feathers ominously bristling. "Are we all perfectly clear?"

"Look, Reg," Bibbie said after a moment. "I don't want to believe it either. But Monk's not going to make a mistake about something like this. He knows Gerald's thaumic signature better than any of us. If he says the shadbolt is Gerald's handiwork, then like it or not we have to accept that."

Good old Bibbie. Tentatively, he stroked a fingertip down Reg's wing. "You think *I'm* happy about this, Reg? Just thinking about it makes me sick."

She rattled her tail feathers, distressed. "I don't understand," she muttered. "It's just not *like* him. Not even that government stooge Sir Alec could convince my Gerald to do something like that—especially to *you*." She took a deep, rallying breath. "So *if* this is true—and I'm not saying it *is*—then something must've gone terribly wrong."

Oh, it had. Because the Gerald who'd prisoned the other Monk in his shadbolt—that Gerald stank of filthy magics. If that Gerald walked into the parlor right now, chances were he wouldn't recognize him. Not on the inside. Not where it counted. And even though nothing in the world next door had anything to do with him he was suddenly scalded by a terrible, angry grief.

What did you do, Gerald? What the bloody hell did you do?

"Rats," said Melissande, her chin coming up. "I've just had a thought. What if we're looking at this round the wrong way?"

With an effort Monk shook himself free of grief and made himself pay attention to the girls.

"How d'you mean?" said Bibbie.

"Well . . ." Mel snuck a look at the other Monk. "Aren't we making a few assumptions here? And don't we all know what happens when one assumes?"

"Yes," said Reg. "One makes an ass out of you and anyone who doesn't happen to be me. *My* assumptions always turn out to be right."

"Yes, Reg, of course they do," said Mel, with admirable restraint. "*Blimey*. But see, the thing is, because that's Monk—sort of—passed out on the sofa, we're all assuming he's telling the truth. But what if Reg's stupid joke is true? What if this Monk really *is* like an evil twin and he's come here with some dastardly plan to destroy us? Don't ask me why. Or—or maybe he's an escaped convict. You did say shadbolts were used on criminals."

"Madam could be right," said Reg, unflatteringly surprised. "This other Monk Markham could be a rotter. It would certainly explain why his Gerald had to restrain him."

"Monk?" said Bibbie, anxious. He couldn't remember seeing her anxious before. He hated it. "What do you think?"

"You're right," he said cautiously. "It's a theory." But not one he was terribly willing to embrace.

And why's that? Because I can't see myself as an escaped criminal on the run? Because I can't be the villain, I can only be the hero?

No. It wasn't that. According to Uncle Ralph he was already a perishing villain. It was the oppressive, metallic after-taste of the other Gerald's thaumic signature that revealed the horrible truth. And he'd tell the girls that. He would. As soon as he was sure he could get the words out without heaving up his supper . . .

"The problem is," said Bibbie, grimmer and older than he'd ever seen her, "we could keep dreaming up theories until the cows come home—which would get us exactly nowhere. So we don't have a choice. We have to get that shadbolt off him. It's the only way to find out for sure what's going on."

Reg rattled her tail feathers. "True, ducky. But taking off a shadbolt's not like wriggling out of a corset, now is it?"

Monk gave her a look. "You're asking me?"

"Trust me, sunshine, the last man in the world I'd ask about corsets—on or off—is *you*," Reg said coldly. "Now *shadbolts*, on the other hand . . ."

The trouble with any kind of conversation involving Reg was that it was far too easy to get distracted by the insults. She seemed to shed them effortlessly, like lice. How Gerald lived with it he would never understand.

Bibbie cleared her throat, not looking at the bird or Melissande. "Ah—Monk? Perhaps we should—"

"I know," he muttered. "Bloody hell."

"Bloody hell?" echoed Melissande, instantly suspicious. "What d'you mean *bloody hell*? What's going on? Why is it that every time someone mentions *shadbolts* the pair of you turn *green* and nearly jump through the roof?" Arms folded, toes tapping, she treated them to her best prime ministerly glare. And then she blinked. "Wait a minute. Emmerabiblia Markham, does this have *anything* to do with why you were looking as sick as a goose when you finally turned up at the office this morning?"

Bibbie tried to smile. "Ah—would you believe the breakfast milk was off?"

The look Melissande gave her could've shriveled rock. "*No.* Monk, you were here last night. I don't suppose anything of a shadboltish nature happened after Reg and I went home?"

He swallowed. *Bugger.* "Mel, honestly, it's not as bad as—"

"Reg," said Melissande, her all-too-knowing gaze not leaving his face, "about these shadbolts. Exactly how tricky *are* they to remove?"

"If you don't have the incant designed to unravel 'em?" said Reg. "Hmm. Ever dropped a watermelon off a very tall tower?"

Melissande shuddered. "No, actually. And now I'm pretty sure I never will. Tell me, can they be removed without a specifically designed unlocking hex?"

"Depends," said Reg, her eyes gleaming.

"On what, pray tell? As if I didn't know."

"On whether you've got someone a bit thaumaturgically special hanging about with nothing better to do."

"I see," said Melissande. Her toes were tapping again. "And when you say *special*, you mean you'd have to be a Monk Markham."

Reg shrugged one wing. "Or a Gerald. You know. Someone like that."

"Yes," said Melissande. "I rather thought that's

what you meant. So. Monk. Here's my last question—
did you *by any chance* put a shadbolt on Bibbie last
night?"

Damn. "Look, Mel—"

"Melissande, don't," said Bibbie. "The shadbolt
was my idea, not Monk's."

Melissande looked like she wanted to say every last
appalling word she'd ever heard in her life. *"Emmerabiblia Markham!"*

Reg sniggered. "How's your blood pressure doing
now, ducky? Hmm?"

Seizing Bibbie's shoulders, Melissande shook her
with outraged despair. "Bibbie—*Bibbie*—what were you
thinking?" She flung out an accusing, pointing finger.
"Surely you realized you could've ended up like *him*?"

Bibbie pulled free. "Well, yes, I knew it was risky,
but Monk needed my help."

"Oh, I see," said Melissande, rounding on him. "In
other words it was *her* idea but *you* went along with it!
Monk, how *could* you?"

She was furious with him. Melissande Cadwallader, the love of his life, the woman who'd proven
love at first sight did exist. He was having some trouble catching his breath.

Please, Mel. Don't be mad.

Turning back to Bibs, Melissande grabbed her
hands. If anyone ever doubted she'd come to love
Bibbie like a sister . . . "Are you all right, Bibbie?
Have you seen a physician? You really did look awful
this morning. Have you—"

"I'm fine, Mel," Bibbie insisted. "I *promise*."

Mel let go. "I don't believe you," she said flatly.
"You'd say anything to keep Monk out of trouble."

Turning again, she stabbed him with her most accusing glare. "And clearly you'd *do* anything to prove a thaumaturgical point."

"That's not fair!" said Bibbie. "I *told* you, the shadbolt was my idea. And it had nothing to do with one of Monk's experiments."

"Then what was it about?"

Bibbie looked at him. "Tell her, Monk."

"Bibs—"

"Monk, you tell her or I will."

He swallowed a mouthful of his own bad words. So this was how Gerald felt, eh? Backed into a corner, badgered into revealing his secrets . . .

"Fine," he sighed, and told her.

"Blimey," said Reg, when he was finished. For once the bird actually sounded impressed. "Not bad, Mr. Clever Clogs. Not bad at all."

"*What?*" said Melissande, as close to a shriek as he'd ever heard. "Don't tell me you *approve* of this madness?"

Another decisive tail-rattle. "Don't be a noddycock. Of course I do. Desperate times call for desperate measures."

"Yes, well, there's *desperate* and then there's *demented*," Melissande retorted. "And in this case I think we all know which is which!"

Monk knew better than to try to soothe her with platitudes. "You're right. What Bibbie did was crazy and what Gerald and I did was dangerous. But it worked. Thanks to Bibbie I broke the other shadbolt this afternoon. We got some important information."

"Really?" said Bibbie, delighted. "Monk, you plonker, why didn't you *say*?"

"You were never meant to know about any of it, Bibs," he said. "Officially you still don't. Officially what happened here last night never happened."

She pouted. "Oh, but—"

"Quit while you're ahead, ducky," said Reg. "Basking in the glow of being an unsung heroine's not so bad. I should know. I've been doing it for centuries."

As Bibbie made scornful scoffing noises, Melissande sighed. "Just tell me this much, Monk. After all the unpleasantness with your Uncle Ralph, tell me this latest escapade hasn't caused you more grief."

He recalled Mr. Plummer's expression after being discreetly taken to one side and told in a tone that brooked neither contradiction nor negotiation: *"So anyway, here it is. I can break this bastard's shadbolt, sir, and I'll do it for you here and now—on one condition. No awkward questions afterwards. Just nod and smile and send me back to R&D."*

And because Mr. Plummer wanted results more than he needed explanations he'd accepted the outrageous condition and never once made mention of the second shadbolt's disappearance.

"No grief," he told Melissande . . . and prayed devoutly he was right. Because for all he knew, Mr. Plummer's gratitude came complete with an expiration date.

She nodded, trying to hide her relief. "Good. All right—so counting last night and this afternoon, how many shadbolts have you broken altogether?"

He exhaled sharply. "Two."

She wasn't the only one who found the prospect alarming.

"But two is better than none, Mel," he added.

"True," she conceded, after a moment. "And I suppose this shadbolt will be easier to break because Gerald made it. Since you know his thaumic signature as well as your own, it'll just be a case of reading it, like reading his handwriting. And—I don't know—*over-writing* it?"

"Um . . ." He ran one hand down his face, dreading what he had to say next. "Not exactly. If our Gerald and his Gerald were the same wizard, I could do that. I've broken heaps of Gerald's hexes now and some of them were utterly diabolical."

Reg, listening intently, pointed her beak at him like a shooter aiming his rifle. "Eh? What d'you mean *if* they were the same wizard? The last time I looked you were busy bleating over my strenuous objections that they *are* the same wizard. Now which is it, Mr. I'm-the-instant-expert-so-don't-argue-with-me Markham? Make up your bloody mind!"

"Okay," he said, after some frantic thinking. "This is all theoretical . . . but it seems to me that *that* Monk's world and *our* world were running on parallel rails, like—like trains going in a straight line side by side. Same speed, same direction. Same lives, pretty much. Only then something different happened in *his* world and now our worlds are running on two different tracks."

Bibbie was nodding. "Sounds right," she murmured. "As a theory it's metaphysically sound." She pulled a face. "Well. As sound as anything as crazy as this can be. So—what happened? What caused his world to veer off while ours kept going straight ahead?"

"Monk?" Melissande prompted, when he didn't answer. "Monk, what aren't you telling us?"

Sickened again, he folded his arms tight to his chest. He could feel his heartbeat, thudding right through his sleeves. "All I can be sure of," he said, unable to meet her eyes, "is that it's got something to do with the other Gerald. It's something he did. Something . . . not good."

"Pishwash," Reg snapped, feathers ruffling. "I'll never believe it and you can't make me."

"Look, Reg, I don't want to believe it either," he snapped back. "But I felt the other Gerald's thaumic signature in that shadbolt and I'm telling you it's *changed*. It's *wrong*."

"Wrong how?" said Bibbie. "You're going to have to be specific if you want us to believe you. This is *Gerald* we're talking about, remember?"

"I can't be specific, Bibs!" he said, not trying to hide his hurt exasperation. "It's a feeling, isn't it? It's touch, it's taste—I can't put it into words. It's like asking me to describe what Melissande's singing sounds like. The word is *off-key* but that hardly encapsulates the entire hideous experience."

Melissande stared, then slapped his arm. "Do you *mind*?"

"Now, now, ducky," said Reg. "Enough of that. You can't go around hitting people for telling the truth."

He was not, under any circumstances, going to rub his arm. "I know you don't want to hear this," he told them. "Trust me, I don't want to be saying it. But I felt something *rotten* in the other Gerald's thaumic signature. I just think we need to be prepared, that's all."

"Prepared for what?" said Bibbie. Her voice wasn't steady. "That the other Gerald—*his* Gerald—is *bad*?"

Monk slid his arm around her shoulders and held her close. *Oh, lord.* "Who knows? But Reg said it, didn't she? Our Gerald would never put a shadbolt on me."

"Maybe he wouldn't," said Melissande, glaring. "But believe me when I tell you *I'm* getting awfully tempted."

Coughing, the other Monk stirred on the sofa then tried to sit up. "Melissande? Bibbie?"

He returned to his inconvenient twin's side. "It's all right. We're still here."

The man wearing his face, who'd stopped living his life and started living a nightmare, looked up at him with haunted eyes. "We're running out of time, Monk. Right now he's distracted—there's a plan—but he won't stay distracted forever. If I'm not where I'm supposed to be when I'm supposed to be there—" His thin face twisted—even saying that much must have woken the shadbolt. "I can't—I can't—"

Sickened, Monk dropped to one knee beside him. *That's how I look when I'm writhing in pain.* "You mean Gerald, don't you? He's . . . gone rogue."

Gasping, the Monk from next door nodded. "I'm sorry."

So am I. "What's his plan?"

The other Monk was running with sweat now, his dreadful eyes turning glassy. "I can't. I can't." He shuddered, groaning. "Get it off me," he whispered. "*Please.*"

"All right," he said to the man on the sofa. "I'll

try my best but—you know it's not going to be easy, right? And you know it's going to hurt like hell?"

On a gasp, the Monk from next door nodded. "Been living in hell for months now, Debbie. You do what you have to."

Debbie. Short for Debinger. One of his middle names and Aylesbury's favorite childhood taunt. Nobody knew that, not even Bibs. He'd never told anyone. His childish shame had been too great. So if he'd had any doubts left . . . if he'd thought that maybe, just maybe, none of this was really real . . .

Oh, bloody hell, Gerald. What a stinking mess.

Pushing up to both knees, he cradled the other Monk's sweat-slicked face between his hands. "You ready, mate?"

"Don't be stupid," the other Monk said, trying to smile. "But since when has not being ready ever stopped us?"

"Right," he muttered. "Right. So here goes nothing. Hold on."

Mel, Bibbie and Reg had come to stand behind him. He could feel them, warm as flames at his back. Not a word spoken. There was nothing to say. But their silent strength strengthened him. Gave him heart. Gave him hope.

His second plunging into this other Monk's damaged aura was no better than the first. Especially since he didn't let himself dwell on the blue and the gold but made a beeline for the black parts, the twisted parts, the parts distorted by the crippling shadbolt. A shadbolt that wasn't like any other he'd ever seen. Not that he could see this one. Not yet. Sense it, yes. It was setting off all his thaumaturgic alarm bells. But still it remained hidden from his etheretic eye.

Bloody hell, Gerald. I thought I was the inventor.

Circling warily, keeping his *potentia* tightly leashed, he eased himself in for a closer look. Straight away he felt the other Monk flinch. Heard him groan. But he couldn't let that stop him. He had to keep pushing, no matter the cost. And there was going to be a cost. A bloody steep one.

The other Monk's sharp discomfort increased. He could feel it now, in his own flesh, a weird kind of echo. Because they were the same man, sort of? More or less? Or because he'd sunk himself so deeply into the man's etheretic aura that he was starting to lose track of where it ended and his own began?

Either way he'd have to be careful. This was dangerous magic—even for him.

Gritting his teeth he gathered his own *potentia* closer. Imagined it thin and sharp like a needle, poised to pierce the invisible shadbolt's poisonous heart. Where was it, anyhow? He could feel it. He could taste it. It was here. Why couldn't he *see* it?

Come on, you filthy thing. Come out, come out, wherever you are.

Images were starting to form in his mind. Shards of glass. Sharpened knives. Bits and pieces of barbed wire. Twisted and tangled and embedded in flesh. And the hand that had forged them—the wizard who'd dreamed them, had turned his dreams into a lethal reality—

Gerald. Oh, Gerald. What happened to you?

Achingly familiar, abhorrently strange, Gerald's despicably altered thaumic signature tainted every thread of the shadbolt. No doubt about it now. No way to hide. This was Gerald's doing. The other Gerald. This Monk's Gerald. He felt a trembling clutch of fear.

I don't know if I can break this monstrosity. I don't know the man who made it.

From a long, long way distant he heard himself sob, once. A sound of despair and impending defeat. Then faintly he heard a voice.

"Don't you dare give up, Monk Markham. We both know you can do this."

Melissande, being bossy and regal the way only she could. Taking heart from her snippiness, taking heart from *her*, he steadied his ragged breathing and looked again at the cage in which the other Monk was trapped.

Something tickled his attention. Something familiar. Outlying semi-cants, like the shadbolt he'd broken on Mr. Plummer's prisoner. Not the same thaumic signature but the same wicked design. Either it was a coincidence—or Gerald and their mysterious black market wizard had been reading the same books. Even though this was awful, he nearly laughed.

His Gerald had told him exactly how to break through this kind of lock. After doing it twice he was practically an expert. And once the correct sequence of semi-cants was triggered, the rest of the shadbolt should just . . . melt away. All he had to do was work out the correct order.

Except last time it was Gerald who'd identified the right sequence. Sure, he'd figured the proper timing to break them, but without the correct order—

If he can do it, I can. I have to. Come on, Debbie. Prove that pillock Aylesbury wrong.

The other Monk was weakening. The strain of this was proving too much for him. They were both running out of time now.

Come on, come on, come on.

With a surge of his *potentia* he pushed through the wardings and the barriers surrounding the shadbolt, roughly pulling them apart. The other Monk screamed, the most hideous sound. He felt the pain sear through his own body and screamed with him. He couldn't help it—but he didn't let it stop him, either.

Twelve semi-cants. Three groupings. Twenty-four different timings. And oh bugger—what was that? A buzzing, a burning, a warning shudder through the ether. *No.* He'd set something off. Some kind of thaumic booby-trap. Hell. Why hadn't he sensed it?

Damn you, Dunwoody! When did you get so sneaky?

Now the race was really on. Desperately he threw his *potentia* at the tangle of incants. But even as they fell, their timings haphazardly staccato, he could feel the other Gerald's thaumic booby-trap expanding, spreading like acid spilled from a filthy glass.

Come on, Markham, come on, come on. Are you a bloody genius or aren't you?

Six hexes down. Seven. Eight. Nine. The other Monk was howling. *God, somebody shut him up.* Ten. Eleven.

The twelfth semi-cant resisted. Because it wasn't a simple semi-cant. No, of *course* it wasn't. It was a triple-hexed double-looped terto-cant. *You bastard.* He and the other Monk were howling together now, blood and bones and flesh on fire. The booby-trap had nearly reached its critical tipping-point. No more minutes left, only seconds remaining.

No time for kindness. No time for finesse. He ripped apart the shadbolt's final incant like a wolf falling on a lamb. And then, as he pulled himself free of the Monk from next door's tattered aura, he managed to extinguish the booby-trap before it finished its job.

Take that, Gerald, you maniac. Whoever you are.

CHAPTER FOURTEEN

The other Monk's cries of anguish were unspeakable. Hands pressed to her face, Melissande turned away. "I can't bear this," she muttered to Reg on her shoulder, feeling like the worst kind of coward. "I can't."

"Come on, ducky," said Reg. Her claws were close to drawing blood, she was clutching so tight. "It can't go on much longer."

No, it couldn't. Because if their Monk didn't break the shadbolt in the next few seconds the other Monk would surely die—or else go totally mad.

Hurry up, Monk. Hurry up. Saint Snodgrass, help him.

Still hiding behind her hands, she could hear Bibbie's harsh, choked breathing. Poor Bibbie. She shouldn't have stayed. This was too cruel.

And then the two Monks let out a blood-curdling yell. She spun around so hard and so fast that Reg nearly lost her perch. Swearing and flapping, the bird managed to hang on. Bibbie leaped for the sofa, her ivory-pale cheeks drenched with tears.

"Monk! Monk! Are you all right? *Monk!*"

Limp as an overcooked Yok Tok noodle, Monk slid all the way to the parlor carpet. His nose was bleeding, thick red splatters on his chin and his shirt. Eyes rolled up in his head he sprawled on the floor, looking entirely too close to dead for comfort. Only the rasping of air in his throat reassured them that he was actually alive.

"Monk, you idiot!" cried Bibbie, and hauled him into her lap. "Please, please, don't just lie there. *Say* something!"

Monk made a nasty gargling sound without any words in it. Bibbie choked back a sob and held her wretched brother even tighter, heedless of the blood smearing from him onto her.

Reg chattered her beak. "You'd better check on the other one, ducky. And cross your fingers while you're at it, because if the bugger's dead we might never know what the devil's going on."

Reg was right. Of course. She was nearly always right. It was quite possibly her most aggravating trait. "Hop off, then," she said, twitching her shoulder. "I'll have no hope of giving him the kiss of life with you breathing down my neck giving me points for technique."

Ordinarily that would've provoked a flood of sarcastic commentary, with bonus insults, but even Reg was flattened by this latest turn of events. The bird hopped to the sofa's arm without so much as an inelegant snort.

Stepping over and around her Monk and Bibbie, Melissande perched on the edge of the sofa beside the other Monk. He looked utterly dreadful, so pale

he was gray except for where he was splodged with
blood. She couldn't see him breathing. Trembling
with nerves, heart racing, she snatched off her spectacles and held them over his slightly parted lips. Held
her breath—held her breath—then let it out in a sickeningly relieved *whoosh* as his slow exhalation lightly
fogged the lenses.

"Saint Snodgrass be praised," she whispered, and
leaned close. "Monk. Monk, can you hear me?"

The other Monk stirred, his stubby eyelashes flut-
tering. Beneath his closed eyelids his eyes moved
from side to side, restless.

She rubbed her spectacles clean on her sleeve and
shoved them back onto her face. "Monk. It's Melissande. *Monk*, can you hear me?"

"Is he alive?" her Monk croaked from the floor.

"Well, he's not dead," said Reg, always helpful. "But
I won't pretend I've not seen healthier corpses."

"Monk," Melissande said again, and pressed her
palm to the other Monk's cold, clammy cheek. "It's
all right. It's over now. You're quite safe."

Her Monk groaned. "Help me sit up, Bibs. I've
gone all rubbery."

"No, no, you shouldn't move," said Bibbie, still
tearful, clutching him closer. "You should rest a bit
longer before—"

"There isn't time, Bibs!" said Monk. "Please."

Swearing under her breath, Bibbie helped him
sit up.

Melissande gave him another sideways glance.
"Bibbie's right. You should be lying down."

"Don't you start!" he snapped, then shook his
head. "Damn. Sorry."

She turned her attention back to the other Monk. "Doesn't matter." Leaning close again, she patted his cheek. "Monk. Monk?"

Reg rattled her tail feathers. "Oh for pity's sake, woman, stop pussyfooting around and slap him, would you?"

"Don't you dare!" said Bibbie, crowding close. "Shut up, Reg. You're no bloody help at all!"

"Well, at least I'm not impersonating a watering pot!" Reg retorted. "I mean, if you want to turn a hose on him, ducky, turn a hose on him and be done with it. Splashing him with a few maidenly tears isn't going to—"

Bibbie turned on her, ferocious. "Oh, you horrible bird, how can you be so *callous*? After what he's just gone through? Sometimes, Reg, I wonder—"

"Hey," said the other Monk, and opened his eyes. "I thought paradise would be a little more peaceful than this."

Pulling her hands back to the safety of her lap, Melissande managed a wobbly smile. "Not if Reg is there with you, it won't be."

"I think you might be right," said the other Monk. His voice was thready, almost no air behind it. And then his sunken, bloodshot eyes warmed. "Hello, Mel."

Oh, Saint Snodgrass. "Hello."

He fumbled for her hand. She let him. His fingers held hers, weakly. "It's so good to see you. I haven't seen you for so long."

Really? Why not? But she couldn't ask him.

"God . . ." His voice broke. "Melissande, I've missed you."

No, no, no. She couldn't begin to have that conversation. "You and your bloody inventions," she said, seeking refuge in scolding . . . but didn't pull her hand free. "You never learn, do you?"

He shook his head. Smiled. Shattered her heart. "Apparently not."

"Monk," said her Monk, behind her, and put a hand on her shoulder. "Can you talk now? The shadbolt . . . it's gone?"

The other Monk closed his eyes again. Coughed, a horrible rattling sound. "Yes," he murmured. "Feels . . . strange." His eyelids lifted slowly. "Thanks, mate."

Melissande heard her Monk make a funny little sound in his throat. "Don't thank me. You know—"

"Yeah. I know," said the other Monk. "Not your fault. Had to be done."

"What?" said Bibbie, alarmed. "What's not his fault?"

The other Monk looked at Bibbie, his eyes washing over with tears. "Oh, Bibs. I wish you'd listened to me. I wish I'd known what to say. How to say it. I'm so sorry. You deserved so much better."

"Than what?" said Bibbie. "Monk, you're frightening me. What are you talking about, why are you sorr—"

"It doesn't matter," the other Monk whispered. "It's not the same here. You'll be all right."

"No, tell me," she insisted. "I want to—"

"Bibbie, don't," Monk said quietly. "There isn't much time."

Bibbie stared at her other brother. "What?"

"Open your eyes, ducky," said Reg, impatient on

the sofa's arm. "Something went a bit wrong breaking that bloody shadbolt." She looked at Monk. "Didn't it, Mr. Clever Clogs Markham?"

Melissande felt her Monk flinch. "I did my best."

"He did," said the other Monk, his voice hoarse. "It's all right. I always knew—"

"Knew what?" Bibbie demanded. "Monk—both of you—*either* of you—what's going on?"

Ignoring her, Monk grasped his other self's forearm. "How long?"

"Soon," whispered the other Monk.

"Tell us what you can," said Monk. "Quickly. When did everything go ass over elbows?"

The other Monk groaned. His eyes were starting to cloud. "New Ottosland. Lional and his dragon. Gerald swore to stop them."

"We know," said Bibbie. "And he did. He made another dragon and—"

"No," said the Monk on the sofa, sickly pale and sweating. "That didn't happen. Not in my world. My Gerald made a different choice. He—"

A surging wave of pain silenced him. And as he fought his way through it—

"Oh, blimey bloody Charlie," said Reg, with a violent rattling of tail feathers and a great flapping of wings. "*And* his bunions and his *piles*!"

Monk looked at her. "Reg?"

"The palace roof, sunshine. Remember?" said Reg. Her tail was still rattling and her eyes were wide with horror. "Just before Shugat and his swanky sultan turned up? Gerald was all set to help himself to Lional's manky grimoires."

"And you talked him out of it."

"Yes, *I* did," Reg retorted. "But the *other* me didn't." She looked at the Monk on the sofa. "Am I right? I'm right, aren't I?"

Wheezing, the other Monk nodded. "And by the time we got back from Ottosland, it was too late," he whispered. "My Gerald had . . . turned."

Melissande, looking at him, could have wept for his pain. He blamed himself. Gerald was his best friend and in his mind, he'd failed him.

How close did we come to his fate, I wonder? Was it serendipity that saved us, or something else?

"But—how does that work?" said Bibbie, breaking the stunned silence. "Gerald's Gerald, isn't he? He can't decide to do one thing here and another thing—"

"Ha," said Reg. "'Course he can, ducky. Don't tell me you've never been in two minds about something. *I've* seen you in front of the icebox."

"So that was the moment when our worlds diverged," Monk said, frowning. "Our Gerald made his own dragon and defeated Lional in thaumaturgical combat. Whereas *his* Gerald—"

"Corrupted himself," said the other Monk. "He was trying to do the right thing, but—what was in those grimoires, combined with his unique *potentia*—"

Monk ran a shaking hand over his face. "Bloody hell. No wonder his thaumic signature felt so wrong. Your Gerald, mate, he's got to be—"

"Stopped," whispered the other Monk. "I know. Why d'you think I'm here? He's convinced the world needs saving, and only he can save it. By ruling it. He won't listen to reason. And the things he's done— the things he's doing—what he *plans* . . ." Another shuddering, indrawn breath. "Everything's falling apart so fast. My world's on the brink of war. Half the member states of the United Magical Nations have banded together and delivered an ultimatum. Ottosland must stand down from its demands or face an all-out punitive response."

"And oh wait—let me guess," Reg said darkly. "The other half's agreed to join your Gerald's team in return for a share of the international spoils. *Politics*."

"Exactly," said the other Monk. "And he could win. He's powerful enough, and—and—"

"And you've been helping him?" said Monk, his voice tight. "A few new inventions? A nifty little thaumaturgical gadget here and there?"

The other Monk flinched. "I did try to stop him. We were friends." Another flinch. "I thought we were friends. I thought I could reach him. I never *dreamed* he'd—and once the shadbolt was on I couldn't get it off and every time I tried to argue with him—reason with him—" A terrible, ghastly travesty of a smile. "He really doesn't like it when people say no. This ultimatum, Monk—he'll never surrender. He really will plunge my whole world into war first."

Melissande felt herself go cold. *I don't believe it. He can't be talking about Gerald. Gerald Dunwoody's the most moral man I know.* Glancing at Reg, she saw that the bird was—amazingly—lost for words. Bibbie was trying hard to blink back tears. And Monk—*her* Monk—*Oh, Saint Snodgrass. I never imagined I'd ever see him terrified.*

"How long?" he said, staring intently at the other Monk crumpled on the sofa. "Before the UM nations who haven't gone rogue attack Ottosland?"

"They gave us a week," said the other Monk. "That was four days ago."

"*Four days?*" said Reg, feathers bristling. "And what have you been doing since then, sunshine? Lolling about getting manicures?"

"Reg!" Bibbie looked close to violence. "Shut your beak, you horrible bloody bird! You've got no right to—"

"I'm sorry," said the other Monk. "I worked as—" Abruptly his breathing turned to more coughing, and fresh blood-pink froth bubbled on his lips. "I worked as fast as I could," he said, once he'd caught his breath. "But I had to get my hands on the portable portal and figure out how to tweak it without him noticing and then I had to come up with a plausible reason why I needed to be left strictly undisturbed in the lab and—"

Monk dropped to a crouch beside the other Monk. Took hold of his shoulder and held on tight. "Don't. It's all right. Which nations are on your Gerald's side, d'you remember?"

The other Monk pressed his knuckles to his forehead, grimacing. Another cough. More blood on his lips. "Sorry—it hurts—"

Melissande leaned close. "Try, Monk. Please. I know it's hard, I know you're in pain, but if you want us to help you then you have to help us."

"I know," he grunted, nodding. "Believe me, Mel, I know. Jandria. They were first to join him."

She exchanged a jaundiced look with her Monk. *Well, yes, of course bloody Jandria. Never a crisis brewing that they're not interested in heating up.*

"Fine," she said, trying to sound encouraging despite the churning nausea. "Who else?"

"Oh ducky, forget the laundry list," said Reg. With another flapping of wings she launched herself off the arm of the sofa, landed on the other Monk's knees and stabbed him with her steeliest glare. "Let's just leap ahead to the punch line, shall we? To cut a depressing and abbreviated story even shorter—you came here to fetch our—*my*—Gerald to your world so he can snap his fingers and janitor away your troubles, didn't you?"

The other Monk frowned, muzzily. "Janitor? What? I don't—"

"Never you mind playing the dimwit!" Reg snapped. "Do you expect *my* Gerald to clean up *your* mess or don't you?"

Face screwed up with pain, the other Monk nodded. "I had to come. He's our only hope. Gerald's the only wizard I know who can stop Gerald. The only rogue thaumaturgist in either of our worlds."

"And that's another thing," said Reg, unyielding. "Why pick this world? Why pick *my* Gerald?"

"Sorry," said the other Monk, close to wheezing. "This world was the only one I could find."

"Then all I can say is you didn't look hard enough!" Reg retorted. "Perhaps if you *had* then—"

"Reg," Melissande said softly. "Please. Can't you see he's—"

"Of course I can bloody see!" said Reg, eyes blazing. "I can see he's got no more common sense than *your* Monk, madam! Because how, exactly, does he think *my* Gerald's going to help him? *My* Gerald's not corrupted himself with any of that manky grimoire magic and I'll tell you right now, ducky, he's not going to either." She glared down at the other Monk.

"So your world's going to have to sort *itself* out, Mr. Markham from Next Door. Everybody knows charity begins at home. So you can just pop yourself back there and clean up your own mess."

Shocked, Melissande stared at her. "Reg—how can you *say* that? Gerald's in trouble, he—"

"*His* Gerald. Not mine," Reg snapped. "*My* Gerald would never soil himself with that muck. *My* Gerald *didn't*. And believe me, madam, whoever that is in his world wearing my Gerald's face? He stopped being Gerald months ago."

Monk cleared his throat. "She's right about that much. The Gerald who made that shadbolt—I don't know him. That Gerald Dunwoody's not my friend."

"Maybe he is and maybe he isn't," said Melissande. "But for all we know that Gerald is—is trapped inside those awful magics, just like this other Monk was trapped inside that shadbolt. And if that's true we have to help him!"

"Mel's right," said Bibbie. "He's still Gerald, just like this is still Monk."

"I know," Monk said reluctantly. "And as much as I hate to agree with myself, knowing what I know of *our* Gerald's abilities? If he really did decide to get creative the only wizard I know who could stop him *is* him. And that means—"

"Aren't you noddyheads listening?" Reg screeched. "I said *no* and I meant *no!* You are *not* getting my Gerald mixed up in this!"

Monk dragged his fingers through his hair. "Look, Reg, when you think about it he's already mixed up—"

"One more word out of you, Mr. Clever Clogs, and

I'll do more than bloody poke you in your insignificant unmentionables!" said Reg. Her dark eyes were alight with a fury none of them had ever seen before. "I'll fly to your Uncle Ralph's poncy establishment and tell him what you've been up to lately. *All of it*, sunshine. Chapter and verse. By the time this little canary's finished singing you won't be able to show your face past your front door for ten years! That's if Uncle Ralph doesn't throw you in a dark cell—and trust me when I say I'd bloody cheer if he did!"

Bibbie leaped to her feet. "Oh, really? Is that so? Just who d'you think you're messing with, you washed-up old has-been? We're the *Markhams*, we are, *ducky*, and you don't want to mess with *us!* I'm warning you, Reg—you try hurting my brother and I'll have a go at lifting your hex and then *I'll* be the one cheering while *you*—"

"*Bibbie*," said Melissande, reaching out a hand. "Don't. Can't you see she's terrified?"

"Good!" Bibbie retorted. "And so she should be. I'm not a witch to be trifled with and—"

"Bibbie, *shut up!*" she said. "She's not scared of you. She's scared that if *his* Gerald could risk using those grimoires then so could *our* Gerald, which means—"

"He would not!" Bibbie said hotly. "How can you even suggest it? Our Gerald's too smart for that. He *proved* he's too smart for that by not using them the first time. *His* Gerald must've had a screw loose or something. Or maybe the other Reg drove him bonkers with all her nagging. But whatever the reason, I won't—"

"Bibbie," said Monk, quietly. "Melissande's right. Now do us all a favor and hush up. Reg—"

"Monk Markham, you're Gerald's best friend," said Reg, hopping from the other Monk's knees to the sofa-back as Bibbie turned away, flushed pink with affronted misery. "You *know* what he's like. Show him a lame dog and he won't care what it costs him to save it. Look how he was with that pillock Errol Haythwaite. Bent over backwards to see him proved innocent after every mean and nasty thing the plonker said and did to him. And now you want to—"

"No, Reg, I don't want to," said Monk. "Believe me, I *don't*. But it's not up to me. And it's not up to you, either. This is Gerald's decision. We don't have the right to make it for him."

Melissande looked at her. "We don't, Reg. You know we don't."

"Where is he?" said the other Monk, stirring. "Your Gerald? I need to see him. I need to—"

"He's not here," she said. "Sir Alec sent him on assignment. Do you know your world's Sir Alec?"

The other Monk shuddered. "Not well. And not for long. Melissande—" His beseeching eyes, cloudier now, fixed their gaze on her face. "Please. Get Gerald. *Quickly*. Time's running out. If we don't stop him—" He sat bolt upright, shuddering harder than ever. "Monk—"

"I'm here," Monk said, his voice rough. "It's all right, mate. I'm here."

Leaning forward, the other Monk grabbed his arm pulled him close, eyes alight with an almost fanatical glitter. "You felt him. In the shadbolt. You felt what he is now. He's not your friend. He'll kill everyone. He won't stop until the world's drowning in blood. Stop him. You and your Gerald, Monk. Promise me that. *Promise*."

"I don't know if I can," said Monk, sounding helpless. "I mean—you're me and you couldn't stop him. How am I supposed to stop him if you couldn't?"

Melissande felt her throat close hard. She'd never heard Monk so desperate. So despairing. She'd never seen such a look of distress on his face. And the other Monk's face—his face—

"Reg!" she said alarmed. "Something's wrong—something's happening—*Monk*—"

The other Monk's eyes were flickering back and forth, madly, and he was shuddering so hard his teeth were chattering. No, this wasn't shuddering. He was having some kind of *seizure*. Monk was holding on tight, trying to steady him, but it wasn't doing any good. The other Monk shook and shook, teeth chattering, hair flopping, blood pouring from his nose like water from a tap left on full.

Bibbie went to pieces. "Monk, *stop* it! Monk, *do* something! Help him, call for an ambulance, Monk—"

"Shut up, you silly bint!" Reg shrieked, flapping into her face. "Pull yourself together! Is this any way for a witch to behave?"

"*You* shut up, Reg!" shouted Bibbie, and batted her aside. "That's my *brother*, you gobby old crow!"

And even though she was wrong, even though that *wasn't* her Monk—*their* Monk—in the most horrible and confusing way, yes. It was.

"Come on, mate—come on, mate—" her Monk

was crooning. "We can fix this. Hang on, hang onto me. We'll get you some help. We'll—we can—"

Melissande, one hand pressed to her mouth, watched through hot tears as her Monk did his best. But his best wasn't enough. There was too much blood. Too much wrong. The other Monk shuddered again, one last huge convulsion, then sagged into stillness. Slowly, disbelievingly, her Monk lowered him to the sofa's cushions.

The other Monk's eyes opened, slowly, in his dreadful, dead-white and blood-daubed face. He saw her. Breathed out, softly. His bloodied lips curved in a smile.

"Melissande. I love you."

A moment later, he died.

Reg flapped from the drinks trolley back to the sofa. Looking down at the other Monk, she tipped her head to one side. "Bugger," she said heavily. "That's all we need."

Ignoring the wretched bird, Melissande dropped to her knees beside Monk. He was staring into the dead man's face as though caught in some hideous dream. "Monk . . . Monk?"

"It's my fault," he whispered. "The shadbolt—there wasn't time to be careful. I had to—and there was a trick in it—I did my best—but it was a bastard, Mel. I've never seen anything like it. I thought I could do it. I thought I could free him *and* save him but—" His voice broke. "I did my best."

She slid her arm around his shoulder, her eyes burning. "I know you did. And so did he. He knew it was a risk and he wanted to take it. Monk . . ."

Horribly he laughed, then shrugged her arm free.

Shoved to his feet and stared down at the dead man. "So here's the thing, girls. Here's the big question. What just happened—was it murder . . . or suicide? Can any of you tell me? 'Cause I'm jiggered if I know."

Melissande. I love you. Aching, she risked a hand on her Monk's arm. "It was neither. Monk, you can't blame yourself." She gulped. "This was his Gerald's fault. There's no use dwelling. The question that needs answering now is what are we going to do about this?"

Sighing, he scrubbed his hands over his face then got up to perch on the edge of the sofa. The other Monk—the dead Monk—stared at the ceiling with blank, cloudy eyes. In the fireplace, flames danced and crackled.

Monk looked up. Met her stony gaze briefly, then turned to Bibbie. His sister stood still and slender and silent, fresh tears drying on her cheeks.

"We're going to call Sir Alec," he said grimly. "We're going to get Gerald back here. And then we're going to take care of the madman who's responsible for this."

Sir Alec took a deep breath and furiously throttled the fear. Tried to throttle it—but the fear fought back. The last time he'd been this frightened was during his final janitorial field assignment. The one that had taken him out of the field permanently and thrust him with mixed emotions behind a desk. Since then, fear had become something of a memory . . . but, by God, he was bloody frightened now. Oh, yes. That heart he tried so hard to pretend he didn't have was knock, knock, knocking against his broken-more-than-once ribs.

Bloody hell, Dunwoody. Where did you go?

Thanks to the bane of Ralph's life, his irrepressible and annoyingly irreplaceable nephew Monk Markham, Nettleworth's top secret tracking equipment was the best in the world. Barring certain atmospheric hiccups and the occasional idiosyncratic etheretic fluctuation, with the flip of a switch he could pinpoint the location—via thaumic signature—of every agent in his charge. Thanks to Monk Markham he knew where they all were tonight, every last one of them—save Gerald Dunwoody. Who wasn't in Grande Splotze. Who—if that cryptic message was to be trusted—had never so much as set foot in Grande Splotze.

Which means he never made it all the way through the portal. I watched him walk in—but he never walked out.

Not being a portal mechanic he hadn't driven back to the farm. It would have been a criminal waste of his time. But he'd sent his Department expert out there, was waiting even now to hear his report. But surely, *surely*, if there'd been some kind of catastrophic portal malfunction some alarm *somewhere* would have been triggered. If nothing else positive had emerged from the Wycliffe affair, Ottosland now boasted the best portal diagnostic and warning systems known to thaumaturgics.

It was the height of folly, but he couldn't help it. Abandoning his office with its cheerfully crackling fire and small round crystal that remained stubbornly silent, Sir Alec made his way back down to the monitoring station and went in search of Gerald, again. Passing through the main office he noted that Dalby was still here, in the cubbyhole considered his by virtue of him being—well, Frank Dalby. *Mr.* Dalby. Scourge of the new recruits. Aloofly distant Sir Alec's trusted right-hand man. But Frank, thank God, was nobody's fool. One look at his superior's face and he kept his nose well out of the way. If he was wanted he'd be called for, and that was good enough for him.

Baffled—and when the hell was the last time he'd been *baffled*—he stared at his Department's exclusively upgraded thaumic monitor. Twenty-six steadily burning little blue lights. Twenty-six living, breathing agents, scattered all around the globe. Look, there was Frank, upstairs with his mug of ghastly stewed tea and an asphyxiating cigarette. *And look. There's me.* But nowhere, *nowhere*, could he see Gerald Dunwoody. He wanted to swear. To stamp. To pound his fist in someone's face. All his uncivilized impulses, roaring to be set free.

When Felix Saltman's signal was lost the alarm had triggered seconds after his heart stopped beating. But no alarm had sounded for Agent Dunwoody. So either the monitor was malfunctioning—unlikely—or Gerald wasn't dead, he just wasn't registering on the etheretic plane.

But that would mean he's no longer in this world. And that simply isn't possible. Not even a wizard as powerful as Gerald Dunwoody can step between dimensions as though walking into another room.

Thwarted, he scowled his way back upstairs to his office. The phone started ringing just as he slammed the door.

"What?"

"Tokely, Sir Alec. Portal checks out. No malfunction."

He stared at the phone's receiver, disbelieving. "That can't be right. Check it again."

"Checked it three times, sir."

To argue further would be ridiculous. When it came to portal thaumaturgics, Tokely was the expert's expert. But—"Are you saying you found *nothing* unusual?"

"Didn't say that, sir. There is a slight blip. And of course we've got one incomplete journey. Can't say I've ever seen that happen before. Not without finding—well, you know. Remains."

"You're saying my agent simply vanished halfway to his destination?"

"Sorry, Sir Alec." Now Tokely sounded defensive. *"I know how it looks, but that's my finding. You want a second opinion, call one in. You'll get the same answer."*

"No, a second opinion's not necessary. Written report to me soonest, Tokely. My eyes only. This one's off the books, yes?"

"Whatever you say, sir."

He replaced the receiver, heart knocking hard again. So Gerald really had disappeared on his way to Grande Splotze, with no alarms triggered here or at the DoT. How was that possible? Who could *begin* to—

No, surely not. Not even Ralph's nephew is stupid enough to try something like this. Is he? By God, if Monk Markham's behind this I'll—

On the corner of his desk his crystal marble buzzed. Swamped sickeningly with relief, he snatched it up and hexed open a channel.

"Dunwoody? Dunwoody, where the *hell* are—"

"Um, actually, no, this isn't Gerald," said a thin, nervous voice. *"This is Monk, Sir Alec. Monk Markham. I need to see you urgently. At home. Can you come?"*

"Markham?" he said, incredulous. "How the devil did you get this—" And then he ground his teeth together. "Never mind. I'm on my way."

He was too angry to bid Frank a very late goodnight. Barely nodded at Chawtok, the agent on front desk duty. Swathed in coat and scarf and gloves and hat, he slammed out of the building and into his car and drove at reckless speed through the dark night streets, out to South-West Ott and Chatterly Crescent.

Monk Markham, the incorrigible reprobate, was waiting for him on his charming establishment's front doorstep. "I'm sorry, Sir Alec. I didn't know who else to call."

There was blood on Markham's face. Dried, but recent. His usually cheerful, slightly anarchic demeanor was absent. He was tense, his face pale, and there was something approaching dread in his wide eyes.

Raging temper receded, slightly "This had better be good, Mr. Markham."

Ralph's nephew swallowed. "Actually, sir, it's pretty bad. Please—come in. You won't believe me until you see it for yourself."

So he followed Ralph's nephew inside the old, comfortable house, through to the parlor where he found—surprise, surprise—not only the young troublemaker's precocious sister Emmerabiblia but Melissande Cadwallader and the bird.

And another Monk Markham, dead and stiffening on a couch.

"I'm sorry?" he said, looking at them one by one. "Is this some kind of ridiculous joke?"

"Do we look like we're laughing, sunshine?" said the bird. "Would you say this is my *hysterically amused* face?"

Ralph's appalling nephew wiped his hands down his front. "It's all right. I can explain," he muttered. Then he sighed. "Um—well, actually, I can't. Not really. But I can tell you what's happened, Sir Alec. And then—I hope—you can tell us what to do about it."

He listened to their story, growing colder by the minute. Some small, rational part of his mind was screaming, very rationally, *This is not possible. There are laws of thaumaturgics. They can't be bent like this.* And then he remembered with whom he was dealing and he felt like screaming again, not rationally at all.

"So you see, sir," said Ralph's regrettable nephew, when his insane tale was finished, "I really think we need to get Gerald back here. You know, from wherever you sent him. Because if ever there was a case for your best janitor to work on, I think this is it."

He was so angry he felt perfectly calm. "You constructed an interdimensional portal opener? By accident? And you failed to declare it?"

"He only used it the once," said Ralph's equally regrettable niece, firing up. "It's been in his sock drawer ever since. And it was the other Monk—" she pointed without looking, "—that one, who got his opener to work between worlds. And he only did that because his Gerald's gone insane and has to be stopped. So really it's lucky our Monk made his, isn't it, or he'd probably not understand how this other one works, would he? And then Gerald would have no way of getting through to the other world and stopping his mad self before he kills everyone. So—so you might remember that before you start being mean."

"Really?" he said. "That's your informed, experienced opinion is it, Miss Markham?"

As he'd intended, Miss Markham wilted.

"Sir Alec," said Miss Cadwallader, her chin lifted, her green eyes grim. "I appreciate you're upset but you need to focus on what's relevant. This might be a mess but for once Monk didn't make it. Not our Monk. He didn't bring this poor man here and he's not responsible for what's gone wrong in the other world. But now that we know what's happening there, I believe we *are* responsible for stopping it."

He raised an eyebrow at her. "Are we?"

"Legally? No, of course not," she retorted. "But morally? Ethically? Now that we know people are suffering and dying? Absolutely. So please, recall Gerald so we can sit down and work out how to fix this before it's too late."

She was an eminently reasonable, sensible and decent young woman. They were all of them, at heart, decent young people—well, except for the bird—and while they might frequently drive him to raving distraction they weren't actively evil. Well, with the possible exception of the bird. But none of them seemed to have grasped the true import of these remarkable events. The shock of the other Monk Markham's death, no doubt. Not that the reason mattered. What *mattered* was that if one man could breach the boundary between worlds then who was to say there wasn't another coming close on his heels?

And if the next man turns out to be their Gerald Dunwoody . . . twisted by grimoire magic, his mind overturned by a lust for power . . .

"Given the circumstances," he said, knowing it would be a long time before he slept easily again, "I would agree that our only viable course of action is to recall Mr. Dunwoody from his current mission and apprise him of these startling events. Unfortunately—" He cleared his throat. "Mr. Dunwoody has disappeared. And at this particular moment I have no idea where he is."

CHAPTER FIFTEEN

It was the teasing and flirtatious scent of perfume that woke him. Perfume? In Grande Splotze? In his bachelor guesthouse room in Grande Splotze? Surprised—and just the slightest bit alarmed, because during his training there'd been any number of pointed lectures about *inappropriate personal dalliances while on janitorial assignment*—Gerald kept his eyes closed and waited for recent memory to return.

I was in the car with Sir Alec. There was a farmhouse, somewhere in the middle of nowhere. And a portal. I got into the portal. Sir Alec was operating it. I got into the portal. I had an overnight bag. Sir Alec gave it to me. Something to do with a yellow cravat. I got into the portal.

Hmm. There was a theme developing here. He got into the portal and then—

And then what happened? Did I reach Grande Splotze? Did I meet up with my contact? Perhaps my contact was a woman. Perhaps it's her perfume I can smell. Perhaps things got a bit cozy. Were they supposed to get cozy? I don't recall Sir Alec mentioning it. There was something about elk stew. But elk stew doesn't sound terribly cozy. Actually it sounds bloody awful.

Slowly and carefully, still not opening his eyes, he groped around under the blankets. No. Perfume or no perfume, he was definitely alone in the bed. That was a relief. He couldn't begin to imagine how he'd explain an inappropriate personal dalliance to Sir Alec. Not after all the other things he'd had to explain.

I got into the portal . . .

But did he get out again at the other end? Try as he might he could *not* summon the memory. Recollection ended with the secret Department portal in that remote, abandoned farmhouse and the dry, self-contained look on Sir Alec's never—well, almost never—communicative face.

I got into the portal . . .

Well, obviously he *must've* got out of it again because he was lying in a bed now, wasn't he? So the real question was, whose bed and where was it? And the only way he was going to find the answer to those questions was to stop delaying the inevitable and open his eyes.

"Hello, Gerald," said Bibbie Markham, lounging nearby in a silk-covered chair. She was wearing something startling and not altogether proper in red. No. *Scarlet.* "I was wondering how much longer you were going to keep up the charade."

"Bibbie?" he said blankly. "What are you doing here?" *Dressed like that. In Grande Splotze. In my bachelor guesthouse room in Grande—*

And then he looked past Monk's unexpectedly alarming sister to the wallpaper behind her—muddy beige with mustard stripes—and realized—

Wait a minute. That's my wallpaper. In my room in Monk's house. In Ott. So—I'm at home? How did that happen? And why is Bibbie waving that cigarette holder? She doesn't smoke. Does she? Something's not right here. I think I'm in the middle of a very strange dream.

"No, you're not," said Bibbie, cheerfully. With a tap of one elegantly manicured fingernail she ignited the cigarette in the gold-inlaid ivory holder. "You're wide awake, Gerald." And then she laughed. "How odd, having to call you Gerald. I might have to think up another name for you. Pity your parents didn't give you any spares."

What? What the devil was she talking about? Nonplussed, he stared a little closer at Monk's sister. She looked . . . subtly different. Like Bibbie, and yet not. A thin stream of cigarette smoke curled ceilingwards in front of her face. Her—her *painted* face.

Good lord. I must be dreaming. Bibbie's wearing makeup.

But how could that be possible? In Ottosland only socially inferior theatrical ladies and those fallen girls who regrettably sold their—their—charms—to unscrupulous gentlemen put paint and powder on their faces. A respectable girl who—who—what did they call it? Oh, yes. *Tarting up.* A respectable girl like Bibbie who tarted herself up would be subjected to the most *astringent* criticisms. From what he could understand, even tweed trousers were preferable. With her face painted like that, Markham or not Bibbie would be an instant social outcast. Her family would come down on her like the proverbial ton of bricks.

Reg disapproved of the restrictions, of course. Called them fuddy-duddy and anti-female. She'd worn her war paint every day when she was queen. Nothing wrong with it. Looking her best was the birthright of every woman and bugger the old sourpusses out to rain on the parade.

But Bibbie refused to listen to Reg's demand that she take the fight for female suffrage that next important step. At least, he thought she'd refused to listen. But here she was in his bedroom with powder on her cheeks and paint on her lips and something on her eyelids and lashes that made her blue eyes almost too beautiful to bear. Wearing scarlet.

Bloody hell. How long has it been since I got into that portal?

Bibbie was grinning now, and at least that hadn't changed. Her smile could probably power entire small countries. "Poor thing. You do look confused."

"Um—probably because I am," he said. With a glance down at his chest—good, he was wearing a nightshirt, except—*Oh, lord, who put it on me?*—he cautiously eased himself to sitting and rested his back against the knotty old bedhead. The chamber's curtains were closed, and his clock was missing from the bedside nightstand. "What time is it?"

Bibbie waved the cigarette holder. Smoke wafted through the air, the smell of burning tobacco unpleasantly mingling with her muskily floral perfume. "Oh, yes, well, *time*," she said, disparaging, and inhaled deeply on her unlikely cigarette. Tipping her head back, she proceeded to produce seven perfectly round smoke rings and then pierced all seven with a startling smoke arrow. "D'you know—Gerry—I think we've more important things to talk about than *time*."

She'd done something different to her hair, too. On first glance he'd thought she'd just twisted it up in a new style but now, as she turned her head to watch her smoke rings on the arrow dart about the room, he could see that she'd *cut* it. Cut off her long golden hair and—and—slicked it down with some kind of feminine pomade. And there was something else, too. Something . . . unwholesome . . . that had nothing to do with face paint and cigarettes. A sour tang in the ether.

But that can't be right. Bibbie would never get her thaumaturgical hands dirty. Not like that. Not Bibbie.

Dismayed, he stared at her. "*Bibbie*—enough nonsense, all right? I want to know what time it is—what *day* it is—*and* I want to know what's going on!"

She flicked him a cold glance. "You'd be wise not to take that tone with me, Gerry. I warn you, taking that tone will get you into trouble."

His jaw dropped open. "*What?* Emmerabiblia Markham, are you *squiffed?* Or running a desperately high fever? Or is that not exactly tobacco you're smoking? And anyway, since when do you *smoke?* And—and—wear *makeup.* And *scarlet.* And when did you cut off all your *hair?*" Fed up with the disadvantage of being in bed, like a child, he flung back his blankets and faced her on his bare feet. "Look, either I *am* dreaming or the world's been turned completely upside—"

With a blast of raw thaumic energy the bedroom door blew open and banged against the wall.

"Ha! So he's awake at last!" said the man framed in the doorway. "*Excellent.* Now we'll *really* have some fun!"

"D'you think so, Gerald?" said Bibbie, pouting. "Because so far he's not been any fun at *all*."

Dumbstruck, Gerald watched as Bibbie undulated out of her chair, sashayed across the bedroom floor and—and entwined herself around—around—

Me! That's me! But—but—how can that be me? I'm me. Aren't I?

And then, with a second shock that punched right through his middle, he realized: *No. That's not me. At least—not any more.*

The man lounging in the doorway wore his face. They were the same height, the same weight. All right, the man in the doorway had a—a—*gloss*, a *polish*, that he absolutely lacked. Nevertheless, on the outside—except for the two good eyes—they were the same man.

But on the inside? Thaumaturgically? Oh, Saint Snodgrass . . .

The man—the other Gerald—had a *potentia* that choked the room. It reeked of death. Of murder. It stirred his blood with a visceral dread.

Heart thudding, he looked at the Bibbie before him, with her short hair and lipstick and the powder on her face. At the gold-and-ivory cigarette holder and the sheer scarlet silk dress clinging to those curves that day after day he made himself not notice. He looked at the man she'd called Gerald, whose familiar face hid a heart he couldn't recognize. Who wore the most extraordinary, outlandish scarlet and black full-length silk dressing-gown embroidered with gold dragons, and on his fingers exquisitely wrought and fabulously expensive onyx and ruby rings.

And whose brown eyes burned with a flame he'd

not seen since the last time he faced mad King Lional of New Ottosland.

Lional . . . *Lional* . . . bloated with stolen *potentias*, his greedy mind teeming with the worst kind of incants ever devised and contained in the grimoires he'd kept by his bed, for handy reading.

Terrible memones woke, searing him. The man in the doorway stank of *Pygram's Pestilences*, unforgettable after nine days in that cave. He reeked of *Grummen's Lexicon* and other foul grimoire incants whose names he'd never learned because the texts Lional stole from Pomodoro Uffitzi had been confiscated without him ever laying eyes on them.

I had the chance to use those grimoires and I didn't. But he did. So if this isn't a dream—if he's real, and he's not me, and that's not my Bibbie, and this isn't my bedroom . . .

Sickened understanding crashed over him, so he had to sit on the bed.

Oh, bugger. So much for the theoretical part of theoretical thaumaturgical metaphysics and the postulated existence of parallel worlds.

When Sir Alec found out about this he was going to go *spare*. It was hard enough keeping *one* world safe from thaumaturgical villains. And as for Monk, well, he'd likely explode with excitement. *Monk . . .*

Oh, God. Don't tell me he's gone rotten too.

The thought was enough to make the room spin and his belly heave.

No. No. I don't—I won't—believe that. Not Monk. I have to have one friend left in this place.

The other Gerald was grinning. "I knew you'd work it out. No flies on us, Professor Dunwoody."

He felt like an idiot in his striped flannel nightshirt, but it couldn't be helped. All that mattered now was getting answers . . . and getting home.

"So I'm right? This is a parallel world? An alternative reality? You're some kind of copy of me?"

"No, Professor, it's the real reality," said the other Gerald, a snap in his voice. "*Your* world's the impostor. And so are *you*."

His double's anger lit up the room like sheet lightning. *Right. Yes. So not to be making him cross, Dunwoody.* "Sorry. Sorry," he said hastily. "Poor choice of words. So . . . how did you do it? How did you bring me here?"

His—his—*counterpart*—examined fingernails as beautifully manicured as Bibbie's. "Oh, I can do a lot of things, Professor," he boasted with airy self-congratulation. "Things you can only dream of."

He decided to take a chance. Nothing ventured, nothing gained. "Monk didn't help you?"

"Monk?" The other Gerald raised an eyebrow. And then he smiled. "Oh, Monk. Good old Monk. Yes. Our Mr. Markham's been *wonderfully* helpful."

Bibbie giggled. "Wonderfully."

He had to wait for the nausea to subside before he could speak again. That horrible smile . . . and he'd never, *never* heard Bibbie giggle like that. Sly, like a nasty child. Even her voice had gone breathlessly girlish. The other Gerald's hand trailed suggestively, possessively, up and down her bare arm. He almost squeezed his eyes shut, because that was so *wrong*. But even as he felt repulsed a little part of him thought: *Lucky bastard.*

Time for a distraction. *There really is only one explanation . . .* "It was the portal, wasn't it? You pulled me through to your world using the Department's unregistered portal. While I was traveling to Grande Splotze."

And if that's the case he must have tripped an alarm. Sir Alec will know I've gone missing. Everything's going to be fine.

The other Gerald smoothed his hand over Bibbie's hair. "Look at that, Bibs. We're so clever, aren't we?" He turned. "Yes. It was the portal."

"But—how is that possible? I thought—"

"Oh, Professor!" The other Gerald's eyes opened wide. "Portal thaumaturgics are *amazing*. Convenient travel is just the tip of the iceberg."

"But you're—*we're*—not portal thaumaturgists," he said warily. "That's a highly specialized strand of metaphysical study."

"True," said the other Gerald. "But it so happens I have at my disposal most of the finest thaumaturgical minds in the world."

"Really?" He swallowed. *Oh, lord. This isn't going anywhere good, is it?* "In my experience, getting thaumaturgical experts to work cooperatively makes herding cats look like child's play."

Bibbie giggled again. "Oh, no, it was easy. Gerald's very . . . persuasive."

He took a deep breath and pushed back to his feet. "Yes. I'm sure he is."

"And in case you're thinking—and I know you are," added the other Gerald, "that snatching you from the portal triggered an inconvenient alarm? Sorry, Professor. I'm far too good for that."

Oh. Bugger. Still, it couldn't be helped, so no point dwelling. "I'm sure you are. In fact—"

"You're curious, aren't you?" said the other Gerald, almost taunting. "You're dying to know about my . . . thaumaturgical improvements. Jealous too, no doubt."

Really neither. Not even a little bit. "When did you do it?" he demanded, trying to keep the anger and despair from his voice. "*Why* did you do it? You had to know that you'd be—*changed.*"

And not for the better, but he didn't dare say that.

Instead of answering, the other Gerald put a finger under Bibbie's chin, tipped her face up to meet his and devoured her lips in a long, savage kiss. When at last he released her, blood glinted in the corner of her painted mouth.

"Wander down to the kitchen, Bibs, there's a good girl. See how Melissande's coming with breakfast, and tell her we've got an extra mouth to feed."

Gerald felt the name jolt through him. Melissande? She was here? In the *kitchen*? But—

Does that mean Reg is here, too? God, I almost forgot them. Watching him and Bibbie, it's scrambled my brain.

Bibbie was pouting. "Oh, Gerald. Can't you just—"

"*Bibbie.*"

She went very still. Beneath the thin scarlet silk her breathing was shallow, and fast. A frightened pulse fluttered in the hollow of her throat.

The other Gerald flicked the end of her nose. "There's a good girl."

She left the bedroom without another word.

"When did I enhance my natural abilities?" said the other Gerald, as though there'd been no tense interlude. No primal, punishing kiss. Pushing away from the door jamb he strolled into the room.

Wandered to the window and opened the curtains with a careless wave of his hand. Dull light spilled onto the carpet, sunshine filtering through gathering cloud. The other Gerald frowned. "It's going to rain. Bloody weather. Y'know, once I've got a few other little things sorted out I think I'll look into some meteorological thaumaturgy." He glanced over his shoulder. "Want to help? It could be fun."

"Ah—yes. Why not?" he said carefully. "You're right, that—ah—does sound like fun. But just getting back to what—"

"Forget it," snapped the other Gerald. "The diffident act doesn't fool me. *Nothing* you do will fool me, Professor. Not only because you *are* me—well, the old me, anyway—but because since we took our different paths I've worked very hard to develop my skills. My *potentia*. So don't waste your time. We've got better things to do than shadow box each other."

Gerald let out a shaky breath. "All right then. Straight talking. I can do that. I'm thinking it was New Ottosland. You ignored Reg's advice and got your hands on Lional's collection of grimoires, didn't you?"

The other Gerald's lips curved in a small, scornful smile. "And you didn't."

"No. It wasn't necessary. I still defeated Lional."

"So I gather," said the other Gerald, so disparaging. "And all your victory cost you was your sight."

Unbidden, his fingers came up and touched the skin beneath his blind eye. "Only half of it. I manage. And I'd rather lose my eye than my humanity."

"Oh, please," said the other Gerald. "I give you fair warning, Professor—being lectured puts me in a very bad mood. And whoever's doing the lecturing tends to end up pretty damned sorry."

It felt like the air in the bedroom had chilled by a swift ten degrees. "D'you know," he said softly, "you sound uncannily like Lional when you say things like that."

The other Gerald shrugged. "Then don't lecture me, old chap, and you'll be spared the trip down memory lane."

He wiped a hand across his mouth, trying to banish the foul taste of bile. "So what happened? Did you lose your nerve? Doubt yourself? You shouldn't have. You shouldn't have let fear make—"

"Be careful, Professor!" the other Gerald snapped, and raised a clenched fist. Bright blue thaumic power danced over his skin, crackling the air. "I don't permit anyone to speak to me like that." His lips bared in a snarling smile. "Not even me."

Gerald straightened his spine. The important thing was not to show weakness. *Rabid dogs always attack when they scent fear.* "Something tells me you wouldn't have brought me here only to kill me ten minutes after we met."

"Kill you, Professor?" His counterpart's eyebrows shot up. "Don't be ridiculous. But it's only fair to point out I've no problem with hurting you."

He braced himself, waiting for something terrible to knock him to his knees. But nothing happened. Instead, the other Gerald sighed again and lowered his fist. "This is silly. We're meant to be *friends*. How can we not be friends when you and I have so much in common?"

And that was the question, wasn't it? Just how

much *did* he and this—this other Gerald have in common? Take away the dark magic and how alike were they, really? If the theories and suppositions were correct, he and this man who looked like him had at least started out the same person.

So are we still alike enough for me to reach him? Alike enough for me to stop whatever insane plan he's cooked up, that he wants me to be part of?

He had no idea yet. He needed more time—and more information. "You took them all in, didn't you? Every last incant in those grimoires Lional stole from that criminal idiot Uffitzi."

A small, crimson flame flickered deep in the other Gerald's shining eyes. "Yes, I did, Professor. And let me tell you—it was the best decision I've ever made. I mean, I had power before. I had lots of power. But until those grimoires I had no idea what to do with it."

"And now you do?"

"Yes, Professor," said the other Gerald, and laughed. "Now I do."

He cleared his throat. "Congratulations. Don't suppose you'd like to let me in on the secret?"

The question was bold. Almost aggressive. He half-expected another threat—or worse. Instead, his counterpart thrust his hands in the pockets of his expensive silk dressing-gown and considered him in silence, through half-lidded eyes. Then, after a nerve-shatteringly long pause, he smiled.

"All in good time, Professor. All in good time."

Bugger. It was never encouraging when villains said things like that.

And is that what he is? Is that what I became here? A

villain? Is this Gerald the kind of wizard I'd be hunting, back home?

Stupid question. Of course he was.

I don't understand. My didn't Reg stop me? How could she stand by and let something like this happen?

Reg. Oh lord, he had to ask. And whatever the answer, he'd have to bear it. "And where's our little feathered friend?"

"Who? Reg?" the other Gerald said carelessly. "She's around somewhere. I'm sure you'll see her sooner or later. Why, did you think—" He blinked, as though genuinely surprised. "Oh, Professor, come on. Anyone would think I'm a *monster*. But really, how can I *possibly* be a monster when I'm *you*?"

Dizzy with relief, he closed his eyes. It was crazy to care so much, of course. The Reg in this world wasn't his Reg. Just as the woman in the thin scarlet silk dress wasn't his Emmerabiblia. And yet . . . and yet . . .

It doesn't matter. I still have to save them from what's happening here. I have to save him, from himself if nothing else.

But to do that he had to survive. And to survive he had to play along, at least until he had a better idea of what he was dealing with. Until he'd found this world's Monk, and seen Reg, and Melissande. If they were still themselves then he might have a chance. But if they weren't . . . if they'd turned, like Bibbie . . .

No. No. I'm not going to think about that.

He opened his eyes. "All right. Bottom line, Gerald. Why the hell did you bring me here?"

The other Gerald heaved a theatrical sigh. "Well, it's about time. I was beginning to wonder if you'd *ever* get to the point. Was I always this slow on the uptake, I wonder? Or is this simply a by-product of interdimensional travel?" He pulled a face. "Gosh. I hope not. When Monk emerges from his inventorly trance we'll have him test you, or something. Because if traveling between worlds has fried your synapses, Professor, *I'm* going to be forced back to the drawing board. *Again*."

"Monk's inventing something? What?"

"I'm not telling you," said the other Gerald, horrifyingly playful. "It's a surprise. Now come on. Get dressed. It's way past time for breakfast and I'm starving."

The old, ornate mahogany wardrobe opposite the window was identical to his own. But the clothes inside it . . .

"I can't wear *these!*" he protested, looking at the boldly colored velvets and silk brocades. "They're not me. I'll look like a bloody—"

"Yes?" said the other Gerald, fingers caressing his black-and-gold silk lapel. "Like a bloody what, Professor?"

"Idiot," he said, feeling suddenly reckless. "You can wear what you like, Gerald. That's your business. But I wear tweeds or twill or wool. And if you don't like it, feel free to send me home."

The other Gerald tapped a finger against his chin. "Hmm. I wonder, does that petty little outburst mean you're going to be difficult, Professor? I hope not, because I've enough on my plate without you getting temperamental on me."

"What d'you think?" he retorted. "Since you know me so well."

"I think you're thinking there must be some way to—I don't know—*redeem* me," said the other Gerald, shrugging. "Because I remember that look. That stupid, soft, *I need to save the world* look. But you don't have to, because that's *my* job. And *my* way is much, much more effective. I've gone far beyond the notion of saving it one tedious compliance violation at a time."

He managed a smile of his own. "Funny you should say that, Gerald. So have I."

"Yes, well, whatever it is you're doing these days, I can promise you it'll pale into insignificance compared to *my* feats," the other Gerald retorted. "So I suppose it's only fitting that you wear *tweeds* or *twill* or *wool*." With a great flourish he clapped his hands above his head. Power ripped through the ether, rattling the windowpanes and flapping the curtains. "There you go, Professor. Happy now?"

He looked at the drab brown worsteds, the dull green tweeds, the gray twills and the definitely unsilky white shirts. Good, plain cotton.

"Lovely. Thank you."

"Then get dressed," snapped his counterpart. "We've got a very busy day ahead of us."

Since feeling awkward about dressing in front of himself was clearly ridiculous, he pretended he didn't feel any such thing. Once he'd swapped the striped flannel nightshirt for underdrawers, a singlet, and a dull-as-dishwater worsted suit ensemble complete with braces, white cotton shirt, brown tie, brown socks and brown leather shoes, he looked at his incredibly unlikely captor.

"All done."

"Hideous," said the other Gerald. "I can't believe I used to dress like that. I like *this* so much better."

Another flourishing hand clap—another blast of thaumaturgic power—and the dressing-gown was gone, replaced by a supremely elegant royal blue silk suit and a white silk shirt so dazzling it looked like a snowfield at noon on a cloudless day. The ruby rings were gone too, replaced by diamonds and sapphires.

"You see, Professor? One can be elegant and stylish without being pretentious," said the other Gerald, severely. "You of all people, a tailor's son, should know that. I mean, if Father could see you now he'd roll in his grave."

He felt the blood drain from his face. "That's—you're not—roll in his grave, that's just a figure of—"

"'Fraid not," said the other Gerald, pulling a face. "In my world we're orphans, Professor. Mother and Father's round-the-world trip? In hindsight, the little detour to Ling-Ling wasn't such a good idea." He sighed. "Tragic, isn't it? Now for pity's sake, come *on*. Breakfast's going to be *cold*! And we both know how I feel about cold bacon and eggs."

There was an even nastier shock waiting for him in the kitchen. Their kitchen, his and Bibbie's and Monk's and Reg's. Well, Monk's mostly, but his careless, anarchic friend did love to share. This one was exactly the same, old and cozy and comfortable, right down to the scarred wooden table that only moments ago, it seemed, he and she and Monk and Reg had sat around, laughing and eating pancakes, while Melissande stood at the old-fashioned cooking range whipping up yet another bowlful of batter and pretending their compliments meant nothing at all.

Oh, she was there, this world's Melissande. Short and stocky and red-haired and aproned. But she wasn't laughing and trading quips with Monk and Reg. Instead she was braced against the bench under the window, eyes closed behind her spectacles, head slightly turned away . . . from Bibbie. Bibbie in her scarlet dress, laughing as she plucked whole eggs from the empty air and tossed them at Melissande with a careless cruelty that stopped his heart. Egg yolk and albumen dripped down Mel's face, dragging bits of eggshell with them. The conjured eggs were rotten, their stench thickening the kitchen's air, painting over the proper breakfast smells of bacon and coffee and hot bread and fresh eggs nicely fried.

Worst of all, Melissande was wearing a shadbolt.

"Bibbie!" snapped the other Gerald as he led the way into the kitchen. "If you've started playing before she's finished cooking—"

The other Bibbie's laughter stopped. "No, Gerald. Of course not."

Unappeased, the other Gerald scorched her with a look. "Honestly, did the eggs *have* to be rotten?"

"Well, yes," said Bibbie. "It's not nearly as much fun otherwise, is it?" Pouting, she crossed to him and stroked a teasing finger down his nose. "Come on, don't be a spoilsport. *You* get to punish naughty people. Why can't *I*?"

The other Gerald caught her finger in his mouth and sucked on it, his gaze burning into her eyes. She laughed again, in her throat, and pressed up against him. Plucked her finger from his mouth and brushed it over his lips.

"Was she naughty, Bibs?" the other Gerald murmured. "Why? What did she do?"

Gerald didn't want to know. Shaken, he walked past them straight to Melissande, who hadn't moved or made any attempt to clean herself. Behind the egg-fouled spectacles her eyes were still tight shut. This close to her the stink was overwhelming. If there'd been food in his stomach he'd be heaving it all out. But the stink wasn't important.

"Hey," he said gently. "Melissande—"

At the sound of his voice she flinched and whimpered. Melissande, whimpering? *Oh, Saint Snodgrass. This is so wrong.* "Melissande," he said again, and risked a light touch to her arm. "Please. It's all right. Open your eyes."

She obeyed him, instantly. As though disobedience was too dreadful to contemplate. And seeing him, she sucked in a small and shocked gasp of air.

"What? *What?* I don't— Who are you? Where did you come from? How can—"

"I know," he said. "It's a bugger, isn't it? But you're not dreaming. It's real. *I'm* real." Hesitating, he glanced behind him but the other Gerald and his Bibbie were still lost in each other, stroking and murmuring and laughing under their breaths. He looked back and lowered his voice. "And Mel? Here's the thing you need to believe. *I'm not him.* All right? I'm a Gerald who never read Uffitzi's grimoires. Does that make sense?"

"Yes," she said, choking, her fingers twisting in her ruined apron. "Well, no. Not entirely. But if you say so. Only . . . what does that mean?"

Even in her worst moments, in the cave, when she finally realized what her mad brother had become, she'd not sounded like this: beaten down and hopeless and shackled to fear. But then, in the cave, she'd not been wearing a shadbolt. He didn't dare tamper with it, or even look too closely. A cursory examination showed him it was brutal, though. No wonder she'd not tried to defend herself from the eggs.

"Mel, where's Monk gone? Do you know? And Reg? Is Reg all right? He said she was around, but—"

"Please don't," she whispered. "You mustn't ask me any questions. I'm not allowed to talk to anyone but them."

Tears had started leaking from her green, haunted eyes. Her nose was running too. They'd broken her to pieces.

"Sorry, sorry," he said quickly. "All right. I won't."

Any moment now he'd start weeping himself.

He did this? How could he do this? Is this all because of the grimoires, or was it in him all along? Oh, God. Is it in me? Am I capable of this?

In rejection, in revulsion, he summoned his power out of sleep. Stepped back from weeping, egg-soaked Melissande and undid what cruel, scarlet Bibbie had done. Even as the incant wiped away the rotten muck, cleaned her hair and face and spectacles and apron, sweetened her to roses and blanched the stink from the air, he felt a shiver in her shadbolt. A warped and darkened version of his own *potentia* had made the disgusting thing and now power called to power. A reflection in a mirror.

"Well, Professor, aren't you gallant," said the other Gerald behind him. "Never mind. I'll soon cure you of that. Still, I suppose it had to be done. That *stench*—I was about to lose my appetite."

With a last, reassuring glance at Melissande, he turned. "Glad to be of service, Gerald."

The other Gerald smiled, his arm tucked close around Bibbie. "That's good to hear, Professor. Just the attitude I'm looking for. Now, shall we be seated so the uppity wench can serve us? I like to breakfast in the kitchen. It's so cozy and unpretentious."

Could he eat, after this? He suspected not, but he'd have to try. For one thing he was going to need all his strength . . . and for another he just knew that to refuse this Gerald's hospitality would be a very big mistake. So he took his place at the table, opposite this world's dreadful Gerald and Bibs, and looked at his plate so he'd not have to look at them.

Oh, God. What do I do now? How do I get out of this?

CHAPTER SIXTEEN

He'd thought that in the final analysis, dining with Lional would prove to be the worst culinary experience of his life—but apparently he was being far too optimistic.

Breakfasting with himself was a hundred times worse.

Melissande was so frightened, serving them, that she spilled coffee on the table. The other Gerald's shadbolt punished her, driving her to the floor where she trembled with pain.

"For pity's sake, Gerald!" he protested. "What's the *matter* with you? It's only coffee. You're not even splashed! Let her go!"

The other Gerald considered him. "You're being gallant again, Professor. How bloody tedious!" Then his eyes opened wide. "God, don't tell me you and your Melissande are *canoodling* back in your world?"

He stared. "What? No. We're friends. Good friends. But even if we weren't I'd never do *this* to her. I'd never do this to *anyone*. Now *let her go*."

The other Gerald sighed. "Oh, all right. Just this

once. *Enough*." Melissande slumped, gasping. Sitting back in his chair, he reached for Bibbie and linked his fingers with hers. "As for thinking you'd not slap a naughty wrist, Professor, well, don't be so sure. You and I might've taken different paths back in New Ottosland but as I've already said, we're still the same man. Whatever I can do, believe me . . . you can do it too."

Released from punishment and clambered back to her feet, Melissande set about cleaning up the mess from the dropped coffee pot and the tiny trickle on the table. Gerald watched her closely, his stomach churning. He could still feel her pain, fading tremors in the ether. Then he locked gazes with his counterpart and shook his head.

"You're wrong, Gerald. I'm not the same as you. I never touched those grimoires. We're two different men now."

His counterpart shrugged, unperturbed. "We'll see. Now hurry up and finish eating. We've got things to do and places to go."

Ignoring his unquiet belly, he ate. Conversation languished. He had questions but he knew this Gerald wouldn't answer them, so there was no point asking and he lacked the intestinal fortitude for idle, carefree chitchat. Besides, the other Gerald and his Bibbie were so busy canoodling he doubted they'd have heard him even if he tried. And talking to Melissande was out of the question. At least it was in front of them.

The dreadful meal ended, eventually. As Melissande started to clear the table of plates and cutlery, the other Gerald gave Bibbie one last, lascivious look then stood. "Right. Run along upstairs, my dove, and make yourself beautiful. You know it's important to dazzle the locals."

Bibbie blew him a kiss and sauntered out of the kitchen.

"And as for you, Professor—"

"I'm going to help Melissande with the dishes," he said. "You can come and fetch me when it's time to go wherever it is we're going."

The other Gerald looked at him in stony silence, then abruptly smiled. "Fine. Suit yourself. Have a cozy chat. But she's not going to tell you anything that could possibly hurt me."

"I never thought for a moment she would."

Standing, the other Gerald laughed. "Liar. Oh— and if you were thinking about making a run for it? I wouldn't. The house is quite secure, Professor." The kitchen door closed gently behind him.

Secure? What did that mean? He reached out, cautiously testing the ether, and winced. Oh. Right. He'd been too distracted before to feel it, but a tangle of incants bound the old house in Chatterly Crescent like lights strung on a Solstice tree. How odd, feeling his own *potentia* in the hexes, knowing he hadn't created them. They were vicious. If he was idiot enough to try leaving the premises without the right thaumic password he'd be ripped to bloody shreds the moment his fingers touched window or door.

Very slick. Very nasty. Score one for Gerald.

"You're a fool to push," said Melissande, running hot water into the sink. "People are like bugs to him now. He squashes them without thinking."

He fetched a fresh tea towel from the drawer and

threaded it through his hands. "He won't squash me. He needs me for something."

Melissande started washing the dishes. "What?"

He shrugged. "I don't know. He won't tell me."

"Well, *I* can tell you this much . . . whatever it is, it won't be good." She put the first clean plate into the dish rack. "So he's kidnapped you from an alternative reality, has he?"

Of course she'd worked it out. She was one of the three smartest women he knew. "'Fraid so," he said, taking the plate and drying it. "I just wish I knew how. You don't suppose—" He hesitated. "Would Monk have helped him? Your Monk, I mean."

"I expect so," said Melissande, watching him return the clean plate to its rightful place. "You know, that's really quite off-putting. You've never set foot in this kitchen, yet you know where the tea towels are and where the plates live. I wonder if life could get any more peculiar?"

"I'm sorry," he said, seeing the pain in her set face. "What you've been through—what you're going through—" He shook his head. "I'm sorry."

"Why? None of this is your fault," she said, trying to sound indifferent. "It's just the way things turned out. For us, anyway."

She set two more plates in the rack then handed him a third. Drying it, watching her, he thought she was going to ask him something. But then her lips firmed and she gave a tiny shake of her head, as though she were having a silent conversation with herself.

"What?" he said, holding the dried plate and tea towel. "Go on. Ask. It's all right."

The look she gave him was full of fear and sarcasm. "Really? How would you know?"

The imprisoning shadbolt was sunk deep in her etheretic aura. Given her limited *potentia* it was a far more powerful binding than was necessary. Much crueler. He could *feel* it waiting for her to trip up, say the wrong thing or wear the wrong expression, so it could tighten its grip on her and make her pay.

Shamed, he turned away. "Sorry. You're right." He put the plate in the cupboard. "I don't know anything."

She didn't contradict him. Instead she made short work of the dirty cutlery then reached for the bacon pan. But halfway through scrubbing she stopped, her spectacles foggy. "Your world," she said, her voice low. "Is it better than this one?"

"Yes," he said, when he could speak past the lump in his throat. "Much."

"You and me . . . after New Ottosland—we stayed in touch?"

He nodded. "We certainly did."

"And am I happy there? In your world?"

The note of hope in her voice nearly broke him. *How can I tell her without making things worse? But then how can I lie? She deserves the truth.* "Very. At least, you are when you're not worrying about the agency or rousing on Monk for being reckless or scolding Reg for—"

"No, don't mind me," she said, one hand raised and dripping suds, even as tears rolled down her thin cheeks. "I'm glad for me. Honestly. Your me. I'm glad for you, that things are good in your world." On a deep breath she got back to scrubbing. "I hope you make it home again, Gerald. I hope—" Another deep breath. "I hope she knows how lucky she is."

"Melissande . . ." he said, aching. "If there's any way I can help you, I will. If I can get that bloody shadbolt off you, I will. I'll—"

She shoved the scrubbed pan at him. "That's sweet, really. It's easy to forget you used to be a kind and decent man."

He didn't know what to say to that, so he took the pan and tea-toweled it dry.

"There's nothing you can do for me, Gerald," she said calmly. "I mean, I'm sure you could get rid of this shadbolt but he'd only replace it with something worse. And then he'd make you very sorry that you interfered. Don't interfere with him, Gerald. Don't get in his way. Nothing good happens to anyone who gets in his way."

"But—" He stared at her. "I can't *help* him, Melissande. Not if what he wants me to do means people will get hurt."

She snorted. "Trust me, Gerald, if he shadbolts you then you'll not have a choice. D'you honestly think *Monk* wants to help him? He's shadbolted just like me."

Oh, lord. Monk. "Where is he, Melissande? And where's Reg?"

"I don't know," she said, scrubbing at the last pan. "I haven't seen either of them for nearly six months."

Feeling sick, he took the cleaned egg pan from her. "He said they were alive. Do you think he was lying?"

"About Monk?" She shook her head. "No. He

needs Monk for his thaumaturgics. As for Reg, who knows? I mean, she's Reg. He loves that stupid bird. Or he used to. But the last time I saw her she was still trying to change his mind, and these days Gerald doesn't like being challenged. He's got a new motto, you see. *Be reasonable and do it my way.*"

"Oh." Heart sinking, he put the egg pan away with the other pots. "Melissande . . . how bad is it out there?" He nodded at the window, at the unknown world beyond it. "What can I expect to find?"

She pulled the sink's plug then fetched another tea towel. "Misery," she said, starting on the cutlery. "Fear. Our Gerald's got all of Ottosland gripped tight in his fist. And the only way you'll get him to let go of it is by cutting off his hand." Her eyes glittered. "Or better yet, his head."

He swallowed. "You hate him."

"Of course I do," she said. "And so would you, if you were me."

Yes, he probably would.

"I hate Emmerabiblia, too," she added. "Even if she is Monk's sister. Sly little trollop." Her mouth pinched. "In your world, are you and she—"

"No," he said, and had to clear his throat. "But I like her. In my world she's—ah—well. She's different. In my world you like her, too. In fact—"

"Stop," she said, turning away. "Don't tell me any more about your world. I can hardly stand my life as it is."

Oh, lord. "I'm sorry."

"And stop *apologizing*," she snapped. "This isn't your fault. Like you said, you aren't him."

I really bloody hope not. "Look—getting back to him,"

he said diffidently. "What about the government? Surely he didn't just . . . stroll in and take it over?"

"Actually?" She shrugged. "That's exactly what he did. Very nicely at first. He only wanted to help. He solved a few sticky problems and everyone was thrilled. Solved a few more, and still everyone was thrilled. And then he started . . . butting in. So people started having second thoughts, but by then it was too late. And when you're the only rogue wizard in the world, Gerald, and you've got more thaumaturgical firepower at your fingertips than a hundred regular wizards rolled into one, and no conscience at all, well—I'm afraid you can do pretty much what you like."

He felt as confused now as when he'd first opened his eyes in the bedroom that wasn't really his bedroom. "But—but—what about the United Magical Nations? Surely someone's *reported* him. I mean, those grimoires Lional stole from Uffitzi, they're on the proscribed list. They're *illegal*. There are sanctions for using them. Surely *someone* must've—"

Sighing, Melissande put down the tea towel and the forks she was drying. "Gerald . . ." She took her hands in his. "You're not listening. He's made himself *untouchable*."

"I'm sorry," he said. "I don't believe that. *Nobody's* untouchable. Somebody somewhere is fighting him. They have to be. Surely you've heard *something*, a whisper, a—a rumor even, of—"

She let go of him and stepped back, shaking her head. "You really don't grasp the enormity of what's happened here, do you? Gerald, I've not left this house for seven months. Aside from him and Bibbie, you're the only person I've spoken to since I was shadbolted and prisoned beneath this roof. For all I know there *is* no more government and Central Ott's nothing but a smoking ruin."

"Oh, but—surely there has to be a government," he protested. "I mean, every country has a government, Melissande. You know. Lords and ministers and bureaucrats and pen-pushers. We're bloody overrun with them back home. A country can't *function* without a government. You know that better than anyone. You used to be a prime minister."

"For a brother who got rid of his government, remember?" she retorted. "I wouldn't be at all surprised if Gerald's not taken a page out of Lional's instruction manual and done the same thing." Frowning, she reached for the dried cutlery and began putting it away. "Gerald . . . about Lional . . . your Lional, I mean . . ."

Oh, *lord*. "I'm sorry," he said. "But he died."

She nodded, closed the cutlery drawer then picked up the tea towel. "Here, too. Gerald killed him." She looked at him. "Did you . . . ?"

"I'm sorry. I tried not to. I did. But . . ."

"I know," she said, shrugging. "I don't blame you. He'd gone quite mad."

It was her dull resignation that broke his heart. "Look, Melissande—I can't believe there's no hope of fixing things here. What about Kallarap? I know Shugat's not big on getting involved in anything not Kallarapi but under the circusmtances you'd think—"

"Rupert asked," she said, grimacing. "More than once. It was no use. And I made him promise that no matter what happened he wouldn't try helping me on his own. There's nothing he can do, anyway. He's not a wizard and New Ottosland's weak. Gerald . . ." Stepping closer, she rested her hand on his arm. "It's awful you've been dragged here, into our mess. And if there's the slightest chance of you escaping back to your own world, you should take it. Reg was right. The magic in those grimoires ruined you. In a way it killed you. So don't be a hero. You can't save us. Nobody can. But it would make living this nightmare more bearable if I knew you were home safe. If I knew that somewhere I had a life worth living."

"Oh, *Mel*," he whispered, and pulled her to him in a desperate hug. "How can I do that? I can't leave you here alone with—"

The kitchen door crashed open. "Oh, stop groping that silly cow, Professor, and come on!" snarled the other Gerald. "Thanks to Bibbie, who insists on doing her makeup by hand, God alone knows why, we're running late. And I'm expecting a *very* important call this morning. I swear, if I miss it because she can't make up her mind about bloody *lipstick* . . ."

Still holding on to Melissande, he kissed her cheek. "Don't give up hope just yet," he said softly. "I know things look bleak but . . . please, don't give up."

"*Professor,*" said the other Gerald. He sounded dangerous now.

He let her go and turned. "Yes. All right. I'm coming."

"You'd be wise not to try me, you know," said the other Gerald, slamming the kitchen door shut behind them and stalking off along the corridor. "My plans have reached a critical phase and waiting puts me in a very bad mood. So don't make me testy. Because while it might not suit me to hurt you I can always hurt *her*. Cross me and I will. My word as a wizard." A scathing backwards glance. "Do you believe me, Professor? Say you believe me."

Oh, lord. "Yes, Gerald. I believe you."

"Good," said the other Gerald, and picked up his pace.

Bibbie was waiting at the old house's front door, changed out of her scanty scarlet dress into an exotically shimmering neck-to-ankle garment made entirely of multi-colored Fandawandi silk. To complete her decorous deception she'd added a hat that seemed to be adorned with enough bits of parrot to render an entire flock extinct.

"There you are," she said, seeing them, her shiny pink lips pouting. "All that shouting and waving your arms about and now here I am twiddling my thumbs while you—"

"Put a sock in it, Bibs," growled the other Gerald. "Before I put a sock in it for you."

Bibbie wilted. "Sorry, Gerald," she murmured, and meekly followed him outside.

Gerald, his heart painfully thumping, fell into step behind the appalling pair. Parked outside the front gate was an enormous gleaming silver car, the most luxurious and expensive-looking model he'd ever seen. He couldn't be sure, but he thought it was a Kingsmark. Remembering Monk's dilapidated and unreliable jalopy, and despite his current predicament, he couldn't help a soft whistle of admiration.

The other Gerald flicked him a disdainful look.

"What, you were expecting a clunker? Hardly. You can ride in the back."

He nodded. "Of course, Gerald. Whatever you say."

And that would have to be his mantra for the next little while. Until he knew what his other self wanted from him . . . and he'd worked out a way to make sure the mad bastard never got it.

As well as being a stunning example of automotive design, the other Gerald's expensive car—like the house—was hexed, smothered bumper to bumper in powerful incants designed to deflect both physical and thaumaturgical attack. Interesting. It surely suggested that even with his fist gripping tight, he still had powerful enemies. Or was afraid he might have powerful enemies. Something certainly worth bearing in mind.

If I can find out who he's scared of—make contact with them—maybe we could work together. I'll work with anyone to see him brought down, even Errol Haythwaite. Because the enemy of my enemy is absolutely my new best friend.

The Kingsmark's engine turned over smoothly, purring like Tavistock. Behind the wheel the other Gerald pulled away from the pavement, Bibbie pretty and poisonous at his side.

Gerald let his head fall back against the seat.

Bloody hell, Reg. Wish me luck, ducky, wherever you are.

"All right, Professor," said the other Gerald, after they'd been driving for about twenty minutes. "The time has come for you to close your eyes."

Now there was an idea. If he closed his eyes maybe

when he opened them again he'd find himself back in his real bed, in Monk's real house, at home in real Ottosland. That would be nice.

Oh, give it a rest, Dunnywood. This really is happening. You're never going to wish it away.

Looking out of the passenger window had proven pointless—every piece of glass save the windshield was hexed to keep the world beyond it a mystery. It was like traveling inside a luxurious shoebox. He'd done his best to peer between the front seats and out of the more lightly-hexed windshield, but the other Gerald had sworn at him and told him to bloody well sit back and stop wriggling or else. Still. He'd seen enough to know that they were definitely heading down to the city center. And what was there? Government House. Various ministry buildings, including the Department of Thaumaturgy's stately home. The Botanical Gardens. The Old Parade Ground. The Mint. The National Art Gallery. The Opera—

"Eyes *closed*, Gerry," said Bibbie, squirmed around in the front passenger seat and frowning at him. "Aren't you paying attention?"

Dear lord, she was *appalling*. How could she possibly be related—thaumaturgically or otherwise—to his own sweet Emmerabiblia?

"Sorry," he muttered. "Eyes closing now."

But slowly, so he could try to snatch one last glimpse of the world outside their car. As his eyelids drifted shut he caught sight of the city's world famous Botanical Gardens, and with them a corner hint of the Department of Thaumaturgy building. Above and beyond them a tiny snatch of airship floated in the cloudy sky, he thought above the Grand Ott

Portal Station. *Ha. Maybe it's one of Ambrose Wycliffe's, if he's still alive here.* And then, because he couldn't stall any longer, he let his eyes close completely and the world beyond the windshield disappeared.

He felt the car take a right-hand turn, away from the Gardens and his old stamping ground, the DoT. And that meant—that meant—what was in this specific direction? Oh yes. They must be heading for Ott's big ceremonial parade ground, smack bang in the middle of the sprawling metropolis. Not that it was used for ceremonial parades anymore. At least, not often. Not in his world anyway. Back home the empty space was used for open-air theatrical productions and Keys to the City ceremonies and War Remembrance services. Jolly civic get-togethers like that. What it was used for in this Ott, he couldn't imagine . . . although *nothing jolly* seemed a pretty safe bet. Whatever the truth was, he was starting to think it would turn out to be something else he really didn't want to know.

And what I do want to know, this Gerald won't tell me.

While he sat silently in the back seat, feeling stupid with his eyes closed, Bibbie prattled on about some upcoming grand society reception. A glittering event, all the important people coming. She started to name names but her Gerald shut her up. After a moment's frightened silence she started prattling again, her voice brittle beneath the gaiety. This time she was careful to talk only of clothes and jewels and who was yet to be invited and what she wanted on the menu. Then she and her Gerald started arguing about the merits of smoked salmon and caviar.

With his captors momentarily distracted, he grabbed his chance with both hands and took a closer look at Bibbie's aura. He had to know what she'd done to herself. She was nowhere near as rotten as this Gerald, but she'd warped her sweetness somehow. If he could work out what incants she'd absorbed then maybe, just maybe, he could undo the damage. If he could restore her to the Bibbie he knew and—and cared for—perhaps he'd have found his first ally.

God knows I need all the help I can get.

And the thought of leaving her like this, twisted and distorted, was more than he could stomach. But before he'd managed to identify the first dark incant tainting her etheretic aura the other Gerald shushed Monk's sister with a sharp word and started to slow the car.

"All right, Professor," he said, so abominably *cheerful*. "We're here. And we've just enough time to spare to have ourselves a nice little stroll around."

"Stroll around?" he said, lifting his eyelids. *Ha, I was right. This is the parade ground.* "In public? Don't you want to keep me under wraps? I mean, aren't I going to be a bit difficult to explain?"

Looking over his shoulder, the other Gerald smiled the blood-chilling smile that rendered him a perfect stranger. "That won't be a problem. I've had the area closed. Come along!"

So Melissande really hadn't been exaggerating. This Gerald had the power to arrange the city's workings to suit himself. Even incomplete, the picture was getting worse and worse. Beneath his plain cotton shirt and his drab brown suit his skin was sticky with sweat. He had to wait for his counterpart to unhex his door and open it.

"Just one more thing, Professor," the other Gerald

said, out of the car now and leaning down, his hand on the rear passenger door's handle, his body blocking escape. Deep in his eyes, the crimson flames flickered. "You'll notice that as a courtesy I've not restrained you. No shadbolt. No booby-traps. Not even a little *docilianti* to keep you at my heels. I'm going to assume you appreciate that gesture. I'm going to assume you'll not disrespect my hospitality or betray my trust by trying anything stupid—say, like running away."

Keep him sweet, keep him sweet . . . "Of course not, Gerald."

"Good," said his counterpart. "Because I wasn't joking. I will make Melissande pay for your mistakes. And if those mistakes are big enough, well, I'll kick your ass too. And you might as well know now, Professor, so there aren't any misunderstandings. Compared to me? Lional of New Ottosland was a slobbering sentimentalist."

A bolt of the darkest, purest fear he'd ever felt shafted through him. "This is crazy," he whispered. "Gerald, what *happened* to you? What went wrong? We weren't brought up to be cruel, or—or despotic. Our parents are—were—lovely people. And we were—we were *good*. I can't believe that even *Grummen's Lexicon* and those other grimoires could've changed you *this* much."

The other Gerald laughed. "Don't be an idiot. You think I stopped there? Uffitzi's paltry library was only the beginning."

"Oh," he said blankly. "Well. That probably explains it." He swallowed. "So . . . we're talking the entire Internationally Proscribed Index?"

"And one or two collections that slipped through

the cracks," said his counterpart. "Let's just say I'm the most well-rounded wizard *you're* ever likely to meet. And that I can deal with you as easily as swatting a fly."

He nodded, bacon and fried egg churning in his guts. "It's all right. I believe you." *Except—if that's the case, then why do you need me? Whatever you're planning, Gerald, why don't you just get on with it?* "And like I said, I won't try anything. I promise."

"*Excellent,*" said the other Gerald, and stepped back from the car. "But you know—just in case you're trying to pull a swifty? If you're thinking you might, I don't know, bide your time and try something foolish when my guard's down? There are one or two things I really need you to see."

Which means I really don't want to see them, doesn't it?

But he had no choice. All he could do was play along until he had a chance to come up with some kind of plan.

Because there's still the Monk in this world. I have to believe that Melissande's right and he's not let himself be corrupted too. And my Monk, he's a bloody genius. He'll work out what's happened and he'll find a way to get me home. Bibbie—my Bibbie—she'll help him. And Sir Alec. The whole Department. All the janitors—even Mr. Dalby. I'm not alone. It just feels that way.

Steeling himself, he clambered out of the posh car—and nearly fell on his ass.

"Bloody hell!"

What had been an open air civic gathering place was now a forbiddingly-walled enclosure, the red brick barriers standing some fifteen feet high.

Enormous wrought-iron gates guarded a locked entrance, and frozen over the gates in a nightmare greeting—or warning—

His counterpart sighed. "Magnificent, isn't she? Quite the souvenir if I do say so myself."

She was the dragon he—they—had made for Lional. Even in the glum, cloud-filtered light the creature's crimson and emerald scales flashed brilliant. Suspended in mid-air, wings spread wide, lower jaw unhinged to display its full array of fearsome, poison-slicked teeth, tail poised to lash, taloned feet outstretched, the dragon reared above the wrought-iron gates so lifelike, so terrifying—

"God," he said, turning. "It's dead, isn't it? Tell me it's dead!"

Bibbie giggled. "You big baby. Of *course* it's dead."

"Dead and thaumaturgically preserved," added the other Gerald. "For posterity. Because she really is bloody beautiful, isn't she?"

The last thing he wanted to do was agree, but he had no choice. Indeed the dragon was—had always been—beautiful. He nodded. "Yes."

The other Gerald sighed. "Such a shame I had to replace two of the teeth with thaumaturgical fakes."

"They got broken?"

"Sort of."

Oh. Well. All moral considerations aside it was a shame, really. Like a magnet the dragon drew his horrified, fascinated gaze. Cautiously he stretched out his *potentia*. The strength of the incants surrounding the creature did knock him back a step, but he managed to keep his balance and stay on his feet.

Beneath the complex network of preservation and

immobilization hexes he could feel decaying remnants of the *Tantigliani sympathetico* . . . and mingled with that, a lingering memory of Lional.

He felt his belly turn over as bile flooded his mouth.

The other Gerald laughed. "You know what they say, Professor. Look, but don't touch."

He pulled back his *potentia*, shaking, and waited for the churning nausea to subside. "It's very impressive."

"Isn't it?" said his counterpart, smugly pleased. "What did you do with your dragon, Professor? No—wait—don't tell me. You buried her. Right?"

He nodded, his gaze still riveted to the horribly magnificent beast overhead. "Of course. Thanks to the *sympathetico*, Lional and that thing were inextricably bound. To bury him without the dragon would've been like burying him without an arm, or a leg."

"Or a head," said the other Gerald. "But then, since my Lional's not buried either it isn't something I need to worry about."

"Not that you needed to worry at all," added Bibbie. "I mean, he was a rotter and he deserved what he got."

Gerald felt a cold shiver skitter over his skin. "And what did he get? If you don't mind me asking."

"All in good time, Professor," said the other Gerald briskly. "Let's get cracking, shall we? I've a lot planned for today."

With a snap of his fingers he unhexed the lethally hexed wrought-iron gates, which silently swung open to admit them. Gerald hung back, letting his counterpart and Bibbie lead the way. Once they were just comfortably far enough ahead he followed and, trying not to appear eagerly curious, looked around the enclosed parade ground. It seemed they were alone. He couldn't see anyone else. But there was a scattered collection of large, opaque domes. They looked like enormous upended, smoked-glass soup bowls. Most peculiar. But he didn't dare poke at them to learn exactly what they were. Everything in here was hexed, he could feel the incants skittering against his skin. Poke too hard, or at the wrong thing, and he might set off a thaumaturgical booby-trap.

The wrought-iron gates clanged shut behind them, their hexes reigniting as metal kissed metal. He felt that, too, a deep shudder in his *potentia*. The air reeked of coercive magics, a sour tang aftertaste with every breath he took. So unlike his own city of Ott was it that he found it hard to believe they'd ever been the same place.

Like me and this Gerald. We have no common ground.

So how he was supposed to reach him, get him to turn back from his dark, destructive path, he had no idea.

But I have to try.

CHAPTER SEVENTEEN

The other Gerald strode ahead, Bibbie by his side, clearly enjoying himself. Like a child on an outing. Then, realizing he'd left his reluctant guest behind he slowed and, not turning, raised his right hand. "Come along, Professor. I hate people who *dawdle*." He waggled a finger and the air sizzled, suggestively. "Chop chop!"

"Sorry," he muttered, and prudently lengthened his stride.

To his surprise Bibbie slowed her pace until he'd caught up with her. Even more surprisingly she fell into step beside him and linked one silken arm through his.

"Now tell me, Gerry," she said, archly playful. "The Bibbie in your world—is she as pretty and as scintillating and as fascinating as me?"

"Um . . ." He looked down at the gloved hand tucked into the crook of his elbow, then glanced at the other Gerald, sauntering ahead. Every instinct told him the man would be . . . possessive. But if he snubbed her, the other Gerald would probably take offense. And if he praised *his* Bibbie, this one would probably slap him—or worse. *Talk about tap-dancing on eggshells.* "My—I mean, the other Bibbie? She's—ah—she's different. You know. She's her own person."

"Hmmph," said Bibbie, wrinkling her perfect nose. "*Different.* I know what *that* means. *I* used to be repressed too. Oh, I *thought* I was daring, flouting the rules, playing with stupid stuff like ethergenics. Ha. As if silly ethergenics is the cutting edge of witchcraft. But then you—I mean *he*—came back from New Ottosland and . . ." She sighed. "Well. Everything changed."

"For the better?" he asked quietly, and looked at her sidelong. Beneath the polished confidence, could he sense doubt? And if he could . . . *I have to risk it. I might not get another chance.* "Bibbie—sometimes what starts off as fun and games can turn into something else. Something frightening. If you're not happy—if you're having second thoughts—"

She snatched her arm back. Scorched him with her eyes. "Don't be silly. I've never been happier. The things I can do now—all my dreams are coming true! If you think I have any regrets, *Gerry*, then it's clear as glass you don't know me at all."

Soft laughter in front of them. "Now, now, Professor," said the other Gerald, spinning around to walk backwards. His eyes were glittering with a gleeful malice. "Don't you be naughty. She's *my* Emmerabiblia. If you didn't get anywhere with yours, well, that's too bad. You've missed out on quite a treat. But in case you're forgetting, you and I are singletons. Spoiled only children. And everybody knows only children don't share."

He made himself hold his counterpart's intimidating gaze. "We used to."

"Oh, come *on*, Professor," the other Gerald retorted. "This is *you* you're talking to, remember? We only shared then because the cousins were bullies and we were too afraid to fight back. But I'm not afraid of bullies any more. Even better, I'm not afraid of myself. On the contrary, I've *embraced* myself. I *adore* the new me." A quick, sly smile. "And you will too. In time. I promise."

Angry despair robbed him of speech for a moment. *No, I'm pretty sure I won't.* But there was no point arguing. He cleared his throat. "Look— Gerald—what are we doing here, exactly?"

"We're on a tour, Professor," his counterpart said brightly, still walking backwards, as light and confident on his feet as a circus performer. "Trust me, the exhibits here are marvelously educational. The way I see it, they might even save your life."

Exhibits? That's what those opaque domes were? So had this Gerald turned the ceremonial parade ground into some kind of open-air museum? As his counterpart spun around to face forward again, fingers summoning Bibbie to his side with an impatient snap, he took another look at the dome directly ahead.

This close, the level of ambient thaumaturgics in the ether was much higher. So high, in fact, that the air felt almost syrupy. A little hard to push through. Whatever was hidden within that opaque dome it was surrounded by impressively powerful incants.

His own *potentia* was twitching in response—but until this moment he hadn't noticed. Instead he'd let himself be distracted by the Gerald and Bibbie strolling in front of him. Damn. He really was off his game. And why was that? The shock of his abrupt transdimensional dislocation? Or maybe the equally disconcerting effect of suddenly being turned into a twin. Seeing Melissande shadbolted, and Bibbie being cruel. And then he shook himself.

It doesn't matter why. You can't afford to be off your game, Dunnywood, so bloody well pull yourself together. You're a trained professional troubleshooter. A janitor. Situations like this are meant to be your meat and drink.

True. Except what he was facing here and now felt like having to drink dry an ocean and swallow a continent's worth of cows.

"And here we are!" announced the other Gerald, halting. "At what you might call Exhibit A, Professor. Or—as I prefer to think of it—Object Lesson Number One." He laughed. "I'll give you three guesses what's inside."

He stared at the shimmering, impenetrable dome. "You could give me thirty and it wouldn't make a difference. If you want to show me something, Gerald, then show me. I don't understand why we need to play games."

That earned him a sharp look. "Trust me, Professor, I'm not playing. Just ask Lional if you don't believe me."

A fingersnap, one whispered word, and a moment later the opaque dome turned to mist and blew away. The ether sighed with the release of thaumic stresses. Heart thudding, Gerald stared at what was now revealed.

Just ask Lional . . .

Who, like his precious dragon, was dead and preserved with powerful incants. Dead and staked to a rectangle of turf, pinned in place with dragon teeth. Dead with the blood still fresh, with the wounds that killed him still gaping, dead with his mouth open in one last, frozen scream.

"Oh, Professor," said the other Gerald, watching. "You feel *sorry* for him? After the *cave*?"

Slowly he lowered his hand from his mouth. Took a deep breath, even though the syrupy air stank of foul incants, and shook his head. "No, Gerald. Not for him."

His counterpart laughed, incredulous. "For *me*? Really? Do I look like I need your pathetic pity?"

Sickened, he risked another glance at Lional. "No."

"Professor . . ." The other Gerald ran a hand over his hair, everything about him impatient and irked. "I'm disappointed. I never would've pegged you as a hypocrite. You admitted it yourself—the Lional in your world is dead. So what—you expect me to believe he choked on a fishbone?"

Gerald shook his head. "No. I killed him. Him and the dragon together. But afterwards I gave him to Mel and Rupert for a decent, private burial. I didn't—I *couldn't*—" He had to wait until his voice was trustworthy. "Why is he here? Like *this*. Why have you—"

"Oh, *Professor*," snapped his counterpart. "Why d'you think? Because a picture is worth a thousand words, isn't it?"

"The parade ground's only empty this morning,"

Bibbie added. She seemed completely unconcerned by the mutilated man—corpse—at her feet. "As a special treat for you, Gerry. Ordinarily it's jam-packed, you know. Because it's the law that everyone in Ott comes to visit at least once a week, every week. And if you don't live in Ott it's once a month, which I think is very reasonable." She stroked the other Gerald's arm. "Kind of like church, really, only far less boring."

Dazed, he stared at them. "Everyone? You mean even the children are—"

"Oh, *especially* the children," she said, her beautiful blue eyes wide. "It's very important that they understand."

Understand what? he wanted to scream. *That you and your young man are stark staring bloody bonkers?*

"So, anyway," said the other Gerald, and snapped his fingers again. Instantly that smoky opacity began to reform, bowl-like, mercifully obliterating Lional from sight. "That's what happened to Lional. Good riddance to bad rubbish, as they wisely say. And now let's keep on, because the day's not getting any younger and like I said, we've a lot to do!"

Oh, Saint Snodgrass. He didn't want to see inside another one of those domes. He knew, he just *knew*, that as bad as Lional was, he wasn't the worst.

What if I just stand here and dig my heels in, like a mule . . .

"Professor," said the other Gerald. The glitter was back in his eyes. "Did your sideways leap through the portal scramble your memory? Ottosland isn't exactly short of housekeepers. So unless you fancy writing me up a good Positions Vacant notice . . . ?"

Melissande. He could still feel her dreadful fear, a choking constriction in his throat. That shadbolt was capable of inflicting the most horrendous pain . . . "I'm coming," he said, his voice thick. "There's no need for threats."

The other Gerald raised an eyebrow. "Actually, there is. You'd be surprised how dim some people can be." He held out his hand. "Come on, Bibbie. And you, Professor—keep up."

As they headed for the next dome a huge shadow flitted over them. Gerald tipped his head back and stared at the sky, to see a sleek and streamlined airship gliding high above. The cloud cover briefly parted, and its silver and scarlet skin shone brilliantly in the sunshine, which bounced brightly off the—

"*Guns?*" he said, grabbing at the other Gerald's arm. "You've got *guns* on *airships*? Are we—is your city—under attack?"

Halting, the other Gerald looked at him. "Let go."

With a yelp he snatched his fingers free and leaped aside. Soundlessly, no hint at all, his counterpart had surged something sharp through his etheretic aura. He shook his hand, fingers stinging. "Answer the question. Is there trouble? Is Ottosland at war?"

"Blimey, was I really this much of an alarmist?" the other Gerald mused. "I didn't think so—but how embarrassing if I was. No, Professor, Ottosland isn't at war. I'm just a big believer in an orderly society."

You mean a terrified society. But with Melissande hostage to his good behavior he didn't say it, just in case. "Oh," he said instead. "Well. That's good to know."

"Isn't it?" said his counterpart, showing his teeth in a smile, and slid an arm around Bibbie's shoulders. "Because there's nothing like sleeping safely at night." He kissed Bibbie's cheek. "Is there, Bibs?"

She shook her head fervently. "Nothing."

"And believe me, Professor," the other Gerald added, "there's nothing I won't do to make sure things stay that way."

"Oh, I believe you, Gerald," he said. "I mean, I have to, don't I? If *I* can't tell when I'm being sincere, who can?"

"Exactly," said his counterpart, and laughed. "On we go, then—and let's not have any more interruptions or you'll miss out on some of the best exhibits. And you wouldn't want that, Professor. Would you?"

Are you kidding? I'd love it. "No, Gerald," he said obediently. "I wouldn't at all."

Far too soon they reached the next opaque dome.

"Now," said the other Gerald, "here's another really useful object lesson." He snapped his fingers, and the obscuring mist before them began to dissolve. "I like to call this one *You Do Have A Choice.* Because he did. He really did. Didn't he, Bibbie?"

Bibbie smoothed down her short, sleek hair. "Yes, he did, Gerald. And he made the wrong one."

"And d'you know, I was pretty bloody reasonable," said the other Gerald, sounding aggrieved. "I gave him three chances to join me. It was a damned nuisance he'd been shadbolt-proofed, I can tell you."

With an effort he kept his face blank. *A nuisance. Yes. I mean, Saint Snodgrass forbid you should ever be inconvenienced.* Then, as he opened his mouth to say something that could be interpreted as supportive, the last of the obscuring mist melted . . . and he saw who the other Gerald was whining about. He saw, he heard, he smelled . . . and his mind and body rebelled, recoiling in horror.

Oh. Oh—good lord. No. No—no—no—

He heaved up his half-digested fried eggs and bacon in a splattering mess, all over the parade ground's pristine flagstones.

"What?" said the other Gerald, surprised, his voice raised above the steady crackling and the terrible screams. "Do you know him? Really? That's . . . unexpected."

Gerald dragged his sleeve across his foul-tasting mouth. *Don't look again. Don't look. Turn away.* But he couldn't. He owed it to Sir Alec—even a Sir Alec who'd never met him, or fought for him—to bear witness to this most despicable act.

The other Gerald muted the awful sounds. "It's a pretty ingenious incant, even if I do say so myself," he said. "I wish I could take full credit for it, but I can't. It's what you might call a joint effort. I dreamed it up, but Monk's the one who made it work. Y'know, I might be the world's most powerful wizard but Saint Snodgrass's *bunions*—he's its greatest inventor and thaumaturgical technician. What I wouldn't give to have his kink in the brain."

He could taste blood in his mouth, he was biting his lip so hard. *And what I wouldn't give to be completely blind and deaf and senseless right now.* For a moment he thought he'd be sick again, but somehow he managed to keep his stomach where it belonged.

"It is a bit gruesome, though," said Bibbie, sounding petulant. "I do wish you wouldn't keep making me come back to see it."

"Well, of course it's *gruesome*, Bibbie," said the other Gerald. He sounded miffed. "It's *supposed* to be gruesome. What kind of an object lesson would it be if it didn't make you want to claw out your eyes, stuff corks in your ears and shove cotton plugs up your nose?"

"Well . . . yes," said Bibbie, unconvinced. "I know. You're right. I suppose."

"And I thought you were proud of me for thinking this one up," the other Gerald added. "You *said* you were proud. You *said* you thought it was fantastic."

"I do, I do think it's fantastic," Bibbie protested. "Only a genius could've dreamed this up. But I'm sensitive, Gerald, and this must be the fiftieth time I've seen it. *Fifty times.* Isn't that enough?"

As his counterpart and Bibbie launched into a bitter bickering match, he made himself face what they'd done to Sir Alec. Looking at him not only with his one good eye, but with his sharply honed thaumaturgic senses, too.

If I can see how the incant's put together maybe I can break it. Maybe I can set the poor bastard free.

Because what this world's Gerald and Monk had done, between them, was imprison their Sir Alec within an infinite temporal loop. Chained to a stake, surrounded by ignited oil-soaked wood, enigmatic, mysterious and oddly compassionate Sir Alec was burning alive. Worse, he was trapped in the last hideous heartbeats before death that now, thanks to Monk's genius, stretched on and on to infinity. A death without end. A death lasting forever.

They show this to children. They make children see this. How can I help him? I can't help him. I don't want to. I want him to die.

Through blinding tears he battled to understand the construction of the incant. He'd never encountered anything like it, a combination of the darkest magic he'd ever tasted and his own *potentia* warped almost beyond recognition, shot through with Monk's inimitable, irrepressible thaumic signature.

How could you, Monk? How could you do this?

And then he felt a rough hand on his shoulder, shaking him. "Oh, for pity's sake, Professor! Now you're *crying*? What are you, a girl? Even Bibbie's not boo-hooing. Who is this Sir Alec to you, that you'd give a toss that he's dead?"

It was no good. He couldn't begin to break this incant. Not here and now, anyway. Probably not ever. Pulling away from the other Gerald, he dried his face on his sleeve.

"But he's not dead, is he? Gerald—"

"He tried to kill me!" the other Gerald shouted. "All right? This isn't murder. It's self-defense. It's *justice*. When someone tries to kill you—"

"You have them arrested!" he cried. "You don't—you don't—"

"What, like you had Lional arrested?" retorted his counterpart. "Really? You're going to stand there on your high horse and lecture me with your Lional's blood all over your hands?"

He shook his head. "That was—"

"If you say *different*, sunshine, I'll bloody knock you on your ass!" said the other Gerald. "Besides, I told you, I gave Sir Alec three chances. I was prepared to forgive him for trying to kill me—if he'd join me. But he wouldn't. And like I said, I couldn't shadbolt him. So Gerald, I'm telling you, he brought this on himself. And now I'm tired of discussing it." A savage fingersnap, and the dreadful sight of endlessly dying Sir Alec disappeared inside a smoky dome. "Now if you don't mind we've a few more exhibits to look at, and then we've somewhere else to be. So do yourself a favor and just look where I point and no more wringing your lily-white hands. Or I'll bloody forget how much I need you and I *will* do you a mischief. Understood?"

Numbly, he nodded. "Yes, Gerald. Understood."

"Fine," snapped his counterpart. "Then come on. We're running late."

Their nightmare visit to the parade ground took nearly three excruciating hours. By the time it was over, every single monstrous exhibit examined, its history lovingly detailed, Gerald wanted to crawl into a hole and never crawl back out again. *Depravity* would no longer be an abstract word.

"Do cheer up, Professor," said the other Gerald briskly, as they made their way back to the car. "Nothing you've seen here will happen to you. Well. You know. Probably."

They piled into the glamorous Kingsmark and drove next to Government House. And if the rest of the exhibits on the parade ground had been appalling, what had been done to Lord Attaby—no, make that Prime Minister, he was wearing the official chain of office—and his colleagues was unspeakable.

Standing in the lavish blue and gilt Cabinet room, with Bibbie's arm once more threaded possessively—controllingly—through his and the other Gerald standing to one side, gloating, Gerald looked at Ottosland's vanquished leadership and its senior civil servants, shadbolted to a man—and felt the enormity of the situation threaten to crush him like an avalanche.

I can't fix this. How am I supposed to fix this? If I had an army of janitors behind me I don't think I could fix this.

One of the shadbolted officials was Monk's Uncle Ralph. The change in him was dreadful. The Sir Ralph Markham of his world was a wily and powerful First Grade wizard. Forthright, no nonsense—but a man with hidden depths and inconspicuous influence. Fierce in his defense of both family and country. *This* Sir Ralph was a defeated man, with fearful, haunted eyes and a tic in his cheek that leaped and leaped without ceasing.

Sir Alec was his friend. Was he made to watch what was done to him? Does he spend every waking minute wondering if he'll be next?

Knowing the answer, sickened, he looked at the rest of the Cabinet and its servants. All in all some thirty men, crowded into the Cabinet room like bullocks in a butcher's yard. As a janitor he was vigorously encouraged to stay well out of politics, a stricture which didn't bother him in the least. But even so, some three-quarters of the group before him looked familiar, echoes of portfolio and junior ministers back home. Thanks to his short-lived career as a probationary Department of Thaumaturgy compliance officer he even recognized some of the permanent Secretaries and Under-Secretaries—the men whose busy paddling kept their nation afloat.

But look at them now. They're as paralyzed by fear as they are by those shadbolts. Even if I could reach them, I doubt they'd be any help. They're too far gone. I think their minds are close to breaking.

And of course he could never blame them for that. Not when he still visited his own breaking in bad dreams.

Who knows about this? Have the ordinary, everyday people noticed there's something terribly wrong with their government? What about the Times? *Its journalists always sticking their noses into things. I can't believe they've not sniffed this out. I can't believe they aren't shouting protests from the rooftops.*

A flicker of shadow. A vibration of glass. A deep, almost subliminal thrumming in his bones. Through the vast, uncurtained Cabinet room window he watched an airship sail majestically past the building. Up this close its guns looked particularly lethal.

Yes. Right. Next stupid question, Dunnywood?

As Bibbie continued to cling like a barnacle, the other Gerald regarded the assembled Cabinet as though they were exotic exhibits in a zoo. "Politicians, Professor, should be seen and not heard. Father used to say that all the time. D'you remember? I did this for him, you know. Well. Mainly for me, but it's a hat tip to him too. I like to think that wherever he is, he knows I still think of him."

From what he could tell without getting any closer, these particular shadbolts turned people into compliant puppets. The convoluted incants woven into them were composed of various compulsion and direction hexes. Not a single, simple hex to prevent the answering of inconvenient questions, or a choke-chain kind of shadbolt, like the one inflicted on Melissande, but a cobwebbery of thaumaturgics designed to control what its victim said and did. Brilliant . . . and diabolical.

Prime Minister Attaby, his Cabinet and his civil servants were staring at him in shocked silence. Not only because they were shadbolted, but because the sight of him was surely unexpected and probably terrifying. Look, gentlemen! It's your lucky day. Two torturers for the price of one! He wanted to reassure them, to tell them, *No, no, don't worry, I'm not here to hurt you.* But the other Gerald wouldn't take kindly to that, so he had to content himself with throwing the occasional loathing glance at their tormentor when their tormentor wasn't looking.

"It turns out they're proving wonderfully useful," the other Gerald added. "Which is hard to believe, I know, seeing as how they're politicians and pencil-pushers. But it's true. They're making sure Ottosland creaks along until everything else is in place. Ensuring the general populace isn't too alarmed by the changes. And of course keeping up appearances in front of various international heads of state. Because *that's* a situation still in flux,

Professor. Which of course is why I brought you here. To help me de-flux things, as it were."

Bloody hell, he really has fallen in love with the sound of his own voice, hasn't he? When I get home I'm going to give Reg strict instructions to poke me in the unmentionables if I ever turn into a tosser like him.

Oh, lord. Reg. Traipsing around that appalling parade ground, being confronted by atrocity after atrocity, he'd been convinced that at any moment he'd be brought face to face with Reg. Dead or worse than dead, like poor Sir Alec. But she wasn't there. It was the only good thing that had happened since he'd opened his eyes at the house.

"Professor, are you listening?" said the other Gerald, sharply. "Because you've got that look on your face again. The one that says your mind's wandered off. Don't do that. It's rude."

Ignoring Bibbie's scolding little shake of his arm, he swallowed. "Sorry. I was only wondering when I'd get to see—"

"I *told* you. *Later*," said his counterpart. "But if you don't shut up about it you won't see her at all."

Before he could think up a suitably groveling answer the large crystal ball at the center of the Cabinet room's conference table hummed, then started flashing bright green.

"Hmm," said the other Gerald, his frown deepening. "Y'know, if that's not President Damooj calling to accept my terms I'm going to be bloody pissy. Attaby! Answer it! You know what to say."

Moving jerkily, like an animated marionette, shadbolted Prime Minister Attaby stepped forward to the conference table and accepted the incoming communication. The green light stopped flashing, the crystal turned cloudy, then cleared a moment later to reveal a man with robust silver muttonchop whiskers and a thin face, dark as ebony and set into an expression of grim intractability.

"Bugger," said the other Gerald, standing well out of vibration range. He was scowling. "*Not* President Damooj."

Attaby tugged at his tie. "Viceroy Gonegal."

"Prime Minister," said Gonegal. "On behalf of the Directorate of the United Magical Nations, I wanted to see if you'd made any progress regarding our list of demands. As you're surely aware, your deadline expires soon."

"Ha!" muttered the other Gerald, and grinned. "See, Bibbie? I told you. I've got the cowards running scared. They don't have the guts to attack me. They know if they try I'll wipe them out of existence."

Bibbie went to him and stroked his arm. "They're fools."

"I regret, Viceroy, that our answer remains unchanged," said Attaby. He was sweating, fat drops rolling down his cheek and off his chin. "You have no right to threaten this nation, or dictate our friendships and political alliances. We stand firm in our commitment to Ottosland's territorial sovereignty and repeat our warning to the UMN: attempt to set foot on Ottosland's home soil or breach her airspace or indeed harm any nation who supports us and you will face our fierce and merciless retribution."

Gonegal's pale blue eyes blazed with sudden anger. "Prime Minister, I do assure you—any merciless retribution will be faced by you and your innocent population. Ottosland is a founding signatory member of the UMN Charter. If you flout our authority, if you presume to—"

"Oh, *shut up*, Gonegal," said the other Gerald, and shoved Attaby aside. "You can't honestly think I'm actually *scared* of you and your little box of tricks? Your charter and your rules mean bugger all to me. So why don't you stop huffing and puffing and making threats we both know you can't keep and get your nose out of my private business!"

"I beg your pardon, sir," said Gonegal, after a long and frigid silence. "But I don't believe you and I have been formally introduced."

"We haven't been formally anythinged," said the other Gerald. "But who cares? It doesn't matter who I am. All that matters is what I want. And what I *want*, Viceroy, is for you to bugger off. I'm expecting an important communication and you're getting in the way. Don't call again unless it's to discuss how you and the rest of the UMN are going to serve Ottosland's interests."

Gerald, trying hard not to swallow his tongue, watched his counterpart disconnect from Viceroy Gonegal with a snap of his fingers, then sweep Bibbie into his embrace for an extravagant kiss. Far from being embarrassed by such intimacy in front of practically an entire government, and only one of them family, Bibbie laughed and wound her arms enthusiastically around his neck.

Attaby closed his eyes and waited, like a brutally trained dog.

Turning away, because while he did want Bibbie he did *not* want that, Gerald thrust his fisted hands into his pockets and crossed to the window. He could feel the shadbolted men's hungry, disbelieving gazes follow him.

For pity's sake, don't look at me like that. I can't help you. I'm sorry.

Letting his sweat-damp forehead come to rest against the window's cool glass, he stared down into Government Street many stories below. He knew it was Government Street because he could see the Treasury Building, with its distinctive red and blue sandstone bricks and enormous, imposing brass-bound front door. If not for that, though, he'd have been hard-pressed to name it. Government Street was one of Ott's main thoroughfares; he was used to seeing it chockful of cars and carriages and businessmen and civil servants and government officials and messenger-boys racing up and down on foot and pushbike, tending to weighty matters of state. Even on working days the foot paths were clogged with sightseers ooohing and aaaahing and pointing excited fingers. But this Ott's Government Street was eerily empty. Three carriages, one black car, a handful of scuttling pedestrians—and no sightseers. Was it his imagination or even so high up, and inside this impotent Cabinet room, could he feel the city's ambient fear? He thought he could. He thought that if he closed his eyes and listened hard he'd be able to hear the weeping and the stifled gasps of terror.

Another armed airship ghosted by, its shadow blotting out the fitful sun.

How long has it been since New Ottosland, and Lional? Just over a year? How could so much go so wrong in a year? Are we truly so fragile? Do peace and safety really dangle by such a brittle thread?

Apparently, they did.

Behind him he heard Bibbie utter a deep, petulant sigh. "Gerald, I'm hungry," she complained. "It's past lunch time, you know. Government House has a dining room, doesn't it? Why can't they feed us? They really should feed us."

"Bibbie, don't be a nuisance," said the other Gerald, impatient. "Weren't you listening? I'm expecting a call from President Damooj!"

Another sigh. "Yes, Gerald, I know you are. Only have you forgotten it's practically midnight in Babishkia? President Damooj will be fast asleep."

The ether trembled with the other Gerald's displeasure. "He's got no bloody business sleeping. Not when I'm here waiting for his oath of fealty."

His *what*? Gerald turned around. "You're expecting Babishkia to cede its sovereignty to you?"

The other Gerald smiled. "Actually, I'm expecting a lot of things, Professor. But yes, that would be one of them."

"And if they refuse?"

"Well, let's hope for their sake that they don't," said the other Gerald. Then he looked at Bibbie. "You're really hungry, Bibs?"

Bibbie pouted. "*Famished.* My stomach thinks my throat's been cut."

"Oh dear," said the other Gerald, grinning. "We can't have that, can we? All right. We'll go to the dining room and they can feed us an extravagant lunch. You, me and the Professor. But if after that President Damooj *still* hasn't called?" Another ominous tremble in the ether. "Well. All I can say is I'll be glad that *I* don't live in Babishkia." He snapped his fingers. "Come on, Professor. We're going to eat."

The thought of food was revolting, but there was no question of refusal. Silent and nauseous, not looking at Ottosland's shadbolted government, Gerald followed them out.

CHAPTER EIGHTEEN

Because they didn't know what else to do with him, they'd put the other Monk in Gerald's bedroom, on his bed, covered him head to toe with a respectful sheet and closed the door. Then they'd gone back downstairs to the kitchen, where Melissande made tea and buttered toast and they sat around not drinking or eating and waited for Sir Alec to tell them what to do next.

Brooding over his cold, greasy bread, Monk made himself not stare at the kitchen ceiling.

I'm dead. I'm dead up there. That's not right. He didn't come all this way just to die. He came so I could save him. But I didn't. I think I killed him.

"Oy," said Reg, slumpingly perched on the back of the chair beside him. "Don't you dare start with that nonsense, sunshine."

He blinked at her. "How could you possibly know what—"

"Don't make me laugh," the wretched bird retorted. "I can read your face with my eyes closed, can't I?"

"She's right," said Bibbie, quiet and composed with tears running and running and running down her face. "It wasn't your fault. It wasn't anyone's fault."

"Yes, it was," said Melissande, beside her. "It was the other Gerald's fault."

Oh, God. *Gerald*. Midnight was hours behind them. It would be dawn in a while. The sun was going to rise on a world without Gerald Dunwoody in it.

Reg hiccuped, hunched and feather-fluffed. "My poor boy. I always said he never should've got himself mixed up with that government stooge. Didn't I always say it? Didn't I say nothing good would come of him gallivanting around the world sticking his nose into other people's nefarious business?"

"Yes, Reg, and you keep *on* saying it, but that's not what happened, is it?" said Bibbie. Did she know she was crying? It didn't seem that she did. "At least, we don't know for sure. I mean, it's not like you've any proof this is Sir Alec's fault."

Reg rattled her tail feathers. "Oh. Right. Don't tell me, let me guess. You've decided to go sweet on him, have you, ducky? The dashing and mysterious older man mistake." She sniffed. "And here's me thinking you were smarter than that."

"*What?*" said Bibbie, outraged, and threw a discarded teaspoon across the table at her. "Sweet on Sir Alec? Are you out of your mind?"

"Oh, don't even *start!*" snapped Melissande. "Put a sock in it, the pair of you! It's bad enough we don't know what's happened to Gerald. But if you two are going to carry on like *children* you can bloody well go to your rooms!"

As Bibbie opened her mouth to argue, Monk raised a challenging eyebrow at her. Pulling a face she gave up, and slumped a little deeper into her chair.

"Look," he said, "I don't know about the rest of you, but I'm thinking it can't be a coincidence that the other me turned up here around the same time Gerald disappeared on the way to Grande Splotze. Especially since everything points to him not being in our world any more."

"So what are you saying?" said Bibbie. "That their Monk crossed over here—and our Gerald crossed over there?"

"I think it's absolutely possible, yes."

"But how?" said Melissande. "The other you jiggered his portable portal opener to get here. Exactly how many ways are there to open a door between dimensions?"

He shrugged. "I honestly don't know."

"Well, *could* you travel between worlds using a regular portal?"

"I don't see why not," he said, after a moment's thought. "It'd be bloody tricky trying it with one of those big commercial portals but the basic thaumaturgics are the same."

"And what about trying it with a small, unregistered portal?"

Like one of Sir Alec's? "Sure," he said, nodding. "You could jigger one of those if you had some serious thaumaturgic juice."

Melissande looked at him, her green eyes somber.

"Serious as in rogue wizard? Monk, are you saying Gerald isn't missing at all? That he *left*?"

"No," he said quickly. "Of course not. But we've got more than one rogue wizard in play, haven't we? And we all heard what the other me said about *him*. I'll bet you anything you like he's the one behind our Gerald's disappearance."

"Ha! I don't give a fat rat's ass what that other Markham boy blathered!" said truculent Reg. "I'm telling you, sunshine, I know my Gerald. And I don't care *which* version we're talking about, he would *never* stoop to kidnap or—"

"Or shadbolts?" he said, frowning into his cooling mug of tea. "Enough, Reg. Face facts. Somewhere out there is a wizard wearing Gerald's face, possessing his rogue thaumaturgic abilities but none of his conscience or decency. A wizard who's souped himself up on so much dark magic there's a pretty good chance he's not strictly human any more."

"Don't you say that!" Reg shrieked, all her feathers sleeking and her tail ferociously rattling. "Say that again, Monk Markham, and I *swear* I will poke out your eyeballs and—"

"*Hey!*" He shoved his mug away so hard that it tipped over, flooding the old, scarred kitchen table in a tidal wave of tea. "You think I *want* to say it, Reg? Or even think it? But I was *inside that other Monk's head*. I *felt* what his Gerald did to him. Only someone who's completely lost their humanity could do that. And if you think I want to think that about my *best friend* you're mad!"

Melissande, who'd leapt up from the table and

fetched a cloth to stem the tide of tea, paused in her mopping. "Don't, Monk. She's upset."

"And I'm *not*?" Glaring, he sat back and folded his arms. "Melissande—"

"Oh, shut up, Monk," said Bibbie. "Reg is upset, you're upset—we're all of us upset. This isn't about who can boo-hoo the hardest, it's about getting our Gerald back from wherever he's been snatched to."

"And finding out what's going on," Melissande added, carrying the tea-sopping cloth over to the sink. "I mean, don't you think this is all a bit odd? If this other Gerald's so amazingly powerful, what does he want with *ours*?"

"I don't know, do I?" he said, dangerously close to snapping. At *Mel*. "How am I supposed to know? The other Monk didn't say and I'm not a bloody mind reader. The only thing we can bet on is that it won't be anything good."

"Exactly!" said Reg. "Which means for once in her frivolous life your scatterbrained sister is talking sense. Enough of this sitting around on our asses. We've got to nip over to the world-next-door and drag our Gerald back here by the scruff of his neck!"

"And how are we supposed to do that?" said Melissande over her shoulder as she wrung out the cloth. "Wish on a star and hope for the best?"

"What d'you mean *how*?" Reg demanded, staring. "The answer's right under your silly freckled nose, ducky. We've got that other Monk's jiggered-up portal opener, haven't we? That's as good as a battering ram, that is."

Monk cleared his throat. "Except we haven't got it any more."

"*What?*" Reg rattled her tail feathers. "D'you mean to tell me you let that manky Sir Alec get his sticky fingers on it? Monk Markham, how could you be so stupid?"

"Sorry," he said, shrugging. "Maybe I should've asked you to swallow it, Reg."

"You'll be swallowing your own eyeballs if you're not bloody careful!" she snapped. "Our one advantage and you let that sneaky government stooge run off with it? What were you thinking? Were you trying to save your own hide at the expense of—"

"No, Reg, he wasn't!" said Melissande, whipping around. "How can you even suggest it? Of course he gave the other Monk's portal opener to Sir Alec. He didn't have a choice. And anyway, since we're the ones who got Sir Alec involved in the first place it'd be pretty stupid of us to hide crucial evidence from him, don't you think?"

She and Reg glared at each other, then Reg looked away. "I'm telling you, ducky, the man's not to be trusted. He'll use that other Monk's portal opener as a paperweight, you mark my words."

Rolling her eyes, Bibbie crunched a piece of her cold toast. "Yes, yes, Reg, I'm sure that's terribly likely. What about *your* jigged-up portal opener, Monk? Will that get the job done?"

"No," he said, and dragged his fingers through his hair. "Because Sir Alec's confiscated it too and anyway, I have no idea how to double-jig it to open a door into a parallel world. *Any* parallel world, let alone the right one."

"You don't know now," said Bibbie. "But if you had some time I'll bet you could work it out. And what do you mean, Sir Alec's confiscated your portable portal opener too?"

Feeling like a little boy again, he scowled at the toast crumbs she was scattering on the table. "While you and Mel were—were making the other Monk tidy," he muttered. "He asked for it, so I gave it to him."

Now Melissande was staring. "Just like that? Monk—I'm starting to think Reg has a point. It's one thing to hand over the opener the other Monk used to get here, but *why* would you give up the only advantage we have?"

"Well, I could hardly say no, could I?" he retorted, not liking the way they were all looking at him. As though he were the village idiot's even dimmer cousin. "Not after I told him about it. Not after he came rushing out here to help because I contacted him using the super secret password I'm not even meant to know exists."

Bibbie tossed her half-eaten piece of toast back on its plate, her eyes lit up with a dangerous gleam. "And is he going to give it back? Because Monk, that's your invention. It's your intellectual property. He's got no right—"

"And you think that's going to stop him, ducky?" said Reg, rousing out of her funk. "That superior secret government stooge? That stuck-up, autocratic, officious pen-pusher? That—"

"Reg," Melissande said gently, and perched on the table-edge beside her. "Don't. You're not angry with Sir Alec. You're angry with Gerald for disappearing without a trace. You're angry with that other Monk for putting the cat among the pigeons.

And you're furious because he died in such a horrible way."

Silence. Reg sank her head into her shoulders and grieved. Bibbie, the tears still sluicing her cheeks, dabbed up her toast crumbs with the tip of one unsteady finger. Monk, looking at Melissande as she gazed out of the window, thought he'd never loved her more. *Say it. Say it.* But he couldn't. This wasn't the time. On the wall beside the window the kitchen clock quietly ticked. It felt like the ageing night was holding its breath.

"What are we going to do with him?" Bibbie whispered at last. "I'll want to bury him, won't I? I mean, his sister will. Even if she's—" her breath caught, "—different? She'll want to say goodbye."

Leaning forward, he touched his fingers to her wrist. "We'll work something out, Bibs. We'll get Sir Alec to help us."

She looked at the closed kitchen door. "What's he doing, do you think? Is he even still here?"

"Of course he's still here," said Melissande, wearily. "He wouldn't leave without telling us." She bit her lip. "Would he, Monk?"

There wasn't much point asking him. Sir Alec was mostly Gerald's problem. The few times he'd crossed paths with Uncle Ralph's mysterious colleague everything had been strictly business. Whatever Gerald's boss was or wasn't likely to do he didn't know him well enough to hazard a guess.

But the girls were waiting for an answer, touchingly certain he had one. At least, Mel and Bibbie seemed touchingly certain. The glint in Reg's eyes suggested she was happily waiting for him to fall on his face. Or better yet his ass.

"I don't think so," he said at last. "I expect he's around here somewhere."

"Yes, all right, but what is he *doing*?" Bibbie persisted. "Why isn't he in here with us, making plans?"

He managed a tired smile. "Because Sir Alec put the *secret* into secret agent, Bibs." Muscles complaining, he pushed to his feet. "I'll go and see what he's up to. You three stay put. And *don't* try anything thaumaturgical, all right? We've got enough trouble to contend with as it is."

The fact that not one of them had a go at him for saying something so blatantly provocative was a depressing reminder of how much trouble they were in.

Bloody hell, Gerald. Where are you?

When he couldn't find Sir Alec anywhere in the house, he looked outside. Finally ran the man to ground out the back, in the old stable yard, where he was sitting on the rim of a large ornamental flower pot smoking a cigarette. Its tip glowed a bright and oddly comforting orange in the moonless night's star-pricked darkness. The scent of burning tobacco tinted the cold air.

"Here's some unsolicited advice, Mr. Markham," said Sir Alec, not turning. Lamplight from the open mud-room door brushed him with warm soft strokes, like an antique oil painting. In profile his face was remote and severely economical. "Never start smoking. The damned things are too tempting when the world's gone and turned itself ass over elbows."

"Thank you, sir," he said, halting a few paces distant. "I'll try to remember that."

Sir Alec inhaled, then blew out another thin stream of smoke. "So. Have you given any thought as to Mr. Dunwoody's whereabouts?"

He shoved his hands in his pockets. "We reckon the other Gerald's kidnapped him."

"Do you?" Sir Alec slid him a sideways look. "Interesting."

"You don't?"

"Did I say that?"

"No, sir."

"Well, then."

Bemused, he watched intensely enigmatic Sir Alec smoke a little more of his cigarette. "Ah—Sir Alec—"

"Yes, Mr. Markham?"

"Did you know?"

Sighing, Sir Alec stubbed out the cigarette on the side of the flower pot and carefully placed it on its weed-choked dirt. "About the existence of parallel worlds?"

"Yes. Did you know?"

"The notion is hardly groundbreaking, Mr. Markham. I'd be surprised if you'd not bandied it about yourself." Sir Alec snorted. "I'd be surprised to find one thaumaturgical undergraduate who hasn't. It's a popular theme in certain types of literature, I believe."

Oh, this *bloody* man. He stamped his feet a little against the creeping cold. "Sure, yeah, but—that's just theory. That's just mucking about, you know, playing *what if*. What I want to know is whether anyone in the government knew for sure there are—other realities mirroring ours. I want to know whether anyone knows that they're dangerous."

That earned him a wry look. "You're under the impression thaumaturgics are *safe*? My, my, Mr. Markham. It seems I've overestimated you."

In his pockets his fingers clenched to fists. "Just *answer* me, would you? *Does anyone know?*"

"I think," said Sir Alec, after a long silence, "that what you're *really* asking me, Mr. Markham, is whether anyone in the government is working on ways to access these parallel worlds."

Somewhere in the neighborhood a cat yowled and a dog barked. The waning night was so still and quiet the squabbling animals sounded quite close, even though they were probably streets and streets away.

"Well?" he said, his heart erratically thumping. "Are they?"

"Mr. Markham . . ." Sir Alec turned up his coat collar, his only concession to the cold. "At the risk of inflating your already highly-evolved sense of worth, I'll say this: if the Ott government was working on such a project you would know all about it because you would be heading it. When it comes to experimental thaumaturgics there is Monk Debinger Aloysius Markham . . . and then there's everyone else, eating his dust."

Monk felt his face warm. "Oh. Sir Alec, I—"

"Which is *why*," Sir Alec added, ruthlessly severe, "your thoughtless rompings are so frowned upon, young man. If we worry about the wrong people getting their hands on Mr. Dunwoody, you can believe we worry no less about *you*." He shook his head, exasperated. "Dear *God*, you invented an interdimensional portal opener! By *accident*. Young man, you are *lethal*."

"Um . . ." He cleared his throat. "Well. You know. Not on purpose."

Sir Alec's lips twitched. "The answer, incidentally, is no, Mr. Markham. The existence of parallel worlds is held to be nothing more than a fanciful, far-fetched theory."

"Yeah," he said. "All right. Only . . . there's a dead man upstairs that proves the theory's a fact."

"Indeed there is, Mr. Markham," said Sir Alec, most pensive. "But I suggest we tackle one hurdle at a time." He rubbed the side of his nose. "I suppose the appalling bird is demanding that you all go charging off to rescue Mr. Dunwoody?"

"Yes, sir," he said. "Although, to be fair, Reg isn't the only one afraid of sitting around doing nothing. We all want to get Gerald back home safe and sound. I'm assuming you do too."

Sir Alec reached inside his coat and pulled out one of the confiscated portal openers. Tossed it sideways without looking. "Catch."

He snatched the innocuous stone mid-flight and wrapped his fingers tightly around it. Felt the sizzling tingle of powerful thaumics embedded deep in its igneous heart.

"So whose is that one?" said Sir Alec, contemplating the distant, twinkling constellations. "Yours? Or his?"

The trick, Gerald had told him once, was never to let Sir Alec get the upper hand. "Can't you tell?"

Sir Alec's lips twitched again, in what might have been a dry smile. "Pretend that's the case."

"His," he said, and felt a funny little catch in the back of his throat.

"And how can *you* tell?"

Blowing out a breath, watching it mist the air, he rubbed his fingers over the other Monk's extraordinary invention. "There's a—a twist in the thaumics," he murmured. "The operating incant's matrix, it's—different. More complex. Same principles as what I did with mine, only—expanded. And a lot trickier."

Sir Alec nodded. "Could you get it to work, do you think?"

"Oh, yes. Absolutely. I mean, it's keyed to my—I mean his—thaumic signature. Which *is*, y'know, my thaumic signature. Why? Did you want me to—"

"No, no," said Sir Alec. "That's quite all right. I believe you, Mr. Markham."

"Fine, only if we are going to rescue Gerald then—"

Sir Alec stabbed him with a look. "*I said no*, Mr. Markham. First things first, understood?"

He swallowed. "Yes, sir. Understood."

"I wonder," said Sir Alec, his voice soft again, one pale brown eyebrow quizzically raised. "How long would it have been, d'you think, before you put the same thaumic twist into your own unsanctioned interdimensional portal opener?"

He felt his fingers fist again. "I can't help it, you know. I mean, it's not like I sit around twiddling my thumbs and thinking of ways to get up the Department's nose. I don't go out of my way to flout authority."

"No?" Sir Alec slid his hand back inside his coat, withdrew a slim silver case and a lighter and took a moment to extract then ignite a fresh cigarette. With case and lighter returned to his coat, he inhaled deeply, then exhaled fresh smoke. "And if we went upstairs to your attic right now, Mr. Markham? What would we find?"

"Look," he said, feeling another hot rush of blood to his face. "You don't understand. Ideas come to me. I can't stop them. Even while I'm sleeping, they fill up my skull. They never leave me alone. And if I don't—if I don't *do* something with them, if I don't turn them from dream to reality, it's like—" Frustrated, he yanked his hands out of his pockets and folded his arms. "I suppose you're going to tell Uncle Ralph?"

Sir Alec looked at him, cigarette idly balanced between the first and second fingers of his left hand. His chilly gray eyes were lazily intent. "Just as a matter of interest, idle curiosity, no more than that—what *are* you working on, up in your attic?"

And now he knew how a rabbit felt, frozen in the middle of the road with a car bearing down on it . . .

If I tell him he'll make me pull the plug. But if I don't tell him he'll—

"Relax, Mr. Markham," said Sir Alec, his regard still intent. "I'm not a compliance officer. I only want to know because it's likely we'll soon be engaging in some . . . questionable . . . thaumaturgics. Given the delicacy of our situation I'm concerned we don't inadvertently mix our etheretic messages.

The last thing we need tonight is a complication of consequences."

Questionable thaumaturgics? What did *that* mean? "Oh. Right. Well, I've got a few things percolating at the moment, as it happens, but only one big project." He swallowed. "A multi-dimensional etheretic wavelength expander."

Sir Alec stared at him. "Really?"

"Yes."

"A multi-dimensional *expander*."

"Yes."

"And you thought that was a good idea, did you? In some fevered flight of deranged fancy you thought that tampering with the etheretic boundaries between dimensions was a productive use of your time? Is that it?"

Oh, bugger. "I don't know if I'd put it quite like that, sir, but—yes."

"Why?"

"What?" he said, blinking.

"Why did you think it was a good idea, Mr. Markham?"

There was another flower pot handy and he really wanted to sit on it, but he didn't dare. The look in Sir Alec's eyes had him sweating.

"Sir Alec—it's what I do," he said, feeling helpless. "I make improbable things probable. I—think outside what's known and accepted. That's what Research and Development *is*. And when I ended up disproving Herbert and Lowe's notion that sprites are just another postulation of theoretical thaumaturgical metaphysics, well, it got me thinking and—"

"I'm sorry, said Sir Alec, one finger raised. "You proved the existence of *sprites*?"

He swallowed again. "Well, yes. But not on purpose."

Sir Alec took a deep breath and pinched the bridge of his nose. His cigarette, forgotten, slowly burned itself to death. "No. Of course not. And tell me, Mr. Markham, whose cherished theory were you intending to accidentally disprove with this wavelength expander of yours?"

"Nobody's," he said warily. "I just thought it might be a good idea to get a stronger grasp of interdimensional thaumaturgics. You know. What with the sprite, and everything."

"Yes," Sir Alec mused. "I find it's the *and everything* part that has me pissing my pants."

"I'm sorry," he muttered. "But—well—it's not like anybody's been hurt. And anyway, this is about exploration, Sir Alec. Exploration is always risky."

Sir Alec nodded. "That's true. But what is also true, Mr. Markham, is that you walk a fine line between *bold* and *reckless*. Genius is not infallible. Brilliance does not guarantee success."

As if he didn't know that. "So. Sir. *Are* you going to tell Uncle Ralph?"

"Perhaps," said Sir Alec. "It depends."

"On what?"

"I don't know yet. Tell me, Mr. Markham . . . *would* you have done what your alternative self did? Fiddle with your portal opener until you hit the right etheretic harmonics in the right sequence at the right time to punch a hole between this metaphysical reality and the next?"

"Honestly?" He scuffed his heel to the cobblestones. "I can't say. I might've done. Maybe not deliberately. Just—thinking about it, and jiggering. I might have."

Sir Alec looked away. "As I said, Mr. Markham—you are a dangerous young man."

"Not as dangerous as the Gerald next door, I promise you."

Silence, as Sir Alec contemplatively smoked what was left of his cigarette. When it was consumed he stubbed the butt against the flower pot's rim. "I imagine it was . . . disconcerting . . . to watch yourself die."

That was one word for it. He felt the broken bits inside him shift, and stab. "A bit."

"You're all right?"

And that wasn't a question he'd been expecting. Taken aback, he stared at his best friend's unfathomable superior. "Yes. No. I will be. I'll be fine once Gerald's home. Sir Alec—"

Sir Alec stood. By his best guess there were some thirty years between them, if a calendar was used. But looking at the man's face in the mud-room's washing lamplight he realized, with a sickening swoop in his guts, that when it came to experience—and disconcerting experiences—the two of them were more like centuries apart. There was a grim endurance in Sir Alec that he'd never noticed before. And beneath that, a thin blade of sorrow that never lost its edge.

"Sir Alec," he said again, and didn't care how young and frightened he sounded. "What are we going to do?"

"What do you think we should do, Mr. Markham?"

He wanted to shout and stamp and wave his arms around.

Me? Me? Why are you asking me? You're the one who cloak-and-daggers his way through life and takes afternoon tea with Lord Attaby and Uncle Ralph and is on a first-name basis with at least ten world leaders. Don't ask me! I'm terrified and I don't have a bloody clue!

But since he obviously couldn't shout or stamp or wave his arms or say *any* of that, he pulled a face. "I think we need to find out what the Gerald next door has up his sleeve. Only short of actually going next door, I don't see how we can. And I don't see Lord Attaby giving us the nod to go sight-seeing around a parallel world. But even if he does give us a green light and we go—if *I* go—and it has to be me, since I won't meet myself there—Sir Alec, it's a bloody huge risk. I could get taken and if I get taken I'll get used. That shadbolt . . ." He shivered. "Only how can I *not* go? We've got to get Gerald back. But if I *am* going I'd be mad to go in blind. Somehow we have to find out what I'd be walking into. Only I don't have the first idea how."

Another brief, dry smile. "A largely incoherent but not inaccurate assessment, Mr. Markham."

"Thank you, sir." *I think.* "So . . . you agree with me? You think I should—"

But Sir Alec wasn't listening. "There's something I need. I don't have it with me. I must go and fetch it. While I'm gone, Mr. Markham, I suggest you study that other Monk Markham's portable portal.

Familiarize yourself with its incant matrix but *under no circumstance* attempt to activate it. The life of your friend—and perhaps the fate of our world—is absolutely depending on you controlling yourself. Is that clear?"

Chilled, he nodded. "Yes, sir."

"Also, you might like to refresh your memory on the construction of shadbolts," Sir Alec added. "If you're tempted to twiddle your thumbs before I return."

Shadbolts? Why shadbolts? "Yes, sir. Um—Sir Alec—we are going to rescue Gerald, aren't we?"

Sir Alec looked at him. "Yes. If it's warranted."

"If it's *warranted*?" he said, incredulous. "And what the hell is *that* supposed to—"

"It means, Mr. Markham, that my job is frequently distasteful."

"But Sir Alec—"

"Mr. Markham," said Sir Alec, his cold eyes abruptly weary. "Save your breath. We both know Mr. Dunwoody will never again spare himself at the expense of other, innocent lives. You must come to terms with the notion we might not get a happy ending this time." He glanced at his watch. "It's nearly four a.m. How many hours has it been since your visitor expired?"

Stunned and dismayed, he had to think for a moment. "Ah—about five."

Sir Alec frowned. "That's cutting it fine but we should be all right. Back inside with you, Mr. Markham. I'll be as quick as I can."

"Well?" Reg demanded as he walked into the kitchen. "You were gone long enough. What's going on? When do we go after Gerald? I hope you know I'm coming with you. You'll need a good pair of eyes, and the wings'll come in handy too. A flying spy, that's what I'll be." She peered behind him. "Where's that manky Sir Alec got to? What are you playing at, Mr. Markham?"

Abruptly exhausted, Monk dropped into the nearest chair. The other Monk's portable portal was in his coat pocket, weighing him down. "Reg, I'm not playing at anything," he said, around a face-splitting yawn. "I'm following orders."

"What orders?" said Bibbie, still sitting at the table with her head propped in her hands. The long night was telling on her too, purplish shadows shading under her tired eyes. But at least she'd stopped weeping. He supposed that was something. "I'm with Reg on this one, Monk. What the devil's going on?"

Melissande, being Melissande, had already washed their tea mugs and toast plates and was now doggedly blacking the old-fashioned kitchen range. As though tedious domestic tasks could somehow alleviate anxiety and grief. Blacking had smudged itself on the end of her nose and across one freckled cheek. Unlike Bibbie, she never could keep herself clean.

"At the risk of being accused of ganging up on you, Monk," she said, "I'm going to throw in my lot with Reg and Bibbie. No more mysteries, please. Not tonight."

"Sorry," he said, and rubbed at his burning eyes. "Mysteries are all I've got. If I knew what was going on I'd tell you, but I don't so I can't. Sir Alec's buggered off to fetch something. He didn't say what. He wants me to get familiar with *this*—" He pulled the other Monk's portable portal from his pocket and placed it on the table. "And brush up on shadbolts, the construction thereof. And *no*—" he added, as Reg opened her beak. "He didn't explain why."

Reg closed her beak with a snap, rattled her tail feathers and snorted. "I think I've had about as much of that Sir Alec as I can stomach," she growled. "It's time that young whippersnapper was put in his place."

"Really?" Bibbie dredged up a grin. "Make sure you give me plenty of warning. I'll sell tickets."

"No," said Melissande, and dropped the blacking tin and polishing cloth into the kitchen's cleaning box. "You won't. He's only doing his job."

"Ha!" said Reg, rolling her eyes. "And there she goes defending the bureaucrats again. I swear, ducky, there are days when I can't tell which side of the bread you've spread your butter!"

Oh, bloody hell. He looked at Bibbie, who heaved a put-upon sigh then stood. "We've some books on shadbolts in the library," she said. "Mel, come and help me find them, would you?"

As she and Melissande left the kitchen, he looked at Reg. The bird was hunched painfully on the back of a chair, feathers fluffed out again as though she were cold, or ill. He'd long ago given up trying to understand Gerald's attachment to her—or her fierce devotion to him, for that matter. For himself he hardly knew how he felt about her. She was unbearably autocratic and sweepingly opinionated, given to tantrums and hectoring. But then in the next breath she'd be so funny and so wise, supportive, protective. Heart-stoppingly brave.

Talk about enigmas. She makes Sir Alec look as complicated as a blank sheet of paper.

Leaning sideways, he stroked his fingertip down her drooping wing. "We'll find him, Reg. We'll get him back."

She rattled her tail again. "'Course we will," she said, in a tone of voice that meant, *Are you sure?*

No. He wasn't. But if he admitted that out loud he'd hex their chances for sure. "Hey," he said. "I've always wondered—if I can ask—why Gerald? Of all the wizards you've come across since you were—" He cleared his throat. "In all this time. Why did you pick Gerald to adopt?"

For a moment he thought she wasn't going to answer. Then she sighed, sleeked her drab brown feathers close to her body, and stared into the distance as though watching the sweet unfolding of a memory.

"He reminds me of someone," she said softly, her eyes warm. "Someone I knew a long time ago." Then her gaze sharpened, and she looked down her beak at him. "As for why he let me adopt him, Mr. Nosy Markham, and why he puts up with my crotchets and moods, you can ask Gerald that yourself when he gets back."

If he gets back. If I can get him back. If Sir Alec lets me try. But he didn't say that aloud. Instead he crossed to the sink, collecting the kettle on the way. "I could use a cup of tea," he said, pretending he hadn't seen the fear in her eyes. Pretending she couldn't see the fear in his. "One to drink, this time. Do you fancy a mug?"

"Why not?" she said, after a moment. "Just make sure you warm the pot first." She sniffed. "The man hasn't been born who remembers that."

CHAPTER NINETEEN

Crouched on the library floor trying to read book spines, Bibbie sighed. "Melissande, you're staring."

Melissande winced. *Rats. And there's me thinking I was being so surreptitious.* "Sorry."

"If you want to know something, ask," said Bibbie, sitting back on her heels. "I mean, I might say *none of your business* but that's not the same as biting your head off."

"True." She pressed her finger against the last book checked so she didn't lose her place. "All right. So here's the thing. I was wondering if you—that's to say, I've been feeling somewhat—you see, there's this—"

"Yes, Mel, Monk cares for you," Bibbie said kindly. "And no, I'm sorry, I've no idea why he's not made a formal declaration. All I can tell you is, well, don't give up hope. He's never once looked at anyone the way he looks at you. He's just slow on the uptake. He is a man, after all."

Suddenly ashamed, she stared at the old library

carpet. "You must think I'm awful," she murmured. "Worried about my silly feelings while Gerald's missing and there's a dead Monk upstairs and—" She bit her lip, shatteringly close to an inappropriate emotional outburst. "It's just—I can't bear to think about any of that. About how we might never see Gerald again."

Bibbie's blue eyes narrowed. "Don't you dare, Mel. Of course we'll see him again."

"Bibbie . . ." She cleared her throat. "About Gerald. Do you—"

"Quite a lot, actually," said Bibbie. Her chin trembled. "But you mustn't tell him I said so. He's got this ridiculous notion he can't be happy because he's a rogue wizard. And a janitor. That he's too dangerous for me to love. All nonsense, of course, but there's no point in me trying to convince him. I just have to wait for him to work it out on his own."

"Wait for how long?" she said, after a moment.

"Well—as long as it takes, of course," said Bibbie, surprised. "What a silly question."

Yes. Of course. Very silly.

"Ah *hah!*" said Bibbie, and pulled a book from the shelf. "Here we go. *Shadbolts Through The Ages*. Technically it's a restricted text but I'll say this for Great-Uncle Throgmorton—he didn't give a toss about silly rules." She tossed it onto the library's deep, wingback reading chair. "I'm sure there's at least one more, so come on, Mel. Keep searching. Sir Alec could come back any tick of the clock and I want to be ready for him. I don't think I could stand one more of his withering looks." She pulled a face. "I'm a girl, not an amoeba, but I don't think he's noticed."

She had to smile. "Don't be so sure. I mean, he's middle-aged, Bibs. Not blind."

"Oh, *you*," said Bibbie, shifting to the next bookcase. "You're as bad as Reg, *you* are."

"Now, now," she said, still smiling. "I'm sure there's no need to get *nasty*, Emmerabiblia."

Bibbie pouted. "Spoilsport."

"Well, you know. I try my best."

A cheerful fire crackled in the library's small fireplace, throwing warm light and dancing shadows. Its four walls were lined ceiling to carpet with bookcases, and the bookcases were crammed tight with books. It was her favorite room in Monk's house. Most of the collection he'd inherited from his rule-breaking great-uncle Throgmorton, a noted thaumaturgical bibliophile. His own books he'd jammed in around the edges, which was making the search for shadbolt texts something of a challenge.

The library door opened as she moved on to the next row, and Monk came in carrying a tray with a teapot, and four mugs. Reg flapped in behind him and landed on the back of the nearest chair.

"Did you remember biscuits?" said Bibbie, turning.

"No," said Monk, and scowled at Reg. "Why didn't you remind me?"

The bird rolled her eyes. "Because, sunshine, and I quote: *'Offer me one more piece of advice about how to make a bloody cup of tea, Reg, and I swear I'll transmog you into a boot.'*"

"Never mind," said Bibbie. "I'll fetch some."

"Not without me, you won't," said Reg. "You always pick the ones I don't like."

She and Bibbie left the library, bickering. Monk held out the tray. "The red mug. Milk and three sugars."

Taking her tea, Melissande perched on the edge of the wingback chair. "Tell me the truth, Monk. Do you really think we can get Gerald back?"

He put the tray on the library's low table, then shoved his hands in his pockets. "If he is where we think he is . . . I think there's a chance."

She felt her stomach lurch. "Only a chance?"

"Mel . . ." Ignoring his own mug of tea, Monk rubbed a hand over his tired face. "If he is where we think he is—" He shook his head. "It's very bad."

"I understand that, but—he'll have me, won't he? I mean, the other me. And he'll have the other Bibbie. And Reg. He won't be alone."

"Mel, you heard the other Monk as well as I did," he said, looking at her with eyes full of not-quite-stifled fear. "The other you, the other Bibbie . . . something's not right there. We can't assume he's got anyone to help him."

Fingers wrapped tight around the red mug, she took a sip of tea. The heavy porcelain chattered against her teeth. *I heard him say he loved me.* "Then that's more reason to help. You are going after him, aren't you?"

He shrugged. "I don't know. I hope so."

"You don't—" She leaped up, heedless of the tea splashing her shirt. "Monk, we can't *leave* him there!"

"D'you think I want to?" he demanded. "D'you think I can bear thinking we might? But Mel, we're not even certain that he *is* in the other Monk's world.

And even if he is, I don't know if going after him is possible."

"What? Of course it's possible. You've got the other Monk's portal opener, haven't you? You could go to his world right now, if you wanted. So what are you waiting for? Open the door!"

"Mel . . ." Monk folded his arms as though his chest was hurting him. "I can't. Sir Alec said—"

"Oh, *bugger* Sir Alec!" she retorted. "What does *he* know?"

Monk pulled a face. "A darn sight more than he's letting on, I'm guessing. Melissande—"

"Don't you *Melissande* me, Monk Markham. Gerald's your best friend and he saved my country. We can't abandon him, Monk. We *can't.*"

"Now, now, ducky," said Reg, flying into the room ahead of Bibbie, who had biscuits. "Untwist your knickers." Settling herself on the reading chair's high back she looked down her beak, so irritatingly condescending. "Nobody's abandoning anybody. Not while I'm around."

"Hear, hear," said Bibbie, dumping the plate of biscuits beside the tea tray. "What are you guffing on about now, Monk?"

Frustrated, Monk turned away and stamped over to the fireplace. "I'm not *guffing,* Bibbie, I'm—I'm trying to be objective. I'm trying to look at this mess with cold, hard eyes. And like it or not, *all* of you, this is what I see—just because we *want* to rescue Gerald doesn't mean we *can.* We could do the right thing for the right reason and end up making things worse. And if you think it doesn't bloody well *kill* me to—"

Melissande took a breath, ready to challenge him,

but Bibbie beat her to it. "Of course it does, but that's not the point, is it? What you're saying is balderdash. Since when do you get cold feet, Monk Markham? *We* are Witches Incorporated and *we* can do anything we set our minds to." Eyes glittering, she tilted her chin defiantly. "So drink your tea, eat a biscuit, then do as Sir Alec asked you and brush up on shadbolts. We're going to be ready for that sarky bugger when he gets back."

Impressed, Melissande watched Monk's tense shoulders slump. Sighing heavily, he turned. Even in the warming firelight he looked pale. "Fine. But when he does get back, Bibbie, we're going to do *exactly* what he says. Because what we've stumbled into—been dragged into—it's bigger than anything we've come up against before. This isn't only about our Gerald."

Melissande looked at him. "What—you think the other Gerald has plans to come and visit us?"

She'd surprised him. If she weren't so sad and tired she'd be a bit insulted.

"I wasn't sure if you'd thought that far ahead," he admitted. "I think it's possible. Don't you?"

"Yes. What does Sir Alec think?"

"We didn't discuss it. But I'll bet he thinks it's possible too," said Monk, his own tea forgotten. "Which complicates everything. Because if we charge into this half-cocked, if we make the wrong choices? Not only could we end up getting Gerald killed, we could cause the destruction of that world *and* this one."

Nobody spoke for a while. Even the flames in the fireplace sounded subdued.

Melissande looked at Bibbie. "I hate to say it,

Bibs, but he's right. Not about not rescuing Gerald— but we do need to take this one step at a time." She picked up *Shadbolts Through The Ages* from the seat of the reading chair and held it out to him. "Come on. You can start with this."

"Good idea," said Reg, and rattled her tail feathers. "Plop your ass down here, Mr. Markham. I'll read over your shoulder and explain all the big thaumaturgical words."

Despite the tension, everyone laughed. Well, everyone except Reg. "Thanks, Your Majesty," said Monk, crossing to the chair. "I don't know what I'd do without you."

"Trust me, sunshine," said Reg, sniffing. "Neither do I."

Melissande felt herself shiver as Monk's fingers brushed hers, taking the book. He gave her a small smile, resigned and affectionate. Smiling back, she hoped he couldn't tell how hard and fast her heart was beating.

He will end up going. I can feel it in my bones. Oh, lord. Oh, Saint Snodgrass. Please, please . . . bring them back.

He kept the object in a hexed and lead-lined box in a secret storage pit at the bottom of his East Ott garden. Seventeen years ago, when he'd found the appalling thing, this had been his father's garden. This had been his father's house. But that hadn't mattered. Prompted by an odd premonition, he'd built the hidey-hole two years before that, and never once did his father suspect it was there. His father had been a useful wizard, but no match for the obfuscation incants he'd learned from the Department. In the long years since his finding and hiding of the object, Father remained blissfully ignorant of the object's existence.

How bitterly did he wish he'd been granted the same respite.

Being an only child, in due course the property had come to him. As well as sorrow, he'd felt relief. Unlike his father he lived a solitary life. With no regular parade of visitors the hidey-hole was almost certainly safe from discovery.

Because he was a janitor, traveling the world's less savory places, over the years, from time to time, other things had been stored at the bottom of the garden . . . but none approached the malevolence of the object in the box. To this day—especially on this day—he did not regret his failure to report what he'd found, nor his decision not to surrender it to the man who, in that time, had headed his Department. Harfield Gravesend had been a good man, a trustworthy man, and competent enough in his unimaginative way. But Gravesend had been too quick to trust his political superiors. Too bullishly convinced that the government was and would ever be an instrument of good. Whereas Alec Oldman was born a cynical child, and subsequent experience had only honed his wry suspicions.

Besides. Some things were so tempting they should never see the light of day.

The obfuscation hexes around the old hidey-hole melted like mist at his command. Kneeling on the damp grass, his fingers chilled by the rising dew, he unhexed the hole's lid and eased it open. Immediately he felt the tingle of incants binding the lead-lined box within. And even though they shrouded the thaumic signature of the object, still in his imagination he could feel its sinister touch. Twice, he'd used it, and had nightmares for days after. Remembering those dreams, which returned now and then, usually after a particularly vexing case, a prickle of sweat broke out on his skin. If he did indeed ask Monk Markham to use the object he'd be condemning the young wizard to a lifetime of dismay.

Which hardly seemed fair. Ralph's nephew wasn't one of his agents. And this time he'd not willingly become involved in grim affairs. This time his only crime was being friends with Gerald Dunwoody.

Which only goes to prove the old saw right: there is no good deed that finds itself unpunished.

With a tiny shiver of distaste he reached into the hidey-hole and withdrew the heavily hexed and lead-lined box housing the object. Thrust it into the thick felt bag he'd fetched from indoors, re-sealed the otherwise empty hidey-hole and returned to the car with his burden. Threatened by dawn, the world's rim was growing light. Soon now there'd be traffic, and an expectation that he could be found behind his desk in his office at Nettleworth. Knowing that expectations were about to be confounded—and that more problems would arise because of it—he drove with unwise speed back to the Markham madhouse, where Ralph's nephew and niece and two unlikely royal women were waiting. Where a dead man who should not exist lay stiffening with rigor on the bed of a man who also, some believed, should not exist.

Was he doing the right thing? He had no idea. But, like his hiding of the object, he was doing the only thing he could live with. And for better or worse, that was the best he could do.

Monk and the ladies greeted his return with wary courtesy. Cautious, untrusting, belligerent and afraid. They showed him into the old house's library where a fire burned with inappropriate cheer, and a scattering of books about shadbolts suggested that at last Ralph's intractable nephew was learning to do as he was told.

The other Monk's portal opener sat on a low table, outwardly innocent, wholly repellent. He withdrew the object in its lead-lined box from the thick felt bag and put it on the same low table. Then he unhexed the box and flipped back the lid, revealing the object's existence for the first time in years.

"Blimey," said Monk Markham, peering down at it. "That thing's got a kick to it."

He nodded. "It has."

Stepping back, Markham's sister shivered. "I don't like it, Sir Alec."

He flicked a glance at her. "Nor should you, Miss Markham. This is a thaumaturgical abomination. Created by a man afflicted by . . . interesting ideas."

As Monk Markham winced, the appalling bird tipped her head to one side. "Oh yes? In that case, sunshine, what's it doing in our library?"

He'd often wondered just how much Mr. Dunwoody and his friends knew about the former Queen of Lalapinda. He had to believe—very little. For if they'd known what he knew they would hardly be so relaxed in her company. If he weren't convinced she'd been hexed into comparative harmlessness he'd not be relaxed either.

Miss Cadwallader, as she so quaintly insisted she now be called, stood stiffly behind the wingback chair on which the bird perched. "I appreciate that in your profession, Sir Alec, a certain amount of circumspection is required. But really, given our current dilemma, I hardly think it's appropriate."

"In other words, ducky, get on with it," said the bird. "In case you haven't noticed, the sun's about to rise."

And that was true. With nowhere to sit he dropped to one knee beside the low table, and the box. "This device," he said, tapping its lead-lined container, "is the only one of its kind. At least, as far as I know. I've never come across another and it's my devout hope I never will." He swept his gaze around their faces, slowly, and let them see what that meant. "Until this moment I was the only one who knew of its existence. The wizard who created it is long dead and while he lived he kept it a secret. In revealing it to you four now I imperil not only my own career and quite possibly my life, but yours as well."

"Without asking?" said Miss Markham, frowning. "Thanks for nothing, Sir Alec."

He nodded. "You're welcome."

"So this long dead wizard you nicked it from," said the bird. "Killed him, did you?"

"Is that relevant?"

Her disconcertingly human eyes gleamed. "No. But it's interesting."

"It's ancient history," he said flatly, and looked again at Ralph's inconveniently brilliant nephew. "Mr. Markham. There is a short time after death during which echoes of the deceased's experiences remain imprinted on his or her etheretic aura. This device will allow you to read them."

"Bloody hell!" said the bird. "No wonder you kept that thing under wraps. In the wrong hands it could do a bit of mischief."

He gave her a thin smile. "Precisely."

Monk Markham and his sister were staring at the object with oddly-alike expressions: shock mixed with a cautious and regrettable admiring excitement. The term "cut from the same cloth" might have been coined just for them.

Ralph, Ralph. Does your brother know about his children?

Miss Cadwallader folded her arms. "You want to read our visitor, don't you?"

"Not . . . exactly," he said. "I want Mr. Markham to read him."

"Me? Why me?" said Ralph's nephew, startled.

He shrugged. "Because much of the information gained through this device is, for want of a better word, intuitive. And given that you and he are the same man in many respects, it seems likely you've a better chance of connecting with his memories. Especially since he's been dead for some time."

"Fine," said Miss Cadwallader. "Say our Monk connects. What do you intend to do with the information?"

"Whatever I must in order to avert disaster," he replied, with another thin smile. "That is, after all, my job."

Melissande Cadwallader was a perspicacious young woman, with a spirit forged in fires the heat of which thankfully few would ever know. She stared at him in silence, her green gaze measured and cold. One by one the others, even the bird, turned to look at her.

"Mel?" said Ralph's nephew, a young man in love. "What's wrong?"

"I'm not sure," she said. "Maybe nothing. Maybe everything. Sir Alec . . . nobody official knows you're here, do they?"

Ah. Very neatly, very deliberately, he clasped his hands on his bent knee. "No."

"Do they know Gerald's missing?"

"No."

"Do they know about the other Monk?"

"No."

"In other words, whatever you're planning to do isn't sanctioned."

He nodded. "Correct."

"And are you going to tell them? Your political masters?"

Political masters. Oh, how he disliked that term. "In my opinion this situation is too complicated for a politician to grasp. If we're going to act we must act quickly, decisively, with a minumum of interference."

"So, in *other* other words," she said, still so cool and watchful, "you want to go on keeping your secrets." She nodded at the lead-lined box and its contents. "Like that thing."

"Yes. That is, if you've no objection, Miss Cadwallader."

Her lips tightened. "Have you heard of the saying, Who watches the watchers?"

"We watch each other, Miss Cadwallader."

"Ha!" scoffed the bird. "Then why weren't you watching my Gerald?"

"Are you suggesting I should've anticipated the manner of Mr. Dunwoody's disappearance?"

"He didn't disappear, sunshine, he was kidnapped!" said the bird. "Right from under your sleeping nose!"

"Reg," said Miss Cadwallader, and nudged the chair with her knee. "Be fair."

The bird subsided. Interesting.

"Miss Cadwallader," he said, "is there a point you're trying to make? If so, please make it. Every minute we delay makes Mr. Markham's task more difficult."

"My *point*, Sir Alec," she retorted, "is that you should stop treating us like children and instead spell out exactly what you've got in mind."

"You tell him, ducky," the bird snapped, and chattered her beak. "Bloody government stooges. They're all alike and they *never* change."

Mr. Markham cleared his throat uncomfortably, hands shoved deep into his pockets. "Look. Sir Alec. I know when it comes to your dealings with us the road so far's been a bit bumpy. I know that one way or another we haven't always followed the rules. At least, not as they're written. But that doesn't make us the enemy. We might be unorthodox but I promise, you can trust us."

Sighing, he shook his head. "Mr. Markham, if I didn't know that already then instead of remaining here in your comfortable house you and your sister and your unorthodox friends would be under lock and key in an undisclosed location."

"Oh," said Ralph's nephew, blinking. "Right."

The bird cackled. "So now that you've put us all at ease, Sir Watch-Me-Throw-My-Weight-Around-Because-Intimidating-Civilians-Is-So-Much-Fun, why don't you cut to the chase and lay your dog-eared cards on this nice antique table?"

He looked at the bird and the bird looked back. Bright eyes, dull feathers, and deeds long behind her that would make these children weep.

Does she weep, I wonder, in the dark of night, with her memories?

"My cards," he said, and looked again at Ralph's frustrating, well-intentioned, oblivious nephew, "are indeed dog-eared. And my plan, such as it is, might well be regarded by some as insane."

"Yes, but will it get us Gerald back?" said the bird. "Because that's the only thing any of us give a rat's ass about, sunshine."

"I don't know," he said, after a long, considering pause. "All I can tell you is that I believe it's his only hope. Our only hope. And that if we don't do something—even something insane—every instinct informs me we will most certainly live to regret it."

Nearly half an hour later, with Sir Alec's insane plan explained and them all shifted from the library up to Gerald's bedroom, Melissande took Monk's arm and drew him aside. "Look," she said, her voice strategically low. "I realize I'm probably wasting my breath saying this but—you do understand there's no way he can force you into using that infernal device?"

With an effort he dragged his gaze away from the sheet-covered body on Gerald's bed. Tried to pretend that Sir Alec and Bibbie and Reg weren't standing a small stone's throw away. "I know. But how else can we find out what's happening in this world next door? Short of just barging through the portal, of course, and for once I'd prefer to look before I leap."

Her eyes were anxious. "But after you've looked you'll be leaping, won't you? Monk . . ."

"What? So now you're saying we *should* leave Gerald stranded there? Give him up for dead?"

"*No*," she said, flushing dark pink. "But—but Monk, what happened to being objective?"

"It's overrated."

"And what if something goes wrong while you're using that device? You heard Sir Alec. It's sent men *mad* in the past."

"Yeah, well, I'm mad already, aren't I? So I should be safe."

She shook his arm. "Monk, please. It's not just the device, it's the rest of it as well."

Wanting to kiss her, he patted her hand. "I'll be fine."

"You don't know that!"

True. "Maybe not, but here's what I *do* know. If I don't follow Sir Alec's plan a lot of people could die. Sure, it's going to be tricky, but—"

"Tricky's one word for it," she said grimly.

Sir Alec cleared his throat. "Mr. Markham. Time is a factor here."

Time was always a factor. When were they going to run into a nice, *leisurely* crisis? He stared again at the shrouded shape on Gerald's bed. *"Are you all right?"* Sir Alec had asked. And of course he'd said he was, because admitting weakness to that man would be the gravest of tactical errors.

Except I'm not all right. I watched myself—felt myself—die. It was probably my fault. I was pretty rough dismantling that shadbolt. But I can live with that if I rescue Gerald. I think.

"Mr. Markham . . ."

He glanced at the bedroom doorway, where Gerald's superior stood with Bibbie and Reg. "I know."

"Then stop piss-assing about, sunshine," said Reg, hunched on Bibbie's shoulder. "I'm losing so much beauty sleep waiting for you I'm going to have to put a bag over my head come morning."

Oh, Reg. He managed a sort of grin. "Yeah? Well, if you're looking, we keep them in the second-bottom kitchen drawer."

Fingers tugged on his arm. "*Monk . . .*"

He knew his Melissande pretty well by now. She was fighting fear and embarrassing, unroyal tears. Ignoring Reg's bubbling kettle impression, he brushed his knuckles against his young lady's cheek.

"Don't worry, Mel. I'm just going to rummage through what's left of the poor bugger's memories."

"And after that?" she demanded, unmollified. "Monk, please, at least don't let Sir Alec send you alone. You need us to come with you. There's safety in numbers."

Who cared if they had an audience? He kissed her chastely on the forehead and then, on impulse and far less chastely, on her severe, unhappy lips.

"No. It's far too dangerous for you to go. Hell, it's too dangerous for *me* to go—and I *really* wish I didn't have to. If you came with me and something went wrong—I can't afford to lose my focus. I have to get to Gerald."

"*Mr. Markham!*" Sir Alec snapped. "When I say time is a factor, do you imagine—"

"Sorry," he said, turning. "I'm ready."

"Come and stand with us, Mel," said Bibbie kindly. "You'll only be in the way if you hover."

His little sister never ceased to amaze him. First that shadbolt business, and now this. She cared a great deal for Gerald, and for him. She was afraid for both of them. But she was also excited and fascinated by the realm of thaumaturgic possibilities opening up before them. He was starting to wonder if she wasn't the maddest member of the Mad Markham clan. In a good way, of course.

"Bibs is right, Your Highness," he murmured. "Go on. I'll be all right."

Frightened and resentful and nearly killing herself not to show it, Melissande left him alone at the bed. With a last glance at Sir Alec, who nodded once, his expression forbidding, he put her—he put all of them—out of his mind, dragged the bedroom chair closer and dropped himself onto it.

The body was so . . . still.

His hand unsteady, he tugged off the covering sheet and let it fall to the carpet. His breathing wasn't steady either, and his heart was galloping like a speed-em-up hexed racehorse. It felt like any moment it was going to burst against his ribs.

Settle down, Markham. You're a genius, remember? This'll be a doddle. A walk in the park.

The dead Monk's face had taken on a bluish-gray pallor, and most of the heat had leached out of his flesh. He felt odd to the touch, like cool, uncooked bread dough. How could anyone ever mistake sleep for death? Even a man deeply stuporous, barely moving, didn't look like this. Empty. Uninhabited. The spirit flown away.

I'll look like this one day. Sooner than I was planning if this plan of Sir Alec's goes ass over ears.

The device—Sir Alec's object—was already threaded onto the fingers and thumb of his left hand. A beautiful plaiting of copper, bronze and gold, it linked them together and turned his hand into a starfish. The incants that had forged the device hummed quietly against his skin. They weren't out-and-out dark magic, not like the filthy hexes that had given birth to this Monk's shadbolt. No, this magic came from the *potentia* of an amazing wizard who'd chosen to use his extraordinary power for personal gain. Sir Alec refused to say who he was, or what had happened to him.

But I reckon Reg was right. I reckon he died because of this thing.

He took a deep, shaky breath and glanced again at Gerald's boss. "I'm ready."

Sir Alec nodded. "Take it slow and steady, Mr. Markham. If you rush you might well miss a crucial detail. And don't forget your recording incant."

Damn. He nearly had. Hastily he triggered his own tweaked version of the bog-standard hex and embedded it in the bad cloak-and-dagger novel on Gerald's nightstand. Whatever he said as a result of his reading the dead Monk's memories would overwrite the book's printed text, giving them a permanent record of any information retrieved.

He swallowed self-doubt. For someone like Sir Alec to chance his career, his reputation, maybe even his freedom, on such a dangerous, maverick plan . . . to trust *him* . . .

"All right," he said, his mouth cotton-dry. "Wish me luck."

Closing his eyes he held the device over the dead Monk's solar plexus and slowly lowered it until living and dead flesh came close to touching. A shock of thaumic power jolted through his fingers, then along the robust bones of his hand and wrist and arm. He heard himself gasp, air catching in his throat and chest. Felt the drumming of his blood along constricting veins and arteries. His eyes burned hot in their sockets, his skin goosebumped shivery and cold. His *potentia* twisted, protesting. What he was doing wasn't natural and every thaumaturgic instinct he possessed was rising in rebellion against it.

Sir Alec did say it wouldn't be easy.

Breathing harshly, sweating, he made a conscious effort to stop fighting the device. The moment he surrendered, his thundering heart steadied and he stopped gasping for air. Cracking open his eyelids, he saw that the plaited metal imprisoning his fingers now shone fiercely, like a sun. He couldn't feel any heat from the device, though. Maybe he'd feel it later—but he couldn't worry about that now. What had Sir Alec told him? Oh, yes. He had to empty his mind completely and allow the memories stirred up by the incanted metal to flow into him through the incanted metal and out again through his mouth. He mustn't react to them or fight them or try to examine them as they appeared. He was merely a conduit. A tool.

So what's new? These days every time I turn around somebody's trying to use me.

No, no, he had to stop thinking. This wouldn't work if he couldn't clear his mind. It might not work anyway—the other Monk had been dead for hours. For all they knew his memories had already escaped him like water seeping through a sieve. But Sir Alec said there was a chance—so he'd take the chance. He had to. He'd open his own mind and—and—

A burst of light. A rush of heat. And he fell face-first into someone else's life.

CHAPTER TWENTY

M onk. Monk? *Monk*, can you hear me?"

Groggily he opened his eyes and looked up at his sister. She was kneeling beside him, her face hovering above his, and he was—where was he? On the floor? Why was he on the floor? And whose floor was he on? God, nobody's embarrassing, he hoped. Was he dressed? *Please, God, please, let me be dressed.* And then it all came rushing back. The other Monk. Sir Alec's device. Sir Alec's crazy plan . . .

"Bibbie, what are you *doing?*" he demanded, trying to bat her away. "You're not supposed to be talking to me! The device won't work if you're—Bibbie?" He blinked. "You're crying. Why are you crying?"

"I am *not* crying," said his sister, and smeared her sleeve across her wet eyes. "Witches don't cry. *I* don't cry. I'm a Markham. Besides, it's unprofessional."

His head was aching viciously. Someone had hammered a railroad spike through one ear and out the other. "All right. Have it your way. Then why are you *not* crying? Seriously, Bibs, Sir Alec's going to have a fit if you don't let me—"

She pressed her fingers to his lips. "Shut up and listen, Monk. You've done it. The device worked. You've been talking non-stop for nearly an hour."

He had? Really? Oh. Well, that might explain why his throat felt like a gravel pit.

Except . . . "Are you sure? Because I don't seem to—" He frowned. "Did I say anything useful?"

"I think so," said Bibbie. "Monk, stop talking. You're not looking very good. You're all pasty. And a bit green around the edges."

He wasn't surprised to hear it. He was *feeling* green around the edges. A train was roaring along that damned railroad spike—and then there was the matter of his body's other shrill complaints.

"Here," said Melissande, abruptly appearing at his other side with a cup. "Drink this. Don't gulp."

Having tumbled off the bedroom chair, he used it to help him sit up. The room swooped around him and his mind swooped with it. He felt Bibbie grab his shoulder. "I'm fine. I'm fine."

She sniffed. "No, you're not. Now be quiet and drink."

Still dazed, he took the cup Mel handed him and swallowed a mouthful without looking first. Nearly spat it out again, gagging. "*Warm milk?* Bloody hell, woman! Are you trying to poison me?"

Melissande's eyes were watery and her nose was pink, sure signs that she'd been weeping too. He decided not to mention it.

"Stop moaning," she said, her chin tilted. "And anyway, it's got whiskey in it."

He took another tiny mouthful, grimaced, then swallowed. "Thank you. I think," he muttered.

Sharp pain continued to pound through his temples. He looked down at his left hand, where the device sat quietly on his fingers, no sign of brightness or any thaumic activity at all. "All right. So if it worked does that mean I can take this bloody thing off now?"

Bibbie glanced around. "Sir Alec?"

"Give it to me," said Sir Alec, coming forward with the lead-lined box.

Monk looked at Uncle Ralph's friend closely. *No, he hasn't been crying. Well, of course he hasn't. He's Sir Alec. But something I said gave him a bloody nasty shock.* He handed the cup back to Melissande, then unthreaded his fingers and passed over the device. To his unsettled surprise he felt a shock of loss, surrendering it.

"Here," said Melissande, pushing the cup back at him. "Finish your milk."

Grudgingly sipping, he watched Sir Alec return the device to its lead-lined container, hex the small box impenetrably closed then slip it back into its felt bag. Finally, that done, Sir Alec put the thing on Gerald's dresser and gave him a small nod.

"Good work, Mr. Markham."

A compliment? From Sir Alec? *We must be in worse trouble than I thought.* "Thank you, sir."

"There," said Melissande, plucking the emptied cup from his fingers. "At least you've got a bit of color in your face now. How are you feeling?"

"I *told* you. I'm *fine*." But that wasn't quite true. The pain in his head had only eased, it wasn't defeated. Likewise his other rowdy aches and pains. And he had a horrible, lurking feeling in the pit of his stomach. He might not remember what he'd learned through that device, but even so . . .

I don't need Sir Alec's face to tell me none of it was good.

The bedroom's curtains had been opened. The window, too. Fresh cool air and barely-past-dawn light washed into the chamber. Puzzled, he looked around. Someone was missing . . .

"Wait a minute. Where's Reg?"

"Stretching her wings," said Melissande after a moment. She exchanged inscrutable glances with Sir Alec. "Some of the things you said. I'm afraid they were a bit . . . harrowing."

He frowned. "Oh. I'm sorry to hear that."

"You really don't remember any of it?" said Bibbie, sounding uncertain—and displeased. "But that's not right. I thought—" She turned to Sir Alec. "You said he'd—does this mean it didn't work? Or did something go wrong? You gave him the right instructions, didn't you? How is he supposed to do *any* of this if—"

Sir Alec raised a hand. "Patience, Miss Markham," he said quietly. "It can take a little time. Using the device is a confusing experience."

Using the chair again Monk clambered to his feet, grunting. He'd had more than enough of sitting on the floor. From the corner of his eye he caught a glimpse of the other Monk. Somebody thoughtful had recovered his corpse with the sheet.

And now somebody else—whose name rhymes with Sir Alec—is going to have to take him away. See him decently buried because we can't risk taking him back to his own world. Will that mean I'll have to make visits to the graveyard? No. No, I don't think so. Even for me, that's too macabre.

Resolutely turning his back on the sheet-covered body—*my body, but I really, really don't want to think about that*—he folded his arms and looked at Sir Alec instead. "Look, I don't mean to be rude but it's my brain that's buzzing, and not in a good way. And the rest of me feels like the football at the end of the game. So for once can you please give me a simple answer to a simple question? How long before what I just did pays us dividends? Because right now I'm a blank slate, Sir Alec. I don't remember a bloody thing."

Sir Alec sighed. "Mr. Markham, there is no simple answer. The device is idiosyncratic. All I can tell you with any degree of certainty is that it worked. You *did* retrieve memories from the late Monk Markham and they *will* manifest themselves in due course. But stamping your feet like a two-year-old in a tantrum *isn't* going to make that happen any faster."

"That's uncalled for!" said Melissande hotly. "He's not having a tantrum, he's expressing a perfectly legitimate concern. You saw what he went through, using your precious device. If it turns out he's suffered for nothing, Sir Alec, I'll—I'll—be *very* displeased."

"And so will Reg," added Bibbie. "And trust me, you do *not* want that. Because *she's* got a long beak and *you've* got unmentionables."

Sir Alec stared at the girls in silence, clearly regretting his decision to involve them . . . and possibly the fact they'd ever met.

"Oh, come on, girls," he said, taking reluctant pity on Gerald's beleaguered boss. "It's not his fault."

Scowling, Bibbie opened her mouth to argue that—

but instead stopped scowling and smiled. "We're idiots, all of us. You don't need to remember, Monk. You recorded the whole thing." She reached for the book on Gerald's nightstand. "See? All you have to do is—"

"No!" said Sir Alec. "Miss Markham, don't—"

Ignoring him, Bibbie tossed the hexed book. "Here, Monk. Instant memories!"

He reached for it. Fumbled it. The book thudded to the carpet, the impact knocking it wide open. He bent down to pick it up . . . and his eye caught a random line of hexed writing.

And then he said, "Trust me, I have everything under control. You've got nothing to worry about, Monk. The world will never have to fear a Lional of New Ottosland again."

He blinked, startled, as a bright light seemed to explode before his eyes. And then his breath caught, and his heart slammed, and sweat started pouring down his spine.

Oh, bugger. Oh, bloody hell. I remember.

A firestorm of images swirling sparks and flame inside his skull. Sights and sounds and memories that weren't his . . . and yet were.

Horrified desperation. *No, Gerald—don't do this. It's wrong. You know it's wrong. Please, mate. Let me help you. It's not too late, we can—*The death of hope. Betrayal and torture. *It's a shame, Monk. You mustn't think I'm not sorry. But I can't do this without you and we both know that's not the kind of help you meant.* Searing pain as the shadbolt took hold. Disbelief and defeat and a sister lost to the dark. *You're so stubborn, Monk, I could slap you. Why didn't you say yes? What Gerald can do?*

It's marvelous. I'm having so much fun. If you'd only said yes we could've had fun together. Pity and horror. *My God, Gerald, oh my God, what have you done?* Heartbreak at yet another casual cruelty. *Mel, Mel, I'm so sorry, I'd help you if I could.* Defiance, so fleeting. *Forget it, Gerald. You can't ask me to do that. I won't—I won't—* Pain beyond bearing. Craven capitulation. But at its battered, beating heart—a seed of revolt. *I'll stop you, mate. I don't know how, but I will. I owe it to the Gerald you used to be. The Gerald you killed.*

Other memories, tumbling. Bursts and snatches of the other life he'd never lived. Chaotic. Disordered. A nightmare patchwork quilt. Fading now, fading quickly, the thaumic power was dwindling. His tongue raced to keep up. The other Gerald's crazy dreams. His wicked hopes. His terrible plan. And then one final, heartbroken thought.

He'll help me. I know he will. Or I don't know myself.

Monk felt the hexed book slip from his nerveless fingers. Heard its papery bounce on the carpet, and Melissande's alarmed cry. The dead man wearing his face lay so still upon the bed. No-one would guess, looking at him, what terrible things he'd seen and done.

A shocking pain jolted through him as his knees hit the floor.

It was Sir Alec who crouched beside him. Sir Alec who took hold of him and lent him some strength. "Steady now, Mr. Markham," he said sharply. "We've no time for histrionics."

The hand painfully gripping his shoulder gave more comfort than he could ever have expected. And Sir Alec's clipped voice and cool gray eyes helped too, far more than warm soft womanly sympathy. Or tears. They would've undone him.

"I'm all right," he said, after a short struggle. "Sorry. It just—it was—it hit me a bit—I wasn't expecting that."

"No," said Sir Alec, removing his hand and standing. "It does come as a shock."

Something in the way he said it, some odd note in his voice . . . *Ha. I thought so. He's used the device too.* "I'm all right," he said again, looking at Melissande. She was holding the hexed book gingerly, as though it might bite. Or explode. "But Sir Alec's right. We have to get cracking on this, now, we have to—"

"No, Monk, don't listen to him," said Bibbie, shoving Sir Alec aside without hesitation. "We can't rush this. We can't even be sure you can cobble together a shadbolt that will fool the other Gerald. Not if he's as awful and powerful as—as you said the other Monk remembered. And—and what about his portal opener? I know you've both got the same thaumic signature, but what if you can't make it work? What if—"

"Bibs . . ." Sighing, he hung his head for a moment, then let her pull him to his feet. Briefly touched his forehead to hers. "Don't. Of course we have to rush this. The fate of two worlds *depends* on us rushing. That other Gerald could come looking for me—*his* me—any tick of the clock."

She smoothed his collar with trembling fingers. "Well, yes, maybe, but—"

"And if he's not where he's meant to be—if *I'm* not there, being him?" He captured her fingers with his. "Bibs, there'll be no hope of stopping the mad bastard. He'll find a way to make our Gerald finish that bloody machine and once it's finished—once it's working—well. That'll be it. We can kiss each other goodbye. Because if he succeeds there's no wizard *anywhere* strong enough to stop the kind of power he'll have at his fingertips."

Pulling away from him, Bibbie turned on Sir Alec. "So you're just going to stand there, are you, and say *nothing*? You're going to let him *do* this? It's not enough that you've probably sent Gerald to his death, now you want to send my brother after him? Well, I suppose that'd solve a few problems for you, wouldn't it? No more embarrassingly powerful Gerald Dunwoody and no more inconveniently brilliant Monk Markham. That'd save you a lot of money in headache pills, wouldn't it?"

Sir Alec's lips tightened, just for a moment. "Miss Markham—"

Monk cleared his throat. "Excuse me? She's my sister, Sir Alec. Let me talk to her."

"Talk quickly, Mr. Markham," Sir Alec snapped. "Or I'll have no choice but to seek out Lord Attaby and apprise him of everything—which isn't something either of us wants, is it?"

No, it bloody wasn't. As Sir Alec took the hexed book from Melissande and started leafing through it, he tugged Bibbie over to the old mahogany wardrobe. That left Mel stranded—so she occupied herself by putting the bedroom chair back where it belonged, beside the window. Her expression was forbiddingly self-contained.

"I know what you're going to say, Monk, and I don't care," Bibbie muttered, her expression mutinous. "Not after what I just heard. Sir Alec's lost his marbles if he thinks you can handle this on your own. This is the kind of thaumaturgic catastrophe that needs all the help it can get. He just wants to keep it quiet to save his own skin."

Not since she was a baby had he seen her so upset. "Come on, Bibs—that's not true and you know it," he said gently. "Sir Alec's right. If we can handle this situation discreetly we should. We *must*. My God, can you *imagine* the uproar in parliament if what's happened here got out? And it wouldn't stay a secret, either. News like this would spread around the world. And mass panic would only make it easier for the other Gerald to come in here and take over."

"Maybe, but you don't know that's what he's planning, Monk," Bibbie objected. "The—the other you didn't even know his Gerald was going to kidnap our Gerald."

"No," he said, after a moment. "But if he'd had the time, he would've figured it out." He managed a small, painful smile. "He was pretty smart, you know. Okay, not as smart as *me* but—"

"Oh, *Monk*," said Bibbie, and slapped his chest. Suddenly her eyes were full of tears. "Monk . . . you *died*."

"No, no, no, Bibs," he said, and held her tight. "*He* died. And that's not the same thing."

She pulled back. "You don't believe that."

He didn't have time to work out what he did or didn't believe. "Bibs, please," he said, catching hold of her small, cold hands. "It may only be a theory but we have to assume it's fact. If we don't he could win. I can't let that happen."

"But Monk—" Blinking back her tears she tugged her hands free of his grasp. "You're not a *spy*, you're a theoretical thaumaturgist. You aren't *trained* for this."

"Trust me, Bibs, I *know*." Then he pointed to the body on the bed. "But the moment he crossed from his world into ours, that was it. None of us stood a chance of not getting involved."

She looked at him with enormous eyes. "No. I don't accept that. Let Sir Alec send one of his janitors. This is their business, not yours."

"Oh, Bibs . . ." He tucked a strand of her glorious golden hair behind her ear. "I wish I could. I wish it was that easy. But even if I could doppler hex one of Sir Alec's people into me, I can't doppler my thaumic signature and the rest of it, can I? I'm the only Monk Markham we've got. That other Gerald will accept no substitutes."

Her face crumpling, his little sister flung her arms around his neck and burst into tears. "Promise me you'll come back, Monk," she sobbed. "Because if you don't come back that means I'm stuck with Aylesbury and if I'm stuck with Aylesbury I won't care if that horrible other Gerald takes over the world! I might even *help* him just to end the pain!"

"Oh, *Bibbie*," he said, voice breaking, and held her tight again. From the corner of his eye he caught Melissande staring at them, vulnerable in a way he wasn't used to seeing. As for Sir Alec, he was frowning. He nodded. *I know, I know.* Gently he disentangled himself. "Here's an idea, Bibs. Why don't you and Mel go see where Reg's got to? Do something irritating so she can scold you. That always cheers her up."

Sniffing, almost laughing, Bibbie gave him a half-hearted slap. "Cheeky bugger."

"I do my best." He shifted around. "Melissande . . ."

Like magic, her Royal Highness returned. "Don't worry, Monk," she said, formidably composed. "We'll hold the fort here. And if things don't go the way we want them to, over there, well—that other Gerald Dunwoody will be in for a nasty surprise. Forewarned is forearmed, after all. I can promise you, we'll be waiting for him."

He felt his heart thud. *Bloody hell. I love her.* "I know you will, Mel."

The bedroom door closed behind the girls, and it was just him and Sir Alec and the body on the bed. Sir Alec put the hexed book on the dresser, beside the hexed box, his movements restrained and deliberate. Whatever he was feeling he was keeping it to himself.

"So, Mr. Markham," he said. "We reach the point of no return. You understand the risks of what we're about to attempt?"

His mouth was dry. He swallowed. "If you mean do I realize I could fry my brain like an egg, then yes. I understand."

Sir Alec crossed the carpet to the bed then clasped his hands in front of him like a meek civil servant. "You can still decline. We both know I'm in no position to insist."

No, Sir Alec really wasn't. His position, to put it mildly, was professionally precarious. And how did it feel, knowing his future rested in the hands of a wizard young enough to be his son, who'd never been one for slavishly following the rules?

Bloody awful, I'll bet.

"I don't know how to do this," he said, wishing he could sit down. Wishing he couldn't feel a tremble in his knees. "I don't think it's ever been done. Has it?"

Sir Alec raised an eyebrow. "No, it hasn't. Or rather, to the best of my knowledge it hasn't. And if it has, then it's certainly never been documented. Not that I've seen. But I'm sure we'll work it out, Mr. Markham. Rumor has it you're a genius—and how often does rumor lie?"

Bloody *hell*, he was a sarky bastard. How did Gerald stand it? "Are you sure it doesn't matter that the shadbolt's on a—a corpse?"

A breath, a whisper, of a mordant chuckle. "Sure? Not at all. But I'm moderately optimistic. After all, Mr. Markham, it is a *fresh* corpse. Well. Fresh-*ish*. Not decomposing, at any rate—so that's all to the good."

He'd like to kiss whoever had recovered the dead Monk with the sheet—even if it had been Sir Alec. It was a very thoughtful gesture. He never wanted to look at that empty face again. "And you're sure there's enough left of the shadbolt to transfer?"

Another soft snort of dry amusement. "No."

Saint Snodgrass save him, he was starting to feel sick. "But you have transferred a shadbolt before?"

"I have," Sir Alec said, after a long hesitation. "From one living subject to another. And if I had the choice I wouldn't do it again."

"And what if even a rumored genius like me can't cobble together what's missing well enough to fool the other Gerald?"

"In that case, Mr. Markham, your little vacation will most likely take an interesting turn."

Well, that was encouraging. "So—this incant you've got shoved down—" Hesitating, he reconsidered his choice of words. "Up your sleeve. The one that lets a wizard disguise his own thaumic signature as somebody else's. Is that—y'know—legal?"

Sir Alec held his gaze steadily. "Your point, Mr. Markham?"

"Blimey," he breathed, awestruck. "Sir Alec, you're a fraud. You're no more a rah-rah team player than *I* am. Does Uncle Ralph know the truth about you?"

"Your uncle, Mr. Markham, knows precisely what he needs to know."

He grimaced. "In other words, my uncle's a bloody good politician."

"And a good man," said Sir Alec coolly. "Who cares deeply for his country and will do what he deems necessary to see it kept safe." A small, wintry smile. "As will I. And you. Which, to my astonishment, places all three of us on the same team."

"Apparently," he said. "Just let me get my smelling salts, would you?"

Another cold smile. "Sarcasm I can live without, Mr. Markham. Now I suggest that we start with you learning the dubious incant I have shoved—where was it again? Oh, yes. *Up my sleeve.*" He pulled a folded piece of paper from his pocket. "Close enough."

He took the incant and read it quickly. Deceptively simple, it had to be one of the most dangerous pieces of wizardry he'd ever come across. *Blimey. Compared to this my bloody portal opener's a kiddy's toy.* He glanced up.

"Right. Got it. Now what?"

Sir Alec gave him what Reg liked to call an

old-fashioned look, crossed to the wardrobe and took out two of Gerald's shirts. "Now, Mr. Markham, we see if rumor is, in fact, fact." Choosing at random, he turned one shirt from white cotton into green, then tossed him both garments. "Match that."

Feeling faintly ridiculous, Monk closed his eyes and sank himself into the ether. Sir Alec's thaumic signature was piquant, like a freshly cut lime. Strong. Even intimidating. Interestingly it reminded him of Gerald's. Not in power, of course, because nobody was as powerful as Gerald. But in its complexity and subtle shadings there was a definite resemblance.

So maybe Gerald was born to be a janitor and it was only ever a question of how he got there.

A provocative notion. One he looked forward to dissecting with his best friend, over a beer. Soon.

"Mr. Markham . . ."

Bloody hell. "Right, right," he muttered, and summoned the masking incant to mind. Tightened his fingers around the hexed shirt, closed his eyes, and focused on the fabric's altered thaumic signature. The trick was in the balance between the two incants: the easy-peasy color change hex and the quicksilver slippery incant that would fool another wizard into thinking Sir Alec had hexed both shirts. They had to trigger simultaneously or the masking element wouldn't take.

Tweak this one here . . . nudge that one there . . . a little push . . . some more pull . . .

As the shirt changed color he felt the masking incant click into place as though a key had turned in a difficult lock. Surging through him, a sense of release. An odd, shivering quiver in his *potentia.* He opened his eyes and looked at the shirt. It was now the same shade of green as the other one. The only difference between them was the badly reattached top button on the one he'd hexed. He doubted Sir Alec had noticed.

He jumbled both shirts behind his back, then tossed them to Gerald's superior. "Which one was yours? Can you tell?"

"No," said Sir Alec, after a considering pause, and smiled. "Well done."

Stupidly, he felt a warm rush at the compliment— and on its heels, resentment. He made it a point never to get carried away by praise. Anyway, why should he *care* what this cool, self-contained and ruthless bastard thought of him?

Because he's a wizard whose respect is worth having. Because I get the feeling he's done things that mean I get to breathe free air. Because—because—

Well. Just because.

And then he remembered what the other Monk had helped the other Gerald do to their Sir Alec.

"Mr. Markham?"

He shook his head, bile burning his throat. "It's nothing. I'm fine. All right, so what's next?"

In Sir Alec's gray eyes, a hint of sympathy. "Next, Mr. Markham, we get you fitted with a shadbolt."

And once more his mouth sucked horribly dry. *I swear, when this is over I am never leaving my lab again.* "I'm ready."

"I doubt it," said Sir Alec. "Nevertheless. If I might have your assistance?"

"To do what?" he said warily.

Sir Alec looked at him as though he were dim.

"Rearrange the body. You need to be in close proximity to the original bearer of the shadbolt, and I need access to both of you to effect the transfer."

"Wait—you want me to share a bed with my own *corpse*?"

And that earned him another look, even less patient. "Yes, Mr. Markham. Since under the circumstances it seems unlikely you'll be able to sit side by side."

Bloody hell, Dunnywood. The things I do for you . . .

He helped Sir Alec wrangle the other Monk's body until it was lying in reverse on one side of the bed, then gritted his teeth and arranged himself beside it, his head where his feet should go. He kept his gaze pinned to the ceiling and tried to pretend he was somewhere—anywhere—else. Outwardly composed, Sir Alec knelt at the foot of the bed. But underneath his self-contained exterior there was anxiety. Definitely some doubt. And that wasn't something to fill a wizard with confidence—even if said wizard was rumored to have genius-like qualities.

"Right," said Sir Alec. "Deep breath, Mr. Markham, and remain as relaxed as you can."

At first he felt nothing except Sir Alec's hand on his head, lightly pressing. But then, after a few moments, he felt a stirring in the ether. A low, ominous tremble that raised his thaumaturgic hackles. His skin goosebumped again, unpleasantly. His teeth jittered on edge. He could feel the body, too close beside him, begin its own discomfiting shudder. A tainted tang in the back of his throat promised worse to come.

"Steady, now, steady," Sir Alec murmured. "Lower

those defenses, Mr. Markham. Don't fight what's happening. Almost there . . . almost there . . ."

Oh, hell. Oh, bloody hell. This is going to hurt.

The skill required to lift the shadbolt off the dead Monk and place it on him was shocking. The pain of its attachment was a hundred times worse. He heard himself scream as its thaumic claws sank into his etheretic aura. Even damaged, the shadbolt knew its job. Frantically scraping at his face he rolled off the bed and hit the floor hard. The temptation to bash his head on the carpeted floorboards overtook him. But it didn't change anything. The shadbolt wouldn't let go.

Bibbie—Bibbie—no wonder you screamed.

Cursing, Sir Alec scrambled beside him. "Mr. Markham, stop it. *Monk, that's enough!*"

With his hands imprisoned and a knee planted on his chest, he stared up at Sir Alec. "I can't—this won't work—I can't—please, God, *get it off!*"

"Give it a moment," said Sir Alec. His eyes were pitiless now. "Give it a moment, Mr. Markham. You can do this. You're strong enough. If the other one stood it, then so by God can you."

The other one. The other Monk, who'd borne this for *months*. The shamed thought helped him steady his breathing. Helped him not to howl again, but instead sit up like a sane man.

"Bloody hell," he said, shuddering. "It's like—I'm being *watched*."

"And so you are, in a manner of speaking," said Sir Alec. "But we don't have time for a shadbolt tutorial. Take a good look at the thing, Mr. Markham. Can you see the gaps? Can you fill them in sufficiently so that our target's suspicions won't be aroused?"

Our target. *The other Gerald. The man he wants me to kill.* "I don't know," he said, feeling so sick. "I'll try."

He tried and succeeded, more or less, but the effort gave him a nosebleed and stirred his headache to skull-exploding point. The other Monk hadn't been able to stop himself from examining and identifying the incants used to imprison him. Thaumaturgical curiosity, both Monks' besetting sin—and praise Saint Snodgrass for it. And he'd managed to retrieve enough of those memories so that now he could cobble together the damaged shadbolt. Mask his hasty thaumaturgy with Gerald's familiar signature, which he then muddled and muddied to look more like the other Gerald's.

Bloody hell, this is rough, mate. You'd better be able to help me fix it when I finally track you down.

"That's it," he said at last, panting. "That's the best I can do."

"Then let's hope your best is sufficient," said Sir Alec. "Right. On your feet. It's nearly time to go."

He let Sir Alec help him up. Needed the assistance, though he'd never admit it. "Where's the portal opener? Do you have it?"

Sir Alec nodded. "But first you need to complete your transformation."

It took him a moment to twig. But when he did— "Oh—no. No, I'll hex my own clothes to look like his. I am *not* dressing up in a dead man's underpants! He's *dead*, Sir Alec. Dying—it's *messy*."

"I'll see to the . . . details," said Sir Alec, obdurate. "But there's a detectable etheretic variation at the thaumic sublevel of his clothing, Mr. Markham. It's as good as a dimensional fingerprint for anyone who thinks to look. You can't fake it in your own clothing, so quickly—strip off."

"If there's an imprint in the clothing, doesn't that mean there's an imprint in him, too?"

"Yes," said Sir Alec. "But if the clothing is genuine, then—"

"Then that might be enough to discourage a deeper look," he said, and sighed.

Wonderful. Bloody brilliant. For all our sakes you'd better be right.

Hating Sir Alec, he did as he was told as Sir Alec, without ceremony, divested the corpse of its clothes. Cleaned them with casual competence then handed them over.

When he was dressed again, his flesh shrinking and crawling, he held out his hand. "The portal opener?"

Sir Alec pulled the small, innocent-looking stone from a pocket. "You're clear on how this works?"

"Yes."

"And you remember where he was when he operated it? Where it will return you to, and what you're supposed to be doing there?"

"Yes. I remember. You're sure it'll be the same time there as it is here?"

"As sure as I can be." Sir Alec hesitated, then handed him the portal. "So. Mr. Markham. The moment of truth. Are you confident you can do this? The enemy wears your friend's face."

I don't know . . . I don't know . . . "Yes. I can do it."

"Good. Then go."

He made himself look at the dead, naked man on the bed, who'd given his life to save two worlds.

"I don't—I can't—" He took a deep, steadying

breath. "The girls. I can't—will you tell them I'll see them soon? Please?"

Sir Alec nodded, very proper, very formal. No unseemly emotions on display. "Of course. Good luck."

He activated the portal opener. Watched in wonder as a patch of air in the bedroom began to shimmer, sparkling with blue and red lights. Shivering, he felt the ether twist in answer. The patch widened— widened—nearly big enough—almost—

Oh, God. Oh, Gerald. I'm not ready for this.

The portal opened in a silent flash of cobalt and crimson. Sweating, trembling, he started towards it. He could feel the wild thaumic currents churning in his blood. But as he took his first step towards the unknown a feathered whirlwind hurtled into the bedroom through the forgotten open window, shrieking.

"Are you out of your *mind*, sunshine? You aren't going anywhere without me!"

Reg.

Oh, bloody hell.

But before he could grab her . . . the portal swallowed them both alive.

CHAPTER TWENTY-ONE

Abandoned in Government House's swanky Cab-inet dining room, Gerald stared at the ornate clock on the wall. Just over five hours had passed since he'd first opened his eyes in this place. Five of the worst hours of his life—which was an alarming commentary on the state of his life, these days.

I really should've been a tailor. If I'd just followed in my father's footsteps instead of chasing a dream . . .

Lunch sat in his belly like a lump of ice. Not because the food hadn't been spectacular. This was Government House, of course it was spectacular. But digestion, it seemed, was beyond him at the moment. Breathing evenly and not screaming—that was about all he could manage right now.

Of course, I could run. I wonder how far I'd get before he found me? For God's sake, he found me in a portal in an entirely different world. And then he pulled me out of it, with about as much effort as hooking a fish from a lake. What can't he do, I wonder? What won't he do in his mad pursuit of power?

Someone must be looking for him by now, surely.

Sir Alec had to know he'd never reached Grande Splotze. A bugger, that. Perhaps their only solid lead on the black market wizard who'd sold one killing hex to Permelia Wycliffe and another to someone who wanted the tycoon Manizetto dead—and maybe it was lost. So yes. With so much at stake Sir Alec would be keeping a close eye on his janitor. He'd have to know by now that Dunwoody had vanished.

But has he told anyone? He'd have to tell Monk, surely. Like it or not, he'd have to know his best chance of finding me lies with Monk.

Only . . . how was Monk going to figure this out? Sure, he and Sir Alec would suspect a kidnapping. Kidnap was an occupational hazard for janitors. But kidnap to an alternate reality? Not even Monk was likely to dream up that scenario.

So I have to face it. I am stuck. On my own. Unless . . .

But he was starting to think he'd never turn this world's Bibbie. For one thing he was never going to get her alone. Not with Gerald jealously hovering. And anyway, she was in love with him. She was in love with the power. Even afraid, she was still in love.

She's not going to listen to me. Which leaves me with this world's Monk and Reg . . .

Except Reg wasn't a witch any more and this world's Monk was wearing a shadbolt.

Oh, God. Is he going to shadbolt me? He has to sooner or later, surely. He can't honestly think that when push comes to shove I'll stand by and let him slaughter tens of thousands, even to keep my two dearest friends safe.

Although . . . maybe he did. Maybe this Gerald was by now so lost to himself that he really had forgotten his lesson in the cave.

So yes, it seemed likely there was a shadbolt in his future. He wasn't immune. The *docilianti* incant Lional had used on him in New Ottosland was a shadbolt's kissing cousin, and it had worked just fine. Unless . . . could it be a question of thaumaturgics? Perhaps whatever this world's Gerald wanted him to do had to be done without a shadbolt's interference.

Bloody hell, I wish he'd tell me what it is. I wish he'd get this over with. I wish I had the first idea what to do.

But when the other Gerald finally did reveal his plan . . . what then? Chances were good it was going to be monstrous. Unspeakable. A violation of every wizarding oath.

And I know, I just know, he's dreamed up a way to make me go along with it. Lord, if only I could throw myself out of the nearest window. That'd put a spoke in the mad bastard's wheel.

But he couldn't. He wasn't sitting alone here with the trifle and cream. The Cabinet dining room was hexed tight with a dozen binding incants and though he'd tried until his nose bled, he couldn't break them.

All he could do was sit at the table . . . and wait.

Tired of being stared at, sick of their miserable, pathetic faces, he banished everyone but Attaby back to their desks. Attaby he sent to sit in a side room, so that he and Bibbie had the Cabinet room to themselves. He took her on the Cabinet conference table, knowing Attaby could hear them, glorying in her wantonness and the flouting of society's rules. Sometimes he wondered if she'd do it without the wild magics he'd found for her. But every time the thought crossed his mind he crushed it. What did why matter? She did it. She was his.

The Cabinet room's crystal ball remained stubbornly silent. If Damooj didn't call soon . . .

Finished making herself ladylike again, Bibbie perched on the edge of the table and considered him. "Gerald . . ."

"What?" he said, arms folded in front of him, chin propped on his wrists. The afterglow was fading fast, chased away by impatience and doubt.

"The other Gerald. When you look at him . . . what do you see?"

He flicked her a look. "Opportunity. Why?"

"No reason," she said, shrugging. "I was just wondering. It's odd. You're the same age . . . but he looks younger than you. Even with his horrible poached eye."

"That's because in every way that counts, he's a child."

"I suppose . . ." She slid off the edge of the table and wandered to the nearest window. The clouds had lowered and thickened. Any minute now they'd start vomiting rain. "Gerald . . . it is going to work, isn't it? Your grand plan?"

"Of course it's going to work," he said, stung. "Are you *doubting* me, Bibbie?"

"No, no, no! Of course not!" she said quickly. "Only—well, we're cutting things awfully close, aren't we? The UMN's deadline is almost on us and the machine's not finished yet and—" She traced a fingertip down the windowpane. "When are you going to tell Gerry about the machine?"

He pulled a face. "Later. Once I've dealt with that pond scum Damooj."

"Don't worry," she said, glancing over her silk-clad shoulder. "He'll toe the line. He doesn't have a choice."

"I know that!" he snapped. "I'm not an idiot!"

"Of course you're not" she said, fingers clenching. "Sorry. I didn't mean to—sorry."

He flung himself back in his chair and scowled at her. "I should think so."

The first splats of rain struck the window. Turning her back on them, Bibbie sat on its sill. "What are you going to do about Gonegal?"

He felt his belly tighten. *Gonegal.* That arrogant pillock. Him and the other nations of the UMN who were too stupid to read the writing on the wall.

Threaten me, would you? You've no idea what you've done. When I'm through with you, Viceroy, you and your little friends, you'll look at Sir Alec and think he got off easy.

"What do you think I'm going to do, Bibs?"

She smoothed her outrageously short hair. He'd been so cross at first, when she'd cut it. Now he rather liked the look. "Oh, I think you're going to make him pay. Provided . . ."

"What?" he said, sitting up. "Provided *what,* Bibbie?"

For once she didn't back down when he bit. "It's just—well, everything's riding on the machine, isn't it? On Monk being able to build it properly in the first place and then you being able to convince Gerry to help you work it. I mean, what if Monk *can't* finish it? And what if Gerry won't cooperate?"

He smiled, then smiled wider when she flinched. "Of course Monk can finish it, Bibbie. He knows what'll happen if he fails. Besides—since when did Monk Markham *not* finish what he started? People don't call him a genius just to see him blush."

"And Gerry?"

"The Professor?" He snorted. "The only thing that Gerald Dunwoody and I have in common is our rogue *potentia*. Otherwise he's so weak I could snap him like a twig. Did you *see* him nearly burst into tears over Melissande? He'll do exactly *what* I want, *when* I want it and *how* I want it. To the letter. Because he knows I'll make other people sorry if he won't."

She slid off the window sill and walked to him, every footstep a promise. "And when you say *other people* . . ."

You mean me. She didn't say the words aloud but he could read them in her eyes. She adored him and feared him. It was the perfect combination. Reaching for her, he pulled her roughly into his lap. "I mean other people, Bibs," he murmured against her cautious lips. "Why? What did you think I meant?"

Before she could answer, the Cabinet room's crystal ball chimed. He pushed Monk's sister onto the floor. "Attaby! Get in here!"

Shadbolted Attaby, so delightfully obedient, appeared in the doorway. "Sir?"

He nodded at the chiming crystal. "Answer it. If it's Damooj, you know what to say. *And* you know what I want to hear."

"Sir," said Attaby, wooden as a pine tree.

With Bibbie standing beside him, tossing him

reproachful glances, he sprawled in his chair and watched Attaby answer the call. The chiming stopped, the green flashing stopped, and the image of a familiar face formed deep in the clear crystal. It looked wonderfully frightened.

"Prime Minister Attaby. I've called to give you my country's response to your . . . request."

Attaby nodded. "President Damooj. We were beginning to think silence *was* your answer."

Damooj's pale skin flushed an unbecoming dull red. Since his last communication his yellow hair had been cropped close to his skull. It gave him the look of a man suffering from a rampaging fever.

"No, no, not at all, Prime Minister," he said. His voice was cracked and close to breaking. "But these matters—they must be discussed—debated—mulled over—put to a vote. You understand, sir. They cannot be rushed."

Attaby closed his eyes briefly. "Yes, President Damooj. I remember."

"I'm sorry?" said Damooj, frowning. "I don't—"

He rapped his knuckles on the conference table, making Attaby jump. And when the shadbolted fool looked at him, he raised a warning finger. It was all he needed; Attaby shuddered, nearly swaying with fright.

"President Damooj, I am a busy man," he said huskily. "Give me your answer."

"You already know my answer," said Damooj, through gritted teeth. "We capitulate. Babishkia's wizards and witches are being rounded up as we speak."

"To be held under thaumaturgical lock and key?" said Attaby. "In a secure and secret location?"

A bead of sweat rolled down Damooj's cheek. Or

was it a tear? It was hard to tell the difference through the crystal. "Yes. As directed."

Attaby nodded. "That is satisfactory. Continue the good work. A—a—representative of my government will be contacting you in due course. Well done, President Damooj. You've made the right decision."

Damooj didn't answer that. He just disconnected the call.

"Oh, *Gerald!*" squealed Bibbie, and kissed him. "It's happening. It's really happening. *Everything* is falling into place, just like you said."

Delighted, he leaped up from his chair and romped her around the Cabinet room in a fast waltz. Ending the impromptu dance with a dip and a kiss, he then turned to Attaby.

"We have our military on alert? And the portals locked on to Babishkia?"

Attaby nodded. "Yes, sir."

"What about their portals?"

"Disabled, sir, as you ordered."

"Excellent. Then as soon as Damooj confirms their arrests are complete give the order, Prime Minister."

Attaby nodded. "Yes, sir."

"Oh, Gerald, this is so exciting," said Bibbie, clapping her hands. "Ottosland's very first invasion."

Yes. And once Babishkia fell, the other lesser nations would fall twice as fast . . . provided he was able to hold off Gonegal and his short-sighted allies in the UMN.

But failure wasn't something he thought about. He couldn't fail. He was Gerald Dunwoody.

He slapped Bibbie's temptingly rounded behind. "Go and fetch the Professor, Bibs. Taking Babishkia won't help us if the machine's not ready. It's time Gerry rolled his sleeves up and got down to work."

Bibbie's hand on his shoulder startled him out of his doze. Seeing her sweet face beside his, smiling, he thought for the briefest moment that it really had been the worst kind of dream. And then he blinked . . . and the Cabinet dining room swam back into one-eyed focus.

The disappointment was so sharp that he gasped.

"Come along, Gerry," said the Bibbie with short hair and makeup. "Gerald wants you."

In numb silence he followed her back to the Cabinet room, where his counterpart was sitting in a chair with his crossed heels on the conference table. His only company was shadbolted Prime Minister Attaby, whose dull stare was carefully trained upon the carpet.

"Ah! Professor!" said the other Gerald, with a genial smile. "There you are. Ready to go?"

He was desperate to know what they'd been up to while he twiddled his thumbs in the dining room. He wanted to ask, but something dangerously brittle in the other Gerald's voice dissuaded him. Whatever had happened, he thought it had sickened Attaby. There was some new strain in the shadbolted man's gray face . . .

The other Gerald swung his feet to the floor. "Right. So, now that things are under control here for the next little while, you and I and Bibbie are going to—"

On the conference table, the large crystal ball chimed.

"Damooj again?" said the other Gerald, surprised.

"My word, that was fast." He glared at Attaby. "Well, come on man, don't stand there like a noggin. Find out what he wants!"

"Yes, sir," said Attaby, and accepted the call.

The crystal ball's flashing green light was replaced by a man with a wolfish face and bright blue eyes full of disdain. Gerald felt his blood leap. Tambotan of Jandria. *Jandria?* What the devil was this?

Attaby flicked an anguished glance at the other Gerald and eased a finger between his collar and his throat. "Ah—Prime Minister Tambotan. Greetings, sir."

"I do not care for your greetings, Attaby," Tambotan snarled. "I want to speak to him. Send for him immediately."

Bibbie sighed, rolling her eyes. "Y'know, Gerald," she whispered loudly, "I'm beginning to think it was a mistake to pay Jandria any attention at all. Tambotan can't seem to grasp he's not in charge."

Standing, the other Gerald cupped his hand to the back of her neck and kissed her, hard. "Don't fret, Bibs. He'll grasp it soon enough. But I do appreciate you getting all . . . hot and bothered . . . on my behalf."

Bibbie laughed, but she was blushing. "I'll always get hot and bothered for you, Gerald."

"Glad to hear it," the other Gerald said. "Now shut up. Like politicians, beautiful women should be seen and almost never heard." Abandoning dumbstruck Bibbie, he approached the crystal ball. "What d'you want, Tambotan? I thought I made it clear I wasn't to be bothered again."

"And I thought *I* made it clear," retorted Tambotan, "that there would be no alliance with Jandria unless certain conditions were met."

The other Gerald was smiling, but he wasn't amused. "I met the conditions I was interested in meeting. You can wait for the rest."

"Why should I?" demanded Tambotan.

"You haven't proven yourself trustworthy, that's why," the other Gerald retorted. "Once you've lost a few dozen of those airships I helped you build, defending Ottosland from the UMN, then I'll think about giving you something else."

Tambotan's glare should have ignited the ether. "At least give us the weapons you promised. The thaumaturgically-enhanced guns."

The other Gerald heaved a put-upon sigh. "You see, Professor?" he said, turning. "This is what happens when you give people things without getting something in return. They start taking you for granted. I swear, the way he keeps putting his hand out you'd think I was a genie in a magic lamp."

Gerald cleared his throat. "You gave the Jandrians airship designs? Didn't you have the war here, too? When they used airships to—"

"Yes, yes, but that was then and this is now," said his counterpart impatiently. "Now they're fighting *with* us, not against us. At least that's the idea." He turned back to the crystal ball. "All right, Tambotan. You can have the souped-up guns. I'll make the arrangements. Just you be ready, you and the others, in case the UMN won't take bugger off for an answer. Right?"

Tambotan, his eyes narrowed, touched his forehead in formal salute. "We'll be ready."

"Of course," said the other Gerald, once the

crystal ball connection was severed, "what Tambotan doesn't know is that I've embedded an incant in the weapons that means one word from me and they'll go up like fireworks. Never give a man a gun unless you've made sure he can't point it at you, Professor. Bibbie!"

Bibbie roused out of her slouching sulk. "Yes?"

"How long has your brother been shut away in his lab, now?"

"Um—" She frowned at the ceiling. "Three days, twelve hours and twenty-four—no, make that five—minutes."

"Really? Is it that long?" said the other Gerald briskly. "Gosh. I'll bet the poor chap's lonely. I think he'd like some company, don't you?"

"Oh, yes," said Bibbie. The sly smile was back, as though she and the other Gerald were sharing a private joke. "I'm sure he would."

"Then let's pay him a visit and see where he's up to. For his sake I hope he's got the job done, as promised. Professor—"

He let himself feel the depth of his relief. *Monk. Oh, thank God.* "Yes, Gerald?"

"Anything you wanted to say to this fool before we go?"

He stared at silent Prime Minister Attaby, whose chain of office was a sad and terrible prank. "No. No, not really."

The other Gerald laughed, and slapped himself on the head. "I'm an idiot. *I* wanted to say something. Attaby?"

Attaby stood to attention, his eyes frightened. "Sir."

"This is Gerald Dunwoody," said the other Gerald, waving his hand. "Don't let the silver eye fool you—" He glanced sideways. "Did you know the color-incant's worn off, Gerald? Anyway—remarkable as it may seem, this man is me. More or less. To be strictly accurate, he's another version of me. And that's all you need to know about *that*. He's here to work with me, to ensure Ottosland's supremacy. Which means that you'll be answerable to him too. In due course. That's all. I just wanted to keep you apprised of developments. You can get back to work now."

Attaby bowed. "Yes, sir."

"Right then," said the other Gerald, turning away as though Attaby had ceased to exist. "Off we go. I can't wait to see what Monk's come up with. Although—" Heading for the door, he glanced behind him, one arm draped around Bibbie's shoulder. "I should warn you, Professor—our good friend's looking a little the worse for wear these days. Try not to go on about it. Turns out Mr. Markham's a bit more sensitive than we thought."

"Oh," said Gerald faintly, following. "I see. Well. Thanks for letting me know."

Bloody hell. You bastard. What have you done?

They drove through the almost empty, rain-splattered streets to the Department of Thaumaturgy building, where they were waved through to an empty underground garage. Feeling sick again, dreading what he was about to find, Gerald followed his counterpart and Bibbie up three flights of basement stairs and into the building proper. Looking around, he recognized his own Monk's Research and Development laboratory complex—but it seemed deserted. He couldn't sense the presence of any other wizards. Even the ether was silent, no eddies and currents of thaumaturgic activity. It didn't feel like R&D at all. So where was everyone?

I don't think I want to know.

Noticing his confusion as they headed down the central corridor, the other Gerald grinned. "Don't worry, Professor. The Department's other wizards aren't dead. They're just—otherwise occupied." The grin widened. "Bloody Errol Haythwaite. Is yours still alive?"

He nodded warily. "Yes."

"So's mine, more's the pity," said his counterpart, leading them out of the main corridor into a maze of shorter, narrower corridors linking a series of small thaumaturgic labs. "I keep hoping he'll give me a reason to squash him like a bug, but he doesn't. God, I hate him."

"You need a reason to squash him?" he said, remembering those other awful exhibits in the parade ground. "I'm surprised."

Spinning so he was walking backwards again, his counterpart frowned. "Watch it, sunshine. I'm the only one who gets to be sarcastic around here."

He bit the inside of his cheek. "Sorry."

"You will be, if you're not careful," said Bibbie. "We might need you, Gerry, but that's not to say there's bits of you that can't be dispensed with at a pinch." She smiled that sly smile. "And then there's Melissande, don't forget."

The other Gerald gave her a pleased nod. "That's my girl."

The trick was not to listen when they said things like that. "So why haven't you squashed Errol? Made him part of your outdoors amusement park?" he said. "Since you hate him so much, and since I can't imagine he didn't try to interfere with your plans—why *isn't* he dead?"

The other Gerald heaved a sigh and spun around to walk face-forward again. "You tell me, Professor."

How much do I hate that I know how he thinks? "Because you never know when a top-notch First Grade wizard might come in handy."

His counterpart laughed. "You're a fiendishly clever man, Gerald Dunwoody."

"So where is he?"

More laughter, rich and filled with a genuine delight. "He and his dear friends Kirkby-Hackett and Cobcroft Minor, shadbolt-shackled to the eyeballs, the bastards, are currently slaving as kitchen hands in the greasy bowels of Government House. In fact, they're probably washing our lunch plates as we speak. And to think—Errol used to be one of Ottosland's premier airship designers. How's that for revenge?"

He couldn't help it. He laughed. The idea of superior, elegant Errol up to his elbows in dirty pots and pans . . .

"I thought you might appreciate the notion," the other Gerald said, grinning. "What's he doing in your world? Something menial, I hope."

He stopped laughing. *Bugger.* "I—don't know. Errol and I lost touch."

"I never liked him either," said Bibbie, her eyes smoldering with remembered resentment. "At parties he always used to try and look down my dress."

Stunned, Gerald stumbled. She'd said that before. No. *His* Bibbie had said it. At home. In the parlor. Bibbie and Monk and Mel and Reg and him, working together to solve the mystery at Wycliffe's.

God. What is wrong with me? I can't laugh with these people. She's not my Bibbie. I'm not their friend.

The other Gerald frowned. "Something the matter, Professor?"

Oh, only everything. "No."

"Not feeling sorry for Haythwaite, are you? Because if anyone deserves a good shadbolting, he does." They'd reached the end of the latest corridor, and a massively hexed door. Halting, spinning around again, the other Gerald smiled beatifically. "Saint Snodgrass be praised, Professor. I bloody *love* a good shadbolt."

With an effort he kept his breathing slow and steady. "I've noticed. So why aren't I wearing one?"

"Because, Professor," said his counterpart, smile fading, eyes sharply watchful again, "as you know perfectly well, you're shadbolt-proofed. Just like Sir Alec. *Exactly* like Sir Alec, actually. I don't suppose you'd like to explain that, would you?"

I'm what? Since when? "No, not really."

The other Gerald considered him closely. "Blimey. You *didn't* know you were shadbolt-proof, did you? How's that possible, a wizard with our *potentia?*"

Sir Alec must've done it—or had it done—at some point during his janitor training. Sneakily, and undetectably. Probably during one of those interminable tests. Was Monk a part of it? He gave new meaning to the notion of sneaky and undetectable. But why do it and not tell him? What would Sir Alec have to gain by keeping it secret?

When I get back home, he and I are going to have some words . . .

His heart thudded. *When I get back home.* But the way things were looking he wasn't going to get back, was he? Barring some kind of miracle he was trapped in this appalling, madhouse mirror world. And if that miracle didn't come in the shape of one Monk Debinger Aloysius Markham, then he was pretty sure it would never come at all.

"Professor?" said his counterpart, seeming more alarmed than cross. "Your wits are wandering again. Should I be taking you to see a doctor?"

Bloody hell, if he so much as suspects I'm a janitor that'll be it. I'll have no hope of escape.

"What?" he said, trying to sound harmless. "No. I'm fine. I'm just—" *Discovering how good I am at tap-dancing on eggshells.* "I'm trying to remember when it could've happened. The shadbolt-proofing."

The other Gerald raised an eyebrow. "And?"

Cover story, cover story, he needed a plausible cover story . . . *A good janitor, Mr. Dunwoody, knows how to think on his feet.*

"Well, I can't be certain," he said slowly, "but—I think it might've been when I was still a compliance officer. I needed money. You remember how skint we were. R&D was starting some paid double-blind thaumaturgic trials. Monk never told me what they were, just said they were perfectly safe. The boffins must've been testing a new shadbolt-proofing incant. They never explained either, and I didn't ask. R&D—they're so bloody hush-hush. It was about a month before the accident at Stuttley's. You didn't—that didn't happen here?"

"The accident happened," said the other Gerald. "Not the R&D trial."

He shrugged, doing his best to look innocent and bemused. "Oh. All right. Odd, isn't it, the bits and pieces of our worlds that don't fit? Well, anyway, that's the only explanation I can think of."

And truer words have never been spoken. At least not by me.

"It makes sense, Gerald," said Bibbie, slumped against the corridor wall and trying not to look bored. "Now honestly, can we see where Monk's up to and then go? Because I'd really like to—"

His sharp look having silenced her, the other Gerald folded his arms and tapped his fingers, edgily thoughtful. "What is it you do these days, Professor? Back in your world?"

Ah. Right. *Damn.* His counterpart's lack of curiosity had always been too good to last. *What do they say? The easiest lies are the ones we tell ourselves?* "I . . . consult, Gerald. Solve problems of a thaumaturgical nature."

"And how is it you know Sir Alec Oldman?"

Careful now, careful. "Well, I wouldn't say I *know* him," he said, casually dismissive. "We're slightly acquainted. We crossed paths after I got home from New Ottosland." He shrugged. "Sir Alec was just one of a long line of government busybodies I had to put up with while the dust was settling. Look—how come you don't know this? I mean, if you've got the wherewithal to pluck me from my world into yours, how can you not know who I am there?"

The other Gerald smiled thinly. "The *plucking*, as you call it, Professor, is a brand new feat. As it stands

I wouldn't call the technique precisely *refined*. But don't worry. Once Monk's taken care of a few other tasks I have in mind he'll be turning his prodigious talents to the reading of alternative dimensions. In fact, we all will. But for now first things first. Just like dominoes, worlds need to fall one at a time."

It was the off-handed way the words were said that made him ill.

Bloody hell. So that's it. That's his grand plan. It's not enough to rule one world. He wants to rule them all.

"What?" said the other Gerald, reading him like a book. "Oh come on, Professor. Don't tell me you're *surprised*."

He didn't know what he was . . . except terrified and sick.

Sighing, the other Gerald unfolded his arms and pressed his left hand flat to the locked door before them. With a blinding surge of power the tangle of warding hexes on the door deactivated, blowing them all back several paces.

"What did you expect, Professor?" said his counterpart, grinning. "Keeping Monk Markham penned isn't exactly child's play." With a snap of his fingers the de-hexed door swung open. "After you."

The first thing he saw, walking into the unsealed lab with the other Gerald and Bibbie on his heels— was Reg. This world's Reg. Crammed into a cage dangling from a tall stand, tail feathers sticking out through its bars, fluffed-up and miserable. Her beak was tied shut with a length of red ribbon. When she saw him she made a strangled sound of surprise.

He stopped dead.

You bastard. You utter, utter, pillocking bastard. I will kill you for this. I swear you are dead.

With a bang and a thaumic blast, the laboratory door swung shut behind them, the warding incants reigniting.

The other Gerald put a hand on his shoulder. "Can't be too careful, Professor. Like I said, this is Monk. And look, there she is. Reg. Didn't I say you'd be seeing her?"

He swallowed acid and bile. "Get her out of that damned cage, Gerald."

"I will," the other Gerald said. "In a minute. Say hello to Monk, why don't you?"

Oh, yes. There was Monk. This world's Monk. Shadbolted like Attaby and the others, and barricaded behind a veritable wall of thaumaturgical apparatus, monitors and etheretic flux capacitors and test tubes and various bits and pieces he couldn't put a name to, wearing an expression that could only be described as *stunned*.

"Gerald . . ." he whispered.

"Actually," said the other Gerald, "to avoid confusion, I'm calling him Professor. Your sister's calling him Gerry. You can call him whatever you like—but I'm the only Gerald here. Understood?"

"What?" said the other Monk. He shook himself like a wet dog. "Oh. Yeah. Sure. Sorry."

The small, windowless laboratory stank of discharged thaumaturgics and the ether quivered with echoes of thaumic activity. A table shoved against the right-hand wall was littered with dirty plates and cutlery. Crowded with discarded mugs. There was a single gas ring in the corner unlit, and an icebox be-

side it. A narrow door in the left-hand wall offered
a glimpse of bathroom. Along the same wall was a
bedroll, a pillow and a heap of blankets. How long
did Bibbie say this Monk had been here? Three days
and counting? The lab was a cage.

"So," said the other Gerald, as his Monk Markham
continued to stare. "How have you been getting on,
old chap?"

Monk blinked. "Getting on?"

"Don't play the idiot, Monk," Bibbie snapped.
"Because you know what happens when you play the
idiot. Gerald gets cranky, you get punished and *I'm*
the one who has to listen to you scream. So if you
love me like a big brother's supposed to, just answer
the bloody question."

"Bibbie," said the other Monk. And now he
was staring like he'd never seen her before. Reg,
in her horrible cage, banged her beak against the
bars. Monk flinched. "Yes. Of course I love you,
Bibs." He looked at his Gerald. "I'm sorry. It's not
finished."

"*Not* finished?" said the other Gerald, his voice silky
with displeasure. "*Why* not? Monk, you told me all
you needed was a few more days in absolute solitude,
so you could focus. You *swore* to me that in a few more
days it would be *done*. So why isn't it *done*? You know
the timetable. You *know* what's expected. Monk, I can't
tell you how disappointed I am. Bibbie—"

Bibbie looked at him. "Yes, Gerald?"

"Now would be a good time to stick your fingers
in your ears."

As Bibbie turned away, clapping her hands to
the sides of her head, the other Gerald snapped his

fingers. And Monk—the other Monk—dropped howling to the floor.

"Stop it!" Gerald shouted, lunging at his counterpart. "Bloody hell, Gerald. *Stop it!* He's your *friend!*"

"Mind your own business, Professor," the other Gerald retorted, and clenched his fist.

The ether surged and he flew through the air to smack into the nearest bit of wall, flicked aside as though he were a pestering fly. He struck the plastered brick so hard bright lights burst before his good eye and all the stale lab air was punched out of his lungs. He fell to his hands and knees, gasping, and watched himself watch Monk's suffering with no sympathy at all.

Reg was banging her head against the cage.

And then Bibbie tugged at the other Gerald's arm. "That's enough. If you need him you can't keep hurting him like this."

The other Gerald spared her an irritated glance then snapped his fingers again. Monk stopped howling.

"You're a bloody idiot, mate," the other Gerald said, sounding weary. "When you know what that shadbolt can do, why the hell did you have to go and disappoint me?"

Sheet-white, the other Monk staggered to his feet. "You think I wanted to?" he said raggedly. "I've been working non-stop, Gerald. I've been slaving around the clock. I need help. This bloody contraption—I don't have what it takes to get the job done. You're the only wizard in the world with the *potentia* to make this work. You'll have to stay and help me. It's the only way you'll have it in time."

"Well, *that's* not going to happen," said the other Gerald, frowning. "I've got about a million things to do, Monk."

Bracing himself, the other Monk lifted his chin. "Then you'll have to stay disappointed, *mate*. Because I'm officially at the end of the thaumaturgical road."

The other Gerald laughed. "No, you're not, Monk. You should've let me finish. Why d'you think I brought you a visitor? *I* can't stay here and help you—but *he* can."

CHAPTER TWENTY-TWO

M e?" Gerald stepped back. "Ah—no. No, I don't think so. For one thing I don't have a clue what he's—your Monk's—working on, and for another—you may have completely abandoned your principles, Gerald, but I haven't."

"Oh," said the other Gerald. "D'you know, Professor, that *hurts*. I mean, you abandoned them for Lional."

"I did," he said steadily. "To my everlasting shame."

"Everlasting *shame?*" The other Gerald raised an eyebrow. "Really? Because it looks to me like you got over it all right. So what's the problem?"

"That," he said, "is a bloody stupid question, and you know it."

"What I *know*, Professor," said the other Gerald, prowling towards him, "is that Ottosland is on the brink of attack. Your country, your countrymen, are in terrible peril. If you don't help me then the blood of countless innocents will run in the streets."

"Not because of anything *I've* done," he retorted.

"From what I can tell, Gerald, you started this fight. And you can finish it by standing down. Besides. This isn't my country."

Halting, his counterpart smiled. "Well, if we're going to talk about saying stupid things, Professor, you'd win a prize for *that* fatuous statement. You can't fool me. You care. You care too much. It's always been your greatest flaw."

"I prefer to think of it as my saving grace."

The other Gerald shrugged. "If I had time for semantics, Professor, I'd happily argue the point. But I don't. So here's the thing. I didn't risk a temporal-dimensional implosion and give myself a skull-shattering headache bringing you here just so you could stand around carping at me like that bloody bird. I risked those things to make sure my plans come to fruition. You *are* going to help me. You *aren't* going to argue. Because if you refuse to cooperate not only will your precious bloody Melissande get the chop, she'll just be one of many victims you can chalk up to your short-sighted, sanctimonious pig-headed lack of cooperation."

"Gerald!" said the other Monk, his voice rough. Close to breaking. "Please. Do what he says. He really will kill Melissande. And I love her, mate. She's the only woman I'll ever love. I'm begging you, Gerald. Don't let her die."

Oh, God. "I'm sorry," he said at last, and made himself look at the stranger wearing Monk's face. "But if your Melissande's anything like mine, she wouldn't want to be used like this. Whatever that machine is you're making for this bastard? It's not good, Monk. It's going to hurt a lot of people. And

I swore after Lional I'd never capitulate again. No matter what was done to me. No matter what was threatened."

As the other Monk turned away, distraught, and Bibbie groaned, so sarcastic, the other Gerald laughed and sauntered to the birdcage. "How tediously bloody *noble* of you, Professor. I swear, I'm crying. Well, I'm crying on the inside. But that's only so I don't have to heave. Saint Snodgrass's bunions! What a dreary pillock *you've* turned out to be!" A finger snap, and Reg's hexed cage door sprang open. "And how bloody glad am I that I didn't listen to this bitch's nagging and face down Lional without some extra ammunition." In a blur of motion he reached into the cage and snatched the other Reg out of it. Held her up by the throat, wings dangling, eyes rolling. "So how noble are you *really*, Professor?" he taunted. "Noble enough to watch me break the bird's neck like a twig?"

"No, don't hurt her!" the other Monk shouted, terrified. "Please, Gerald—don't let him—God, you can't—you *can't*—"

But he had to. He had to make a stand. Make it clear to his mad other self that no matter what there'd be no cooperation. He closed his eyes. This wasn't his Reg, but even so . . .

I'm sorry.

A stir in the ether and an agonized, strangled shout. And then, despite his cruel shadbolt, the other Monk was lashing out, tossing obfuscation incants and slippy-finger hexes and anything else he could think of to make the other Gerald let go.

For all the good it did, he might as well have been spitting.

Laughing, the other Gerald deflected the thaumaturgical attack and retaliated with a brutal strike of his own. The other Monk hit the lab's low ceiling then dropped to the floor with bone-rattling force. Shrieking, Bibbie threw herself under the nearest table. Captive Reg flapped her wings desperately, struggling to get free. And Monk—the other Monk—

The other Monk staggered to his feet, lurched around his lab bench and came straight for him, a mad light in his eyes. "You bastard! *Bastard!* Let Melissande die, would you? Let Reg die? Not while I'm still breathing, sunshine!"

The last thing he wanted to do was hurt this other Monk. He tried to dodge but the lab was crowded with benches and equipment. There was nowhere to run. As the man who looked like his best friend crashed him to the floor he caught a glimpse of the other Gerald laughing as he shoved his Reg back in the cage.

Panting, the other Monk grabbed him by the hair and thudded his head onto the concrete. "I don't know you! *I don't know you!*"

"Markham—you idiot—get off me!" he grunted. "I don't want to hurt you but I will if you don't stop!"

"Hurt me?" shouted the other Monk. "As if you bloody could!"

So he lunged upright, using fists and elbows and knees to fight free. But this other Monk was desperate. Red-faced and sweating, he crushed him close in a suffocating bear hug.

And then that horribly familiar voice was whispering frantically in his ear.

"Bloody hell, Gerald, it's me. The real me. Play along with him, for God's sake. I've got a way out."

Stunned, he went limp, as though the assault had overwhelmed him. Monk shoved him to one side and found his feet. Turned on the other Gerald, sucking great rasping mouthfuls of air into his lungs.

"I'll make him help you! I swear it, all right? I'll make him do whatever you want, Gerald. Just don't hurt Melissande. Don't hurt Reg. *Please*."

Cautiously, Bibbie crawled out from under the bench. "I agree, actually," she said, fastidiously smoothing the wrinkles from her Fandawandi silk ensemble. "It's more fun if they're alive. It won't be the same if I have to throw rotten eggs at a stranger. And you know the bird's harmless, Gerald. It just sits in the cage and moans."

"What?" said Monk, startled. "What did you say, Bibs?"

Bibbie shot him a venomous look. "You can shut up. I don't have to listen to you any more, *big brother*."

Shaken, Gerald stared at the Markham siblings.

Monk? My Monk? How can that be my Monk? Bloody hell, I know he's a genius but . . .

It couldn't be him, surely. This had to be a trick. There was no proof that this man was who he said he was or that he had a way out of this mess.

Bloody hell. I'll have to trust him. I can't afford not to. Because if that is my Monk Markham—

He wasn't going to think about how that made a difference. It just did. He'd worry about the ethics of it later, once they'd got themselves safely home.

If we can. If we don't get ourselves and everyone else in this world killed trying.

The other Gerald, ignoring Monk's staring disbelief and Bibbie's bristling resentment, considered him with narrowed eyes. He stared straight back, making sure to still look shaken. It wasn't much of an act.

But—but if this is my Monk Markham, what's happened to the other one? Oh my God, don't tell me he's hiding in the bathroom!

It took all his strength not to look through the bathroom's open door.

"Professor," his counterpart said at last. "That was stupid. And I am—I used to be—a lot of things but really, stupid isn't one of them. You've read my *potentia*. You know what I can do. You've seen what I *will* do. And you still refuse me? I'm embarrassed for both of us."

He won't believe me if I give in too easily.

"I think you *are* stupid, Gerald," he snapped. "I'm the Dunwoody who didn't lose his nerve, remember? The one who defeated Lional without resorting to Uffitzi's filthy grimoires. In the only way that truly counts, I'm stronger than you. So go ahead. Do your worst. You won't break me."

"Really?" said his smiling counterpart. "You know, I wouldn't bet on it."

And with a snap of his fingers he dropped Monk back to the floor.

"You have to understand, Professor," he said, sounding bored now, "that I can keep this going and going and he won't actually die. He'll want to die. He'll *beg* to die. But he won't. He'll just suffer until you change your mind. Remember the cave? Just like that. Days and weeks and months and *years* of suffering. So the question is—how noble *are* you, Professor, when you get down to brass tacks? How noble is it to let someone else pay the price for your principles?"

Transfixed, Gerald stared at his keening, writhing friend. His Monk. From his world. The man who'd risked his career for him. Saved his life. Made him laugh. Paid for more than his fair share of Yok Tok takeaway.

I'm not an only child. I've got a brother, and his name's Monk Markham.

Bibbie had walked away, as far as she could get, and was standing with her back to them with her close-cropped head lowered and her silk-covered arms folded tight. Beneath her ghastly new veneer she wasn't entirely indifferent. Did that mean there was hope for her? Maybe. Maybe there was.

And then he looked at his counterpart.

But there's no hope for him.

"I might even put him on display in the parade ground," said the other Gerald, still smiling. "Wouldn't that be an exhibit to make folk sit up and blink? Imagine it, Professor—the five year old brought to witness your indifference today could be the grandfather forty years from now, showing his own grandson what happens when I don't get what I want. On the other hand, I could lock you both in here and leave you. How would you like that? Just your best friend and his screams for company, year after year after year after messy, noisy year . . ."

Oh, lord. Eyes stinging, he looked down at Monk,

his jaw clenched so hard he thought it might break. The shadbolt shackling his friend was the worst he'd ever felt. It made Melissande's look like a diamond tiara. Even those he'd sensed on Attaby and the others, they endured *nothing* compared to this. The urge to rip Monk free had him shaking. But he couldn't. He had to play this out, right to the bitter end. This other Gerald would never believe a swift surrender. And if he wasn't convinced—if he suspected a trap—

Hang on, Monk. I'm sorry. Please. Hang on.

The other Gerald was watching him closely. He didn't dare so much as a glance at this world's Reg—but he could feel her looking at him, crammed in that dreadful cage with her long beak tied shut. On the floor, Monk started twitching. The sounds he was making were getting louder. Less bearable. And then he opened his eyes and looked straight at him.

"Gerald, come on," he whispered.

He shook his head. "I'm sorry. You know I can't."

"Yeah, you can. Come on."

He closed his eyes, briefly. "No, Monk. I *can't.*"

Monk sobbed once. "Thought you were my friend. Everything I've done for you."

"You—" He had to fold his arms against the pain in his chest. "You haven't done anything for me. I don't know you. I know the Monk from my world. And he—he wouldn't ask this. He knows what's at stake."

"Bugger that," said Monk, choking. "We're the same man in every way that matters, Gerald, and I'm asking . . ."

He didn't know what to do. How long to let this play out. Sickened, and sickeningly aware of the other Gerald's scrutiny, he half-turned away.

Monk's anguished cry followed him. "Please, Gerald. *Please!*"

Right or wrong, he couldn't do this any more. He let the plea break him.

"Fine!" he shouted, turning to the other Gerald. "You win! For God's sake, that's *enough!*"

"Not quite," said his counterpart. "After all, I am trying to make a point."

"You've made it!" he said, and dropped to his knees. "*You've made it!* You've got me, Gerald. All right? You win. I'll do whatever you want."

His counterpart laughed. "See, Bibbie? I told you. Soft as whipped cream." And then the amusement vanished. "But Professor? Just in case this is a ruse, and you're planning to pull a fast one? Well—just *don't.*"

Monk shuddered once, with a terrible moan. Then the other Gerald snapped his fingers again and released him.

Bibbie turned around. Her eyes were dry but her face was chalk-white. "So are you finished now, Gerald? Can we *go?*"

The other Gerald glanced at her. "In a minute. Professor?"

He dragged his gaze away from silently shivering Monk. "What?"

"Catch," said his counterpart, and tossed him a small, dark red crystal.

"And what's this?" he said, feeling the acid of dark magics sizzle his cold fingers.

"A present," said the other Gerald. "I made it especially for you."

"Really?" He pushed to his feet. "You shouldn't have."

"Oh, it was no trouble."

He could feel his *potentia* stirring, reacting to the incants sunk into the red crystal. "Don't tell me, let me guess. You want me to swallow this?"

A genial nod. "If you'd be so kind."

"Since it's not a shadbolt," he said, feeling his skin crawl, "d'you mind telling me what it is?"

"You don't know?" The other Gerald pretended shock. "Gosh. Are you the world's most powerful wizard or aren't you?"

"I meant specifically, Gerald," he said, glowering. "Under the circumstances *rogue thaumaturgics* is a little vague for my tastes."

The other Gerald's smile went nowhere near his eyes. "Don't worry. There's nothing in there that can hurt you, Professor. I'm just . . . giving you a boost, that's all. So you can help me. Although, actually, when you think about it, you're really helping yourself."

No nightmare could ever come close to this. "Really? And what—you just happened to have this little grimoire sampler lying around? How convenient."

"*Convenience* had nothing to do with it," his counterpart snapped. "I've been planning this for months, Professor. I knew almost from the beginning that I'd need you to make my plan work. Why d'you think I risked what I risked to get you here? Mind you—" He shot a resentful look at Monk, on the floor. "I didn't realize *this* idiot would fail me. But that's all right. I can spare you for a few hours."

"To do what?"

"Bloody hell, Professor," said the other Gerald, exasperated. "Weren't you listening? I need you to help him finish what he started. What he *swore* to me he could build. And then, once it's completed, you and I are going to change the world. *This* world. To start with. Today is what you might call—the overture."

Oh, wonderful. He looked down at the red hex crystal burning his fingers with malign, malevolent promise. "Using this?"

"That's right." Another wide smile, as though he and the other Gerald were friends. As though Monk wasn't curled up on the floor at their feet. "Using that. And trust me, Professor, you're going to thank me for it. Not only will the incants in that crystal help you change the world, they'll give you a taste of what you're missing out on because of some antiquated notions forced on you by men too gutless to take what they want."

He looked at Bibbie. "And that's how you hooked her, is it? How you twisted and—"

The other Gerald raised a finger. "*Careful*, Professor."

Of course it was. This other Gerald had dangled a morsel of forbidden fruit in front of his Bibbie, and his Bibbie—being Bibbie, and fearless—had grabbed it with glee. Because she and Monk were Markhams, and in the habit of . . . bending the rules. Because she was tired of being a *girl* and hearing *No, dear, you can't. Be a good little witch and don't show up the boys.* And of course, once she'd tasted it, she'd wanted more, and more, and more . . .

Oh, bloody hell, Bibbie. It was ridiculous to feel guilty. He wasn't the one who'd tempted her. But still. *Bibs, I'm so sorry.*

"Anyway," said his counterpart briskly, and clapped his hands. "I've got things to do, so let's get on, shall we? Swallow the crystal, Professor. Now. While I'm watching. Nothing personal, I just don't trust you not to flush it down the bog once my back's turned."

"You still haven't told me what incants are in this thing."

The other Gerald rolled his eyes. "Oh, Saint Snodgrass save me. *Fine.* There's a general etheretic enhancement hex. A trebled counter-incant that'll let you—well, never mind. You don't need to know about that yet. There's an incant that gives you the power to control any First Grade wizard—which won't work on me, so don't even bother trying. A bunch of shadbolt matrixes, always useful. A handful of compulsion hexes—and they won't work on me either, so, y'know, don't waste my time. Oh yes, and a couple of nifty punishment hexes. For when your underlings get uppity."

"I see," he said, feeling sick again. "And that's it?"

"For starters," said his counterpart. "But if you're very good, Professor, who knows? There could be more."

He shook his head. "Trust me, Gerald. I won't be wanting more."

The other Gerald laughed. "Yes, well, you say that now. But I think you'll find that once you get a taste of what's possible you won't be quite so eager to sermonize. Or turn me down."

The casually mocking comment chilled him.

What if he's right? What if I like what's in this crystal? It might not be the worst dark magic in the world, but still . . . if I swallow it I won't be me any more. I'll have taken the first step towards turning into him.

He could feel Monk, staring. Lifted his own gaze, just enough. His friend was hunched on his side with his back to the other Gerald. He nodded, the smallest gesture. Twitched his lips into the merest hint of a smile.

Oh, bloody hell, Monk. You'd better know how to purge me if this muck.

He closed his eyes, shuddering, and swallowed the hex crystal. Within moments his mouth filled with a raw and angry heat. Whatever he was tasting he didn't begin to understand it. It tasted of nothing, of everything, of power and pain. He felt his *potentia* stir to life like a banked fire kicked over. Felt the hex crystal's incants unfurling like a seed-pod in spring. All that dark promise uncoiling, expanding, pushing single-mindedly through his blood towards the sun.

"Steady now, Professor," said his counterpart, and took his arm. "Don't fight it. Let it happen. It might tickle a bit. But what's a little pain compared with undreamt of power?"

Bloody hell. A *little* pain? The dark incants and hexes had sharp teeth and claws and they were tearing holes in his etheretic aura. Burrowing into his *potentia*. He could feel himself . . . changing. Could feel a shadow, encroaching.

Oh no. Oh no. What the hell have I done?

He would've fallen, if the other Gerald wasn't holding him up. He felt himself clinging. Heard himself say: *"Don't let go."*

"It's all right, Gerald," said his other self, so kindly. "Don't be frightened. I've got you. You're safe with me. You're safe."

And then the dark magic inside him finished unfolding and caught fire. Seared every nerve and sinew as it flashed through him, incandescent.

"There," said the other Gerald, pleased. "All finished." Letting go, he stepped back. "And doesn't that feel better?"

The pain was gone. That was better. But the shadow—the shadow—

"Yes," he said, blinking. "I'm fine."

"I knew you would be," said his counterpart, who then turned and kicked Monk. "Get up, Markham. You've got work to do."

Slowly, painfully, Monk rolled to his hands and knees. Took a deep breath and staggered to his feet. "Look. I'm going to need him for more than a couple of hours. This bloody contraption of yours—I don't know if you understand how complicated it is, Gerald."

"Thank you, I'm not an idiot," the other Gerald said coldly. "How long do you need him?"

"All night would be good."

"*All night?* Markham—"

"Oh, Gerald, don't go on," said Bibbie. "Isn't it better that he'll be locked in here with Monk? At least this way you won't have to worry about keeping an eye on him. Once the lab doors are hexed that's it. He's just another Reg in a tiny little cage."

"I suppose so," said the other Gerald, grudging. "But let's get one thing clear, Monk—if he's staying the night that means no more excuses. I want to find my machine finished and foolproof when I come back in the morning. Is that clear?"

"Actually," said Gerald, not looking at Monk, "instead of making assumptions that I can help, maybe you should explain what this contraption of yours—"

"Monk'll explain it," snapped his counterpart. "I don't have time. Bibbie—"

"*Finally,*" said Bibbie, going to him. "I was about to die of boredom. You're taking me out to dinner, Gerald. A very expensive, very exclusive, very *rarified* dinner. *And* you're giving me a gold-and-diamond bracelet."

The other Gerald laughed. "Am I? All right."

Gerald looked away as they kissed, not envious any more. Just ill and revolted. He felt Monk's shocked horror like a blow. Poor bugger. Bet he was sorry he'd come, now.

The laboratory door banged closed behind them, and then came an obliterating surge in the ether as the multiple, unbreakable locking-hexes and incants were reengaged.

"Right," said Monk, once the etheretic ripples had faded. "Come on, Gerald. We're getting the hell out of here."

"What?" he said, staring. "Um—no. No, we're not. We can't, Monk. Not yet."

The Reg in the cage started bouncing up and down, banging her beak against the bars so hard she risked hurting herself. Poor thing.

"Oh, blimey," said Monk, and crossed to the cage. "Hang on—hang on—Gerald—unhex the door, would you? I can't. This bloody shadbolt."

Yes. The shadbolt. How the devil had he managed *that*? How had he managed *any* of this?

"Gerald, I'll explain later! Just open the bloody cage!"

Thanks to the dark magics the other Gerald had given him, the filthy incants binding the cage door surrendered without a fight.

"Wait—wait—" said Monk, carefully extracting agitated Reg from her prison. "I don't want to hurt you."

Released from her prison, with the red ribbon gag discarded, Reg shot into the air, an indignant blur of feathers. "Not yet? Not yet? What d'you mean, *not yet*? Gerald Dunwoody, *I want to go home!*"

Stunned, he watched her flap furiously around the lab. That was Reg. *His* Reg. But—but—

I was going to let Gerald kill her. I was going to let him snap her neck. Oh my God . . . oh my God . . .

Furious, he turned on Monk. "Bloody hell, Markham, what's *she* doing here? What the hell were you *thinking*, bringing Reg into this?"

"Hey, don't look at me!" Monk retorted. "I didn't invite her, she invited herself!"

"Then why didn't you *un*invite her? Why didn't you send her packing as soon as you realized—"

"Shut up, the pair of you!" said Reg, landing in a flapping of wings on the top of the cage. "Do I look like a wishbone at the family picnic? Has interdimensional sightseeing scrambled your brains? Monk Markham, get us *out* of here!"

Abruptly exhausted, Gerald headed for the nearest bit of empty wall and slid down it. His head was pounding. "*No!* I told you, nobody's going *anywhere*. At least, *I'm* not going anywhere. I suppose you two can do what you like."

"Bloody hell," said Monk, and scrubbed his fingers through his hair. "*Gerald—*"

"*Don't,*" he snapped. "I've had a *very* bad day."

"It's no use, sunshine," Reg sighed, rattling her tail. "You know what he's like. We'll have to hear him out. Only first you'd better make sure my pathetic twin hasn't carked it."

"Bugger," said Monk. "I forgot about her."

Gerald watched, lost for words, as Monk ducked into the lab's bathroom and came out again a moment later cradling a limp draggle of feathers against his chest. "She's all right, I think," he said. "Just weak."

"Yes, I'm fine," said the other Reg. Her eyes were glazed, and there was no familiar gloss on her feathers. "Just tired. And thirsty."

"Well, don't sit there gawking at her, Gerald," Reg snapped, waspish. "Fetch her some water. Fetch enough for both of us. I'm parched too."

Water. Yes. Right. Good idea. He scrambled to his feet, snatched up two empty beakers and took them into the bathroom. It was empty. No second Monk. Everywhere he turned, another bloody mystery. After filling the beakers with water he went back out to the lab.

"So where is he, then?" he said. "This world's Monk, I mean. You must have him stashed somewhere."

"He's dead," Monk said flatly, perched on the lab's only stool. "Look. Give that poor bird a drink, and Reg, and then I'll tell you what's been going on. Maybe then you'll understand why we have to get out of here before that bastard comes back."

Dead? The other Monk was dead? Then where was the body? "But Monk—"

"Just hear me out, Gerald! I think you owe me that much!"

Right. Right. Monk was upset. "Fine," he said, then looked around the locked lab. "Only, is it safe to talk? He could be listening."

"I've checked," said Monk. "We're safe. Gerald—"

"Yes. Sorry."

Monk had settled the other Reg on the makeshift bed's pillow. He put one beaker down on the bench for his Reg, then sat beside the other one, braced his back against the wall and offered her a drink.

"Thank you," she murmured, after drinking, then almost immediately drifted into a doze.

Bloody hell, she looks rough. I can't imagine what she's been through . . .

Having drunk her own fill, his Reg flapped down from the bench to perch on his bent knees. He stroked a finger down her wing, so pleased to see her. "All right, Monk. I'm listening."

Slumped on his lab stool, Monk started talking. At last, when he stopped, Gerald looked at him. He felt pummeled. No, pulverized. Thrashed to an emotional pulp.

But that's probably nothing compared to what Monk's feeling.

"Bloody hell."

Monk snorted. "You're telling me."

"Are you all right?"

"I'll live."

Oh, very funny. It wasn't remotely true, either. Monk was holding himself together, but only just.

But that's a conversation for another time and place.

"And *nobody* in the government outside Sir Alec knows about *any* of it?"

"Not when I—I mean *we*—left," said Monk. "But the longer we stay away the more likely it is that something'll go wrong and he'll have to spill the beans. If we're not careful, Gerald, we'll walk back into a bloody firestorm. I'm telling you, we need to go and we need to go *now*."

Gerald wiped a hand across his face. "You're not thinking straight, Monk. We can't leave until we've done something about this world's Gerald."

"We *will* do something," said Monk. "As soon as we get home."

"Like what?"

"Like—like—oh, I don't know," said Monk, reckless. "I'll invent something, won't I?" And then he straightened. "In fact—in *fact*—" He snapped his fingers. "*Ha!* I've *got* it! I've already invented the solution, haven't I?"

"I don't know," he said, rubbing his temples. "Have you?"

"Yes! My multi-dimensional etheretic wavelength expander," said Monk, fired up. "The work's practically done for us, mate. All we have to do is iron out the kinks, soup it up a bit, reverse its etheretic polarities to switch its modality from expand to inhibit, add a few extra layers of security and booby-traps and what have you—and hey presto. Instant impenetrable interdimensional barrier. Guaranteed to stop your evil twin from opening a portal to our world ever again."

Letting his head tip back against the wall, he considered his friend with weary affection. "Hey presto, eh? Just like that?"

"Bloody oath just like that!"

He managed a tired smile. "Yeah. It sounds great, Monk. Only you're forgetting one small detail. Evil twin Gerald didn't open a portal to bring me here. He yanked me out of an existing regular domestic transport portal. While I was on my way to Grande Splotze. Can you guarantee your invention can prevent a repeat of that nifty trick?"

Monk opened his mouth, then closed it again. Shook his head. "No."

"Fine. So unless you want to explain why we have to close down our world's entire portal network overnight we can't go home until we've taken care of him."

"Bugger," said Monk, scowling. "I hate it when you're right."

He sighed. "Trust me. So do I."

"Well, then," said Reg, rattling her tail. "So now we've decided the manky git's got to die, if one of you can rustle up a nail file I'll sharpen my beak and stick it right through his maggoty black heart."

"Oh, Reg." He stroked her wing again. "Get a grip. Nobody's stabbing anyone. We'll have to smuggle him out of here, back to our Ottosland. Hand him over to Sir Alec. He'll know what to do."

"Yes," said Reg. "He'll put him down like a dog. But I don't see why our resident government stooge should have all the fun."

Monk pulled a face. "Y'know, she's got a point. Give me a nail file and I'll perforate the bastard myself."

"No!" he said sharply. "Just—shut up, Monk. You don't know what you're saying. You've never killed anyone and believe me—you don't want to."

Instead of answering, Monk slid off his stool and checked on the other Reg. She'd fallen properly asleep, head tucked under one wing, a forlorn drabble of feathers piled on the pillow. Sitting down again, he sucked in air and winced.

Gerald bit his lip. *Lord, he looks bloody terrible. He's had it ten times worse than me.* "I wish I could get that bloody shadbolt off you."

"Not as much as I do, mate."

"I will. The second we get home, the filthy thing's history." He heard his breathing hitch. "I can't believe you let Sir Alec put it on you. I can't believe—"

"What, you thought I'd leave you stranded here?" said Monk, eyebrows lifting. "Thanks. Nice to know you've got such a high opinion of me, Dunnywood."

He sat up, indignant. "What? No—I just—Monk—"

But Monk was grinning, sardonic. "Gotcha."

"Pillock," he said, slumping again.

"Tosser," Monk retorted. "Huh. Y'know what *I* can't believe? I can't believe *that* was *Bibbie*."

"It wasn't," he said quietly. "Monk, forget what you saw. What you heard. You'll go demented if you don't. They might be wearing our faces but they aren't us. All right?"

"Yeah," Monk muttered. "I suppose." He punched his knee. "Except—look—what Bibbie—*she*—said about Mel. Rotten eggs? What did she mean?"

Oh, *hell*. "What did I just say, Monk? They're not us. Forget it."

But Monk never was one to take wise advice. "Have you seen her? This world's Mel? Is she all right? Is she safe? Gerald—"

"She's fine," he said, making himself meet Monk's distressed gaze without flinching. *I have to lie. I have to. It's the kind thing to do.* "She's living in the same house. Our—your—house. She's fine."

Monk let out a long and shaky breath. "Good. That's something. I mean, I know he threatened her to get to you, and I understand what you're saying about us not being them, but still—I mean, in a weird way he *is* you, isn't he? Yeah, he's twisted inside-out with dark magics—I know, I felt them—but—underneath all that, even though he isn't, he's still *you*."

"Yeah, Monk. He is."

And that would be what scares me the most.

"Blimey—" Monk sat forward. "Sorry. I'm not thinking straight. Those dark incants he made you swallow—"

"I'm fine," he said quickly. "I wouldn't even call them dark. Grubby, maybe. But nothing I can't handle."

"Ha!" said Reg, and chattered her beak. "Pull the

other leg, sunshine. If it comes off we know where to find a spare."

Monk was scowling. "Yeah, Gerald. What she said. I saw your face when those incants kicked in."

The shadow slithered through him, a dark snake in the grass. "I can handle it," he insisted. "Rogue wizard, remember? It's under control. Now stop fussing at me, the pair of you, and tell me what it is this world's Monk Markham has been building for my evil twin." He nodded at the sprawl of coils and conductors and thaumaturgic containers and gauges spread out on the lab's biggest bench. "I take it that's it?"

"That's it," said Monk.

"And?"

Monk shrugged. "And it's the most diabolical perversion of a thaumaturgic invention that I've ever come across."

"Oh." He stared at the mysterious thingamajig on the bench. "Why? What does it do?"

Reg chattered her beak. "Nothing yet, because Mad Mr. Markham here hasn't finished the bloody thing. But when he does—"

The other Reg stirred on her pillowy bed, and sat up. "When he does, sunshine, that'll be it. The end of our world. And then the end of yours. And after that . . ."

"It's a weapon?" he said, startled, turning back to the other Monk's untidy invention.

"Not the way you're thinking, Gerald," said the other Reg. "*Gerald.*" Her voice broke. "I never thought I'd see the old you again."

He had to clear his throat. "No. I don't suppose you did. Look, about this—"

"It's a thaumaturgic enhancer," said Monk, his face grim. "Good old Gerald's tired of arguing with people. He's going to shadbolt every wizard and witch in the country—and from what I can gather, it's all thanks to me."

"In other words it *is* a weapon," he said. "So I guess that means we've got some work ahead of us. Because if it's the last thing we do, we can't let him get his hands on it."

CHAPTER TWENTY-THREE

Half-way through his very expensive dinner with Bibbie, Attaby called from Government House. *"What?"* he demanded, striding back into the Cabinet room. His head was splitting. Bibbie hadn't taken at all kindly to her intimate supper being disrupted. Sometimes he wondered about her, he really did. He'd thought she understood what he was doing. The scope of it. The sheer *majesty* of it. But then she'd turn around and whine . . .

"Gerald, when do I get to do some proper magic? Gerald, when do I have a Department of my own? Gerald, you said we'd rule Ottosland together as husband and wife. So when are we going to get married, Gerald?"

She'd started up again on their way to Government House from the restaurant, so he'd doubled back and taken her home. He had enough on his plate without listening to her whine.

I wonder what the Bibbie from next door is like? She can't possibly be more irritating than mine. Maybe I'll swap them. I can't do any worse.

Attaby was staring at him like a mouse facing a cat.

"Sir, there's been another communication from Viceroy Gonegal." A nod at the Cabinet room's crystal ball. "It's recorded."

He felt the blood thundering inside his aching skull. "You dragged me away from dinner for *that* twit?"

Shadbolted Attaby flinched. "Yes, sir. I thought it advisable. Perhaps you should look at the message, sir."

"*Fine,*" he said glowering. "Now bugger off. The sight of your hangdog face makes me sick."

"Sir," said Attaby, and wisely retreated.

He activated the crystal ball. Gonegal's face swam into focus. "I'm told your name is Gerald Dunwoody," said the old fool, his eyes narrowed. "I'm told your *potentia* is unlike that of other wizards. And I'm told you've polluted yourself with grimoire magic. That is unfortunate. You should know, Mr. Dunwoody, that Babishkia is now protected from your predations. You should also know that the United Magical Nations has expelled from its ranks all those member states who have foolishly allowed themselves to be suborned by you. They are now facing . . . sanctions." Gonegal smiled, like a tiger. "That *especially* includes Jandria. Jandria is closely watched. And finally you should know that an armed fleet of airships is poised to bring Ottosland to its knees. Stand down, Mr. Dunwoody. Awaken from your outlandish dream of world domination. Spare yourself and your people the consequences of our wrath."

Fury turned the Cabinet room to scarlet. With a shout of rage he smashed the crystal ball to dust and shards.

"Attaby! Attaby, get in here!"

Attaby came running. "Sir? Yes, sir?"

Bone and muscle burned with his anger. "Get your staff back here. I want every desk manned and every man working. I want every single portal in the country closed down. All portal travel is suspended, is that clear? I want armed airships patrolling our borders and the limits of the city. I want every thaumic monitor pointed at UMN headquarters. Send a message to Tambotan: I want his airship fleet patroling with ours by sunrise, or else."

"Yes, sir," said Attaby, nodding. His eyes were wide and fearful. "I understand."

"Are preparations completed at the ceremonial ground?"

Attaby nodded again. "They are."

"And the unshadbolted wizards and witches?"

"Under lock and key in Ott's main prison, sir," said Attaby. "Ready for transport first thing in the morning."

A little of his anger receded. "Good. That's something. I need a lorry."

Attaby goggled. "Sir?"

He clenched his fist and cracked lightning around the room. "A lorry, a lorry, you know what a bloody *lorry* is, don't you?"

White and sweating, Attaby screwed his eyes shut. "Sir. Yes, sir. Of course I know what a lorry is."

"Well, I want one!" he said, and leaned into Attaby's face. "D'you hear me? I want a lorry and a driver at my front door no later than seven tomorrow morning! Can you manage that, Attaby? Or is that too complicated for a prime minister to arrange?"

"No, sir," whispered Attaby. "I can arrange that."

"*Good!*" he spat. "And I want another car and driver to take Bibbie to the parade ground at eight. Can you manage *that*? Or will doing two things at once give you a nosebleed, *my lord*?"

"No, sir," croaked Attaby. "A lorry and a car. You'll have them."

"I'd better," he said, heading for the Cabinet room door. "Or there'll be one more exhibit gracing Ott's parade ground. Understood?"

Thanks to the curfew there was no traffic to impede him on the way home. Searchlights stabbed the cloudy night sky, illuminating the armed airships as they ceaselessly prowled. His fingers were bloodless around his car's steering wheel. His own harsh breathing filled his ears.

Threaten me, Gonegal? You and your friends at the doomed UMN? Bloody hell, you'll be sorry. You won't know what's hit you.

Bibbie had taken herself off to bed, but Melissande was still awake. She looked up from blacking the cooking range as he strode into the kitchen.

"I want tea."

She put down the blacking and the brush then wiped her hands on a cloth, warily watching him. She was always wary these days. Not without reason. "Yes. All right."

He watched as she put the kettle on, spooned tea leaves into the pot and got a generous mug out for him. Dumpy, frumpy bloody woman. She had no business being a princess. If a woman was a princess she was meant to look like Bibbie.

Gonegal threatens me? My God. How does he dare?

Waiting for the kettle to boil, Melissande slid him a sideways glance. "Where's the other Gerald?"

"None of your business," he said, glowering.

She swallowed. "He's not—you haven't—"

He kicked out a chair from the kitchen table and sat down. "No, of course I bloody haven't. God, you're an idiot. Not much point half-killing myself to get him here just so I can snuff him out, is there?"

She stared at her red and work-roughened hands. There was boot black under her fingernails. "I suppose not."

"And like I said. He's none of your business."

The kettle had started to steam, very slightly. She fetched a jug of milk from the icebox and the sugar bowl from the pantry.

"I wish you wouldn't do this, Gerald," she said quietly. "Whatever it is you're planning to do."

"Really?" he said, drumming his fingers on the table. Fury burned beneath his skin. *Gonegal.* "And what makes you think I give a fat rat's ass about what you wish for?"

"Nothing," she said, flinching. "Never mind. It doesn't matter."

He grinned. "You're right. It doesn't. And neither do you."

Her breathing hitched. "I know, Gerald. You've made that abundantly clear."

The kettle was belching steam now, so she took it off the range and poured water into the tea pot. "He'll stop you, you know." Her voice was barely above a whisper. "The other Gerald. He's not you. He's better than you. He's a good man, a *lovely* man, and he'll—"

"He'll *what?*" he said, as the fury broke free. "What exactly will lovely Gerald do? Save you from *this?*"

But she couldn't answer him. He'd stolen her breath. And as she gasped for air he tightened his fist harder. The shadbolt, tightening with it, crushed her skull like an egg. She hit the kitchen floor like a sack of wet sand.

He finished making his tea and took the steaming mug up to bed. Beautiful in the lamplight, Bibbie lowered her magazine. "So what was the emergency?"

"Nothing I couldn't deal with," he said, shrugging. "No need to worry."

She rolled her eyes. "I wasn't *worried*. I just want to know if it was worth missing dessert for."

Her skin was glowing, translucent like pearl. Her eyes had the luster of the world's best sapphires. And her lips . . . her cherry lips . . .

Suddenly he wasn't interested in tea any more. Suddenly the fury knew where to find a home.

Laughing, pique forgotten, she threw back the blankets. Tossed aside her magazine and welcomed him in. Later, clothed in darkness on the trembling edge of sleep, he pressed her fingers to his mouth and kissed them.

"Mmm?" she murmured, drowsy. "What's wrong?"

"Nothing. It's just I forgot to mention something."

She sighed. "What?"

"That you'll need to find someone else to throw eggs at."

"What? Oh, *Gerald* . . ." Bibbie turned over. "Well, *that's* a bore, isn't it." She yawned. "G'night."

*　*　*

Their counter-plan was terrifying in its simplicity: *kidnap evil twin Gerald before he conquers the world.*

Because if the other Gerald's plan came to fruition he'd succeed in shadbolting every wizard and witch in Ottosland to his service. And once he'd done *that*, he'd have no trouble bending the whole world to his will. With the power of thousands and thousands of *potentias* at his command, nothing and nobody would stand in his way. Not even the combined resistance of those UM nations who'd not sold their souls to side with him would be enough to prevent disaster.

But to kidnap the other Gerald, first they had to get the other Monk's dreadful machine to work. The notion of trying to fool the man was out of the question.

Banished to the thankless role of spectator, at least for the time being, Gerald sat on the bedroll with the other Reg in his arms. Heedless of passing time and how long he'd been awake, Monk worked frantically on stage one of the plan: finishing the instant-shadbolt gizmo so that together they could rig it to judiciously backfire. Their Reg was helping him, passing him tools and bits and pieces of stuff on his barked command, offering unsolicited advice and tolerating his impatient rudeness with remarkable restraint. So far she'd only threatened his unmentionables four times.

Although he was so tired his eyelids kept trying to slam shut, he made himself stay awake. Kept himself alert by catching up on events with the other Reg.

"I don't understand," he said softly, not wanting to distract Monk and his Reg. "I know your

Melissande told her Rupert to keep out of this, but . . . surely someone else in the government could've tried asking Kallarap for help? I mean, the jury might be out on whether their gods actually exist, but there's no denying Shugat's got a lot of power at his fingertips."

Sighing, the other Reg rubbed her beak against his coat, a gesture of affection far more frightening than pleasing. Lord, she felt so fragile beneath his hands. She'd never been a plump bird—vanity saw to that—but with what this Reg had endured since New Ottosland . . . well, she was feathers and skin and hollow bones and not much else.

"Don't be daft, Gerald," she said. "That ratty old holy man Shugat got one whiff of *my* Gerald back in New Ottosland and that was that. He wasn't having any of it. Not even when the Butterfly King found out madam was in trouble and ran bleating back to Zazoor. I think the poor gormless twit thought that since Zazoor and Melissande were almost engaged for two minutes that'd make some kind of difference."

"But it didn't?"

"Of course not," she said, scornful. "Shugat's answer was to seal Kallarap inside one of his poncy magic bubbles and leave the rest of us poor infidels to sink or bloody swim."

He shook his head. "And what did your Gerald have to say about that?"

"Not a lot," she said, after a moment. "He just laughed. *'Shugat and Zazoor can hide, but they can't run. I'll get to them.'* That's all he said."

"Reg . . ." He looked over at his Monk and their

Reg, up to their elbows inside that infernal invention. "None of this is your fault, y'know."

She heaved another mournful sigh. "I never should've gone back to Ottosland with madam and the others. I never should've left you to face that pillock Lional on your own. I deserted you when you needed me the most, Gerald. And look what's come of it. Of course it's my fault."

Gently, so gently, he lifted her until they were eye-to-eye. "*No*. It's *not*. I—*he*—your Gerald—had a choice and he made the wrong one. Nobody twisted his arm. Nobody held a staff to his head and said: *steal Lional's pilfered grimoires or you're a dead man*. He chose to do that. It's on him, Reg. Not you."

Her dull eyes brightened. "Why didn't you choose that, Gerald? Did I—did *she*—"

"I don't know," he said shrugging, and lowered her to rest again in his lap. "Maybe my Reg said something different, or did something different. Maybe Monk did. Or Melissande. I honestly don't know. I don't know why your Gerald lost faith in himself, lost his courage, and I didn't. And I don't suppose it matters now. We are where we are. All that matters is stopping him before it's too late."

"If we can," the other Reg muttered. "He's strong, Gerald. You know, sunshine, you've felt him. He's a rogue wizard with a very bad attitude. In all my years I've never met anything like it." She sniffed. "Speaking of which, how are you doing with that muck he made you swallow?"

He smoothed a finger over her head. "Like I told Monk. I'm fine."

"Ha!" she retorted, with a tiny flash of the spirit

he loved so much. "And *when* was the last time you managed to lie to me?"

"Never," he said solemnly. "And we both know *that's* because you and I only met a few hours ago."

She chattered her beak. "Smart-ass. Gerald—"

"Yes, Reg?"

"Gerald, are you happy?"

"Right now? No, not terribly."

"Gerald Dunwoody—"

Laughing softly, because he didn't want to weep, he picked her up again. "I'm as happy as I can be, Reg, under the circumstances."

"All this rogue wizard malarkey," she said, sounding anxious now. "It's not—nobody's tried to—you aren't—"

"It's . . . complicated," he said at last. "But no, I'm not in any danger." *Or I wasn't before this happened. What I'll face when we get home again is anybody's guess.* "You don't have to worry."

"Good," she whispered. "Gerald—"

He rested his head against the wall and closed his eyes. "Yes, Reg?"

"My Melissande. She's not really fine, is she?"

Damn. "Reg, from what I can see, nobody who lives in this world is fine. Not while my evil twin is free to do what he likes."

"And your Melissande?"

Eyes still closed, he smiled. "Bossy as ever. And no more princessly now than she was the day we first met her."

"A fully-qualified witch, is she?"

He shook his head. "Sadly, no."

"Ha! I told her that Rinky-Tinky woman was just

stringing her along." Reg fluffed her drooping feathers. "And your Emmerabiblia?"

He felt a bittersweet ache in his chest. "Brilliant and brave and beautiful, Reg."

"Ah," she said knowingly. "So have you set the date yet?"

And *damn* again. He looked over at Monk. "How are you getting along there? Nearly done?"

Monk dragged his sleeve over his face. "Do I look like I'm nearly done?"

"I can't see, Monk. That's why I'm asking."

"Yes, he's nearly done," said Reg, perched on the stool. "So maybe you could stop your nattering, sunshine, and pay attention?"

"She's right," said the Reg in his lap. "They're probably getting to the sticky end of things by now. Go on, my boy. Make yourself useful."

She was thin, and her dark eyes were dull and all the gloss had faded from her feathers. But she was still Reg. He kissed her beak, settled her on the bedroll and left her to sleep.

"Right," said Monk, after ten more minutes of tight-lipped work. "So that's that. But your evil twin'll want to know what you did to make this thing work, so I've left half a dozen gaps in the amplification chamber's matrix. You'll need to fill them with the strongest incants you can rustle up. That's the important bit— the ether won't ignite without them. And once you've sorted those, just—tizzy up a few of my incants. You know. Add some extra thaumaturgic decoration."

"Now?" he said, staring at the almost-completed machine.

Monk rolled his eyes. "No, next week."

"Ha," he said. "Y'know what? You've been spending too much time with Reg."

Reg whacked him with her wing. "Cheeky bugger. Put a sock in it, sunshine, and let's get this over with. Saint Snodgrass only knows what those girls are up to behind our backs. Especially with that manky Sir Alec hanging around like a bad smell."

Summoning his *potentia*—feeling anew its taint of darkness—*but I'll be all right. I will. I will*—he sank himself into the ether and looked at the machine. Monk was right, the incants needed to complete its amplification chamber's matrix were daunting. Well . . . daunting for someone who wasn't him. Feeling the surge of power through his blood and bones, he filled in the matrix's gaps then added his own flourish here and there to give the impression he'd done even more work than that.

In passing he felt the ever-so-slightly different thaumic signature of the other Monk Markham. The dead one. Melancholy, he touched it lightly—*Thanks, Monk*—and moved on.

"All done?" said his Monk, once he'd withdrawn from the machine.

He nodded. "All done."

"I'll just have a quick squiz," said Monk. "Not because I don't trust you, mate. Only if that other bugger asks me—"

"Fine. Go ahead. Squiz away."

So Monk squizzed, nodding his approval. "Good. So this bloody thing—" he whacked the gizmo with the back of his hand, "—will, when it's activated, trigger a massive etheretic carrier wave. And once it's triggered, and your evil twin tags it with his favorite shadbolt incant, every non-shadbolted and unprotected witch and wizard in this Ottosland will be instantly shadbolted." He frowned. "Damn. That means we'll need to proof you, Gerald, somehow, in case—"

"No need," he said. "Turns out I'm already proofed. Don't suppose you know anything about that?"

"*Me?*" Monk stared at him. "Why would you think *I*—" And then he understood. "Oh, that's great, Gerald. That's a real vote of confidence. Thanks a lot. Once, *once*, you got clobbered with one of my incants—and it wasn't even my bloody idea!"

"Well, you can't blame me for wondering," he retorted. "Every time I turn around you've invented another crazy gizmo—broken another rule—and if you thought it was for my own good we both know you'd—"

"Do you *mind?*" said Reg, rattling her tail feathers ferociously. "Save the kindergarten fisticuffs for our own backyard. Right now we've got an evil twin to thwart, you plonkers!"

He and Monk glared at each other, and then he sighed. "Yeah. You're right. Sorry."

"*Anyway,*" said Monk, breathing hard, "now that we've finished this infernal machine we can jigger it so it backfires in that mad pillock's face."

"Yeah . . ." He scratched at his chin, which was starting to stubble. "About that. Look, how confident are you that you can hide the bits of jiggering I'm not supposed to have done? Because if that crazy bugger catches so much as a *whiff* of me in the wrong place then—"

"Bloody hell, Gerald, how many times do I have to say it?" Monk snapped. "*He won't.* The masking incant Sir Alec gave me is brilliant. You didn't detect me in this bloody shadbolt I'm wearing, did you?"

"No," he said at last, reluctantly. "But come on, Monk. You can't compare this gizmo and a shadbolt. The amount of thaumic energy it's going to gobble up—the etheretic discharges—the carrier wave itself—what if they blast that masking incant to smithereens?"

Monk shook his head. "I know it's a risk but we have to take it. Because this is it. This is our one shot at spiking your evil twin's guns, Gerald. If we don't stop him with this . . . well. You know what comes next."

Unfortunately he did. He looked at this world's sleeping Reg, then back at his own. "What d'you think?"

"I think you'd be better off ignoring that bird over there," said Reg. "Because when this plan of ours works, and it'll work because he's a genius and you're a rogue wizard and I'm a very intelligent woman, we'll be buggering off home with your nasty double and leaving her behind." She gave Monk an equally sharp look. "That goes for you too, Mr. Clever Clogs. No saving that fallen woman masquerading as your sister, or the Princess Pushy she's got stashed away. They belong in this world, not ours. Our world's already got a Bibbie Markham and a Princess Melissande and a cruelly dispossessed Queen Dulcetta. And you don't know what kind of mischief you could be stirring up, bringing them home with us for good. Bad enough we've got to drag along the other Gerald. It only takes one straw to break the camel's back."

"I hate to say it, Monk, but she's right," he said, after a moment. "We don't dare risk unbalancing the dimensional metaphysics any more than that—especially when we don't have a clue how they work. And anyway—once we've taken care of this world's me, they won't be in danger any more. Will they?"

Monk frowned at his nicked and singed hand. "Right," he said at last. "So, now that I understand exactly how this gizmo works, I'm thinking we need to embed a reverse-thaumic trigger inside the activation matrix. *And* we need to make it target specific. So when that mad bugger switches this thing on, instead of lots of shadbolts imprisoning lots of witches and wizards—"

"—he gets trussed up by his own shadbolt," said Reg. "Neat and tidy and ready for kidnapping. Y'know, Mr. Markham, that just might do the trick."

"Will it, Gerald?" said Monk. "I mean, he is bloody powerful and he's soaked to the gills in all that foul grimoire magic. And you'd have to think he's immune to his own shadbolt incant."

"Well," he said slowly, "as powerful as he is, I can't see him being stronger than the etheretic amplification wave this machine's designed to create. And as for being immune to his own shadbolt—" He shrugged. "Maybe there's something I can do about that."

Monk's eyebrows shot up. "*Maybe?*"

"Let me think about it," he said. "In the meantime, we'd better jigger what we can, quickly. Who knows when that bastard's going to turn up again?"

"Good point," said Reg, and ruffled all her feathers. "So come on, get jiggering!"

He pulled a face at Monk, who grinned. "You heard Her Majesty, Gerald. Chop chop!"

Despite the horrible shadbolt binding Monk's aura and the taint of dark magics in his own blood, despite the thin, downtrodden other Reg asleep on the bedroll—and their own Reg making exploding tea-kettle noises because, in her opinion, they weren't working fast enough—he and his best friend found their tandem thaumaturgic rhythm almost at once . . . and without even having to discuss tactics began jiggering up a storm.

At one point Monk paused and grinned again. "All I know, Gerald, is that after this caper nobody back home whose name rhymes with Uncle Ralph *or* Sir Alec better say *boo* about you and me practicing on my inventions in the attic. Because if we hadn't done that—"

"I know," he said, soberly. The thought was so appalling he couldn't manage an answering grin. "We'd have no hope of doing this."

Monk nodded firmly. "Bloody oath. In fact, they ought to give us a raise."

I'll settle for a whole skin, and our world sqfe. Or at least a decent breathing space between disasters.

"Come on, come on," said Reg, rattling her tail. "That's enough chit-chat. Get on with it!"

With an exchange of eye-rolling glances, they got on.

Weaken the sub-dimensional etheretic link . . . reverse the polarity, on the secondary directional matrix . . . tag the wave amplifier with an amended target . . . and hide every last trace of their tricks. Done and done and done and *done*.

"Bloody hell," Monk muttered, and blotted sweat from his pale face. "Is that it, mate? Please tell me that's it."

"Yeah, I think so," he said, just as sweaty and exhausted. "You all right?"

Monk pressed the heels of his hands against his closed eyes. "This bloody shadbolt," he muttered. "It doesn't half give me a headache."

"I know. But honestly? It won't hurt for him to notice you're in pain. There's nothing he likes better than someone suffering on his behalf."

"Right," said Monk, giving him an odd look. "If you say so." And then he bit his lip. "Look. Gerald. Are you sure about this? Because if you can't handle it—if you're not as good as you think you are? Ass over elbows won't begin to—"

"Monk, I can handle it," he said flatly. "You worry about—"

The hot, sharp stirring in the ether turned both of them towards the hexed laboratory door.

"Is that him?" said Reg, craning her head. "Is he coming back? Bugger. Then tie that old biddy's beak shut again and chuck her in the cage, quick."

He stared at her. *"Reg!"*

"Don't you *Reg* me, Gerald Dunwoody!" she retorted. "I'm the one who's got to hide in that manky bathroom. Quick, can't you feel him? He's in a right state!"

And she wasn't wrong about the other Gerald's angry approach. Still a ways distant, this world's Mr. Dunwoody was burning through the ether like a wind-whipped summer fire through the dry grass. He couldn't feel Bibbie with him—and that was a relief. Even knowing she wasn't really his sister, Monk was distracted when she was in the room. And they couldn't afford any distractions. One false step and they'd be toast.

"I'm sorry, I'm so sorry," he whispered to the other Reg. "But she's right. You need to go back in the cage."

"I know," she said, her familiar eyes warm with a smile. "If she hadn't said it, I would have."

He fetched the red ribbon and started winding it around her long beak. "Look. If this goes right we—we won't see each other again. So I'll wish you good luck, Reg. After he's taken care of there'll be a lot of work to do. I expect your Melissande will be up to her eyeballs in that. She'll need your advice. She'll need you to—to nag her. Will you do that for me, Reg? Nag her and make rude comments about her butt—her behind? Complain about her tweed trousers and her terrible hairstyles and how she walks like a hockey player instead of a princess?"

Bound to silence now, the other Reg nodded.

"Thanks," he whispered, and kissed the top of her head.

"Right, right, so if you've *finished* slobbering all over my third-rate understudy, Gerald," his Reg snapped, her head poked around the bathroom door, "maybe you could get her in that cage before your evil twin kicks the front doors down?"

Ignoring the wretched woman, he returned the other Reg to her prison and re-hexed it. "Monk. The portable portal opener. Is it—"

Monk slapped his chest. "Safe in my pocket, mate."

"And you're sure it's still working?"

"Sure as I can be."

"He really can't sense it?"

A shrug. "He hasn't so far."

"And if we manage to do this and have a shot at escaping, where do we—"

"He was a bit clever, that other Monk," said Monk, not quite smiling. "It'll take us back to the last place it opened. In this case, your bedroom. All very neat."

"And if that's not proof positive it was a different Monk Markham who made it . . . ." Heart pounding, he turned to stare at the hexed door. Raised his voice a little. "Reg, if he's taking us out of here I'll make sure the lab door stays open. Follow us as soon as you can and for the love of Saint Snodgrass, *don't* get caught."

"No, really?" said Reg, from the bathroom. "That's a bugger. Because I was planning on introducing myself and asking for a matching cage!"

"Gerald," Monk said urgently, standing behind the etheretic gizmo. "Gerald, what about—"

But there was no more time for talking. The other Gerald was here.

With a blinding surge of thaumic power the laboratory door smashed open and the other Gerald strode in, pushing a large wheeled trolley. He'd changed out of his royal blue suit and was garbed now in gold and crimson, garish as bullion splashed with fresh blood.

"Well, Monk?" he demanded, eyes glittering with rage. "Is it finished? You'd better tell me it's finished, because if it's *not* finished I'm going to make you *very* bloody *sorry!*"

Monk flinched and gasped, as though a knife had run through him. The shadbolt. "It's finished, Gerald. All right? It's finished!"

"And is it working?" said the other Gerald, silkily

smooth. "Because if it's finished and it's *not* working then I don't see the point. Do you?"

Gerald bit his tongue. Damn. They hadn't tested the wretched thing. There hadn't been time. "Gerald," he said, stepping forward. "It's working, but it hasn't been given a proper test run. That's your prerogative, not ours. Anyway, when did Monk Markham ever build a thaumic machine that didn't work?"

His counterpart sneered. "When did Monk Markham need me to help him build one?"

"Actually—" Monk cleared his throat. "A few times, Gerald. Only I didn't have the guts to admit it. I could hardly admit it to myself. So anything I couldn't do without you, I just—I stopped working on."

Before Gerald could stop himself, he was exchanging surprised looks with his evil twin.

"Huh," said the other Gerald. "Y'know, call me crazy, Professor, but I think that touching declaration had the ring of truth about it. Don't you?"

He nodded. "Yeah. It did."

And when Monk and I are home again, we're going to have a little chat.

"Anyway," said Monk darkly. "The bloody thing's operational. So what happens now?"

Brief amusement fled from the other Gerald's demeanor, and fury poured in after it. "Ideally I'd test that claim for myself, Monk, but I'll have to take your word on it. There's been a slight change in plans. That stupid bastard Gonegal at the UMN had the *gall* to threaten my life. There's a fleet of UMN armed airships on their way here now. He's coming to take me into custody! Crimes against thaumaturgics! Can you *believe* it? I can't *wait* to put a bloody shadbolt on *him*."

Gerald didn't dare risk a glance at Monk. "Armed airships? But—"

"Frightened, Professor?" said the other Gerald, full of contempt. "There's no need. Gonegal's armed airships are no match for ours. And once I've shadbolted Ottosland's wizards and witches and have their harnessed *potentias* at my beck and call?" He laughed. "Viceroy Gonegal and his toadies won't stand a chance."

"Gerald . . ." He risked a step closer. "Stealing other people's *potentias* will make you no better than Lional."

"That's a *lie!*" the other Gerald spat. "Lional was a murderer. He *killed* the wizards whose *potentias* he took. I'm not killing anyone." And then he smiled. "Well. Not anyone in Ottosland. I won't vouch for those pustules from the UMN. If they breach our sovereign airspace then all bets are off. And I'm not *stealing* anything, either. I'm borrowing it. In a good cause. *I'm* not the villain here, Professor. Now shut up. You're wasting my time." He gave the wheeled trolley a shove. "Here. Get my machine on that, Mr. Markham. We'll have to transport it the ordinary way, in case more thaumaturgics upset its calibrations. Quickly! We've got a lot of people waiting for us at the parade ground and I don't want to disappoint them. Thanks to certain troublemakers I'm already running late."

Monk nodded. "Yes, sir. Ah—Ger—sorry, Professor? Would you mind giving me a hand?"

"Good idea," said the other Gerald. "I mean, I'd help but I'm not exactly dressed for manual labor."

Oh, blimey. Puffing and grunting with the effort, he helped Monk manhandle the etheretic amplifier onto the trolley. Touching the gizmo, he could feel its enormous thaumaturgic potential thrumming beneath his hands like a rumbling volcano waiting to erupt.

"All right," said the other Gerald. "That's it. Let's go. Except—" He looked at poor caged Reg, silent and miserable. "Bring the bird, Professor. She really shouldn't be deprived of seeing my moment of triumph. And with any luck she'll choke to death trying to apologize." He smiled. "I'll just unhex the cage for you."

Gerald held his breath, his stomach churning. If his counterpart noticed it had already been unhexed and re-hexed—

But no. Either their thaumic signatures were close enough to fool him or the other Gerald was just too keyed up with angry excitement, because he didn't notice a thing.

Praise the pigs.

"Thank you," he said, and gently took the other Reg out again.

"No, don't untie her beak yet," said his counterpart. "She'll only start nagging. Untie it when it's time for her to apologize. Until then, Professor, we'll bask in the silence."

"Right," he said, and stroked the tip of Reg's wing. Surreptitiously, so his counterpart wouldn't see.

The other Gerald glared at Monk. "Well? Why are you standing there like a lump of dried cowpat? Push the damn trolley! We've got to go!"

Monk flinched. "Sorry. Sorry. Um—push it where?"

"Oh, for the love of Saint Snodgrass," the other

Gerald snapped. "Follow me. Both of you. And you'd better bloody well keep up."

He swept out of the laboratory, crimson boot-heels banging the floor. Gerald, not daring to look at the bathroom, dropped another kiss on Reg's third-rate understudy's head, exchanged a grim glance with Monk, and followed him out . . . making sure to leave the lab door open behind them.

CHAPTER TWENTY-FOUR

A covered, open-backed lorry took them to the ceremonial parade ground. The other Gerald traveled with them, not wanting to let his precious thaumic machine out of his sight. Gerald swallowed frustration. Inconvenient didn't begin to describe it—now there was no hope of discussing his crazy idea for an evil-twin nobbling incant with Monk. So he consoled himself with holding the other Reg and silently promising her that whatever else happened, when this was over she'd be free to fly away.

As the lorry passed through the gates into the ceremonial parade ground, Monk looked up and saw Lional's transfixed dragon.

"Bloody hell!"

The other Gerald stared at him. "What is *wrong* with you? Anyone'd think you'd never seen it before—let alone helped me get it up there!"

"What?" said Monk faintly. "I mean, sorry. No. It's just—it's been a while, hasn't it? I—I forgot what an impression it makes."

The other Gerald glowered. "One more uninvited

word out of you, Monk, and I'll give that bloody dragon a jockey, I swear."

They rode in silence the rest of the way.

"So," said the other Gerald, as the lorry finally ground to a halt. "Here's what's going to happen. You're going to stand with me on the dais, both of you, with my machine. You're going to monitor its status while I begin phase one of my plan. If I don't like the way either of you so much as *blinks*—the bird dies. Melissande dies. And if it comes to that, Monk, your sister dies too." He smiled. "She's not the only pretty blonde witch in the world."

"You mean—" Monk had to moisten his lips and try again. "Melissande's here?"

"No. She's at home," said the other Gerald, straightening his lapels. "But believe me, old chum. It makes no difference. I can kill her with a thought from a hundred miles away."

Gasping, Monk dropped to the lorry floor, eyes wide, chest heaving.

"You see? Just like that." A wide smile. "Saint Snodgrass's bunions. I *love* a good shadbolt."

Gerald set the other Reg on his shoulder then risked touching his counterpart on the arm. "Don't be a fool, Gerald. You need him."

"For the machine, yes," his counterpart snapped. "But for precious little else, believe me! So if he wants to go on living he'll watch his bloody step!"

Released, breathing harshly, Monk shakily sat up.

"Now come along," said the other Gerald, leading the way out of the lorry. "I want this over and done with before Viceroy Gonegal and his pathetic armed airships get here."

There was indeed a dais. It had been assembled in the middle of the ceremonial parade ground. Crowded onto it were the elected government and appointed senior civil servants of Ottosland, every last one of them still shadbolted to the hilt. He could see Lord Attaby, but not Monk's Uncle Ralph. The rest of the walled enclosure was crammed full of unshadbolted witches and wizards, their *potentias* stirring thickly in the agitated ether. Bibbie was there too, at the very front of the dais, resplendent in swathes of vibrant pink silk, pouting because she'd been left alone for so long.

All the smoky half-domes had been removed, revealing the obscene and terrifying exhibits this world's Gerald had so assiduously collected.

"Monk," Gerald said under his breath, as they guided the etheretic wave enhancer on its trolley down the lorry's portable ramp. His friend was walking backwards, bracing it, keeping it straight. "Monk, listen. When you turn around you're going to see some things. Whatever you do, mate, *don't react.*"

Puzzled, Monk blinked at him. "Yeah? All right. Whatever you say."

But then they hit the bottom of the ramp and the trolley rolled over the flagstones and Monk had to wrestle it a bit—and he turned.

There was Sir Alec, still dying, dressed in flames. There was Lional, ripped and slashed and pinned to the ground. There was the witch whose name he didn't know, wrapped in a blanket made of her own flayed skin. And wait—there was a new one—he hadn't seen that one the last time. It was—it was—

Monk staggered. "Oh my God. That's *Uncle Ralph.*"

"Oh, yes," said the other Gerald, turning. "Stubborn

old coot. Y'know, even with a shadbolt he kept on answering back. I didn't want to lose him, I *really* didn't. A First Grade Markham wizard isn't something you throw away lightly. But—he was setting a bad example. He didn't give me a choice."

Uncle Ralph was front and center, directly in line with the dais. Probably the other Gerald had ordered him set there just so Sir Ralph's former colleagues were reminded to hold their busy tongues. Compared to some of the others here he'd been granted an easy death: a swift impalement on a long, thin, sharpened stake.

"Monk, *don't*," said Gerald, and grabbed his friend's arm. "Remember Melissande. And Reg. And Bibbie."

Dazed, Monk shook him free. "Yeah. Yeah. Right."

Still clinging to his shoulder, the other Reg was making angry noises in her throat. He patted the nearest bit of her that he could reach. "I know, Reg," he muttered. "But we can't help him now."

The truck was retreating, chugging steadily away. The sky above the parade ground was clear of cloud but clogged with airships. The early morning sunshine turned their gun barrels bright silver. Some were pointed at the ground, covering the uneasily silent crowd of captive thaumaturgists; the rest were pointed outwards, waiting for the airships of the United Magical Nations.

When they got here—if they got here—there was going to be a bloodbath. There was going to be a bloodbath anyway, of a sorts. All these wizards and witches, waiting to be enslaved.

Sick to his stomach, Gerald turned to the man

in crimson and gold who was wearing his face. He didn't want to take this other Gerald back through the portable portal. The risk to Ottosland was too great. What if he and Sir Alec couldn't contain him? What if this murderous madman got loose?

What was I thinking? I can't risk it. He's too danger- ous. There has to be another way.

"Gerald, listen to me," he said, cajoling. "You don't have to do this. There's still time to change your mind. Deep down I don't think you *want* to do this. All these grand plans, enslaving wizards, taking over the world . . . it's those grimoires talking. It's not you. Let me help. Let me fix this. Someone has to know a way of getting that magic out of you. There'll be questions—and yes, there'll be a tribunal, you can't avoid that—but I'll—I'll testify about how the gri- moire magic changed you."

Monk was staring at him. "What the—*Gerald*—"

"Be quiet, Monk." Desperate, he looked at his counterpart, willing him to listen. "Not all of this is your fault, Gerald. The magics you gave me, in that hex crystal—hardly anything, and I can *feel* them in- side me, changing my *potentia*. A teaspoon's worth of grinwire magic, compared to what you took—and I'm twisted. Only a little bit, but I know the twist is there. I know what you went through. And I know why you did it. You did it to stop Lional, to save New Ottosland. You did the wrong thing for the right rea- son—and that has to count for something, Gerald. I think it counts."

The look on his counterpart's face shifted from bafflement to irritation. "Oh, my God, Professor. You're as bad as the bloody bird. Now shut up before

I shut you up. I might not be able to shadbolt you but I'll bet I can find a gag."

Swamped with despair, he shut up.

I'm a bloody idiot. Talking to him is like talking to Lional. He's too far gone to reach.

And so, just like New Ottosland, this could only end one way. Except this time it wasn't just him and one insane man getting ready to face each other in a thaumaturgic duel. This time there were hundreds of people who could—who would—get hurt in a confrontation. So this time, terribly, he had no other choice.

Oh, lord. Oh, Saint Snodgrass. I really have to take him home.

"Professor Dunwoody! Sir! Sir!"

As one, he and his counterpart turned. "Yes?"

It would have been funny if the situation weren't so dire.

Some kind of junior government flunky was panting on a pushbike across the ceremonial parade ground towards them, brandishing a piece of paper. He was so upset he didn't even notice the horrendous exhibits around him, or the fact that he was staring at two Professor Dunwoodys. Reaching them, he half-leaped, half-fell off the pushbike which clattered onto the flagstones, wheels spinning.

"Sir! Sir! They've been sighted, sir! The UMN airships have crossed the border! *Scores* of them! And they're heading this way, sir, at a right rate of knots!"

Gerald watched his counterpart's face flush red, then drain dead white. The ether stirred dangerously, his warped *potentia* snarling. He snatched the piece of paper from the flunky's hand and read it for himself. Crumpled it in his fist and threw it at the terrified young man.

"And what about the Jandrians?"

The flunky shook his head. "No sign of them, sir," he whispered. "Looks like we're on our own."

Another threatening sizzle in the air. "Send word to the commander of our airship fleet," the other Gerald snapped. "Engage the enemy at will. I don't want to see a single UMN airship over this city, is that clear? And then send a message to Tambotan of Jandria. I want his airships here within the hour. If *one* Ottish citizen is harmed because he fails to keep his word, his streets will run with Jandrian blood and his head will take pride of place above my fireplace mantel. Tell him to tell his feckless allies the same applies to them. Well? Why are you still standing there? *Start pedaling!*"

Almost gibbering with fear the flunky snatched up his pushbike and desperately pedaled away. Behind them, stranded on the crowded dais, Bibbie stamped her stylishly-shod foot.

"Gerald? Gerald! What's going on? I've been waiting for *ages*. Are we going to do this or aren't we?"

"In a minute, Bibbie!" The other Gerald raised an eyebrow. "Well, Professor? Are you ready? I hope so, for your sake. Because it's only fair to tell you that if you and Monk, here, fail to deliver what *you've* promised? I'll be looking for a bigger fireplace, with more room over the mantel."

Gerald risked a glance at Monk, who nodded. He looked back. "Yes. We're ready."

"Then get my machine up to the dais. We've no time to waste."

As the other Gerald wandered away to inspect his latest gruesome exhibit, Monk glanced at the sky. "I can't see Reg," he muttered. "What about you?"

Reg . . . He risked his own quick look around. "No. But she'll be here."

"She'd better," said Monk. "We won't have time to wait. Gerald—" Now he was staring at the cowering crowd of wizards and witches who'd been brought here for a group shadbolting. "I don't get it. Why are they just *standing* there? Why are they letting him *do* this? He's one man, Gerald. It's crazy."

He sighed. "Monk, he's one man who's managed to shadbolt an entire government. He's one man who can rain fire upon their heads with a couple of words and the snap of his fingers. They've got families— and at least once a week they have to walk around here looking at what happens to people who put him in a bad mood. Now come on. I want to get out of here before the UMN fleet turns up. They've got no chance of beating him—which means things are going to get messy, fast."

There was a ramp ready and waiting for them. With the other Reg clinging tight to his shoulder, her beak still tied shut, he helped his Monk wrangle the other Monk's invention into position at the front of the dais. Bibbie watched them, arms folded, her beautiful, painted face set into deep lines of discontent. Would she be heartbroken to lose her Gerald, once they dragged him through the portal? It was hard to believe she could love a man who didn't love her.

She's not the only pretty blonde witch in the world.

He felt his heart break. Felt the burning sting of tears.

I'm so sorry, Bibs. I wish there'd been time to help you.

"What's wrong?" Monk muttered as he checked

the machines etheretic calibrations. "Bloody hell, Gerald. Don't tell me you're getting cold feet."

"No, of course I'm not," he muttered back. "Shut up. Is everything set?"

"Well, it's set from *my* end," said Monk, straightening. "But what about—"

"Don't worry. I've got everything under control."

Except of course he didn't. How could he? This was an entirely unprecedented situation. Not a single hex or incant in his repertoire had been designed to do what he and Monk planned to do here. Not one lecture in his training at Nettleworth had encompassed *this* kind of mission. In all the history of janitoring there'd never *been* this kind of mission.

I'll have to wing it. Just like I winged it with Hal Rottlezinder and his warding hexes. I did it then. I'll do it now. Because I'm Gerald Dunwoody, janitor, and this is my job.

Overhead, the armed airships of Ott methodically criss-crossed the sky. And somewhere beyond the city were UMN airships, just as determined. This could all go ass over elbows in the blink of an eye.

"*Right,*" said the other Gerald, rubbing his hands together as he joined them on the dais. "I think I've waited long enough for this, don't you?"

"*I've* certainly waited long enough," said Bibbie, arms folded, toes tapping. "Honestly, Gerald—"

He silenced her with a look. Then he turned. "Professor, why are you still wearing that bloody bird on your shoulder? You look ridiculous. Put it down."

Oh. Right. *Poor thing. Poor Reg.* "Is the dais railing acceptable, Gerald?" he said, nodding at it. "There aren't any spare seats and if I put her on the ground she might get trodden on accidentally."

"And wouldn't *that* be a tragedy?" said his counterpart. Then he sighed. "Fine. The railing. Just hurry up." He glanced at the sky. "We could have visitors any minute."

As gently as he could, he plucked the other Reg from his shoulder and made sure she was settled safely on the dais railing. Her eyes warm with appreciation, she gave him a little nod. She even managed to rattle her tail.

The other Gerald snapped his fingers and a rain of rose petals fell from the sky. Then, ignoring Reg, he grasped the dais railing with both hands and swept his gaze around his frightened, captive audience.

"Look, everyone, I know you're afraid," he said, his voice clear and carrying. "I know in the last few months there have been many changes which you haven't always understood. And some harsh measures have been taken that have caused some of you pain. I'm sorry about that. Truly. I wish there'd been time to tread lightly and kindly. To explain everything step-by-step. I wish there'd been time for committees and consultations and working parties and resolutions in the house. But there wasn't. I had to act swiftly and I didn't have time to argue every little thing. There are dangers in this world, my friends, terrible dangers. And whether it was by accident, or by some strange thaumaturgical design, I'm the wizard who was in the right place at the right time with the right resources to make us safe. Which is what I'm about to do now. I'm going to make every last one of us safe."

Silence. The captive crowd of wizards and witches looked at each other, then looked back at the dais.

The other Gerald was frowning. "Well, y'know, I think a *thank you* would be nice. *Bibbie*."

Smiling brightly, Bibbie started to clap. After a moment, behind them, Ottosland's impotent Prime Minister Attaby clapped with her. One by one his fellow shadbolted ministers and senior civil servants joined in. Bibbie clapped harder. Ottosland's government followed suit. And at last, grudgingly, the city's captive thaumaturgists followed suit. Nobody in their right mind would call the applause enthusiastic, but it was loud enough to put a smile on the other Gerald's face.

Reluctantly clapping, Gerald kept his own face blank and was careful not to look anywhere near Monk. *Blimey, he really believes it. He believes everything he just said. I don't know if that makes it better or worse.* Trying to be inconspicuous, he stared around the ceremonial parade ground. There was still no sign of Reg. Where the devil was she? Surely not *lost*. Or—oh, God, was she trapped back in the Department of Thaumaturgy building? *No, no, no. Don't let it be that.* Because once the etheretic enhancer was switched on there'd be no going back. She had to be here, ready and waiting.

Bloody hell, Reg. Don't do this to me.

Thanks to Bibbie's enthusiastic example the ragged applause showed no sign of dying down. The other Gerald raised his hands. "Oh, you're welcome, you're welcome," he said, widely smiling. "It's my pleasure. Honestly, my only interest is in serving you all. And right now I'm going to serve you by asking *you* to serve *me*. So everybody please relax. There's no need to panic. You're going to feel a little peculiar—and then *everything* will be fine. I promise. My word as a wizard."

Bibbie stopped clapping, and immediately so did everyone else. With a final smile and a wave the other Gerald stepped up to his precious machine and started flipping switches. Moments later the ether began to stir, thaumaturgic currents agitating as the amplifier's incants came alive. Gerald felt his own *potentia* stir in answer, shadowed eddies an unwelcome reminder of what had been given to him against his will. Felt what he'd have to purge from himself against *its* will, when this was done and he was home again, safe.

He looked at Monk, anxious. His friend would be feeling the machine's effects too, along with every witch and wizard gathered in this horrible place. Monk was holding on, his face rigid with strain. He risked a glance at Bibbie. She was frowning, fingers tightly interlaced against the uncomfortable thaumaturgic roil.

But the other Gerald? His counterpart? He was revelling in it, grinning, drinking the ether's agitation like fine wine. His perverted *potentia* was hungry, and fed on discord. Watching him, Gerald shuddered.

I don't know why that isn't me. I haven't a clue why I was spared.

The etheretic pressure was slowly building to a crescendo. It was nearly time. They had one chance to do this—one chance to stop a madman and save two worlds, maybe more. He looked sideways at Monk, the only man in any world he wanted standing by his side. Poor Monk. Not a trained government agent, just an extraordinary theoretical thaumaturgist. Dragged into this disaster by the scruff of his neck. Condemned by his own brilliance to be the lynchpin of a deluded wizard's megalomaniacal plans.

Bloody hell, Markham. I'll owe you for this.

Meeting his gaze, Monk flicked him a wink. Non-chalant on the surface, but terrified underneath. And he wasn't the only one. If either of them made even the smallest mistake . . .

No. No. Don't think like that, Dunnywood. You can do this. It's your job.

He took a deep breath, then let it out. One more. One more. This world's Reg had turned herself around on the dais railings. She was staring right at him, her eyes full of love. He couldn't look at her. He had to look away.

Oh, God. Reg. Where are you? Come on . . . come on . . .

With a silent peal like thunder the etheretic amplifier's process approached its peak strength. Feeling it, many of the captive wizards and witches cried out. The other Gerald shouted, a raw, shocking sound of triumph, his *potentia* shuddering—and then he started to recite the incant for his planned mass shadbolting.

"*Now, Monk!*" Gerald shouted. Then, as Monk triggered the hexes they'd planted in the machine he spun around to face his dreadful other self. Unleashed his own tarnished *potentia*, lashing out at the other Gerald to throw him off stride and disrupt his shadbolt incant.

Take that, you bastard. Bloody well take that!

But the other Gerald wasn't easily knocked off stride. Shaking with fury, he pointed at Monk and snapped his fingers. Monk dropped, writhing, as his shadbolt woke and sank its claws deep.

Gerald leaped forward but Monk waved him back. "Don't be an idiot!" he grunted, choking with pain. "Stop him while you still can!"

"*Stop* me?" echoed the other Gerald. His wide eyes were mad, promising an appalling retribution. "You bloody idiots. You morons! *You can't!*"

Laughing, he continued reciting the mass shadbolting hex.

Gerald spared one last look at Monk, tormented and shuddering against a dais railing post. And then he banished outrage and anguish and focused on the plan. The machine's etheretic amplification wave was still building but Monk's triggered incant had reversed its direction, sent it seeking, like an arrow, a rogue wizard's *potentia*. He staggered, feeling its power.

Bloody hell, Monk. I hope we know what we're doing.

And then there was no time for wondering, hardly any time to think at all. He'd baited his counterpart's machine with the unique thaumaturgical signature that they shared—and if he could work out how to deflect the amplifier's attention from himself *right now*—before the other Gerald realized—before the wave of power found them both—

Oh bugger. Oh, bugger. I don't know what to do.

He'd thought he could wing it. He'd thought he could make it up as he went along, avoid tumbling headfirst into his own clever trap—

And I can. I can. I've got a knack for improvisation. What do I need? What do I need? Bloody hell, I need not to be me . . .

With a blur of inspiration shooting through him

faster than thought, he turned on his shivering friend and snatched at his *potentia*, as though Monk were a paint pot and he wanted to slather himself green. Not knowing how to do it, precisely, knowing only that he could, even through the mauling claws of the cruel, confining shadbolt. Monk cried out, a sound of fresh shock and pain. Ruthless, he ignored that. For a heartbeat—and a heartbeat—and another pounding heartbeat—he smeared himself with Monk's brilliant thaumic signature. Made up his own masking incant on the fly. Made himself not-Gerald. As good as invisible. He hoped.

Come on ... come on ... come on ...

And all the while the other Gerald, oblivious, lost in a trance of his own grimoire making, wove his web to ensnare a whole world. Hidden in plain sight, Gerald shifted his attention. Now for the second impossible part of the plan. He needed to jigger with that shadbolt hex and in doing so fool the other Gerald's shadbolt-proofing into failure. Trick it into accepting the very incant it was designed to defeat.

On a breath, on a sigh, he eased his *potentia* into the shadbolt's matrix. Just like he'd eased it into Haf Rottlezinder's warding hex. Sneaky—stealthy—he was a janitor's janitor—

An odd thaumic *click*. A subtle etheretic vibration. *Done*. The shadbolt matrix was altered. The shadbolt-proofing would be blind. With a shiver, the redirected amplified etheretic carrier wave began to shift and—

And then—*oh, bloody hell*—things went ass over elbows in the worst possible way.

"Gerald!" Bibbie shouted, pointing skywards. "Gerald, *look!*"

Everyone on the parade ground and the dais was looking and pointing . . . and suddenly the sky had too many airships in it.

"It's the UMN!" cried Attaby. "God be praised! We're saved!"

Abandoning incantation the other Gerald turned on him, ferocious. "D'you think so, you tosser?"

A single word, a clenched fist, and Ottosland's shadbolted Prime Minister dropped dead.

Pandemonium on the dais. Pandemonium in the sky. The other Gerald's armed airships started shooting at the green and black UMN airships—and the city of Ott erupted in noise and fire.

"*Gerald!*" screamed Bibbie, reaching for him. "Gerald, what are we going to do?"

The other Gerald wrenched his arm free and shoved her aside. "Shut up, you silly bitch," he snarled. "I'm going to finish what I started! Once I've harnessed these sheep's *potentias* I'll burn those airships with a *look.*"

Holding his breath, heart racing, Gerald stepped back. Any moment now, any moment . . . the ether was shuddering again, the jiggered shadbolt incant burgeoning. Despite the interruption the other Gerald hadn't noticed. It was all coming together—the plan was going to work—

Hold on, Monk—hold on, mate—we're nearly home— hold on—

The shadbolt incant ignited just as the amplified etheretic wave struck home, enveloping the other Gerald in a giant thaumic maelstrom. Bibbie shrieked, the other wizards on the dais echoed her surprise, and Gerald flung up his arms against the tremendous flash of heat and light. Moments later the ether cleared, and his vision cleared with it. Dizzy with relief, he lowered his arms.

The other Gerald, unshadbolted, backhanded him across the face. "Are you a *moron?* You're a *moron!* Did you think I wouldn't *know?* Did you think I wouldn't *feel* you piss-assing about with my incant? What—you thought you could *touch* me? *Me?* The greatest wizard ever born?"

Choking, Gerald pushed himself off the dais railing. His face was on fire. Over the other Gerald's shoulder he could see Bibbie, avid for revenge. He could see the shadbolted government and its servants, broken by Attaby's death. The air stank of discharged thaumics and burning airships. Battle raged over their heads, gunfire and screaming. The air boomed and blossomed with scalding heat and raging sound. Too soon to tell where victory would belong. From the corner of his eye he caught sight of Monk, up on his elbows. Released from the shadbolt's punishment, at least for now. The other Reg had hopped down beside him, her long beak still bound with ribbon the color of blood.

I want my Reg. The real Reg. Bloody hell, woman, where are you?

Eyes stinging, he looked again at this world's terrible Gerald. "Did you think I *wouldn't* try to stop you?"

"And did *you* think, Professor, that I'd *ever* give you the chance?" Grinning, gloating, the other Gerald snapped his fingers. "Didn't you learn *anything* from what happened in New Ottosland? Didn't drinking wine with Lional put you off swallowing things for *life?*"

Swallowing things? *Swallowing things?* What the hell was he—and then he understood. *The crystal.*

Pain knocked him to his knees.

The other Gerald was laughing, no, *giggling* with his glee. "I can't believe you *fell* for it, Gerald. Bloody hell, you are so *soft*. You were so worried about saving Monk and Melissande and whoever that you forgot to save yourself. I swear, I could weep for you. Thank God I found those grimoires. When I think I could be *you* right now? I swear, I could vomit for a week." Smile vanishing, he clenched his fist. "*Get up.*"

Powerless, he stood.

"Now kill our good friend Monk, Gerald, because he's been a naughty boy. Go on. Not all of the hexes in that crystal were for my use, you know. You've got what you need to squish him like a flea. So come on. *Squish him.* I want to see him bleed."

The taint in his *potentia* stirred. He could feel the shadbolt incant waking, over-riding his own proof against compulsion. Its shadow crawled before his eyes, blotting out the fitful sunlight and plunging him into a nightmare dark. Growing dim, the sound of airships fighting overhead. Growing distant, the sight of Monk at his feet. Growing stronger, the urge to obey.

The other Gerald slapped him again, more kindly this time. "Well? What are you waiting for? I've given you an order. In case you hadn't noticed, we've got a bit of a crisis on our hands. Gonegal and his UMN busybodies, trying to take the country from me. From *us*. We're going to run things together, Gerald. I can't do any of this without you. So *kill* the bastard, would you? He's standing in our way."

Dreamily he nodded. Dreamily he turned. Monk Markham groveled at his feet, eyes filled with terror. The bird was crouched beside him, her eyes hot with rage.

Bloody Reg. Tie her beak with red ribbon and she'd still poke it where it wasn't wanted. He frowned. Reg.

Don't I know something about Reg?

Never mind. It'd keep. Right now he had to kill Markham. Behind him, Bibbie was bleating something. The other Gerald—the *better* Gerald—silenced her with a slap. Bloody Markham shoved himself onto his knees.

"Gerald—for pity's sake—*fight* it!" he shouted. "Fight *him*. This isn't you, mate. If you do this—God, if you *do* this—"

"Put a sock in it, Monk," he said, and raised his fist.

Monk went down screaming. The air itself was screaming. But—no, no, actually that was an airship of the United Magical Nations. Engulfed in flames, it plummeted blazing towards the ground. And that would likely be his problem too—but not yet. Not until meddling Monk Markham was finally taken care of.

"That's it!" said the other Gerald, wildly encouraging. "Finish him, sunshine. We don't need him any more."

No, they didn't, did they? It was time for Monk to go.

"Goodbye, Monk," he said quietly. "Don't fight it. Just let it happen. It won't hurt as much that way."

For the second time he raised his fist. Clenched it tighter—and simultaneously tightened the killing hex. Monk sucked in a deep breath, eyes wide with disbelief. His throat worked—it worked—and blood trickled from his eyes.

A shriek of outrage. A whirling comet of brown

feathers. And then there were claws in his hair and hard wings beating about his head.

"*Gerald Dunwoody, what the hell are you doing?*"

Stunned, he staggered backwards. Monk dropped to the dais again. And then his attacker was yanked away. But—but—it was *Reg*.

"*Two* of them?" said the other Gerald, his eyes narrowed. "How can there be *two* of them? *Two* of them is two too many! How did you get here? Which world are you from?"

This new Reg was suspended in midair, held fast by the other Gerald's thaumaturgical fist. "How do you think, you manky pillock?" she said. "I was traveling in the portal with Gerald. When you yanked him out I caught his coat-tails, so to speak. And I've been in hiding, keeping an eye on him, ever since."

"Is that so?" said the other Gerald, his eyes still narrow with dislike and suspicion. "I find it hard to believe."

"Then how do *you* explain it?" the bird demanded. "You think I hitched a ride here on an interdimensional sprite? You opened a window between my world and yours and I flew right through it. So let *that* be a lesson to you. Next time stay in your own bloody backyard!"

"Actually," said the other Gerald, smiling, "I think I'd rather let *this* be a lesson for *you*."

Feather by feather, Reg burst into flame.

Monk was screaming again, not in pain but in horror. The other bird with the red ribbon beak was flapping and flailing in avian distress. The other Gerald was laughing. In the blue crowded sky airships burned in hot, bright sympathy.

Reg . . . Reg . . . Reg . . .

Gerald felt something inside him twist—and tear—and break. Felt his rogue *potentia* overtake him like a tidal wave come to shore. It obliterated whatever hold the other Gerald had upon him. Obliterated too any sense of decency or restraint. Cast him free of all restrictions and let fury off its leash. Unleashed instinct with it, and a wild, wailing grief.

Reg.

Throwing his head back he screamed to the fiery sky.

"Draconi! Draconi! Draconi revenanto!"

Helpless before his blinding rage the ether seethed and surged and rushed to do his bidding. The other Gerald, startled, loosened his fingers and let the charred birdish skeleton in his grasp tumble to ash.

"Gerald? *Gerald!* What d'you think you're doing?"

Reg.

He had no words for this creature with the two seeing eyes. No words, no forgiveness, no desire to redeem.

Somebody in the crowd of witches and wizards cried out. "Run! Run! It's the dragon!"

Pandemonium again—and this time it won the day. Shadbolted or not every captive in the walled ceremonial parade ground broke free of obedient terror and fled. They stampeded from the dais, they stampeded to the gates. They crushed the hideous exhibits beneath their racing feet.

Bibbie was crying. "Gerald—Gerald, *stop* him. Make him *stop* this. *Gerald!*"

The other Gerald turned on her. *"Shut up*, Emmerabiblia, you stupid whining *cow!"*

"What?" She stared at him, dumbfounded. "What did you call me? How *dare* you, Gerald, after I—"

"I told you to shut up!"

Emmerabiblia, like Lord Attaby, fell dead without a sound.

Hardly even noticing, the other Gerald raised both fists. "Think I'm impressed with your parlor tricks, Professor? Think you can scare me by waving a dead dragon in my face? I *killed* that dragon. I killed the man who had it made. And now, because you're a moron, I'm going to kill *you*."

He shook his head, shuddering. *Reg.* "No, Gerald. You're not."

The other Gerald—his counterpart—absolutely his evil twin—flushed crimson with fury. The ether trembled, twisting dark with his rage. A hot wind stinking of cinders and burned blood whipped up out of nowhere. Above them the airships began to plunge like wild horses.

And riding the scorching thermals came the dragon, reborn.

Feeling it, calling it, Gerald stood silent and stared at himself. Smiled as his counterpart threw curse after curse at him, tried to reignite that controlling incant, tried to set him on fire with a word. He was impervious to all of it, his *potentia* sheathing him like tempered glass. Every killing incant flowed down him, every murdering hex washed away. He was cold, he was so cold, yet something burned inside him. Burned hot, burned bright, burned itself as it burned.

Blimey. I think I'm dying.

But that didn't matter—provided he watched his other self die first.

Reg.

The dragon came screaming, poison pouring from its mouth. Came beating the smoky air with its beautiful emerald wings. He heard Monk say something, and turned his head, and smiled.

"It's all right, Monk. It's not here for you. Stand still, and it'll pass. Stand still. Don't run."

Exhausted, for the moment, the other Gerald let his arms drop. "You're a fool, Professor," he said, his breathing ragged. "I *made* that thing. I control it. It won't come after me."

He smiled. "You made it. You killed it. *I* brought it back to life." Eyes drifting closed, he reached out to the dragon. Whispered sweetly into its dead, empty heart. "He's the one, *draconi*. He's the one who took your love."

"Took *what?* I did *what?*" The other Gerald stepped backwards. "What are you talking about?"

Gerald opened his eyes and laughed. "The *Tantigliani sympathetico*, you moron. It binds man and beast heart to heart. Kill one and you kill both. Kill one, and murder love."

The other Gerald blanched to snow. "You're lying. That's a lie."

He looked up. "Really? Am I? Well, you tell *her* that."

CHAPTER TWENTY-FIVE

The crimson and emerald dragon came swooping. The other Gerald, on a choked cry, threw his strongest incants at her. She brushed them aside like the smoky air. Like they were nothing. Like her bright shining scales were sheathed in tempered glass.

The other Gerald screamed once as the great talons caught him. Screamed again, blood dripping, as the dragon wheeled away.

Still watching, Gerald breathed out a sigh. "I'm sorry," he murmured. "But you were never meant to be."

He snapped his fingers once . . . and where a dragon flew with a wizard in its talons, within a slow heartbeat the sky was full of fresh fire. And in another heartbeat even that vanished, and victorious airships filled the eye.

"Gerald. *Gerald*. Bloody hell, Dunnywood! Come on, mate, we've got to *go!*"

He swung around and there was Monk, the portable portal in his hand. A few feet distant a small bluish-red light, expanding . . . and in the ether a dreadful deep, twisting moan.

"Gerald!" said Monk again, and gestured at the sky. "Are you with me? Get ready!"

The green and black UMN airships were drifting lower, rope ladders unfurling from their underslung passenger pods, close enough now to nearly touch the ground. Behind them the sound of heavy running feet. He turned and saw more UMN personnel, felt their martial *potentias* like iron in the ether.

He nodded, feeling dreamy. Feeling very, very tired. "I'm with you. Just say the word."

There was a pile of charred feather and bone on the dais. He knew it was there, but he wasn't going to look. He wasn't going to look at this world's Bibbie, either, whose lips were painted the same shade of pink as her gown. If there'd been time he might have saved her. *And now I'll never know.* Instead he looked at Monk, who was weeping. Proper tears this time, not blood, as he jiggered with the portal.

"So is that it? Can we go?"

Monk checked the slowly widening vortex. "A few more seconds. We can't afford to get it wrong. Gerald—"

Reg.

"No." He shook his head. "Don't. Not yet."

"Yeah," Monk said roughly. "Gerald—are you all right? You look—"

He shrugged. "I don't know."

The running feet were getting closer. Someone in authority shouted. "You there! You there— Gerald Dunwoody! You're under arrest! Stand where you are!"

"Monk, I *really* think we need to—"

"I know! I know! All right. Bloody hell, we'll have to risk it."

The portal was a ragged blue and crimson hole in the air. Broad enough, certainly, but not quite the height of a tall, upstanding man.

"Bloody hell," Monk said again, nervous, his gaze shifting from the portal to the soldiers. "If we duck we should make it." He blew out a shaky breath. "On three, Gerald. Stay close behind me. One—two—*three!*"

With a strangled grunt Monk leaped into the portal. But as he went to leap after his brilliant friend he heard a dreadful, familiar sound. Tail feathers, rattling . . . and a muted chatter of beak. He spun around. Looked down.

The other Reg, come out of hiding from under the trolley, looked up at him in silence. The tatty piece of red ribbon was still wound around her beak.

"No. *No*," he whispered. His skin was full of tears. "You're not her. You'll never *be* her. Don't you see? It won't work."

Running feet. More shouting. Another gunship fired overhead.

"Oh, *bloody hell*," he said, and snatched her up, and leaped.

Feeling only a little bit trepidatious, Melissande took Sir Alec a cup of piping hot tea. She and Bibbie had spent the night in the parlor, dozing on and off, but he'd chosen to wait it out in the library. No explanation. No apology. Just a closed door in their faces.

Opening it now, she poked her head into the room. "Sir Alec?"

He was standing at the window, contemplating the new day. It promised to be warm and fine. "Miss Cadwallader," he said, turning. "Good morning."

He looked as fragile as she felt, and as rumpled, but he sounded unaltered. Cool and calm and completely self-contained. *No-one would guess, looking at him, how many laws he's broken in one night.* She crossed the book-lined room and handed him the cup and saucer. "No milk, a squeeze of lemon, and two sugars. That's right, isn't it?"

He took the tea. "Yes. That's right."

"I can boil you an egg, if you'd like," she added. "Bibbie and I aren't hungry, but . . ."

"No. Thank you," he said. "This will be fine."

Folding her arms, she stared out through the window. "Nearly a full day they've been gone. Will it be much longer, do you think?"

"I have no idea. I hope not."

"You've taken an awful risk, haven't you?" she said quietly. "If something goes wrong—if Monk and Gerald and Reg don't come back—"

"It will certainly be interesting," said Sir Alec, and stirred his tea.

"Sir Alec . . ." Sighing, she shifted her gaze to him. "I'm not just plain Miss Cadwallader, remember? You don't need to be . . . clever . . . for my sake."

He raised an eyebrow. "What makes you think I'm thinking of your feelings?"

She was exhausted, she was frightened, but she couldn't help a smile. "You're admitting to feelings? Blimey. Wait till I tell Gerald. He'll have to sit down."

And that made *him* smile. But it didn't last long. He sipped his tea, thoughtful, then sat the cup back in its saucer. "You don't approve of my secrecy."

"It's not my place to approve or disapprove, is it?" she said. "You're the government stooge. I'm merely . . . a girl."

His dry look contradicted that assessment, but he didn't reply. Instead he sipped more tea. The clock on the mantel ticked softly as the morning's light slowly brightened.

"You can trust us, you know," she said at last. "We may not like you very much but we do know you're on our side." She pulled a face. "Well. You're not on *their* side. The villains' side. And since we aren't either . . . I suppose it's close enough."

He took a last sip of tea then put the cup and saucer on the windowsill. "I do trust you, Miss Cadwallader. Within narrow parameters."

"Gosh. That's flattering," she said, eyes wide. "*I* might have to sit down."

"I trust that you will never do anything to hurt either Mr. Markham or Mr. Dunwoody," he said, ignoring her sarcasm. "Which means—"

"What?" she said, alarmed by the look on his face. "Sir Alec? What's the matter, what—"

The library door banged open. "Do you feel that?" demanded Bibbie. Her long golden hair flew wildly about her face. "Sir Alec?"

He looked up, at the ceiling. *Through* the ceiling. "Yes, I do, Miss Markham. I suspect—"

But Bibbie was gone again, racing, her shoes thudding on the stairs. Not running, but definitely hurrying, Sir Alec followed. "Come along, Miss Cadwallader. Don't dawdle. Someone's knocking at the door."

There was a glowing, growing blue and crimson hole in the air of Gerald's bedroom.

"Stand back, Miss Markham," Sir Alec said sharply. "I know who we want to see step through that portal, but wanting and getting are two very different things."

As Bibbie retreated one grudging pace, Melissande felt her heart leap. *Oh, Saint Snodgrass preserve us.* "You think this could be the other Gerald?"

"I'd be a fool to think it weren't possible," he said tightly. "Stand *back*, I said, Miss Markham. You too, Miss Cadwallader."

The glowing hole in the air ripped wider. Wider. Reaching out blindly, she clutched Bibbie's hand.

Please, please, please, please . . .

Monk leaped out of thin air. Oh, lord, he looked dreadful. Shattered and terrified and covered in blood.

"Monk!" cried Bibbie, surging forward.

Sir Alec caught her around the waist and swung her aside. "Wait!" he snapped. "*Wait!* The danger's not over yet!"

Monk was ignoring them, had spun around to stare at that blue and crimson glowing hole, the portal. His hands were clenched to fists and he was dancing on the spot.

"Come on—come on—Gerald, you idiot—*come on*—"

And then another figure emerged out of nothing. Melissande heard herself sob.

"*Gerald!*" cried Bibbie. "Sir Alec, *let me go!*"

But Sir Alec didn't let go. Instead he pulled Bibbie further back, one arm still holding her tight, and with his free hand he caught *her* arm and started tugging—

Wild-eyed, Monk shut down the portal then shoved Gerald behind him. "It's all right!" he shouted. "Sir Alec, he's safe! He's *safe!*"

But looking at Sir Alec's face, she wasn't sure.

"How can I trust you, Mr. Markham?" he demanded. "For all I know he's hexed you to his will."

Monk was breathing so fast he was practically panting. "He hasn't. I swear it. I promise, he's safe."

"What are you talking about?" said Bibbie, still struggling. "What do you mean *safe?*"

"Stop thinking like a girl and start thinking like a witch," snapped Sir Alec. "Feel the ether, Miss Markham. Mr. Dunwoody's not himself."

Melissande stared at him. What? *What?* "Monk—"

But before Monk could say anything, Bibbie let out a small cry. "Oh, Saint Snodgrass. *Gerald.* Monk—Monk, what *happ*—"

"I'm tainted, not tongueless," said Gerald, over Monk's shoulder. "Do you mind? I can speak for myself."

"Then speak, Mr. Dunwoody," said Sir Alec, ominously restrained. "You have one minute to make your case."

"I had to play along," said Gerald. Even without the blood, what they could see of him looked worse than Monk. "Take in some grimoire magic. Not much, I swear, not enough to turn me, but—" He shuddered. "Just tell me there's a way to strip it out again, Sir Alec. I'll do whatever it takes. I don't care what it costs. I just want it gone. And I want it gone *now*."

"He's not kidding, Sir Alec," said Monk. "I'm telling you, he's safe. He's still Gerald. You can trust him. You *can*."

After a heart-stopping moment, Sir Alec nodded. "Very well."

Monk turned. "Gerald—sit down, mate. Here—give me—give me—*damn*." He shook his head. "I'll take her."

And that was when Melissande realized Gerald had Reg tucked under one arm.

"Reg!" she said, relief and alarm clashing. There was *red ribbon* tied around her beak. "What's happened to you? Reg?"

"She's not Reg," said Gerald, staring at the bird in Monk's hands. "Reg is dead. She's—that's—she's not Reg."

Silence. One look at Gerald's eyes told her this wasn't a joke.

"Dead?" she whispered. "What do you mean? Dead how?"

"I killed her," said Gerald. "If you really must know. Sir Alec—"

"Mr. Dunwoody?" said Sir Alec. Nothing in his face gave anything away.

"I killed the other Gerald, too. I don't think we need to worry about any more interesting visitors—the other Ottosland's pretty much gone up in flames, and the UMN's moved in to take over—but just to be on the safe side, Monk's come up with a plan to stop any more incursions from alternative worlds."

Sir Alec nodded. "Of course he has. I would expect no less."

Gerald didn't smile. He looked like he'd never smile again. "But first I should get him out of that shadbolt. If you've no objections?"

"None at all," said Sir Alec. Then he glanced at the sheet-covered body on the bed. "But perhaps, all things considered—"

Gerald looked. "That's the other Monk?"

"Yes."

"What are you going to do with him?"

"Bury him discreetly, with honor," said Sir Alec, after a moment. "An unmarked grave, of course."

"Of course," said Gerald. Then he looked at Monk. "You ready?"

Monk shook his head, as though suddenly events were moving far too fast. "Well, yes, but—"

"Good," said Gerald. "Now be quiet. And get rid of—you can't hold—"

"Oh," said Monk. "Um—"

Melissande held out her hands. They were shaking. She wanted to weep. "I'll take her."

Another silence fell. With trembling fingers she untied the ribbon around Reg's—the bird's—familiar beak. She—Reg—the bird nodded but didn't say anything. Good lord, she was so *thin*.

Gerald had one hand on Monk's head and the other on his left shoulder. Eyes closed, breathing deeply, he seemed to sink into a trance. Nothing. Nothing. Just silence. Still nothing.

And then a flash of bluish white light, like a lightning strike. Monk shouted in pain and dropped to the floor.

"Monk!" cried Bibbie, rushing to him.

Melissande held the bird.

"He'll be all right," Gerald said to Sir Alec, as Bibbie helped Monk to his feet. "Headaches for a few days. After we've jiggered his expander he should steer clear of thaumaturgics for a while. A week, at least."

"I'm sure we can arrange that," said Sir Alec. "Mr. Dunwoody—"

Gerald silenced him with a look. "You'll get your report. Just . . . not right now. If you don't mind."

"Tomorrow," said Sir Alec, nodding. "No later. We need this put to bed."

"Buried, you mean," said Gerald. "Like that poor bastard under the sheet."

Monk cleared his throat. "Gerald—"

"I'm fine," said Gerald. But looking at him, Melissande could see he wasn't. Oh, he wasn't. Monk wasn't either. *And neither am I.* "If you're ready," Gerald added, "let's get up to the attic and bloody finish this, shall we?"

"Yeah," said Monk, sighing. "Yeah. We can do that. Sir Alec?"

As Monk followed Gerald out of the bedroom, Sir Alec raised an eyebrow. "It might be best if you ladies . . . sit this one out. I'm sure these thaumaturgics won't take long. And then I'll be on my way."

For once, Bibbie didn't argue about being treated like a girl. Melissande nodded. "Yes. Of course. We'll be downstairs when you're done."

Sir Alec went after the boys, leaving silence in his wake. She stared at Bibbie, and Bibbie stared back. And then the bird in her arms . . . the bird who *was*

Reg . . . and *wasn't* . . . feebly stirred and tried to rattle her tail.

"Blimey bloody Charlie," she croaked. "Madam, I'm starving. Where do you keep the minced beef around here?"

It took him and Monk not quite an hour to re-jig the multi-dimensional etheretic wavelength expander and turn it into a wavelength inhibitor that, once activated, would prevent the opening of portals between their dimension and the next. Well. For the time being, anyway. For the short term, at least. Until Monk could look at inventing a larger and more permanent solution.

And he will. Because he's Monk Markham and that's what he does. It's his job.

With that done, Sir Alec suggested they adjourn to the kitchen and fortify themselves while he . . . explained a few things. Melissande, being Melissande, made tea and cooked them scrambled eggs.

Oh, God.

It took every scrap of will power he had to eat them. The bird sat on a cushion on a spare bit of kitchen bench. He managed not to look at her once.

"The problem is," Sir Alec said, in his quiet, nondescript way, "that as far as I can see, revealing what's happened here can only cause more trouble. Obviously the notion that you've turned metaphysical theory into fact is . . . significant. But the thaumaturgical, social and geopolitical consequences could be grave. Perhaps even catastrophic."

"In other words," said Melissande, eyes narrowed, "you want us to keep on keeping our mouths shut."

Monk snorted. "You realize you're hatching the greatest conspiracy of modern times?"

"Mr. Markham, I'd hazard it's the greatest conspiracy in *history*," Sir Alec retorted. "Make no bones about it: this is irregular in the extreme. But after careful consideration I don't see that we have another choice. At least, not for the time being. Besides . . ." He smiled his small, chilly smile. "You're going to be far too busy inventing new locks for interdimensional doors to be dallying with gossip."

"That's true," said Monk. With that bloody shadbolt gone, and tea and eggs inside him, he was looking a little better. But the fingerprints of their adventure were on him . . . and chances were they'd never quite leave.

We'll have to talk about it. We can't pretend it didn't happen. We can't pretend I wasn't about to kill him.

Only not today. And not tomorrow. That conversation would have to wait.

"But you know, Sir Alec," Monk added, pretending that everything was fine, just fine, nothing to see here, move along, "if I am going to keep the inhibitor running here in the meantime—"

"Don't worry, Mr. Markham," said Sir Alec. Not fooled, because he was never fooled, but prepared to pretend. For now. "You'll have enough thaumaturgic energy at your disposal . . . and no questions asked."

"Does that go for me, too?" said Bibbie, glancing up. "Only I'm working on this ethergenics thing and—"

Sir Alec sighed. "Yes, Miss Markham. I'll see what I can do." He looked at them one by one. "So . . . do I take it you're agreeing to my unorthodox proposal?"

Monk scrubbed a hand across his stubbled face. "Sure. Why not? I mean, what've we got to lose?"

Gerald looked at Sir Alec. *For God's sake, don't tell them.*

Sir Alec nodded. "Thank you. Please don't talk about these events beyond the confines of this house. Of course it would be better if you didn't discuss them at all—but I'm not entirely stupid. I'm prepared to take what I can get." Pushing his chair back, he stood. "And now I'll bid you good day. Mr. Dunwoody—kindly walk me to my car."

It was a pretty morning. Lots of sunshine. Butterflies in the garden and birds on the wing. Sir Alec, holding the driver's door open, looked him up and down with a jaundiced eye. "I'm not going to like what I read in your report, am I?"

"Sir Alec . . ." He sighed. "Come on. You're going to hate it."

But not as much as I will.

"You're taking a bloody big risk, keeping all this secret."

Sir Alec shrugged. "I'm not a stranger to secrets, Mr. Dunwoody." Then he hesitated, and cleared his throat. "I'm sorry about the bird. I know how fond you were of her. And I wonder if it was wise of you, to bring the other one back."

He pulled a face. "I guess we'll just have to wait and see, won't we?"

Abruptly, Sir Alec slapped the roof of his car. "A damned unfortunate mess all around, Mr. Dunwoody. You did well. Again. Take tomorrow off. But I'll want you in my office the day after, with that report. You and I have a lot to discuss.

And then, of course, there's the matter of that grimoire magic."

Which sat inside him, black and waiting, like a wolf.

"I meant what I said, you know," he said, letting Sir Alec see behind his own mask. "I want the filthy bloody stuff *gone.*"

In return, Sir Alec showed him nothing. "I know you meant it, Mr. Dunwoody. And we'll see what we can do." Halfway into the car he stopped, and looked back. "I'll send Mr. Dalby for the other Monk's body. No need for you to be involved."

He supposed he should say thank you, but he wasn't in the mood.

Uneasy, he watched Sir Alec drive out of sight, then turned to go back inside the house. The bird was behind him. She'd slipped out the open front door and was perched on the big flower pot at the top of the steps. Seeing him see her, and hesitate, she fluffed out her feathers. Tipped her head to one side, her familiar—her unknown—dark eyes sardonically gleaming.

"Hello, Gerald."

. . . if you've finished slobbering over my third-rate understudy . . .

"Hello."

The bird sighed. "So. Sunshine. What are we going to do?"

Sunshine. He pulled a face. "I don't know about you, but I thought I might get drunk."

"And then what? Blow your brains out?"

He stared at her. *"What?"*

"Well . . . those are your two basic choices, aren't they? Drop dead or keep walking." She stared without remorse. "So, Mr. Dunnywood? What's it going to be?"

Oh, God. I can't do this. I watched her burn alive. And now here she is, and that's her voice and her feathers and her beak and her eyes . . .

"Your Sir Alec," she said, and rattled her tail. "Bit of a sarky bugger, isn't he? I think you need to watch your step with him, my boy. I don't altogether trust that glint in his eyes."

"He's all right," he said, shrugging. "He's a good man. He's just . . . not very comfortable. And anyway . . . he's your Sir Alec now."

"Ha," she said. "*I* don't want him. I never asked for him, did I?"

"Yes, well, neither of us did, Reg," he said. "It just worked out that way."

Her head tipped again. "Reg?"

It's not the same. It's not the same. But it's not her fault, either.

"What?" With a soft sigh, he held out his arm. "You'd prefer Dulcetta?"

"Ha," she said again, and jumped, and made her way up to his shoulder. "So you like living dangerously. Nice to know some things don't change."

They went back inside, down the corridor to the kitchen, where Monk and Melissande and Bibbie sat with their tea. As they walked through the door, intent conversation ceased. His friends . . . his family . . . stared at him, anxious.

"Gerald," said Monk. Still his friend, despite everything. "Honestly. Are you all right?"

He pulled out two chairs, one for him and one for Reg. "Not really," he said at last, because he owed them the truth. "But I will be. I think I just need some time." Reg hopped from his shoulder to the back of the other chair. She looked at him, and he looked at her. His fingertip stroked the length of her wing. "Monk . . . Melissande . . . Bibbie . . ." He swallowed. "This is Reg."

Silence. And then Reg rattled her tail, eyes gleaming, and tipped her head to one side. "Well, well, well, duckies. Is this different, or what?"

**Look out for the next book in the
Rogue Agent series from Orbit.**

acknowledgments

My wonderful beta readers Mary Webber, Glenda Larke and Elaine Shipp

The fabulous Orbit team, on both sides of the pond

My agent, Ethan Ellenberg

The booksellers

The readers

extras

orbit

meet the author

K.E. Mills is the pseudonym for Karen Miller. She was born in Vancouver, Canada, and moved to Australia with her family when she was two. She started writing stories while still in primary school, where she fell in love with speculative fiction after reading *The Lion, The Witch, and The Wardrobe*. Over the years she has held down a wide variety of jobs, including horse stud groom in Buckingham, England. She is working on several new novels. Find out more about the author at www.karenmiller.net.

introducing

If you enjoyed WIZARD SQUARED,
look out for

THE PRODIGAL MAGE

Book One of the Fisherman's Children series

by Karen Miller

*Many years have passed since the last Mage War. It has
been a time of great change. But not all changes are for
the best, and Asher's world is in peril once more.*

*The weather magic that keeps Lur safe is failing. Among
the sorcerers, only Asher has the skill to mend the
antique weather map that governs the seasons, keeping
the land from being crushed by natural forces. Yet, when
Asher risks his life to meddle with these dangerous
magics, the crisis is merely delayed, not averted.*

*Asher's son Rafel inherited his father's talents, but
he has been forbidden to use them. With Lur facing
devastation, however, he may be its only hope.*

PROLOGUE

The first time Rafel told his father he wanted to travel beyond Barl's Mountains he was five, sailing towards six. When Da said no, Meister Tollin's expedition didn't need any little boys to help them, he cried...but not for long, because he had a new pony, Dancer, and Mama had promised to come watch him ride. And then, ages and ages later, the expedition came back—which was a surprise to everyone, since it was declared lost—and he was glad he hadn't gone with Meister Tollin and the others because while they were away exploring, four of the seven men sickened and died, wracked and gruesome for no good reason anyone could see. Not even Da, and Da knew everything.

Once all the fuss was died down, some folk cheering and some weeping, on account of the men who got buried so far away, Meister Tollin came to tell Da what had gone on while they were over Barl's Mountains. They met in the big ole palace where all the grown-up government things happened, where the royal family used to live once, back in the days when there was a royal family.

He knew all about them grand folk, 'cause Darran liked to tell stories. Da said Darran was a silly ole fart, and that was mostly true. He was old as old now, with an old man's musty, fusty smell. His hair was grown all silver and thin, and his eyes were nearly lost in spiderweb wrinkles. But that didn't matter, 'cause the stories he told about Lur's royal family were good ones. There was Prince Gar, Da's best friend from back then. Darran talked about him the most, and blew his nose a lot afterwards. There was the rest of the royal family: clever Princess Fane and beautiful Queen Dana and brave King Borne. It was sad how they died, tumbling over Salbert's Eyrie. Darran cried about that too, every time he remembered...but it didn't stop him telling the stories.

"You're young to hear these tales, Rafel, but I won't live forever," he'd say, his face fierce and his voice wobbly. *"And I can't trust your father to tell you. He has...funny notions, the rapscallion. But you must know, my boy. It's your birthright."*

He didn't really understand about that. All he knew was he liked Darren's stories so he never breathed a word about 'em in case Da fratched the ole man on it and the stories went away.

He especially liked the one about Da saving the prince from being drownded at the Sea Harvest Festival in Westwailing. That was a *good* story. Almost as good as hearing how Da saved Lur from the evil sorcerer Morg. But Darran didn't tell him that one very often, and when he did he always said not to talk about it after. He didn't cry, neither, after telling it. He just went awful quiet. Somehow that was worse than tears.

When he overheard Da telling Mama about Meister Tollin coming to see him, in the voice that said he was worrited and cross, Rafel knew if he didn't do a sneak he'd never find out what was going on—and he *hated* not knowing. The trouble with parents was they never thought you were old enough to know things. They praised you for being a clever boy then they told you to run away and play, don't bother your head about grown-up business.

He got so cross when they said things like that he had to hide in his secret place and crack stones with his magic, even though Da would wallop him if he found out.

Of course he knew perfectly well he wasn't supposed to do a sneak. He wasn't supposed to do *any* kind of magic, not just stone-cracking, not unless Da or Mama was with him. Or Meister Rumly, his tutor. Da and Mama said it was dangerous. They said because he was special, a *prodigy,* he had to be very careful or someone might get hurt. He thought they were boring and silly, all that fussing, but he did as he was told. Mostly. Except sometimes, when he couldn't hold the magic in any more, when it skritched him so hard he wanted to shout, he danced leaves without the wind or made funny water shapes in his bath. Only playing. There was no harm in *that*.

The time when Da said he and Meister Tollin were going to meet and talk about the failed expedition, that was when he was s'posed to be in his lessons. But the moment Meister Rumly left him to work some problems on his own, and took himself off for a chinwag with Darran, he did the kind of earth magic that helped Mama creep up on a wild rabbit she wanted for supper and fizzled away to the white stone palace. He had to wait until there weren't any comings and goings through its big double doors before he could hide in the tickly yellow lampha bushes beside the front steps. Waiting was hard. He kept thinking Meister Rumly would find him. But Meister Rumly didn't come, and nobody saw him scuttle into the bushes.

Da and Meister Tollin came along a little while after, and he held his breath in case they didn't choose to talk in the palace's ground floor meeting room where Da and the Mage Council made important decisions for Lur.

But they did, so once they were safely inside he crawled on his hands and knees between the lampha and the palace wall until he fetched up right under that meeting room window.

There, hunkered down on the damp earth, yellow lampha blossom tickling his nose so he had to keep rubbing it on his sleeve in case he sneezed, and got caught, and landed himself into wallopin' trouble, he listened to what Meister Tollin had to tell Da about his adventure, that Da didn't want anybody else to hear.

The lands beyond the Wall were dark and grim, Meister Tollin said. Weren't nothing green or growing there. No people, neither. All they'd found was cold death and old decay. Moldy bones and abandoned houses, falling to bits. There wasn't even a bird singing in the stunted, twisted trees. That sorcerer Morg had killed everything, Meister Tollin said. Might be Lur was the only living place left in the whole world. It felt like it. On the other side of Barl's Mountains it felt like they were all alone, in the biggest graveyard a man would ever see.

Meister Tollin's voice sounded funny saying that, wobbly and hoarse and sad. Rafel felt his eyes go prickly, hearing it. *All alone in the world.* Meister Tollin was using tricky words but he understood what they meant. Most every day Mama told him he was too smart for his own good, but he didn't mind that kind of scolding because in her dark brown eyes there was always a smile.

Next, Da wanted to know why Meister Tollin and the others had broken their promise and not contacted the General Council through the circle stones they took with them. They couldn't, said Meister Tollin, sounding cross. In the dead lands beyond Barl's Mountains their magic wouldn't work. Not gentle Olken magic, not pushy Doranen magic. They tried and they tried, but they had to do everything the hard way. Just by themselves, no magic to help out.

Rafel felt himself shiver cold. No Olken magic, the way it was before Da saved Lur? That was nasty. He didn't want to think on that.

Then Da wanted to know more about what happened to the four men who died. Three were Olken, and two of them were his friends, Titch and Derik. They'd been Circle Olken, and helped him in the fight against Morg. Da sounded sad like Darran, saying their names. It was horrible, hearing Da sad. Scrunched so small under the meeting room's open window, Rafel tried to think how he'd feel if his best friend Goose died. That made his eyes prickle again even harder.

But before he could hear what Meister Tollin had to say about those men getting sick for no reason, Meister Rumly came calling to see where he was. His manky ole tutor had a sneaky Doranen seekem crystal that Olken magic couldn't fool. Meister Rumly was allowed to use it to find him. Da had said so.

It wasn't *fair*. There were rules about that for everyone else, about using Doranen magic on folk. There were rules for pretty much *everything* to do with magic and big trouble if people broke them — but sometimes they did and then Da had to go down to Justice Hall and wallop 'em the way grownups got walloped. He hated doing that. Speaking on magic at Justice Hall got Da so riled only Mama could calm him down.

Remembering his father's fearsome temper, Rafel crawled his way out of the lampha bushes and scuttled to somewhere Meister Rumly could find him and not cause a ruckus. If there was a ruckus Da would come out to see why and his tutor would tell tales. Then Da would ask what he'd been up to and he'd say the truth. He'd have to, because it was Da. And he didn't want that, because when Da said *"Rafel, you be a little perisher too smart for his own good"* he hardly ever smiled. Not with his face and not in his eyes.

So he took himself off to the Tower stables and let Meister Rumly find him hobnobbing with his pony. Knowing full well he'd been led on a wild goose-chase, his tutor wittered on and on as they returned to lessons in the Tower. And all the long afternoon, bored and restless, he wondered and he wondered what else Tollin told Da.

That night at supper, sitting at the table in the fat round solar where they ate their meals, his parents talked a bit about Meister Tollin's expedition. They didn't mention any of the scary parts, because his stinky baby sister was there, banging her spoon on her plate and making stupid sounds instead of saying real words like Uncle Pellen's little girl could. He wished Da and Mama would send Deenie away so they could all talk properly.

"So that's that," said Da, who'd called Meister Tollin a fool for going, and the others too, even though Titch and Derik were his friends. "It's over. And there'll be no more expeditions, I reckon."

"Really?" said Mama, her eyebrows raised in that way she had. "Because you know what people are like, Asher. Let enough time go by and—"

Da slurped down some spicy fish soup. "Fixed that, didn't I?" he growled. "Tollin's writin' down an account of what happened. Every last sinkin' thing, nowt polite about it. I'll see it copied and put where it won't get lost, and any fool as says we ought to send more folk over Barl's Mountains then Tollin's tale will remind 'em why that ain't a good idea."

Mama made the sound that said she wasn't sure about that, but Da paid no attention.

"Any road, ain't no reason for the General Council to give the nod for another expedition," he said. "Tollin made it plain—there ain't nowt to find over the mountains."

"Not close to Lur perhaps," said Mama. "But

Tollin didn't get terribly far, Asher. He was only gone two months, and most of that time was spent dealing with one disaster after another."

"He got far enough," Da said, shaking his head. "Morg poisoned everything he touched, Dath. Ain't nowt but foolishness to think otherwise, or to waste time frettin' on what's so far away."

"Oh, Asher," Mama said, smiling. Da's grouching nearly always made her smile. "After six hundred years locked up behind those mountains, you can't blame people for being curious."

Six hundred years. Rafel could hardly imagine it. That was about a hundred times as long as he'd been alive. Mama was right. Of course people wanted to know. *He* wanted to know. He was as miserable as she was that Meister Tollin and the others hadn't found anything good on the other side of Barl's Mountains.

But Da wasn't. He gave Mama a look, then soaked his last bit of bread in his soup. "Reckon I can blame 'em, y'know," he grumbled around a full mouth. That wasn't good manners, but Da didn't care. He just laughed when Mama said so and was ruder than before. "You tell me, Dath, what's curiosity ever done but black the eye of the fool who ain't content to stay put?"

Rafel saw his mother cast him a cautious glance, and made his face look all not caring, as though he really was a silly little boy who didn't understand. "Tollin and the others were only trying to help," she murmured. "And I'm sorry things went wrong. I wanted to meet the people who live on the other side of the mountains. I wanted to hear their stories.

And now we find there aren't any? I think it's a great pity."

With a grunt Da reached for the heel of fresh-baked bread on its board in the center of the table. Tearing off another hunk of it, he glowered at Mama. Not angry at her, just angry at the world like he got sometimes. Da was never angry with Mama.

"I tell you, Dathne," he said, waving the bread at her, "here's the truth without scales on, proven by Tollin—there ain't no good to come of sniffin' over them mountains. What price have we paid already, eh? Titch and Derik dead, it be a cryin' shame. Pik Mobley too, that stubborn ole fish. And that hoity-toity Lord Bram. Reckon a Doranen mage should've bloody known better, but he were a giddy fool like the rest of 'em. They should've listened to me. Ain't I the one who told 'em not to go? Ain't I the one told 'em only a fool pokes a stick in a shark's eye? I am. But they wouldn't listen. Both bloody Councils, they wouldn't listen neither. And all we've got to show for it is folk weepin' in the streets."

Sighing, Mama put her hand on Da's arm. "I know. But let's talk about it later. Supper will go cold if we go on about it now."

"There ain't nowt to talk on, Dath," said Da, tossing his bread in his empty bowl and shoving it away. "What's done is done. Can't snap m'fingers and bring 'em all back in one piece, can I?"

Da was so riled now he sounded like the cousins from down on the coast, instead of almost a regular City Olken. He sounded like the sky looked with a storm blowing up. Even though stinky Deenie was a baby, three years old and still piddling in her nappies, she knew about that. She threw her spoon onto the table and started wailing.

"There now, Asher!" said Mama in her scolding voice. "Look what you've done."

Rafel rolled his eyes as his mother started fussing with his bratty sister. Scowling, Da pulled his bowl back and spooned up what was left of his soup and soggy bread, muttering under his breath. Rafel kept his head down and finished his soup too, because Da didn't like to see good food wasted. When his bowl was empty he looked at his father, feeling his bottom lip poke out. He had a question, and he knew it'd tickle him and tickle him until he had an answer.

"Da? Can I ask you something?"

Da looked up from brooding into his soup bowl. "Aye, sprat. Y'know you can."

He felt Mama's eyes on him, even though she was spooning mashed-up sweet pickles into the baby. "Da, don't you want anyone going over the mountains? Not ever?"

"No," said Da, and shook his head hard. "Ain't no point, Rafe. Everythin' we could ever want or need, we got right here in Lur." He looked at Mama, smiling a little bit, with his eyes all warm 'cause he loved her so much. Da riled fast, but he cooled down fast too. "We got family and friends and food for the table. What else do we need, that we got to risk ourselves over them mountains to find?"

Rafel put down his spoon. Da was a hero, everyone said so. Darran wasn't the only one who told him stories. Da hated to hear folk say it, his face went scowly enough to bust glass, but it was true. Da was a hero and he knew everything about everything...

But I don't believe him. Not about this.

Oh, it was an awful thing to think. But it was true. Da was wrong. There *was* something to find beyond the mountains, he *knew* it—and one day, he'd go. He'd find out what was there.

Then I'll be a hero too. I'll be Rafe the Bold, the great Olken explorer. I'll do something special for Lur, just like my da.